A GIRL IN TRAFFICK

A GIRL IN TRAFFICK

A Novel

Mamta Jain Valderrama

Majavii Press
Los Angeles, CA

Printed in the United States of America

First Printing, 2016.

ISBN: 0692788883
ISBN 13: 9780692788882
Majavii Press
Los Angeles, California
www.Majavii.com

To Arlo—while you patiently wait for a kidney transplant.

For the victims of organ trafficking around the world—past, present, and future—and for the activists who work tirelessly to protect them.

CONTENTS

ACKNOWLEDGMENTS

Thanks to my husband, Steve, who supported my decision to quit my job and write full time. He pushed me to (finally after thirty-seven years) discover the intersection between joy and skill. To our daughter, who shared her first year of life with the birth of this book. Thanks to my parents for giving me the freedom to study journalism when *all* the other Indian students went to medical school, law school, and engineering school. To my sister, Samta Varia, for her continuous support. To my mother-in-law, Sandra Valderrama, who said the story of organ trafficking needs to be told to the world. Without my book club, this novel would not exist. Thanks to Katherine Vogt, Celia Adelson, and Jill Paider. Thanks to my West Coast family for their unwavering support and encouragement: Ranjit Koshy Mathews, Johanna Jacob Kuruvilla, and Dhruv Jacob Mathews; Christopher James Alexander; and Sachin

Jain. To the beta readers who made my book better: Jaymin Patel, Brendan Docherty, Sue Paider, Sharon Yikanen, Caitlin Gremminger, Kiran Srivastava, and Laurie Bryan. Sincere thanks to nephrologist and fellow new mom, Dr. Mandana Rastegar, MD, for your clinical expertise. Finally, heartfelt thanks to Nancy Fulton, founder of Nancy Fulton Meetups, whose invaluable teachings propelled me forward.

PART 1

Juhi

CHAPTER 1
A NEW LIFE

Juhi hoisted herself onto the oversized sofa in Kevin's Santa Monica apartment. When she sat completely against the back, her toes barely stretched to the ground. At fifteen years old and five feet tall, she was petite in America, and she was even considered short in her native country, India. Her body had developed nicely. She was a beautiful young woman; her thin frame bulged only in her feminine parts. She would not gain more height, but Juhi didn't mind. She was content with her small stature—it was easier to find hiding holes and sleeping cells in the shadowy alleys of India's slums, where she'd lived for the last three years. During that time, before her recent move to the United States, Juhi had mastered the art of making herself invisible. It was difficult to hide in the slums, especially when the Delhi sun shone down on her stunning face.

As a slum dweller, her beauty set her apart from everyone else. Juhi was one of the most beautiful girls in all of India, even after she had not bathed for weeks. During her time in the slums, Juhi endured long stares and pointed fingers in her direction. She despised the strangers who stopped in their tracks to admire her as if an angel walked among them. She could not recall a time when she felt like an angel. Her hardened interior mismatched her alluring exterior, which was marked by a long mane of thick, black, unbreakable hair. It swayed behind her head in perfect congruence like a fresh coat of glossy paint on a new car.

Her dark-chocolate skin was supple, yet marred. Where she came from, a lighter complexion was more coveted. Her own mother, and other women in her village, constantly reminded her, "You are beautiful even though you are dark." Juhi thought she was beautiful *because* she was dark.

She had a broad forehead, which drew more attention to her face. It led to her full eyebrows that were formed naturally with a slight arch. Her narrow nose had a point that gently leaned to the right, which made her face a tiny bit asymmetrical but only to the most observant admirer. Her nose made her already slender face look even slimmer. Her pink lips pursed at the center and covered her bone-white teeth. Her smile drove men mad, so she stopped smiling a long time ago. But more than her smile, it was her eyes that mesmerized and captivated friends and foreigners alike. Under her seemingly meter-long eyelashes lay almond-shaped hazel green eyes that glistened by the light of the sun and the moon. She once heard a man describe her eyes as the two most magnificent green-tinted Koh-i-Noor diamonds.

Since early childhood, her classmates, her parents' friends, and people she didn't know shouted to her, "Aishwarya! Aishwarya!" after the Bollywood actress and former Miss World, Aishwarya Rai Bachchan. Aishwarya was famous for her green eyes, but Juhi abhorred the nickname. She didn't like the attention. But the label stuck to her like gum on the bottom of a shoe—until she moved to the United States. When Juhi lived in the Delhi slums, fellow slum dwellers gave her another nickname. They called her "Afghan Girl" after the refugee in the famous *National Geographic* photograph by Steve McCurry. It shocked Juhi that even the most uneducated and destitute people of India recognized that photograph from 1985. Slum dwellers called her that to remind Juhi that she was a penniless orphan. The women who were most jealous of her beauty taunted her and accompanied their verbal assaults with vulgar gestures.

When Juhi lived in the slums, she wished she could hide under a scarf like the Afghan girl. Before her body changed from a girl's to a woman's, her face was already irresistible to men. After her thirteenth birthday, two perfect breasts formed as juicy and pink as the first ripe cantaloupes of the season. Her high, curved backside filled her *salwar kameez* just so its frame was slightly visible. In her presence, practically all men and teenage boys degenerated into animals in heat. The only exception had been her father, who cherished Juhi and his wife—Juhi's mother—more than anything else in the world.

As memories of her past filled her mind, she flipped on the flat-screen television, which filled half of the living room, and turned the channel to the cable news station. The reporter talked about a new tunnel that connected Europe and Asia through something called the Bosphorus Strait. Juhi wished that her own story was the topic of the day. Her parents' photo would take over the screen with the channel's logo in the bottom right corner. Above their photo, they would show today's date: October 29, 2013. The handsome news anchor would refer to her as "India's Harriet Tubman."

But Juhi had never met this news anchor, or any journalist. In fact, her new father, Kevin—the man who adopted her—promised her she would get to tell her story to the media. But she had arrived in the United States three weeks ago. The journalists and pundits told her story on television as if they had lived it themselves. Where they got their information, she didn't know. All she knew was that it wasn't her side of the story, and none of the news was about her parents. Less than one month ago, she was plucked from her native country and transplanted to America. Her parents were murdered in India. Back home, she had no family—no siblings, no grandparents, and no aunts or uncles—and there was a bounty on her head. New Delhi's most notorious crime lord hunted all over India for her, and he would not stop until he found her. Yet India was her home—the only place she had ever known. It held her best and worst memories. *Hindustan* was where her parents were, even if they were dead. Now, in Los Angeles, she was halfway around the world from them—nine thousand miles away and twenty-four whole hours of flying time. Even time zones told her she was left behind in the shadow of their past. The clock on the television read "10:00 a.m., October 29, 2013," but at that exact moment it was already ten thirty in the evening that same day in New Delhi.

No matter how much she longed for India, she knew she would never be safe there again. Video footage of her former captor flashed across the television screen. The slumlord, Sunardas Shetty, was handcuffed and bowed his head to hide from the cameras. At least a dozen police officers escorted him. Even though he was a prisoner, his vast network of gangs and criminals would still hunt for Juhi. With the help of her drawings, she had cast a spotlight on criminal masterminds throughout Delhi and perhaps all of India.

They would seek revenge. As much as they thirsted for her body, they also thirsted for her blood.

She was not safe in India, but she didn't feel safe in the United States either. Juhi had a lingering feeling that one day, once the journalists forgot about her, the devils of India's underworld would turn up at her new Los Angeles home. If they had to, they would chase her across the globe. Kevin had promised her that would never happen. She thought he was stupid to promise things he knew nothing about.

Just then, on the television, Sunardas Shetty looked directly into the cameras. His yellow, bloodshot eyes looked directly at her, as if he knew she was watching. He smiled ominously and held his hand out as if he would grab her right through the television.

She fumbled for the television remote and pounded the "off" button. She shivered and breathed harder. She tried to erase the image from her mind, but she saw his face everywhere, even when she closed her eyes. The hatred in his expression, the determined gaze to find her and to kill her...Kevin couldn't protect her from the images in her mind. She curled into a ball on the couch and wrapped her arms around her small frame.

Since her arrival in the United States, she was forced to meet with dozens of social workers, caseworkers, and politicians. They lied to her, every one of them. They promised her that if she let Kevin adopt her, and if she gave her entire folio of evidence to the Americans, her real parents would get justice. The Americans promised her that Mummy and Papa would be honored and memorialized. They promised Juhi that the world would hear her parents' tragic story. Juhi grew weary of waiting for that time to come. So far, the brand-new "wonderful American life" that Kevin wanted to give her was nothing short of miserable.

Her mind drifted back to happier times in India, when Kevin interrupted her on the couch.

"Good morning, Juhi." He sat next to her but careful not to touch her.

She turned her mouth up in an obligatory grin and looked away.

"Big day today," he said and smiled.

Juhi stirred in her seat. Kevin searched her expression for any hint of emotion. She was a steel trap, and at times it tested Kevin's patience. The harder he tried to connect with her, the less Juhi shared. But he was determined to show his fatherly affection, even if she didn't believe that.

"This you say one week ago," Juhi replied in broken English and a thick Indian accent.

"I know you were upset after we met with the congressional committee, Juhi. I'm sorry. I want to make it right."

Juhi stared out the window.

"Are you nervous?"

Juhi shook her head no, but Kevin saw fear in her eyes.

"Good, then!" he said with too much enthusiasm, attempting to lighten the mood. "Your pant suit is in your room. Why don't you start getting ready? And by the time you're done, breakfast will be here."

Juhi hopped off the couch and went to her room. As she closed the door, she glanced back at Kevin, who already held the receiver to his ear.

"Three orders of fresh fruit, one basket of pastries, and a pot of coffee," he said into the phone.

That was the closest Kevin would come to cooking. He ordered most of his meals and had them delivered to his home. Juhi's most prized memories with her mother were made in the kitchen. She longed to be back in her village, making *dal cheela* (lentil pancakes) spiced with fresh ginger-green chili-garlic paste, and cumin and mustard seeds, sizzling over a drizzle of oil. Mummy added a surprise ingredient—fennel, which gave each cheela a touch of sweetness that balanced the savory flavors. She missed her mummy hunched over the stove, filling the whole house with steam. In that moment, she wanted nothing more than to sip a cup of masala chai with Mummy and Papa.

CHAPTER 2

AN INTRIGUED REPORTER

Kevin and Juhi arrived at the studio a few minutes early. The crew shuffled around the concrete room while they set up spotlights, flash shades, cameras, and then more cameras that were perched on tripods. Max Kray stood in the middle of the room and gave orders: "Move that camera stage right," "Angle the lens lower," "There's too much shadow in this corner," "Where is my fresh shirt?" and so forth. He didn't see them arrive.

A nearby camera grip saw them first. He hopped off his step stool to greet them. He brought them over to Max, whose arrogant, commanding tone completely flipped when his eyes landed on Kevin and Juhi.

"Kevin! Welcome, man!" Max opened his arms wide, and Kevin embraced him. Their exchange reminded Juhi of the boys at her school, the ones who thought they were the kings of the castle. Max turned to Juhi and shifted his tone from fraternity brother to solemn philosopher. "Juhi, I want to personally thank you for being here. Your presence is so important. I am so grateful. Thank you." Max cupped his hands together and folded them over his heart as he spoke to Juhi. She hated him instantly.

Max Kray was a self-described documentary filmmaker/journalist and author/film director/truth seeker/social-justice entrepreneur. In his self-made résumé reel on YouTube, all those words—SOCIAL JUSTICE, DOCUMENTARY FILMMAKER—appeared on the screen in all caps, bold white font against a black background. The animated words started small but grew bigger until they overtook the screen. Max's voiceover read the words and other statements as if they were fact. I AM A TRUTH SEEKER. I RISE ABOVE. *"Rise above what?"* Juhi wondered. Snippets of Max's films and reviews of his work played out on the screen. The reel ended with him looking at the camera, wearing oversized sunglasses with his long, greased, curly hair dangling on his big head. He declared, "If you would like to join my revolution for justice, subscribe to my Facebook page and YouTube channel." Then he folded his hands together as if in prayer, slightly bowed without moving his gaze from the camera, and chanted "Namaste." But he pronounced it the butchered American way, "Nam-aus-tay." Kevin pronounced it that way, too; he learned it in yoga class. Juhi was irritated that the Americans had bastardized one of the most sacred Hindi words. As if she needed another reason to dislike Max Kray, she felt the urge to ask him if he thought he was the reincarnation of a Hindu god.

But Juhi would have to put her feelings aside. Kevin arranged for Max to meet Juhi, and turn her story into a documentary film. No matter how Juhi felt about Max, he was good at his job. He was even nominated for an Academy Award for his film about child labor on chocolate farms. Juhi swallowed her feelings about Max and clung to any hope for her story to be heard.

After Kevin and Juhi returned to Los Angeles from Washington, DC, feeling frustrated and disappointed after meeting with a senate committee, Kevin scrambled to get in touch with Max. At the US Capitol, Juhi expected to honor her parents by bringing awareness to organ-trafficking crimes. Kevin said she might even inspire the American politicians to take action to stem the kidney black market. She was scheduled to testify for four hours. She was being forced to distill three horrific years of her life into half a day. She rehearsed quietly to herself all the things she wanted to say, and it always ran longer than the time she was given. Yet when the day arrived for her to testify, her time was cut in half. The head of the committee, a US senator from the southern part of the country, was running late from his last appointment. But one week later on the news, Juhi saw that same senator on television being chased by journalists as he walked out of a building to his car. He had been late to her testimony because he was getting an expensive haircut, which he bought with tax dollars. After that revelation, it seemed like more and more ugly truths emerged about that senator until he was forced to resign. Juhi's testimony was long forgotten.

In addition to promising her safety in the United States, Kevin swore Juhi would get to tell her story to someone who could help. He knew Max from his days at Logan Studio.

"So, Kevin, I'd like to start with Juhi's story and then get your side of it afterward." Max rubbed his palms together vigorously like a coyote biting a plump rabbit. "We're all set up and ready to go. We'll keep it simple. Just you and me in those chairs over there, with a simple background." Max pointed at three chairs that sat against a light-gray background. Spotlights loomed above and shone down on all three chairs. Next to Juhi's chair, Max left a clipboard with a stack of plain white paper and a few pencils.

"I'll start us off by asking you a few questions, and then I want to keep it open-ended for you to share your entire story, uninterrupted—except for bathroom breaks and for lunch. I only have the studio until six o'clock today, so we'll see how far we get, and we'll pick it up again tomorrow. It can get hot under the lights, so there is water for you, which you're welcome to at any time during filming. I will be filming everything you say in its entirety. The people you see are the crew and cameramen. They will be here the entire time, too. The third chair is for our interpreter, Madhuri Subramanian." A petite woman with long, flowing black hair walked across the room toward Max.

"Kevin told me you speak English," Max explained, "but in case you feel more comfortable talking in your native language, Madhuri has worked as a Hindi-to-English translator in Hollywood and Bollywood for many years."

Juhi eyed the interpreter. She was inclined not to trust her, but then she saw a spark of kindness in Madhuri's eyes.

"Hello, Juhi. *Mujhe aapse milkar khushee hui.*" (I am happy to meet you.)

"Hello," Juhi replied softly.

"Juhi, did you bring your drawings?" Max asked her.

She held up the manila envelope that she held in her hand.

"Great. As we're talking, you can show me your drawings. You can put them on that table. Do you have any questions?" Max looked at Juhi. She shook her head no. "Great, then let's get started." Max gestured for Juhi and Madhuri to take their seats, and Max followed.

The cameras rolled.

"Juhi, thank you for being here today. And thanks for your bravery to share your harrowing ordeal. Let's start by gathering some basic facts. Why don't you tell me your name and age?"

"My name Juhi Gupta. I have fifteen years," she said, in broken English. "I am twelve when Papa's kidney is stolen, and Mummy, Papa, and I kidnapped. Two years, I live in slum and as slave. One year I run away."

Juhi's heart beat so hard that the vibration thumped in her ears and shook her stomach. The cold, recycled air, mixed with the hot air from the lamps, sent a wave of goose bumps up and down her arms. She crossed her legs, squeezed tight, and resisted the urge to urinate.

"I come to you today to tell story of Mummy, Papa, and me. But first I wish to share how US government treat me."

Max looked at Kevin who stood off the camera a few feet away. Kevin shrugged to indicate he was just as surprised as Max. Max let her continue uninterrupted.

"I am promised four hours to share my story. This feels impossible to make three years of life into four hours. Then the time cut to two hours. Now, man who

I told my story is no longer in US government. I am left disappointed. In India, people think America so great. This not my feeling."

"What happened when you went to the US Capitol?" Max asked Juhi.

"I am attacked by photographers and interrupted while I speak."

"That must have been difficult," Max replied. "I would love to hear more."

Juhi sat back in her chair as she recalled that day into her memory. Although she had introduced herself in English, Juhi decided to switch back to her native Hindi. She didn't want to miss her chance to explain all the details and nuances that only came to her in Hindi.

CHAPTER 3

THE UN-TESTIMONY

Juhi started her story by telling Max about her arrival at the Senate chamber. She recalled that the room felt methodical, yet elegant. Carved concrete columns lined the room's perimeter with images of stars and stripes, something called the "Liberty Bell" and a man named "Uncle Sam." The symbols meant nothing to her. The rows of chairs that filled the audience gallery behind her had filled before she arrived. Some people forced themselves into whatever small space they could find, like passengers in sleeper cars on India's trains.

"Who are all these people?" she asked. "Why are they here?"

Kevin shrugged.

"I don't know. But I do know that you're meeting with members of the United States Congress."

She knew from her fifth-grade global civics class that Congress was similar to India's Parliament.

"I can't bring your parents back to life," Kevin told her. "But I can try to bring some justice to them and to you. If you tell those politicians your story, you will help them make sure the same thing doesn't happen to anyone else. But they can't do that without hearing your story."

A pair of heavy industrial doors swung open, and almost in unison, everyone in the room rose to their feet. A single-file line of serious dignitaries entered, as if they rehearsed their entrance ahead of time. They all took their seats at a long, half-oval-shaped table at the center of the room, while cameramen flooded the room with flashes of light. The paparazzi didn't photograph her, which she appreciated. A stern man with a face covered in wrinkles sat squarely in the center of the table.

"Please be seated," he said into his microphone.

Juhi climbed into the leather-lined chair that was as heavy as the oak tree it was made from. She felt mouse-like in the oversized chair and grand hall.

"This is Senate Foreign Relations Committee Hearing five-six-four-one-two," announced the wrinkled man. "This proceeding, scheduled on this day of October twenty-second, 2013, is to take testimony of Juhi Gupta, a victim of organ trafficking in her native country, India. The interpreter seated to the right of the witness will translate the witness's testimony as needed from the witness's native language, Hindi, to

English. To that end, and in order to give the witness as much time as possible, we will skip introductions to the entire committee, as is the normal course of this committee's proceedings. Please make a note of the change on the formal transcription and the explanation for the change."

As the senator spoke, Juhi sat as still as a mummy. She wanted to testify in English, but she felt relieved to have an interpreter in case she got stuck. Her English was good. She knew that the correct pronunciations for "put" and "but" were different, even though they look the same. She knew that "pneumonia" had a silent "p." She knew that "p" and "h" together make an "f" sound. But she recognized that there were some words that she didn't know, and she worried that Americans might not understand her accent.

"Miss Gupta, please stand." He pronounced her name as "Goop-tah."

As she stood, Juhi squeezed her legs tight to stop herself from urinating. She felt hundreds of eyes watching her. Because she was short, and maybe the table where she sat was too high, but when she stood up, only her chest and head were visible over the table. A man stood in front of her and extended a closed, heavy book toward her. He instructed her to place her right hand on it. It felt like sandpaper against her palm. Juhi took an honesty oath and returned to her seat.

"Miss Gupta, on behalf of the American people, I would like to welcome you to the United States and to this chamber here at the Capitol in Washington, DC."

The senator continued without waiting for a response. Each time he referred to himself, he pointed at himself with his right thumb. He had already done that ten times since he entered the chamber.

"Everyone in this room, me in particular," he said, pointing to himself, "is eager to hear what you have to say. But before I turn it over to you, I"—again he pointed to himself—"want to thank you for appearing here today. You're very brave to share your story with us." He pointed to himself. "This committee and I"—he once again pointed to himself—"believe that any sort of human trafficking is deplorable, and we will consider dedicating whatever resources we can to stop it."

His condescending tone washed over Juhi. It reminded her of Sunardas Shetty. She wanted to hide.

The senator continued.

"You have our undivided attention for the next two hours. Rarely do we meet a strong witness and victim such as you. Let's start with your name."

She had rehearsed her introduction with Kevin at his home in Los Angeles.

"My name Juhi—"

But before she could finish, a sea of paparazzi popped up in front of her and flashed boulder-sized bulbs in her face. Juhi screamed and leaped into Kevin's arms. She hated being that close to Kevin, but she had no choice. The flashbulbs practically blinded her. Juhi's head spun as she squeezed her eyes shut. But the paparazzi persisted the more she tried to cover herself. Kevin yelled at them to stop, which only encouraged them. The senator pounded a gavel against a wooden block and yelled into his microphone.

"Order! Order!"

Four security guards surrounded the paparazzi and attempted to cover their camera lenses. Senator Murphy continued to yell for two long minutes until the flashing finally subsided.

Juhi stayed buried in Kevin's arms. He affectionately rubbed Juhi's back as she shook and wept. She was surprised by the affection she felt for Kevin in that moment. It scared her. She climbed off Kevin's lap and stood awkwardly next to him.

"Miss Gupta, it's OK. Don't be frightened," the senator told her. He spoke to her as if she was an infant. "I know that must have been scary for you."

The photographers were still there, waiting to pounce. Juhi recognized men like the senator. Rich. Powerful. Usually get what they want. She had had enough of men like him. And she was outraged by the paparazzi. They misrepresented her in the media ever since she arrived in the United States, and she was tired of them following her. She had a small window of power at that exact moment.

"I not continue with them here," she declared. Juhi pointed at the photographers and repeated herself. "I not continue with them here." The entire chamber gasped at her indignation.

"I'm afraid that's not up to you, Miss Gupta. They have a right to be here as per the First Amendment of our Constitution. Plus, your testimony is part of the deal your father made with the Government of the United States." The senator gazed hard at Kevin as if to implore him to take control over her.

Juhi didn't care.

"This *your* First Amend-a-ment. You made agreement with Kay-win. He not *my* father. I not continue with them here."

Kevin shrugged helplessly at the senator.

"They hurt me. You want story? You send them away," she continued.

"Excuse me? Did you say they *hurt* you?" the senator repeated.

Juhi rose from her chair and stood in front of the table so the committee could see all of her.

"Today, when I arrive, they snapped many my picture when I step out of car. I am blind, but they not move. I could not pass. Kay-win said, 'Move! Move!' but they would not. Kay-win gave me plastic mask to cover face. But they have broken it."

Kay-win showed the senator the shattered mask.

"When I came from car, the photo men yelled in English, but I did not understand. It sounded like strange noises, but then I realize they called my name—'Joo-ey!' 'Chewy!' 'Joey!' 'Joe-heeeee!' 'Ju-high!'"

Juhi imitated them sarcastically and waved her hands in the air to signal the commotion that surrounded the situation.

"My name pronounced Joo-hee. In Hindi, it is jasmine flower. This was my father's best flower. My mother wore fresh jasmine flower in hair every day."

Juhi was remarkably sharp and sharp-tongued for her age but not for the life she had lived. She was living proof that a person lives an entire lifetime in one month in an Indian slum. She continued to recount her altercation with the paparazzi.

"I climbed stairs in front of Capitol; he stabbed me in my back with his long camera! That fat one." She pointed at an egg-shaped man with a dwarf-like face. Breadcrumbs shook out of his facial hair like dandruff when he turned to face the senator. He looked back and forth between Juhi and the senator, like a child caught with his hand in the cookie jar.

"I fell down. I tore my pants and my knee, but they did not stop. No help came. He did not say sorry. He looked stupid at Kay-win and me and snapped more photos. A kind American lady helped me. In the bathroom to wipe the blood. Even now, you will see I continue to bleed. It is also paining." She paused. "In India, we hear America is great. You are not ashamed of these camera people? Send them away. And I continue."

The committee sat speechless and stared at Juhi. She broke the silence.

"I know you think my English is no good. You see me and think me poor and stupid foreigner. You feel sadness for me. Kay-win made promise my drawings. You promised he my new father. I had a papa. I not need a new one. I not need Kay-win. I not need you or anyone. My mummy, papa are no more. I am raped too many times. I stole gold chain right off old lady's neck in Delhi market; otherwise, my master would kill me. I stole *roti* (Indian flatbread) from another child because I too hungry. I survived. Alone. I not need your deal."

Juhi had stopped talking, as if to declare "checkmate." She waited for the senator to make his move. The committee members deliberated for several minutes until they demanded all the photographers leave the room. They declared it a "closed session" in the name of national security, and only the official Senate photographer, videographer, and stenographer would remain. Calling "national security" in the United States was like calling "dibs" to sit shotgun in a car.

An uproar of protest erupted from the photographers who threatened an injunction. But the senator did not care. An injunction would take hours to obtain, and by then Juhi would be done testifying. Security guards ushered the photographers out of the room, and the audience erupted in applause.

The senator struck his gavel several times and turned to Juhi but said nothing. She thanked him and continued.

"My name Juhi Gupta. I from India. I have fifteen years old. My mummy, papa killed in India. Kay-win tell me he is my father now. Now I live here USA, California. Today I tell you how Papa…was stolen."

She explained to Max that while she testified in front of the committee, she forgot the word for "kidney," so she pointed at her back. The translator helped her. "Yes, kidney…stolen and how he die. I have twelve years old at that time. One year I live in Delhi slums, one year I enslaved with slumlord, one year I run and hide."

CHAPTER 4

BIRTHDAY CELEBRATION

Juhi attempted to tell her story, but the senators kept interrupting her, she explained to Max.

"The senator told me he wanted me to share my story, and he would not interrupt, but that is all he did. The first time I mentioned Kabir Singh's name, the senator wanted to know all about Kabir Singh and then about Sunardas Shetty. He did not ask me one single question about Mummy and Papa. Not one. Or about me. He just wanted to know about the criminals from my story. Kay-win told me I would get to honor Mummy and Papa by sharing my story. He said I would feel better sharing the heavy burden I carried. I felt worse after leaving that chamber than when I started the day. Mummy and Papa would be disappointed in me for not honoring their memory."

Well, it will be different here, Juhi." Max spoke to her directly, as an equal. Juhi liked that. "I *do* want to hear your entire story, uninterrupted. I might ask you questions along the way to help me understand, but this is your story to tell in your own words."

"Thank you, Max."

"You're welcome. Please go on."

"Three years ago I was at school, and it was my twelfth birthday. I kept watching the clock. Time seemed to stop in the classroom. While my teacher talked on and on, I sat on the edge of my seat, waiting for three o'clock in the afternoon. I just could not wait to return home to enjoy every minute of my birthday with Mummy and Papa. My classmates had already celebrated with me. They sang, we ate chocolate cake and *besan laddoos*, and my two best friends, Pari and Shilpa, decorated my desk with stars of purple and aqua. Those are my favorite colors."

Juhi took a sip of water and proceeded.

"That day was the final lesson in a two-week series about slavery. During that time, I learned about everything from slaves in Africa to modern-day slavery, such as sweatshops and child labor. Because my teacher was American, she knew a great deal about the enslavement of African Americans in this country."

Juhi pointed at the ground to show she meant the United States.

"I loved the story of Harriet Tubman and the dozens of slaves whom she freed in the Underground Railroad. She showed such bravery, especially as a woman. I liked that she found a way to help others in a nonviolent way. She risked her own life to help others."

"The day before I learned about Harriet Tubman, my teacher showed my class the Kiva website, and we learned about Muhammad Yunus and what we can do to help our own people—Indians—out of poverty. But on that day, my birthday, my teacher didn't teach anything new. She just summarized everything we had already learned, which made me more eager to get home. Please do not misunderstand. I am grateful for my teachers. All day long, they joined in wishing me birthday salutations. The teachers at my school liked me. I could even say I was beloved at my school."

Juhi paused to glance back and forth at the translator and at Max. She knew she might sound arrogant, but her tone was plain and truthful. She didn't detect any judgment from either of them, so she continued in Hindi and let the translator do her job.

"I had the highest marks in most of my school subjects—Hindi, English, social studies, and science. I was good at math for several years, but then I struggled. My teacher said I could have skipped third standard and gone straight to fourth if I was better at math. Even though I did not perform well in math, I excelled in other areas. I played the lead role in the school play every year, and I was one of the stars of the debate team. Mummy and Papa used to say that I was very mature for my age. Mummy thought I studied too much. She feared that in our small village, where most of the men were farmers, no man would think of me as suitable. Mummy used to say that no man wants an educated girl, but Papa told me that I was destined for great things in my life and that no one could stop me."

Juhi loved all of her school activities, but she loved drawing the most. She painted grand murals of scenes from India's epic, Mahabharata, on the classroom walls. She designed sets for the school plays. Drawing was her meditation. She liked the rhythm of a moving paintbrush on canvas. She could draw with anything—pencil, pen, marker, or crayon, either black and white or color. She remembered feeling happy in front of a crisp, blank paper that was full of possibility. It was the only activity that she didn't share with anyone. She had it all completely to herself. The rest—debate team, the school play—were team sports. Juhi enjoyed the quietness and solitude of creating something out of nothing. She was born with long, slender fingers, as if they were designed for drawing. Juhi picked up the clipboard and a pencil and closed her eyes as she started to draw.

"When I draw, it is as if the rest of the world does not exist. Everything is calm. Everything is quiet. It is as if my hand controls my mind and the strokes it makes across the page. The other children at school teased me for closing my eyes while I drew. But I can remember things after I see them. I can see them in my mind like a photograph. That makes it easy to draw them. Papa called it a gift. Mummy called it a curse. Mummy used to say, 'Juhi *beti,* I do not mind that you draw. Just keep your eyes open! People will say you are bad luck! Imagine what stories they will spread all over town with you making such a spectacle of yourself!'"

But Papa encouraged her, and he rarely got upset. But he did have one angry face. His eyes flickered like flames, and his mouth twitched, as if he used every ounce of energy to hold a bucket of anger from tipping over. Juhi's mummy knew to be quiet when he made that face.

Juhi's eyes were still closed as she drew.

"I like to draw people more than anything else, especially faces. I like the lines on foreheads and cheeks and around the eyes. I think about the stories of their lives that are tucked between them. And the detail is important because it is someone's face. I like it because it is delicate, and because I am good at it. I do not like to play cricket, because I am not good at it."

Max chuckled, which prompted Juhi to open her eyes. She held up her drawing toward Max. She had drawn an uncanny portrait of him. A camera zoomed in on her drawing. It looked more like a photograph than a drawing—the likeness was so strong. Max applauded.

"Thank you, Juhi! Wow, you're very talented!"

Max washed away any doubts he had about the authenticity of her drawings. They were real. Every facet of her life story was real. He believed her.

"Thank you," she responded.

Given all her talents, someone might assume Juhi to be arrogant, but she was just the opposite. She could not take a compliment without blushing, and she avoided eye contact. She was quick to compliment others to move the spotlight off her. Juhi's unquestionable talents and her sweet nature made her a polarizing figure at school with the other girls. Her classmates either loved and admired her or were jealous of her. Those were the two options: love or hate. As for the boys, they were all in agreement. Every single one of them, whether older or younger than Juhi, was mesmerized by her sweet grace and easy personality. But mostly, her eyes hypnotized them into adoration. For the girls who hated Juhi, her beauty caused them to dislike her even more, for she was not only stunning but also humble about that.

"Many of the girls at school, who did not like me, used to tease me. They chanted 'Ash, Ash, please dance!' all over the playground. Aishwarya Rai Bachchan, the actress they nicknamed me after, is famous for her Bollywood dances. As much as I excel at drawing, I am equally unskilled at dancing. I do not mind that I am a bad dancer. But I did not like being teased. I did not want to fight with those girls, either. Actually, I never understood why they hated me. I just wanted to hide. I remember that I wished I were invisible. And now, I am an expert at hiding." Juhi paused. Her life in her village felt so far away, as if it never happened.

Papa worked on Kabir Singh's farm. Juhi's friends' fathers worked there, too. Kabir Singh was the richest man in her village, Gantak Mandi. Kabir Singh owned all the farmland and employed most of the village's men. There were some men, though, who had their own shops, like the snack stand or the small market where Juhi and her friends bought candy. Those fathers did not need to work in the fields, and they were the wealthy people in the village. Those men were Kabir Singh's friends, even though none of them was as rich as him.

At school, there was a well-known yet never-discussed division among the students: the *gareeb laug* and the *ameer laug*. In Hindi, *gareeb* means "poor," and *laug* means "people." That is what the rich kids called Juhi and her friends. In return, the rich kids were called *ameer*, which is an insult to a rich, arrogant person. The *gareeb laug* did not mix with the *ameer laug* unless forced.

They had created their own unspoken caste system. At lunchtime, the two groups sat on opposite sides of the mess hall. The *gareeb laug* were forbidden from certain parts of the playground. The girls who teased Juhi were *ameer laug*. Pari and Shilpa said those girls didn't like it when *gareeb laug* outshone them. Juhi was glad to have a group of friends at school. But, sometimes, even the other *gareeb laug* fought with her. They claimed that Juhi thought she was better than them. There were days when Juhi felt trapped and confused, and she wanted to run away from school. But now, after everything that had happened to her, she wished she could go back to the way things were.

"I miss my school. I miss my friends. I miss Mummy and Papa." Juhi drew a deep breath and sipped her water.

She explained to Max that on that day, her twelfth birthday, the *ameer* girls teased her more than usual. They resented the attention she received for her birthday. Thankfully, it was a rare day when Juhi didn't have any after-school activities—no debate class or play rehearsal. Mummy was waiting for her at home, and Papa would try to come home early from the fields. They would sit together on the mat in their "living room," which was the floor in the kitchen, and her birthday present would lie in front of them. Mummy and Papa would try to disguise it with a pillow cover or a sheet, but Juhi always saw it, year after year. Mummy and Papa would be casual, as if it was any other day of the year, until they would reveal the big surprise.

Those moments of anticipation used to annoy Juhi, but now she would do anything to have another birthday with them.

On her eleventh birthday, Juhi received a used computer printer. Papa saved as much money as he could. He wanted her to print her homework, just as the other students did. Most of Juhi's classmates had purchased printers even when they were in third standard, but Juhi's family could not afford one until she was in fourth standard. Juhi was convinced that Mummy and Papa would give her another gift that would further her education.

"Papa was very proud of me," Juhi told Max and the translator. She sat up and puffed up her chest to imitate him. "'She is the first person in our family to read and write in Hindi,' he would say. 'And she knows English too!'"

The other farmers already knew that Juhi excelled at school, but they did not mind listening to Papa brag about her. And Papa did not care if he bored them to the ends of the earth. They loved Papa, and he loved them. He had worked alongside most of them in the fields since they were boys. Although they were not blood relatives, those farmers were Juhi's extended family.

On her twelfth birthday, Ms. Nisha went on and on about the new lesson plan that they would start the next day. They had already learned all about slavery.

For the next two weeks, they would learn about water shortages around the world.

Ms. Nisha looked Indian. She had an Indian name, she ate Indian food, wore Indian clothes, and she practiced Indian rituals and religion. But she was born in the United States, so she had an American accent, and she spoke English better than Hindi. The villagers called her NRI for non-resident Indian. She worked for a nonprofit organization called IndiCorps, and she moved to India for three years to volunteer as a teacher at Juhi's school. Two other NRIs came with her. They were volunteers, too. Juhi liked Ms. Nisha. She was kind and patient, and she taught Juhi English. She encouraged girls to get an education.

Most of the villagers in Gantak Mandi welcomed Ms. Nisha and her friends, but a few people did not like them. They felt insulted by them and said the village didn't need foreign teachers. The people who didn't like Ms. Nisha said that the Americans think they know everything, and anyone who wasn't American was not as important.

But Juhi liked the Americans. She was convinced that her regular teachers would not have taught her about Kiva, Muhammad Yunus, and Harriet Tubman. But that day even Juhi didn't want to listen to any of her teachers, not even Ms. Nisha. She just wanted to see what Mummy and Papa got for her birthday.

When she arrived at home, Mummy was busy in the kitchen as usual. Juhi changed out of her school uniform and washed her face and hands. She sat down on the mat in the kitchen to start her homework, while Mummy continued to cook and hum. Mummy didn't say much, but that was normal when she was distracted by her steaming pans and boiling pots. Juhi did her homework until Papa came home about one hour later. He kissed Juhi on the forehead and Mummy on the cheek, just as he did every day. He went to the bathroom to clean up and change his clothes. They still had not wished Juhi a happy birthday, and she started to wonder if they forgot. How easily she is fooled! They did this every year, yet she fell for it every time!

Papa returned to the kitchen with a box covered with a pillow cover in his hand. Juhi's heart raced. Papa joined Juhi on the mat and placed the box in-between them. But instead of giving it to her, he picked up a letter that came in that day's post and examined it as if he were reading! Juhi's agony must have been written all over her face, because Papa burst out laughing and exclaimed, 'Happy Birthday, *beti*!' He wrapped his arms around Juhi and embraced her in an enormous hug. Mummy joined them on the mat and brought a plate of *kaju katli* and a beautiful chocolate cake with her. Mummy and Papa fed bites of sweets to Juhi, and they put ceremonial *tikka* on her forehead for good luck.

They finally handed her the box. Juhi yanked the cover off and could not believe it. It was a camera. Her very own camera! It was one of those little ones that fits in a pocket or a purse, and it was digital, so she could take as many photographs as she wanted. It had an option to flip the lens so she could take pictures of herself with her friends. The girls at school who had cell phones told her it was called a "selfie." The camera weighed no more than one kilogram. Its shiny silver surface felt chilly in Juhi's hands. But its petite size matched her petite hand; it was easy to carry. She installed the battery and turned it on.

She asked Mummy and Papa to crowd in next to her, with herself in the middle. Juhi held the cake out in front of her with one hand and the camera in the other hand, and *snap!* She took a selfie of the three of them. There they were, smiling on the miniscule screen—Mummy, Papa, and Juhi. She used the wire that came with the camera to connect it to the computer. She printed the picture and gave it to Papa. He examined it and smiled at Juhi from ear to ear. Then he folded it gently and put it in his pocket.

"It is most important to me. I will keep it in my shirt pocket close to my heart where it is safe," he told Juhi.

Juhi's parents embraced her in a hug again, and Mummy and Papa cried with pride. They stayed in their embrace for a long moment and then celebrated with the beautiful meal that Mummy had prepared. It was Juhi's favorite—bhindi masala (okra cooked with spices) and *besan ki khadi* (gram-flour soup). Mummy made Juhi two fresh *parathas* (rolled whole-wheat bread) and doused them in a little extra *ghee* (clarified butter) as a special treat. It was the last meal that they would eat together at home.

CHAPTER 5
GANTAK MANDI

The next day was a normal day in Juhi's village, except that Papa—his name was Satyaraj Gupta—visited the village doctor to have a rotten tooth removed. But instead of removing the tooth, the doctor stole Papa's right kidney. Juhi pointed at her back again.

She spoke clinically, as if reciting facts and statistics from an encyclopedia. Of course, Max already knew her father's kidney was stolen, but he was taken aback by her detached tone. Juhi had already spent every ounce of grief and pain she had inside of her. She was like a dried fig, wrinkled and keeled over with no more juice left to squeeze. She continued to recount her story in a flat, emotionless monotone.

The doctor gave Papa drugs that made him sleepy; then he cut Papa open and took his kidney. Afterward, to hide it from the rest of the village, Mummy, Papa, and Juhi were sold to a slum in New Delhi, hundreds of kilometers away from their village, where both Mummy and Papa died. A slumlord adopted Juhi. He called her his daughter, but he treated her like his pet. At first he was very kind. He gave Juhi new dresses, meals fit for a princess, and all the paper and drawing supplies she could ever want. But later, he grew very mean. He said she was like a fly trapped in his house. Juhi did whatever he demanded, as he threatened to beat her if otherwise. He held a gun to her head several times. One time he pulled the trigger and laughed when Juhi screamed. The gun was empty. He liked it when people feared him. Juhi escaped from him, but a gang of his men chased Kevin and Juhi across India. They chased her because she stole one hundred thousand American dollars from the slumlord.

While she lived in the slum and then with the slumlord, she was beaten and raped. In the United States, Kevin and other people dressed in suits who Juhi didn't know kept telling her that she was safe. But she didn't feel safe. The men who came after her in India were still alive, and Juhi feared that they would try to find her in America.

"I see their faces when I close my eyes," she told Max.

Juhi stopped talking. Her hard exterior began to collapse. Her lips quivered, and her voice quaked as she spoke. The tough girl from a few minutes ago had vanished. Kevin had pushed Juhi to tell her story. He promised her that she would feel better. Now he wondered if he had pushed too hard. He was still there at the studio but in the background, off camera. He walked toward her and wiped her tears from her eyes.

"I'm sorry I brought you here. You don't have to do this. We can go home right now."

"Home?" she replied.

Kevin sighed and squeezed her arm. "I mean my home."

Juhi turned away from him. She didn't know what might come out of telling Max her story, but if there was a chance for her parents' story to be heard, it was worth a try. She wiped her face, sipped some water, and continued. Her voice didn't shake.

"Mummy, Papa, and I were very happy in our village. I wish I could go back there with them and live our lives together the way we planned."

As Juhi spoke, she took out from her envelope a copy of the selfie from her twelfth birthday and stared at it for a few moments.

She told Max how much Papa loved working at the farm. The entire village respected Papa. While some of the farmers struggled with alcohol and drugs and beat their wives and children, Papa and Mummy truly loved one another and were playful and loving toward

each other—and toward Juhi. Music filled their l
every evening. Papa loved the old classics by Jagjit Singh and Kishore Kumar, and he hummed them all the time. Sometimes Papa spontaneously took Mummy into his arms and they danced around the room like a Western slow dance. This made Mummy blush, and she covered her head with her sari and buried her face in Papa's shoulder. Juhi would sit on the sprawled mats on the floor, smiling profusely, until Mummy broke away from Papa. Mummy looked as though she might die from embarrassment. Then she pulled Juhi up to dance with her in this Western style, which made Papa hysterical with laughter.

Juhi smiled faintly and removed several drawings of her parents from the envelope as she spoke. She handed them to Max, who displayed them on the table and pointed at one of the cameras to zoom in.

Papa loved it when Mummy and Juhi danced together. He threw back his whole head, and great bellows of laughter that came from his belly filled the room. Afterward, they sat together on the mats and sipped hot, fresh Darjeeling chai and nibbled on Parle-G biscuits. They were so happy. That daily cup of chai was like hot wax on an envelope that sealed their happiness and kept it safe.

There was a grassy hill behind Juhi's house that she wasn't allowed to play on. Mummy said it was too far from the house and too steep.

Mummy would say to Juhi, "What if something happens to you? Who will run up such a tall mountain?"

"Would you stop her if she was a boy?" Papa asked Mummy.

"That is different!" she declared.

Papa told Juhi it was not her fault she was a girl. It was no one's fault, and it was nothing to be ashamed of.

"Do not ever let anyone tell you that you are less because you are a girl," Papa used to tell Juhi.

Juhi loved the way Papa said her name. It made her feel like she really could climb the Himalayas or become a world-renowned scientist or a doctor who saves lives. Papa told Mummy that he would run up the hill to get Juhi if she needed help. Of course, Mummy wanted to know what Papa would do if Juhi got hurt while he was at the farm, but Mummy knew she wouldn't win, so she kept her question to herself. Luckily, when the day came when Juhi needed to be rescued from the hill, Papa was at home. It so happened that after a round of cartwheels, Juhi landed on some loose rocks, and her ankle popped and twisted like a cap on a medicine bottle.

Juhi shrieked in pain and called "Papaaaaa!"

Papa came running up the hill while he shouted for her.

"Juhi! Juhi!" As he approached, he looked like a Bollywood hero. His hair flowed in the wind, as if he ran in slow motion. "Juhi *beti*!"

He scooped Juhi up into his arms and ran back to the house—back to safety.

Her voice trailed off, and she leaned back into her chair.

"I wish I could remember what 'safe' felt like. I wish I had told Papa that I felt safe that day when he rescued me from the hill. I wish he knew that I felt safe as long as we were together. I wish he was here to make me feel safe again."

She covered her face with her hands, while the cameramen and even Max fought back tears. Kevin walked up to Juhi again and stood in front of her. Juhi collapsed into his arms and released a gush of sobs. Kevin wrapped his arms around her, and together they mourned Juhi's parents. Max stood up and suggested they take a fifteen-minute break.

CHAPTER 6

KABIR SINGH

When Juhi returned to her seat at Max's studio, she walked in with her head held a little higher. She had that same assured feeling that someone gets when driving to a new location for the second time. Juhi sat down and launched straight into her story even before Max could ask her to begin. Madhuri was still there translating for Juhi.

"Every morning I woke to the raucous sounds of pots clanking, spoons swirling, and dal (lentil soup) boiling. Mummy was hunched over the gas fire. She prepared fresh meals for Papa and me every day. By the time I opened my eyes in the morning, she was already sweating as if she had gone jogging. The fragrance of black Darjeeling tea and ginger-cardamom chai masala muted the clatter and helped me gain balance among the morning chaos. Papa and I ate the same breakfast every morning. We sat together on our straw mats, sipped chai, and nibbled on Parle-G biscuits. This was my favorite part of the day—when the day was fresh—Papa was not too tired to ask me about school or to discuss the latest World Cup cricket match. He was playful with Mummy and me, and energetic, which made the whole house—our two cozy rooms—feel light and happy. Papa was kindhearted. But the nature of his work left him weary from the moment he started his walk home from the fields. You see, Papa was a farm laborer his entire life. Papa was an only child, just like me. By the time he was seven years old, he was the man of the house. My grandfather, who also worked on Kabir Singh's farm, was killed in a farm accident. It is funny how life repeats itself; Papa was fatherless by the time he was seven, and I was an orphan when I was twelve." She paused. She thought she had made a harmless joke, but Max didn't laugh.

No one knows what really happened to Juhi's grandfather. Some say he was cut to pieces by the tractor; others say a bull attacked him. The more sinister rumors were that he somehow upset the farm owner, Jagjit Sahib, who was Kabir Singh's father. The rumors were that Jagjit Sahib murdered her grandfather. As she was growing up, Juhi never believed Jagjit Sahib harmed her grandfather, but now—after everything she had been through—Juhi wasn't sure what to believe. Despite the rumors, Jagjit Sahib gave Papa a job on the farm, and Papa worked there for thirty-three years. Juhi's *dadima* (grandmother), a young, uneducated widow, was forced to rely on Papa for her livelihood. They lived a very simple life, and Dadima was eager to get Papa married as soon as he was old enough. Papa married Mummy when he was twenty and Mummy was seventeen. Juhi was born five years later. Mummy and Papa wanted children sooner, but it did not seem to work. Dadima blamed Mummy, and Dadima died resenting Mummy. She passed away before Juhi was born, which was probably for the best. Dadima would have wanted a grandson.

Jagjit Sahib had a son, Kabir Singh, who was the same age as Papa. When they were boys, Kabir Singh attended school. Papa caught glimpses of him playing near the farm in the afternoons. Kabir Singh never worked on the farm, and he never spoke to any of the workers. Papa admired Kabir Singh's clean, pressed clothes; his shiny black shoes with laces; and his perfectly combed hair. Papa longed to be Kabir Singh's friend, and while Papa gathered okra and squash, he daydreamed about the two of them playing together in the fields. Even though they never spoke a single time when they were children, Papa genuinely loved Kabir Singh as an older brother loves a younger sibling. Juhi never understood Papa's affection for Kabir Singh, but Papa always wanted a brother.

Juhi met Kabir Singh several times, and while he seemed like a nice man and a good boss, he did not do anything to earn Papa's love, and he never felt like an uncle to Juhi. He did not visit their home and eat dinner with them like an uncle would; he did not bring Juhi toys and pretty dresses or teach her magic tricks. He did not even look at Juhi when she visited Papa in the fields. But that's just how Papa was—a simple man who was quick to smile, quick to share his heart, and too quick to pledge his loyalty.

Papa's loyalty showed on the farm. He went to work on time every day and was one of the last to go home. He was meticulous in his work, and although he never knew how smart he was—he knew even more about farming than Jagjit Sahib and Kabir Singh! Papa had the natural ability to hear something once and remember it forever. Juhi got her photographic memory from Papa. Papa recited tips and knowledge about crop rotation, how much water to use, how to spread fertilizer evenly, and what time of day to feed the crops. He could have been a successful farm owner himself if he had money—and if he believed he was smart. Sometimes when Juhi visited Papa at the farm, she overheard other farmers encouraging him to save some money to buy a small piece of land. Papa just smiled shyly, shook his head no, and insisted he was just a simple laborer. Besides, he would never leave after Jagjit Sahib saved him and his mother from a destitute life. He gave Papa a job when he was just seven years old! And, of course, later on, his beloved "brother", Kabir Singh, inherited the farm, so there was no possibility of Papa leaving them.

"I will tell you more about Kabir Singh, but I want to tell you about my village, Gantak Mandi. It's important so you can understand my story," Juhi explained to Max.

Gantak Mandi is an endless plain of flat, dry land. Until the time her family was kidnapped, Juhi had never left Gantak Mandi. The village offered everything she and her family needed: food, a decent home, and each other. Juhi attended school for seven years. She was enrolled when she was five years old, and she was forced to leave right after her twelfth birthday when she was kidnapped. Like Juhi, many of her classmates were the first in their families to read and write. The school opened to girls just thirty years ago, but it took some time for girls to attend.

"The girls were smarter than the boys..." she told Max.

Juhi was interrupted by a small burst of laughter from the camera crew. "It is true!" she reacted. "I was glad to be a girl, even though aunties in our village frowned at Mummy for only having a daughter. Pari and Shilpa, my closest friends, had fathers who worked on Kabir Singh's farm, too. We attended school together for those seven years, but I never saw them again after I left Gantak Mandi. I think of them often and wonder if they remember me or if they think about me. I still have portraits of them that I drew just a few weeks before I was kidnapped. Would you like to see them?"

Juhi rummaged through her manila folder for the portraits. Juhi felt proud of her drawings. She missed her friends.

"I remember when I met with the senators, they took my drawings from me and made copies," she said. "I asked the senator, 'Did you copy *all* of my drawings?' The senator looked down at me and spoke slowly, saying, 'We needed all of them to serve as evidence. Do you understand what evidence is?'"

"Yes, I understand," I snapped back. "But no one asked me if you could copy all of them."

"Excuse me?" The senator was offended.

I repeated, "No one asked me if you could make copies of my drawings. I would have given them to you if you had asked. I thought that in this country, people's possessions are not taken without asking, even from children."

"In matters of national security, we," the senator said, pointing to himself, "don't need to ask."

"Hmph! I wonder if that is what the doctor said who stole Papa's kidney," I responded.

"Wow, Juhi. So what did the senator say?" Max wanted to know.

"What could he say? He just stared at me, and I stared back until he looked away. He looked away first; I was not going to lose."

"That was gutsy."

Juhi didn't know what that meant, but she could read from Max's tone that he meant to pay her a compliment.

She smiled and continued to explain to Max that the capital city, New Delhi, was two hundred kilometers southeast of Gantak Mandi. Men used to come in big rusty flatbed trucks to take vegetables to New Delhi from Kabir Singh's farm. It was a five-hour journey each way. The two-lane road was paved in some sections and gave way to dirt paths in other sections. Trucks like the ones that came to Gantak Mandi shared the road with tractors with fat tires that left a wake of dust behind them and billowing TATA trucks that transported supplies and tools between the city and villages. One day, when Juhi visited Papa at the farm, she overheard the truck drivers say that they blast Hindi film songs at full volume on the radio just to stay awake. The terrain is a flat, dry land followed by more flat, dry land, ripe for farming—and for falling asleep while driving.

The deliverymen who traveled that road complained that there was very little to see on the journey. Sometimes they might pass a *dhaba* where they could stop for chai or soda and a samosa or *pani puri*. Juhi didn't know where those dhabas were. She only traveled that road once, on the night her family was kidnapped, and it was dark.

Once she did see a makeshift dhaba in Gantak Mandi, but she saw many in other parts of India after she was left an orphan. They were all similar. They made samosas in a huge, black wok that was burnt from all the years of use. Vegetable oil crackled over a wild blue-and-orange flame that looked as if it would reach out and grab you. Samosas were dropped in the fiery oil one at a time, instantly bubbling, crackling, and rising to the surface like an Olympic swimmer after completing a successful dive. One man hovered over the wok, carefully babysitting each samosa, flipping it in the oil, and lifting it out at the exact right moment. He carried his special spatula, the flat, round kind with small holes that leaked excess oil. He waved it with such pride, like an orchestra conductor. He was the guardian of the samosas.

Juhi saw many samosa woks when she lived in the New Delhi slums. It was like watching flames in a fireplace or like watching a newborn baby. She just could not look away while the soft, doughy shell cooked to a perfect brown crisp.

"My mouth waters just thinking about it." Juhi paused.

She told Max about one of her dhaba visits in New Delhi. Juhi stared at a woman and her children who pointed at the giant wok to pick the specific samosas they claimed as their own. The cook did not say anything and did not look at anyone. He nodded in acknowledgment but his gaze stayed on his precious gems. With a graceful glide, he lifted the chosen one out of the sea of samosas. As steam rose from its surface, he placed it on a little paper tray and scooped a tablespoon of *imli* (tamarind) chutney from a pocket and poured it next to the samosa. I still wonder how the samosa guardians can scoop the chutney without drenching the entire plate."

Juhi turned to the interpreter as if waiting for a reply to her question, but the interpreter just stared back at her. Juhi shrugged and continued.

There was one lucky day when a man had set up a dhaba in the Gantak Mandi market. Papa came home from the fields early to take Juhi there under the guise that they were buying *dal* and rice for Mummy. It was their secret, Juhi's and Papa's, but Mummy was very clever. She smelled the *imli* chutney and fried dough on Juhi. She scolded them for squandering money.

Juhi realized later that Mummy was not upset that they indulged in this small pleasure; she was hurt that they had ruined their appetites. Mummy had a freshly stocked supply of vegetables, lentils, and whole wheat. She especially enjoyed preparing meals on the days that the kitchen felt plentiful. Papa and Juhi had no choice but to eat the meal Mummy had prepared. It was delicious, but their overstuffed bellies ached. It was better to endure that than her wrath if the food had gone to waste. Juhi was up all night, rubbing her aching stomach, but she still looked forward to the next time she and Papa would sneak samosas.

Max smirked.

There are very few records about Gantak Mandi because it was only recently that anyone from there could read or write. No one knows when Gantak Mandi was first settled or how many people made the community. It started as a farming village, and its villagers were proud of their carrots, potatoes, cauliflower, squash, tomatoes, okra, spinach, and many other vegetables.

Kabir Singh, Jagjit Sahib, his father before him, and perhaps his father before him were landowners from the start. Neither Jagjit Sahib nor Kabir Singh beat or abused Papa or the other workers. If a worker needed to be disciplined, Kabir Singh called the worker to the side of the field and quietly explained what he wanted. Kabir Singh didn't make Papa look like a fool in front of the other farmers or harm Papa. Kabir Singh gave his workers vegetables to take home—not all the time but sometimes. Over the years, instead of increasing wages, he would offer the farmers more vegetables. Papa and the other farmers preferred more wages, but no one complained, because although Kabir Singh was benevolent, there were rumors that once someone crossed Kabir Singh, there was no turning back.

In Gantak Mandi, the only job for uneducated men was farming. The closest village was fifty kilometers away, and the villagers in Gantak Mandi believed that that village's farm owner was very cruel. In fact, it was Kabir Singh himself who spread those rumors. Juhi was convinced Kabir Singh made up that rumor just so his workers would not leave. Kabir Singh was shrewd and cunning—and he had complete power over Papa.

As the years passed, the farmers gained experience, so the farm produced more vegetables, and Kabir Singh grew richer and richer. He expanded the farm to cover more of Gantak Mandi, which put him in even more control of the village. Giant flatbed trucks replaced the modest ones. The only thing that stayed the same was the truck drivers.

On one of the days just before Juhi was kidnapped, her school finished early, so she walked to the fields. She thought she might find Papa at the end of his day and that they could walk home together. The delivery trucks were parked on the side of the field, where workers emerged from the fields and disappeared back among the crops. They walked into the fields with empty wheelbarrows, and when they returned, the wheelbarrows overflowed with vegetables. When the farmers kneeled to pour the vegetables onto the trucks, they looked like worshippers who bowed to Lord Ganesh.

The driver sat inside the truck with his leg lazily strewn across the steering wheel. He puffed on a *beedi*, a cigarette that is much more potent than American ones. The smoke filled the cabin. A man sat next to him, looking out the window. He drew on a beedi, too. Two other men stood watch behind the truck and issued commands to the farmers. Their black, leathery skin contrasted against their yellowed eyes and teeth. The driver's front tooth was gone, so when he talked, it was like peeking inside a cavernous black hole. He didn't say much except to bark orders at his assistants, who, in turn, reissued the harsh commands to the farmers. He spoke in a low tone, but the heaviness of his orders was threatening. The first time Juhi saw him, she went home and tried to mimic his style of snapping orders. She liked that it sounded authoritative even when he spoke softly. She thought it might work on the girls who teased her.

Juhi pulled out a portrait of the toothless driver from her manila envelope. In the drawing, he leaned against a clunky old truck.

Papa told Juhi that in Delhi, sellers from the *sabzi mandis* (vegetable market) purchased the crops at a wholesale market. Papa said that a wholesale market is a place where vegetables from all the surrounding farms are bought and sold to various shopkeepers and *sabzi wallas* (people who sell vegetables on a cart, who travel to different neighborhoods to sell). The wholesale market bustles with people, cars, cows, and shops selling every fruit and vegetable you can think of in rows and rows of stalls as long as railroad tracks. Men shout and talk over each other as they bargain, poke, and sniff vegetables. Papa said that even though he had not been to the wholesale market himself, Kabir Singh's vegetables were the best, and they always sold first. Juhi didn't know how Papa knew they were the best, but she never thought to question him.

Mummy spent her day cooking delicious fresh meals with the vegetables that Papa brought home from the farm. She used to squat over the fire, masterfully flipping rotis with her bare hands while stirring dal in a sizzling pot and pouring a rainbow of paprika, ginger, garlic, green chili, garam masala, mustard seeds, and cumin over crackling vegetables. Her purple sari was wrapped over her head, and she clenched the corner between her teeth. She used the excess fabric to from her sari to wipe the sweat from her brow. She was mesmerizing.

Juhi watched in awe as Mummy maneuvered all those moving pieces at the same time, intense smoke filling her eyes. If Juhi went near the stove, her eyes welled up with thick tears like raindrops, and the steam filled her lungs, causing her to cough wildly. But Mummy was immune, and although Mummy once told Juhi that it was disrespectful to say so, Mummy resembled an incarnation of Ganesh. Her long, thin, strong arms were guided by devotion, endless concentration, and intuition.

Juhi showed Max a stack of drawings of her mummy. Juhi paused and breathed in deep as she looked at her mother's portrait. She felt guilty that despite her photographic memory, sometimes she could not remember what her mother looked like, and she had to revisit her portraits to remind her. Juhi's voice shook as she spoke about her mother.

"One night as we ate dinner, Mummy covered her face shyly when Papa and I declared that Mummy was the most beautiful woman in the world." Two silent tears trickled down Juhi's cheeks. She stayed quiet for a long time.

Juhi had already told Max that Mummy and Papa had a difficult time having children. Like Papa, Juhi was an only child. On a hot summer day, when she was walking home from school, one of her classmates, Sudhir, said that Juhi was supposed to have a younger sister. Sudhir's father worked with Papa on Kabir Singh's farm.

"What do you mean?" she asked Sudhir, her temper swelled.

"She was killed when she was a baby!"

It was the first time Juhi hit someone, a precursor to the many other times she would have to defend herself after she left Gantak Mandi. Juhi slapped Sudhir across the face so hard that he was too scared to fight back. He ran home. Juhi fell to the ground after she hit him; her scraped knees bled down her legs, and her school uniform was covered in dirt. She walked home in a daze, wiping tears and dust from her eyes. Mummy searched her eyes for an explanation, and the blood left her face when Juhi repeated Sudhir's story. Mummy wept. Juhi thought Mummy was crying because she was disappointed in Juhi for fighting at school and, that too, with a boy. Mummy helped Juhi clean up and then stroked her hand through Juhi's hair. That was Juhi's signal that Mummy forgave her and that Mummy would not tell Papa. Juhi squeezed onto Mummy as Mummy helped Juhi wash away the dirt. Afterward, Juhi sat outside behind the house alone for a while. Mummy stayed inside the house in a daze. The sound of Papa's footsteps brought Mummy out of her daydream, and she waved away memories of her second child. She squatted over the fire and drowned a ball of moist *atta* (dough) in a bowl of dry flour, as if to bury the memory of Juhi's murdered sister.

Mummy was pregnant once after Juhi was born. When the village doctor, a different doctor than the one who stole Papa's kidney, saw it was another girl, he aborted Juhi's sister without telling Mummy and Papa. He told them that she had miscarried. He decided that he was doing them a favor. Who wants another girl, especially when there are no sons? It was a few years later when Mummy and Papa would come to know the awful truth. A nurse caught the doctor aborting another female baby. Some of the villagers beat the doctor and dumped him in the middle of the night somewhere in the uninhabited land between the Punjab and Pakistan border. He had nothing except two hundred rupees and the clothes he wore. Mummy and Papa did not plan to tell Juhi about her sister. But Mummy was babbling from delirium one day in the slum after they were kidnapped, and it came out. It was also the first time that Juhi ached for a sibling.

It was now noon, and Juhi had already talked with Max for two hours, but she had not talked about her father's kidney. She was visibly ready for another break. Max suggested they have lunch, which he provided for her, Kevin, and his entire crew. It was Mexican food, something Juhi had never tried before. Juhi's stomach growled, and the smell of black beans whet her appetite. She filled her plate with roti-like bread, called tortillas; green and red salsas that reminded her of chutney; and sour cream, which looked like *dahi* (Indian yogurt).

Since she arrived in the United States, Juhi's appetite played tricks on her. She felt hungry at mealtimes, but as soon as she saw food, she could not eat. But she felt hungry today, even after seeing the food. She added black beans and cheese to her plate. Each item sat on her plate in separate sections, and Kevin showed her how to stack the ingredients onto the tortilla, roll it tight, and then bite. She stared at him for a few seconds and decided to try it her own way, the Indian way. She tore a piece of tortilla and used it to scoop the beans and sour cream. In the next bite, she scooped up some more beans with salsa and cheese. As an Indian accustomed to eating with her hands, she dreaded awkward fork-and-knife meals. Mexican food did not require utensils, so she decided it was her favorite type of food, after Indian. She wished the tortillas were not so fat and that they were cooked a bit more. They tasted and felt raw compared to rotis. But she was happy that the entire meal was vegetarian, just like Juhi.

CHAPTER 7
THE BAD MEN

Juhi found new energy after lunch. She actually enjoyed the meal, and it helped her to relax. She returned to her chair under the lights and picked up where she left off. She wanted to talk about her mummy and papa. She wanted them to be the focus of her testimony. She decided that was more important than skipping right to the part of her story when her father's kidney was stolen.

Every morning after Mummy woke Juhi up, and Mummy got busy with her cooking, Juhi bathed and dressed in her school uniform, combed her hair, shined her shoes, and packed her schoolbag. Mummy packed her lunch tiffin (stainless-steel stacked lunch-box) with two rotis, vegetables, and, on lucky days, a couple of spoons of *kheer* (rice pudding) or a chocolate biscuit. Juhi didn't know where Mummy bought those special treats, but like magic, they appeared in Juhi's lunchbox now and again. When Juhi was too young to go to school, Mummy played with Juhi all day. Mummy was uneducated, so she could not teach Juhi math or science, but she did not think those subjects were as important as cooking and managing the home. But she did teach Juhi the importance of practice. Whatever Juhi did, if she wanted to be good at it, she had to practice. So when Juhi wanted to show the other kids in school that she had the quickest feet, she practiced hopscotch for hours until Mummy called her inside for dinner. When her rotis didn't roll in a circle, Juhi rolled a small piece of leftover dough over and over until it was a perfect sphere. Mummy taught Juhi what she knew—how to tell when vegetables were ripe or rotten and how to light the stove without burning the tips of her fingers. By the time Juhi was seven years old, Juhi could make every vegetable dish that Mummy made. Mummy also taught Juhi how to read Papa's mood when he came home from work. If his footsteps were heavy and long, he was sluggish and hungry. If they were fast and short, he was in a jolly mood and would be eager to hear about Juhi's day.

Even though Mummy and Papa filled Juhi's life with love, she spent a lot of time alone. Papa worked all day, and Mummy was tired after cooking and cleaning. To while away the time, Juhi played single-player games like pick-up sticks. She collected rocks from the fields surrounding their house, since she did not have marbles. But secretly she spent most of her alone time drawing. She loved to draw portraits of Mummy and Papa. She captured the lines that surrounded Mummy's eyes from lots of laughter and squinting in the sun, and Papa's wrinkly nose that took up most of his face. The three long, horizontal wrinkles that stretched across Papa's forehead—they were more pronounced when he and Mummy whispered about something they did not want Juhi to hear.

Juhi usually heard them anyway, and the topic was usually money and rent. The bad men visited Juhi's house every month to collect rent. They flashed their red eyes at Mummy. They looked at her in that funny way, as if they were thirsty. Juhi would hide her drawings in her backpack when they came to the house. They took anything that was not nailed to the ground or hidden out of sight. Although Mummy and Papa encouraged her drawing, Papa did complain that she spent *too* much time drawing. He said doctors and lawyers and scientists did not earn those jobs by drawing.

"It is funny that my drawings are the reason that I'm here in the United States today. It is funny that they are the evidence the Americans needed to capture the slumlord and the bad men. Kevin said there is a term for this—irony. I wish Papa was here. He would have been proud that my drawings came to good use after all..." Juhi's voice trailed off.

Aside from drawing, Juhi loved to read and write. In their small village, they didn't receive many letters, so Juhi had little opportunity to use her reading skills outside of school. But Papa used to say that one day Juhi would leave Gantak Mandi for the big city and have a job with her own office. He thought that would excite Juhi, but it frightened her to think about living in a big city. Before she was kidnapped, she had seen big cities in Hindi films. She remembered one movie that starred a young girl who was Juhi's age. The girl's mummy and papa were in a car accident, and in the commotion of trying to figure out whose fault it was, the girl was separated from her parents. She got lost in the maze of the big city and walked all day and night in a daze. She stumbled along the side of the road in the dark as a sea of honking cars whizzed past. Strange men approached her and looked at her the same way the bad men looked at Mummy. The hero eventually reunited the girl with her parents, but that movie haunted Juhi for a long time. She used to wake up shaking and sweating; the room spun around her, the car horns honked in her ears, and the red eyes of the bad men were still in her mind's eye as if they were in her room. Even though she knew it was just a bad dream, her heart pounded in her chest for what felt like an eternity before she could lie down again.

The strange men in the movie reminded her of the real-life bad men in Gantak Mandi. Juhi remembered the shaky buzz of their Maruti van as it approached her house. It made her heart pound as it did in her nightmares. When the bad men turned up at her house, Mummy told Juhi to wait outside while they talked with Mummy. While Juhi waited, she drew pictures of their van—every time it showed up, it had a new dent or scratch, and Juhi came to yearn for the challenge. Her favorite part was to draw the numbers—the license plate (which also changed frequently) and the long line of numbers inside the car near the steering wheel. She started with the side mirror and the crack that grew by a few millimeters each month. She made a perfect blend of white, brown, and red crayons to match the faded paint. On her tiptoes, she snuck into the front seat. It reeked of body odor and flatulence that had been trapped for days. She gagged and quickly rolled down a window. She slid into the driver's seat and located the vehicle identification number. She didn't know what the numbers meant, but she loved to practice writing them. She drew them just as they appeared to her—upside down as if she was the driver.

Juhi passed a drawing of the van to Max.

Inside her house, Juhi heard one of the men grunting repeatedly, and it quickened. Then he squealed, and the house fell silent. Then the fast grunting started again, but it was a different voice. It was the other bad man. Mummy didn't make any sounds. Juhi hid her notebook when the second man squealed like the first one. It meant that they would leave soon. They made those sounds every time they came to Juhi's house. After the second man squealed, Mummy yelled for Juhi to return to the house. The men were still inside and looked much calmer than when they arrived. They both wore crooked smiles that made them appear as dumb as they were. Mummy had changed her sari. She wiped sweat from her forlorn face.

When Juhi walked in, there were bags of groceries in the kitchen—biscuits, dried fruit, and other sweets. Juhi smiled because it meant that she would get an extra treat for lunch the next day. One of the men caught Juhi's smile, and he smiled back. Mummy grabbed Juhi's arm and stepped in front of her, shielding Juhi from him. Even though Juhi had been through much worse, the image of him smiling at her still haunted Juhi. Maybe it was because he was the first man, but not the last, to stare at her that way.

The bad men worked for Kabir Singh. Since he owned most of the land in Gantak Mandi, Juhi's family along with all the other farm workers paid rent to Kabir Singh. Most villagers walked to the farm to pay. Juhi's house was the only one that the bad men visited. On the first day of each month, they came to Juhi's house. After they left, they set up a little desk with stools in front of Kabir Singh's house. Kabir Singh sat in the middle and squinted in the sun, with each of the bad men on either side of him. The mean nature of the bad men seeped out of every one of their clogged pores. They never spoke, only grunted and pointed, as they commanded the villagers to "stand here" or "move over there." There was no reason for those commands, except that the villagers had to do as they were told, and the bad men liked being in charge.

The bad men were disgusting. They smelled worse than the outhouse at the farm. Their yellowed teeth had big, gaping holes between each tooth. It might seem strange, but the thing that frightened Juhi the most was their long, creepy fingers that were like a daddy longlegs spider. Both men had long nails; their nail beds were a bright-pink flesh that came to an abrupt halt at the nail, which was black and covered with dirt. The contrast drew Juhi's attention whenever she saw them. Juhi wondered how they could eat with such filthy fingers. Juhi shuddered and gagged at the thought of it. Max pushed her glass of water closer to her. He got too close, and his hand brushed hers. Juhi involuntarily yanked her hand away. She did not look at him when he pulled back. But she took a sip of the water he had passed to her and hoped that was enough of a peace offering.

"At my school in Gantak Mandi," Juhi explained, "the teacher reprimanded students for poor hygiene. Students were sent home if their nails were too long, if their shoes were not shined, or if their hair was not combed. The bad men would not survive one day at school."

The crew and Max laughed. Juhi liked that they laughed at the bad men.

To this day, Juhi did not know the names of the bad men, but their faces were etched into her memory. Max pulled another drawing of them from the stack that Juhi had already shared. She looked away, as if the bad men might reach through the paper and fondle her. With her eyes closed, she described them exactly as they appeared in the portrait.

One of them was tall and lanky, and he was the boss. She shuddered again and paused.

"Juhi, you are safe. They can't hurt you now."

Juhi wanted to believe him, but when she closed her eyes again, she felt their dirty fingers tracing her arms, their hot breath hitting her face, and the memory of stale alcohol stench filling her nose.

The tall one had thick, black, unwieldy hair and a dark mustache to match. His mustache almost covered his mouth, making it difficult to understand him. He had a long neck and skinny arms and legs. He was already tall, but he was very thin, so he appeared even taller. His nose was covered in little red bumps, and his skin was black leather. He had little craters all over his face, as if he was eaten by bugs and then he picked the scabs. His eyes appeared to pop out of their sockets; the contrast of their yellowness to his dark skin made him repugnant. His lips were blood red, stained from *paan,* (small betel leaves filled with tobacco and spices) that he chewed endlessly. He wore the same brown button-down shirt and black pants every day. Juhi wondered if he had more than one of those brown shirts or if he wore the same one day after day. His faded, wrinkled pants had torn pockets and a small hole on the right near his stomach. There was no life in his eyes; his gaze was distant even when he was right in front of Juhi. Juhi nicknamed him "Mogambo" after the villain in one of her favorite Hindi films, *Mr. India.*

Juhi nicknamed his friend, the other bad man, Gabbar after the notorious bad guy from *Sholay,* because he looked like the actor. They had the same curly black hair and broad torso. He lazily dragged a belt behind him wherever he went. He said it was a whip, but Juhi never saw him use it. Although he was one of the bad men, Gabbar sometimes hesitated when Mogambo ordered him around. He probably spent his whole life taking orders from Mogambo and would not know what to do without him. Even though Juhi hated both of them, she believed that on his own, Gabbar might have been a nice man who was forced to be bad.

Like Mogambo, Gabbar wore the same thing every day—a blue, collared shirt and brown pants. The shirt had a small hole in the right arm just above the wrist. He smelled as bad as Mogambo and chewed the same betel leaves. At first glance, Juhi thought they were mentally ill or disabled. They constantly chewed, spat, and drank from bottles; it made their movements jerky and unpredictable. Whenever they came around, Juhi was careful to dodge out of the way of their spit, which sometimes Mogambo launched directly at her and laughed hysterically as she leapt out of the way. She avoided making eye contact with them. When they looked at her, they saw a piece of candy they wanted to unwrap.

Mummy and Papa physically stood in front of her when the bad men were near, but sometimes Mummy and Papa were not there when she saw the bad men. Sometimes Mogambo and Gabbar drove around Gantak Mandi just for fun. Juhi and her friends saw them as they walked home from school. During those times, both of the bad men had bottles in their hands and drank from them every few minutes. The windows in their truck were wide open, and they both seemed to dangle their arms, poke out their heads from the windows, and shout and yell at no one in particular. They drove in circles that created dust clouds on the footpath. Dust filled Juhi's eyes and made her cough, and the bad men laughed and drank from their bottles and drove faster in circles around Juhi and her friends. Luckily, the bad men didn't do anything else to harm them. But they loved the fear they incited. Everyone in Gantak Mandi hated the bad men, they were powerless to stop them.

CHAPTER 8

THE ROTTEN TOOTH

Dr. Suraj Rao stole Papa's kidney. He was the only doctor in Gantak Mandi. Juhi used to see him in the village, but she had never spoken to him. One day Mummy sent Juhi to the vegetable stand at the village market. It was near his clinic, and Juhi saw him. That was the closest she ever got to him. His long, thick, straight hair swayed as he walked, and it covered his face as if he was hiding from someone. He was tall and muscular and younger than Papa, maybe in his thirties. He had light skin and a narrow nose, which made him look smart. His long eyelashes were almost girlish, but the rest of his face had strong lines and a strong jaw. His eyes were unforgettable. They were so dark that they looked black. Yet somehow they appeared hollow, as if the life they once possessed was squeezed out of them. Juhi drew his portrait on the night that she saw him in the market. She felt lucky that she got a rare and up-close look at him.

She rummaged through her portraits and handed the sketch of Dr. Rao to Max.

Dr. Rao looked as though he wanted to be left alone. He walked with his head down, and he never said hello to anyone. He was not married. He moved to Gantak Mandi when Juhi was seven years old. One of the few things that she knew about him was that he grew up and was educated in New Delhi. Most people leave the village to move to the city, not the other way around. No one knew why he moved from New Delhi to a small village, but Mummy and Papa and the other villagers were grateful to have a big-city doctor in Gantak Mandi.

Papa's back tooth was beyond rotten. By the time the pain grew unbearable, whatever ailed him had spread to his other teeth. Two weeks before Papa's kidney was taken, Papa asked Kabir Singh for a few hours off to visit Dr. Rao, but Kabir Singh refused. It was the peak of the squash season, and Kabir Singh needed all of his workers, especially the experienced ones. Once the peak finished, Kabir Singh himself called Dr. Rao to make Papa's appointment.

"You will be the first patient tomorrow morning," Kabir Singh told Papa. "That way Dr. Rao will be fresh and alert."

As Papa left the farm the day before his appointment, Kabir Singh shook Papa's hand, thanked him for his hard work, and wished him good luck at the appointment. Papa worked on Kabir Singh's farm for thirty-three years. That was the first time Kabir Singh shook Papa's hand. Papa was surprised by Kabir Singh's kindness. He went home singing and laughing.

On the morning that Papa arrived at the clinic, the entire town center was abandoned. A rusty desk and chair sat outside the clinic that faced the dirt road that led to the clinic. Patients typically checked in there; however, that day the post stood empty. Papa waited for a few minutes; he began to feel anxious that Dr. Rao was not there. He waited for a few more minutes, and then out of nowhere, the doctor appeared. Papa followed him into the patient room, and Dr. Rao commanded Papa to wear the patient gown that lay on the exam table. Papa held his breath as he stretched one arm, and then the other, into the squalid gown, which was stained with other patients' sweat, pus, and filth. Papa felt too nervous to ask why he had to undress for a toothache and why he must wear such a horrid gown.

Without introducing himself or asking Papa any questions, Dr. Rao began a full-body exam. He carefully pulled rubber gloves over each of his hands, as if Papa had leprosy. As he lay there, Papa searched the drab room with his eyes. Cracks marked every side of the grey stone walls. In addition to the patient's bed, the room contained a stool, a small table, and a leaky sink. A dusty desktop fan sat perched on the doctor's table. Shattered pieces of the fan's blades stuck out of the holes, like a prisoner pressed against metal railings, begging to be set free. The generator, which kept the room lit, looked like it might slip and break at any minute. Its humming noise mixed with the buzzing of two flies that circled the single light bulb. That was the only sound in the room. Papa could hear his own heart beating, and he could hear its rhythmic *thump thump* in his ears. The gown felt damp as Papa's sweat pooled in it.

Dr. Rao was not dressed the way Papa expected. Instead of a crisp, white lab coat, his wrinkled jacket had a yellow cigarette-smoke hue. He grimaced beneath dark circles under his eyes. He examined Papa's head and face, poked his cheeks, and looked at Papa's scalp the way Mummy sometimes looked for lice in Juhi's hair. He felt behind Papa's ears. Papa was grateful that Dr. Rao wore gloves. Papa was embarrassed for an educated man to touch his sweaty face. Papa opened his mouth, expecting the doctor to look at the black, rotten tooth.

"Shut your mouth!" Dr. Rao snapped. Then he turned his back to Papa and wrote something in a brown notebook. "How old are you?" he demanded with his back still turned away.

Confused and embarrassed, Papa replied, "Forty."

"What medical problems do you have?" barked Dr. Rao.

"Just a toothache."

"Any past surgeries?"

"No. I have had no need for surgery, and if I did, I would not be able to afford it."

The doctor scribbled Papa's responses in his notebook and continued to examine Papa's back and chest. Papa had to breathe in and out heavily three times at Dr. Rao's command while the doctor pressed his cold metal device against Papa's skin. The examination continued, and Papa was forced to lie quietly while the doctor examined his genitals, moving his penis from one side to the other while feeling the whole area. He squeezed Papa's thighs and legs and then checked his feet. When Papa turned over, the doctor listened again through his metal device to Papa's lower back, where he seemed to spend a lot of time. Twenty-five minutes had passed, and the doctor still had not looked inside Papa's mouth. Papa's anxiety grew. He feared that his appointment would take longer than Kabir Singh gave permission for. But he was too worried about insulting the doctor to ask how much longer it would be. Another man entered the room, whom Dr. Rao introduced as his assistant. Papa recognized him immediately as Mogambo. Again, Papa was too sheepish to ask why Mogambo was there acting as the doctor's assistant.

Mogambo handed Dr. Rao a small brown bag filled with medicine vials. The doctor drew two tubes of Papa's blood with no explanation. Without warning, Dr. Rao jabbed another needle into Papa's arm—this one was connected to a vial of medicine.

"Will you be removing my tooth soon...?" Papa's question trailed off, as his eyes grew heavy.

He fell asleep before Dr. Rao replied "no."

When he awoke, Papa still lay on the bed, wearing the soiled gown. His eyes searched the room. He felt groggy and sensed that he was alone. He remembered where he was, and he sloppily moved his tongue to the back of his mouth to feel for the rotten tooth. It was still there! Yet he felt different.

Through the cloudiness that filled his head, he could feel that something had changed. He tried to prop himself up, but he collapsed and screamed piercingly from a sharp pain. He rotated from his stomach onto his side. He shivered from the cold wetness that drenched him from the waist down. He thought it must be his own urine, and he pulled the gown up to his waist and, with painstaking effort, twisted it in front of him. Drops of blood fell from the gown and made a *splat!* as they hit the filthy floor tiles. The gown looked like the *dhoti* he wore last spring to celebrate Holi. The metallic smell of his own blood overtook the room, and as he writhed in pain, dried flakes of blood sloughed off him and slowly drifted to the ground to mix with the pool of wet blood that was still collecting.

He screamed again as he tried to sit up, but it was no use. He leaned over the side of the table and vomited.

He instinctively pressed his hand into his thigh where the pain radiated. Papa traced a long cut that stretched along his inner thigh. He could feel the blood streaming out of the wound, onto his fingers, and collecting in his palm. It still bled. His hand grazed a soaked bandage that only covered half of his wound. It felt rough on the edges, puffy, and tender. He felt the crisscross of stitches. He jerked and howled every time his finger touched between them, but he couldn't stop. He shrieked uncontrollably. He tried to flee, but he was paralyzed. Dr. Rao burst into the room.

"Shut up!" Dr. Rao demanded. Mogambo followed and pointed a gun at Papa. Papa lay there helpless, like a cow about to be slaughtered. Tears ran down his cheeks and mixed with the blood and vomit on the floor. Papa folded his shaking hands together in *namaste* and faced the doctor.

"Please, Dr. Raoji. Please. Do not hurt me."

They ignored Papa. Papa's whole body slumped into despair, and Mogambo still pointed the gun at him. Mogambo struck Papa across the face with it, and Papa's head crashed into the wall. His nose bled, and his watery eyes blinded him.

"Get up!" demanded Mogambo.

But it was too much. Papa could not move. Mogambo struck him again.

"Get up!" This time Dr. Rao yelled at Papa. But Papa did not move. He just wept in despair.

Dr. Rao shoved Mogambo out of the way, lifted Papa, and then dumped him into a wheelchair. The pain proved too much, and Papa fainted. Dr. Rao checked if Papa was still breathing. He stared down at Papa in disgust as he wiped Papa's blood off his fingers. Still in a coma or somewhere between sleep and hell, Papa was wheeled away through a hidden hallway and out a secret back door. They left Papa in an empty alley. It was dark outside. Dr. Rao fanned smelling salt under Papa's nose, and Papa regained consciousness. His first thought was Kabir Singh. Even in his anguish, Papa panicked about how to explain his absence at work to his boss.

Dr. Rao joined a shadow that lurked a few meters away, behind a parked van. Papa strained to see, still delirious and confused but grateful to be out of the blood-soaked room and in the open air. Dr. Rao handed an envelope to the second man who was still covered by shadows. There was something familiar about the second man, but Papa could not identify him. The second man opened the envelope and handed it back to Dr. Rao.

"Count it out loud," the man commanded Dr. Rao.

As Dr. Rao counted each slip of paper and handed it back to the man in the shadow, the shadow grew more clear. It was Kabir Singh. Papa was certain. He knew Kabir Singh's face, his posture, his walk; surely he recognized his silhouette. Dr. Rao continued to count the paper for several minutes, and as Papa's eyes adjusted to the darkness, he saw Dr. Rao pass rupee after rupee to Kabir Singh. When it was done, Dr. Rao disappeared, and Kabir Singh stuffed the money back into the envelope. Kabir Singh turned to walk away, but he stopped abruptly, turned, and marched toward Papa. His face emerged from behind the shadows as he stared down at Papa.

"I expected to get a few more years of hard work from you, but you have slowed down, and you make too many mistakes. You waste too much of the crop. You have disappointed me. But I found a better use for you. But do not worry; you still have one kidney. You are lucky. I usually take both. You should be grateful that I spared your life even after you let me down."

Before Papa had a chance to respond, Kabir Singh turned his back to Papa and vanished into the shadows.

Papa was left stranded in the alley. Horror turned to sorrow and despair as Kabir Singh's words washed over him. His sank deeper into the wheelchair. His breath quickened, faster and faster, into a panic attack. He could not breathe, and he raised his head to the sky like a drowning swimmer, begging for oxygen. He clutched his chest.

"Papa!" Juhi screamed.

Juhi and Mummy were in the van that was parked in the alley. The windows were blackened so no one could see in or out. Mogambo was in the van with them. He slid the back door open, which faced Papa. Mogambo jumped out of the van and wheeled Papa toward the van. The redness of Mogambo's eyes shone in the moonlight like a wolf. Mogambo pushed Papa's wheelchair to the edge of the van. He tipped the wheelchair forward and dumped Papa into the van like a barrel filled with potatoes. He threw Papa's clothes in after him. Mogambo slammed the door shut before Juhi, Mummy, or Papa could shout for help, and locked them into complete darkness.

Juhi and Mummy shifted to the side so Papa could lie down. He gripped Mummy's hand in his. He was relieved to see them and searched their faces for answers. Mummy was silent and looked away. Papa turned to Juhi. Juhi's eyes had adjusted to the darkness, and she saw that Papa's face was overtaken with sadness. He examined the black eye circling the right side of Juhi's face and the dried blood around her nose.

Juhi told Papa what little she knew. She told Papa that they came home in the afternoon and told Mummy and Juhi that they were leaving forever. They forced Mummy and Juhi to get into their van. Juhi and Mummy demanded to know where Papa was, but they wouldn't tell them. When Mummy begged for an explanation, he slapped her so hard her whole body twisted and fell to the ground. Juhi charged him and hit him back, and she knocked him into a wall. The impact set the small cupboard loose, and it crashed on top of him. In the commotion, one of the kitchen knives fell on the ground near Juhi. She grabbed it and tried to stab him. He grew wild with anger, and he punched Juhi in the stomach and the face over and over. Mummy threw herself over Juhi to make him stop.

"Who? Who attacked you?" Papa demanded.

"Gabbar and Mogambo."

Papa stared at Juhi in disbelief.

Gabbar and Mogambo shoved Juhi and Mummy into the van and brought them to the clinic. They sat in the van for several hours, but the windows were blacked out, and they didn't know where they were. They thought they would never see Papa again.

Juhi thrust her body onto Papa and embraced him. He shrieked and writhed in pain. Startled, Juhi pulled away and sobbed. Papa turned onto his side, still wearing the gown from the procedure, and lifted it up to expose his scar. Juhi turned away in horror, and Mummy screamed. Mummy attempted to put a consoling hand on Papa's thigh, but he pushed her away.

"It is too tender. Please do not touch it."

Mummy withdrew her hand and fell back against the van wall. Papa pulled the gown back over his wound, and Juhi turned around to face him. She came closer to him and pressed her hand on his forehead with light pressure. Juhi's tears fell onto Papa's face.

He wiped her eyes and attempted to smile. He hated to see Juhi so frightened.

Papa insisted that he would be OK. After all, he still had one kidney.

"One kidney?" Mummy shrieked in horror. "That doctor took one of your kidneys? Kabir Singh paid for your kidney?"

Papa looked away from Mummy. Juhi had seen news reports about kidneys being stolen and sold to wealthy Westerners who needed transplants. But for every story, there was a government official who swore it off as folklore. Juhi and her parents agreed—no one could be so evil. And while it was happening to them they still couldn't believe that a wealthy white person would pay to have Papa's kidney stolen so that they could live. And there was no way to know if Papa would survive or to confirm that Kabir Singh really only took one kidney.

"How do we know he is not lying? How do we know that you will not die?" Juhi shouted like she had never shouted before.

Mummy grabbed Juhi's wrist and pulled Juhi into her chest. The monotony of Mummy's breathing calmed Juhi. None of them knew what to say. Papa implored Juhi to tell him more about what happened to her.

Through her sobs, Juhi told Papa that she could hear Kabir Singh's voice outside the van, but they could not see him. They heard Kabir Singh ask someone how much money he could earn for a kidney. Then he said he had three more farmers lined up—Sameer Uncle, Govinda Uncle, and Rajeshswami Uncle. All of them were Papa's friends on the farm and were the same age as Papa.

"He sold you," Mummy said to Papa. "The man whom you love like a brother sold you."

Mummy's words stung Papa. His thoughts shifted back and forth between his broken heart and his wound. He wept like an abandoned child, and Mummy and Juhi joined him. They cried until they were wrung dry. Mogambo and Gabbar jumped into the van, and together they sped away into the emptiness of the lonely night.

PART 2

Kevin

CHAPTER 9
DIAGNOSIS

The next day, Max decided it would be better for him, as an artist and journalist, to pause Juhi's interview so he could interview Kevin. Max wanted a simultaneous account from Kevin about how he wound up in India. Kevin agreed to Max's request so Juhi could get a break, even though Juhi was ready to share the rest of her story. Juhi still went to Max's studio with Kevin the next day. She knew most of Kevin's side of the story, but she thought he might say something new. Kevin took his seat across from Max in the same seat that Juhi had sat in the day before. The cameras started to roll, and Kevin jumped right in.

Kevin had a corner office on the eighth floor of Logan Studio in Burbank—just outside of Los Angeles—where the entire marketing department was housed. Kevin's story started on his thirteenth anniversary at Logan Studios. It was also his one-year anniversary in his role as director of marketing for new releases. In Kevin's thirteen years with Logan, he had four different jobs and moved up in title and pay with each new role. He took his first job with Logan when he was twenty-one. He was fresh out of undergrad at New York University, and he started as an assistant. Kevin didn't land his dream job until after he graduated from business school more than a decade later. He'd wanted to do marketing and promotions at a major film and television studio since he could remember.

As a marketing director for new releases, Kevin partnered with some of the largest advertising agencies in the world. They developed swanky campaigns for print, television, radio, and web, all to promote the newest blockbusters and movie bombs that Logan Studios produced and distributed. He used to meet with the actors from the movies that he promoted, and he attended celebrity-ridden red-carpet release parties. The glamour of it all lost its luster after a couple years. Kevin still liked the actual work part of it, though. On the night of his thirteenth anniversary at Logan, Kevin's coworkers organized a celebratory happy hour.

Kevin's colleague, Jeremy, swung by Kevin's office, and they walked out together.

"So thirteen years? Man, you held on tight."

It didn't actually feel that long to Kevin.

"Really? You gotta be joking. How many films have you worked on?" Jeremy asked Kevin.

"At least three or four a year."

"Dude! That's a lot! Don't tell me it doesn't feel like a long time!"

Kevin smiled half-heartedly. "So...where are we going tonight?"

"The usual."

The marketing-department personnel were regulars at the Blue Room, a dive bar one block from Logan Studios. The bartenders and waitresses all knew Kevin and his colleagues. It was their "Cheers."

"We're all coming out for you, so you better have at least one drink!" Jeremy told Kevin. "It's Friday night. I don't want to hear that you have to get up at six tomorrow morning to run a marathon or volunteer at a homeless shelter." In addition to being coworkers, Kevin and Jeremy were friends. Jeremy liked to give Kevin a hard time about being a morning person.

Kevin's coworkers knew that he started his weekends early in the morning with a jog or to meet his self-imposed commitment to volunteer once a month. He did have to wake up early the next day but not to exercise or volunteer. He had to be out of bed at seven o'clock in the morning to make it to the clinic for his seven-thirty dialysis treatment. It was a four-hour treatment, and Kevin liked to get it out of the way first thing in the morning to free up the rest of his weekend.

Kevin was diagnosed with kidney failure ten years ago. He was twenty-four years old and was living in New York City. Kevin remembered the day he got diagnosed, as if it was just yesterday. He remembered every detail—they told Kevin he would need dialysis for the rest of his life.

Kidney disease can be genetic, but as far as Kevin knew, his was a fluke. Kevin didn't know of any family members with kidney problems. His diagnosis felt like he went to sleep one night and when he woke the next day, one of his limbs was gone. Sometimes people have kidney disease for months or years but don't show any symptoms until one or both kidneys start to shut down. Kevin was probably sick for a while but had no idea until one day his entire body swelled like a balloon. He ached everywhere for three days until he couldn't take it any longer. He staggered out of bed, got dressed, and walked down the stairs to the garage. He could hardly descend the steps, and midway down, he collapsed on the breezeway. He had just enough strength to reach for his phone in his pocket to call 9-1-1. Two hours and a trip to the ER later, a nephrologist—a kidney doctor—dropped a bomb on Kevin.

"You have end-stage renal failure. That means your kidneys aren't working the way they're supposed to. Unfortunately, there's no cure. You'll have to start dialysis treatments right away, and you'll have to do them for the rest of your life or until you can get a transplant."

It didn't make sense. Kevin was healthy. He drank homemade smoothies every day. He cut out all processed foods from his diet and alternated between CrossFit and yoga seven days a week. He stopped eating red meat and, over time, turned vegan. At most, he drank one or two beers each week. He even dabbled in meditation on occasion and seriously considered attending a ten-day silent-meditation course in Dharamshala, India, where the Dalai Lama lived. And here was this doctor, Dr. Goyal, telling Kevin he had to do dialysis treatments for the rest of his life?

"I'll send a nurse in to give you instructions. Do you have any questions for me?" Dr. Goyal asked Kevin.

Kevin didn't know where to start. A stream of questions raced through his mind like a stock ticker on fast forward. *What is dialysis? Is it a daily pill? What are the side effects? What will happen if I don't do dialysis? Why is this happening to me? Could I have done anything to prevent it? Can I still have sex? What will Emma say? Can I still exercise? Is this going to kill me? How much does dialysis cost? Will my insurance cover it? Will it impact my work? How can I get a transplant? How long will that take? How much will it cost? I would need a kidney to have a transplant, right? Where could I find a kidney?*

Kevin didn't realize that he was talking out loud. Dr. Goyal put a reassuring hand on Kevin's shoulder.

"Slow down," he said. "Let's take it one thing at a time."

Kevin looked at Dr. Goyal with despair.

"I know this is a lot to process," Dr. Goyal said. His calm voice helped Kevin breathe a little easier. "You're young, incredibly fit, and you're otherwise healthy. This doesn't make sense to you."

Kevin nodded in agreement. It was nice to have a doctor who wasn't socially and emotionally void.

"Unfortunately, medicine hasn't progressed enough to understand why some kidneys fail. There are markers that we can monitor, like if a family member has it, or certain ethnic groups that are at higher risk, such as Latinos and African Americans. People with diabetes are at higher risk, too. But you don't match any of those. I wish I could tell you why this is happening. Like I said, I will have a nurse come in to talk to you about the next steps. She can answer all your questions about lifestyle impact and any transplant questions too. But before I go, dialysis is not a pill that you can take. With normal kidney function, you have two kidneys that work together twenty-four hours a day to clean the toxins from your body. Those toxins leave your body through your urine. People with zero kidney function ultimately stop urinating altogether. You told me you're still urinating several times a day, which means you still have some kidney function. That's great, but it's not enough to keep you healthy. So you need some assistance, which is where dialysis comes in."

"You said normal kidney function is when two kidneys work together. Are you saying I only have one kidney? That I was born with some weird abnormality, and no one noticed?" Kevin panicked.

"No. Not at all. Your ultrasound shows two kidneys. But your creatinine blood test was through the roof. It's one of the primary markers of abnormal kidney function. Have you noticed that your urine looks foamy?"

Kevin actually had noticed that his urine was a little frothy, but he didn't think anything of it.

"There's too much strain on your kidneys; they need support," Dr. Goyal explained. "That's what dialysis provides. If we don't start treatments, you will die. I'm sorry to say it so bluntly, but that's the truth. We all need kidney function to survive. Kidneys aren't extra organs like an appendix. And it's not like losing your eyes or ears. Without kidney function, we can't live."

Kevin thought he might faint. He hunched over the patient bed and put his head between his legs. The doctor put his hand on Kevin's back. "Breathe deep, in and out," he instructed Kevin. "Can I get a nurse in here?" Dr. Goyal shouted into the hallway, and he turned his body toward the door without leaving Kevin's side.

A nurse rushed in and rubbed Kevin's back. Dr. Goyal stepped back but stayed in the room. Kevin sat up again as he felt the blood rush back to his face.

"Are you all right?" Dr. Goyal asked.

"Yeah. I'm sorry; this is just a lot to take in."

"I understand," replied Dr. Goyal. "This is Margaret; she's one of our best nurses. She will tell you about scheduling dialysis and will discuss other options with you, such as a transplant."

Kevin forced a smile.

"Nice to meet you, Kevin. Do you have any family that we can call to help get you home? You will still be here for a while, but you might feel better with a family member? But only with your consent."

Kevin explained to Margaret that he didn't have any family, but he instructed her to call his girlfriend, Emma.

"Why don't you call Emma, and I'll stay for a few more minutes with Kevin?" Dr. Goyal told Margaret.

Margaret looked at the doctor with disbelief. Doctors didn't typically spend that much time with their patients. They were usually in a rush to round on the next one coming through the door. But Dr. Goyal pitied Kevin. Dr. Goyal was only a few years older than Kevin, and he could relate to Kevin.

"You asked about what dialysis is?" Dr. Goyal said. "It's a way to clean out your blood. A machine, called a dialyzer, removes the toxins from your bloodstream, since your body isn't doing it well enough on its own."

"So I have to get hooked up to a machine?" Kevin asked.

"Yes."

"How do you do that?"

"You'll have to go to an outpatient surgery center so the surgeon can create what's called an artery vein graft or AV graft. An AV graft is when your own vein is connected to your own artery. The graft is also called an "access." Once you have an access, it gets connected to a dialyzer with tubes. The dialyzer draws out your blood into the dialyzer. The dialyzer is filled with dialysate, which removes toxins from your blood. After your blood has been cleaned, the dialyzer pumps it back into your body. The dialyzer pumps out "dirty" blood and returns clean blood, simultaneously. It's a continuous cycle of removing and returning your own blood."

Kevin thought he was tough, but the image of his blood being pumped in and out of his body made his stomach turn. He dry-heaved and began to sweat.

"So I just want to make sure I understand," Kevin said. "I'll be able to see this whole thing happening?"

"You won't be able to see the machine actually cleaning your blood, but you will be able to see the blood leaving your body, and the clean blood reentering," Dr. Goyal explained.

That was enough to push Kevin over the edge. He vomited into the tray that Margaret had left for him. Kevin missed a little, and some of it landed on the exam bed. It soaked through the thin paper lining.

"Nurse!" Dr. Goyal shouted again into the hallway. "Why don't you lie down?" he suggested to Kevin as he replaced the soiled bed lining.

Margaret appeared in the doorway a few seconds later and took over. She cleaned the mess and dumped Kevin's vomit into the trash labeled "Biohazard Waste."

"Margaret will assist you from here," the doctor said to Kevin. "You'll be here for a little while longer. My shift is ending and another nephrologist, my colleague, Dr. Mazgar will be on call. I'll speak to her directly about your situation so she will be fully informed when she sees you. Again, I'm sorry that this is happening. Good luck."

Kevin could barely say "thank you" to Dr. Goyal before he vomited again. Dr. Goyal used that moment to leave the room and to avoid embarrassing Kevin any further.

"You poor thing." Margaret moved around the room. "I spoke with Emma. She's on her way."

Kevin had only been dating Emma for a few weeks. This was a lot for Kevin; what would she think? He knew it was wrong to think this, but he couldn't help but wonder if he might cut and run if the roles were reversed. He wouldn't blame Emma if she dumped him.

"Thanks, Margaret. Could I have some water?"

"I wish I could give you water, but I can't. When you have end-stage renal failure, you have to be careful about your liquid intake. See how your fingers and belly are distended?"

Kevin looked at her with confusion.

"You're swollen. That's because the liquid has built up in your body, and you're not urinating enough."

"But I am still urinating, like I told Dr. Goyal."

"Yes, but not enough," Margaret replied. "I can give you a few ice chips to suck on?"

"Sure. Fine. Whatever. Does this mean I have to stop drinking water? I drink at least a gallon of water every day."

"No, of course not. Water is good for you. But you should ask Dr. Mazgar how much is safe to drink."

"This is ridiculous! I don't understand! Doctors have been telling us for years how important it is to drink at least eight glasses of water a day, and now it's not safe?"

Margaret remained silent. Nothing she could say would comfort Kevin. She continued to complete forms at the mobile computer station next to Kevin's bed.

"I'm sorry. I'm not angry with you," Kevin told Margaret. "I…I just don't understand. I still don't even know what dialysis is. I mean, how often do I have to do it? How long does it take? Do I have to come to the hospital to get treatments? Will it make my hair fall out like chemo?"

"I know you still have a lot of questions, and I will answer all of them. I just want to finish a few things so we can get you treated as quickly as possible. Is that okay, or would you prefer to talk through your questions now?"

"No, go ahead and work on whatever you were doing. I'm sorry. I'm just…scared."

"I understand, Kevin." Margaret reassured him. "I'll help you get through it. I need to step out to call over to the social worker's office. I'll be back in a few minutes."

Just as Margaret left, Emma arrived. She must have sped across town; she arrived just fifteen minutes after Margaret called her. She ran to hug Kevin, but she stopped herself.

"Is it OK?"

"Yeah, it's fine." Kevin smiled and held his arms out toward her.

They embraced for a long while. She rubbed his back with one hand and kissed his neck and cheek.

"Are you OK? What happened?" She looked into Kevin's eyes with concern.

Kevin sighed. He didn't know where to begin.

"I…I…I don't know how to say this, but I have kidney failure. It means I have to—"

"You have to do dialysis," Emma interrupted.

"You know about this?"

"My grandfather had to do dialysis for twenty years, until he..." Emma's voice trailed off.

"Until what? Until he died?" Kevin asked matter-of-factly.

"Well...yes. But he was sixty-five years old when he *started* dialysis. You're young and healthy."

"How did he die? Was it the dialysis that eventually caused his death?"

Emma looked away without responding. He died after he chose to stop dialysis treatments. The dialysis itself actually kept him alive. It was the kidney disease that caused his death. But by the time he was in his eighties, dialysis grew to be too tough on his frail body.

"It was, wasn't it?" Kevin said more as a statement than a question.

"No, that's not true. After almost twenty years, dialysis was too hard for him. But when he did dialysis, he came to my graduation and attended my sister's wedding. We had Christmas and birthdays together. He wouldn't have been able to do all that without dialysis." She paused. She knew she sounded patronizing, and that was the last thing she wanted. "He lived a full life by the time he passed away. Dialysis can be hard when you're older. But I remember seeing young patients at his dialysis clinic—people our age—who were healthy.

Dialysis wasn't as hard for them." Emma's voice swelled with hope.

Kevin was quiet. He half listened to Emma, but he also focused on the question that lingered in his mind.

"Look, I know we just started dating, and this is a lot. If you want to take off, I understand."

"You're giving me an out? Are you kidding me?" She was angry.

"I'm not asking you to leave. I'm just saying I would understand if you want to."

"Well, do you want me to? Because if you do, just say so. The nurse who called me made it sound like you wanted me to be here."

"I do. Of course, I do. I don't want you to leave. It's just..."

Kevin didn't know what else to say. Emma was hurt, and he regretted that he even mentioned it.

"I'm sorry. It's just a lot to process. I don't want you to feel like you have to stick around because of all this."

In that moment, Kevin forced Emma to wonder if she cared for him more than he did for her. He loved her as much as she loved him, but neither of them was ready to be that vulnerable. Emma was the best thing that ever happened to Kevin. She was particular about things that he didn't care about, and vice versa. He could be himself, and she didn't judge him. They were best friends with all the benefits.

But because it had only been a few weeks since they started dating, and Kevin subscribed to the ridiculous "relationship rules," he didn't tell her how he felt. He didn't want to come on too strong. In hindsight, he wished that he had told her that he was already in love with her.

"I'd like to stay," Emma said.

"Great," Kevin replied and kissed her hand.

Margaret returned with a wheelchair.

"You must be Emma. Nice to meet you." She turned to Kevin without waiting for a reply. "I'm going to take you to the third floor now. You need to get an emergency catheter and that's where they'll do your dialysis treatment."

"Is the wheelchair necessary?" Kevin asked.

"I'm afraid so."

Kevin's heart pounded. Dr. Goyal said that he would need outpatient surgery to get a graft in his arm. *Were they doing it at the hospital instead? Right now? Was that another way of saying he needed a catheter?* Kevin wondered. His hands shook with nervousness, but he put a brave face on in front of Emma.

CHAPTER 10
ROLLER COASTER

Kevin had a routine by his third month of dialysis. Most people have a bar or restaurant that they frequent, but Kevin was a regular at the dialysis clinic just a few blocks from his SoHo one-bedroom apartment. He shared the apartment with a college buddy. They were roommates at New York University and stayed on together after graduation. Kevin signed up for early morning dialysis treatments before work. That was the least disruptive to the rest of his life. He visited the clinic three times each week on Tuesdays, Thursdays, and Saturdays. Kevin showed up at five o'clock in the morning and was hooked up to the machine fifteen minutes later. The treatments usually lasted three and a half to four hours, so it gave him enough time to hop on the subway and arrive at work by ten o'clock. That might seem late for most offices, but not for Logan Studios and not for Kevin's low rank.

After he graduated from college, Kevin accepted a bottom-of-the-totem-pole marketing job at Logan Studios. He essentially served as a catch-all task and errand runner to the entire marketing department. On the organizational chart, he was half a rung higher than the interns. Like most ambitious and eager twentysomethings, Kevin wanted to do more, and he had the drive and the work ethic. He knew that he could lead a major project, but he would have to put in his dues to earn that kind of trust. But with his dialysis, Kevin also needed flexibility, and given his status, he was easily forgotten on the days that his dialysis ran late.

Kevin struggled in the first month to grow accustomed to dialysis. The treatments drained him, and he needed a nap by the time he arrived at work. The doctors and nurses promised that the fatigue would fade. They swore that his body would normalize to dialysis after six months. That was still twenty weeks away! Luckily, the transition from the catheter to the AV graft was uneventful.

That day at the hospital when he was diagnosed with kidney disease, a surgeon placed a central venous catheter inside Kevin on the right side of his chest. It was a temporary dialysis tube—a stop gap—while he waited for an AV graft. He received a graft one week later at an outpatient surgery center in the city. It had to heal for two weeks, so in the meantime, the dialyzer was connected to the central venous catheter in his chest. Central venous catheters are foreign objects, while AV grafts use a patient's own artery and vein. Sometimes grafts fail after a couple of years, and patients have to either get another one or get another access called a fistula. Fistulas have a whole other bag of potential complications. Kevin was stuck with the catheter in his chest for two weeks. Kidney doctors call it the "death tube. It has a direct gateway to the heart, and it can be deadly if it is infected.

When his graft was created, Kevin juggled the side effects of the dialysis treatments, plus he had to continuously monitor his graft's progress. Fortunately, the graft healed well. The nephrologists and nurses said it looked great. But Kevin hated it. He wore long-sleeved shirts, even during East Coast summers, because he despised the bulge it created in his arm. He would probably have the bulge for the rest of his life. He would still need a graft as a backup even though he eventually had a kidney transplant. Kidney transplants function for the first few years or for decades, but sometimes—not always—they fail. In that case, patients have no choice but to return to dialysis.

While the graft healed, he still had the catheter. Kevin hated the foreign catheter surgically implanted in his chest. It was an invasion of privacy, even for a guy like Kevin who loved gadgets. If he was certain that his devices would still work under running water, he was the guy who would bring them into the shower with him. Sometimes Kevin imagined the worst. What if the catheter or the AV graft had a GPS connected to it and it tracked him? What if it monitored and recorded stuff such as how many beers he drank in a week? What if his health-insurance company used that information against him? What if a small piece of the catheter broke off and traveled into his bloodstream? Kevin recently watched *Star Wars* for the one-hundredth time, and he remembered when Obi Wan-Kenobi told Luke Skywalker that his father, Darth Vader, was "more machine now than man." Kevin had nightmares about the gadget in his chest slowly taking over his body.

Emma reassured Kevin that she didn't mind the lump in his arm, and she didn't notice it after a while. But Kevin struggled with his body image. He kept his shirt on when he was with her. Emma tried to take it off a few times, but he refused, and he even became angry when Emma unfastened a button. Emma accepted it but hoped Kevin would come around. Kevin changed his morning routine. Before he started dialysis, he threw on boxers right after he showered. But with a graft, he put his shirt on first. He had to be more careful about his diet, specifically his liquid intake. If he drank too much liquid, even water, he could bloat and swell and wind up in the hospital. He didn't want to, but he had no choice but to cut down on his physical activity because he was just too exhausted. But there was another reason. The death tube had to stay dry to avoid infection, so too much sweat could kill him. Swimming was a thing of the past.

Kevin hid his depression from the dialysis nurses and from Emma. He didn't even tell his boss or co-workers about his kidney disease or dialysis. He didn't want anyone to know. He didn't want to be treated differently. He cloaked his anger behind a curiosity to learn everything about kidney failure and dialysis. His nurses encouraged him. They called him a "dream patient" because he took responsibility for his health. Emma complimented him for "being proactive" and for "taking the bull by the horns," along with a slew of other clichés.

But resentment toward the world slowly stirred inside Kevin and grew at a snail's pace. He replaced exercise with reading about transplants. He learned a lot, but the big, glossy headline was that it could take years to get a transplant. Where would he get a kidney from? He convinced himself that he would never find a living donor. Most of those donations came from a family member. Kevin's parents had passed away in a car accident when he was in high school. The aunt and uncle who took him in cut him off on the day he turned eighteen. His grandparents died when he was just a child. If his sister were still alive, she would insist on giving him one of her kidneys, but he would never let her do that. Emma was the closest person to family that he had, and he could not ask her for her kidney. He wouldn't know what to say.

So...um...Emma...where do you want to go for dinner tonight? And, oh, by the way, could I have one of your kidneys? I only need one of yours to live. You can keep the other one.

Emma stayed with Kevin despite his diagnosis, but he was convinced that if he ever hinted at asking her for a kidney, she would buy a one-way ticket to another continent. His best option was to register with the Organ Procurement and Transplantation Network (OPTN), the national database of people waiting for cadaver organs. The average wait time for a viable kidney organ was three to five years. He read stories about patients who, after receiving a transplant, traveled the world, attended their children's weddings, and ran a marathon. Some of those patients waited for a viable kidney for only a few months, while others waited fifteen years. If he did find a match, it would depend on how his own kidneys matched with the donor's, how often matching kidneys became available, and where he was on the waiting list compared to others. There was also the issue that each state or region had its own waiting list. The waiting list in New York was longer than places like Montana. Even if his name moved to the top of the list, a lot of other things had to fall in place to get a kidney.

Kevin's blood type had to match the donor's. Luckily for Kevin, his blood type—O positive—was the most common in the United States. Almost 38 percent of Americans shared his blood type. If the blood types matched, then the doctors would look for matches of human leukocyte antigens. Every person inherits three antigens from each of his parents, for a total of six. The more antigens that matched between Kevin and the donor, the longer a transplanted kidney would function. If any of the antigens matched, the doctors would test antibodies, which measured the likelihood that Kevin's body would accept or reject the organ.

Kevin felt like his chances to find a match were slim to none, but he added his name to the wait list anyway. At least Emma and his dialysis nurses would stop nagging him about it. Kevin read that antirejection pharmaceuticals had improved in recent years, which implied that more kidneys with fewer matching antigens could be successfully transplanted. But Kevin didn't hold his breath.

Six years passed in New York. Kevin grew more accustomed to dialysis but continued to fall into occasional downward spirals of depression. He did his best to manage it by staying true to who he was before dialysis. He was still the guy at work whom everyone liked, when they remembered him. His buddies still called him when they wanted to grab a beer and watch football. He continued to volunteer every month. He had a regular exercise regimen, because he could do more with a graft than he could with the "death tube" catheter. He learned to control his diet, and he even traveled. He just had to coordinate it ahead of time with his nurses, who arranged treatments for him at clinics wherever he traveled. Kevin and Emma traveled to friends' weddings, they dashed off to the Hamptons during summers, and they spent a week in Paris.

Kevin and Emma were going strong for all those years. They moved in together three years into their relationship, into a one-bedroom loft in the Meat Packing District. They were great together. She loved to cook, and he cleaned. He despised clutter as much as her, and they both preferred to spend money on food and experiences rather than stuff. She supported him during rough patches with dialysis. He helped her find direction in her career.

Emma worked in the entertainment industry too but, on the creative side, as a professional hair and makeup artist. She started out as a costume designer, but cosmetics and hair were her true passions. Kevin encouraged her to leave her job at a costume studio to do freelance makeup. Over time, she landed a few high-profile gigs for commercials and music videos. She got a couple of referrals for bigger jobs with big-name celebrities. Eventually, her business grew so much that she had to turn down gigs. Kevin helped her set up her own business and eventually launch her own training school where she could build her brand and bench strength.

He loved helping Emma with her business. He had started to feel useless at his own job, and Emma gave him a purpose. Kevin knew he needed to make a change in his career, but if he wanted to move up the ladder in marketing at Logan, it became obvious that he would have to move to Los Angeles. He was surprised about a recent trend that most marketing executives went back to school to get a master of business administration. MBAs weren't required, but it could take two or three times longer for him to move up with just a bachelor's degree.

But Emma was so successful in New York, so Kevin didn't bring up the idea of Los Angeles, even though part of him knew she might be up for it. A few of her gigs called her on location to Los Angeles, sometimes for weeks at a time. When she returned to New York, she came back with a smile, a tan, and a handful of new tofu and kale recipes. She sounded Californian, with her complaints about the blustery New York winters and her longing for the Santa Monica sand and surf—not to mention all the great job opportunities that Los Angeles had waiting for her. She had earned a good reputation in both New York and Los Angeles.

But Emma was in the middle of a few long-term projects in New York, and she wanted to see them through. Plus, Kevin didn't have any job prospects out West, and it was too risky to move across the country without an offer.

There was also the issue of the kidney waiting list. In six years, Kevin's name moved up a few notches. He would have to start from the bottom of California's very long list. He was glad he stuck it out in New York, because one day at work, he received the call that he had been waiting for.

"Can I speak to Kevin Whitman?" a woman with a heavy Bronx accent blasted into the phone.

"This is Kevin Whitman." He held the phone away from his ear.

"I'm calling from the New York office of the OPTN. You're a match for a kidney that became available this morning. Can you come in right away?"

"Um...yeah...sure. Where should I go?" He reached for a sticky-note pad and a pen. His hands shook.

"New York Memorial Hospital. At the main entrance, check in at the front desk, and tell them you are there for a kidney transplant. Do you understand?"

"Y-yes," he replied, his voice quivering. "I can be there in thirty minutes."

"Perfect. Best of luck to you."

He was so nervous that he knocked over his iced coffee.

"Fuck!" he shouted.

Susie, the intern who sat in the cube next to his, shot up from her desk and peered at Kevin.

"Are you OK?" She reached over the divide between their cubes with a roll of paper towel.

"I'm fine." Kevin looked up at her and grabbed the roll. "Thanks."

Susie noticed his hands shaking, and then she saw his face. He looked like he saw a ghost.

As Kevin wiped up the coffee, he pushed his phone off his desk, and it landed on the soaked carpet.

"Fuck! Fuckity fuck fuck!"

Susie slid out from her cube and walked over to Kevin.

"What's going on? Is everything OK?"

"Yeah, sorry. It's great, actually." Kevin paused. "They found a kidney for me. I have to go to the hospital right now, but now I have to clean up this shit."

Kevin had finally told his coworkers about his kidney failure after four years of dialysis, and everyone knew he was waiting for a kidney.

"What? That's amazing! Don't worry about this, I got it. Seriously. You need to go." Susie stepped into Kevin's cube and took the paper towel roll out of his hand.

"Really? Awesome, thank you so much. I just need to call for an Uber."

Kevin had to tap the app three times to get it opened, because his hands shook.

"Here, why don't I do that, while you shut down your MacBook and pack up your things?" Susie took his iPhone. "All right, my friend. You're going to show up in style with a super fancy UberLux."

Kevin looked at her as if she was crazy. He just needed to get to the hospital. He didn't need black-car service.

"It was the closest one. I figured you wouldn't care that it costs three times more than the other cars." She smiled. "Hey, one more thing. While I have your phone, can I text Emma to call you in ten minutes? You'll be on your way to the hospital by then. Let me do this for you. You look like you'll forget."

"Good call. Yes, please. Thanks." Kevin continued to pack up his backpack. "Could you do me another favor? Could you let the boss know that I had to go?"

"Of course! No problem. Anything else I can do?"

Kevin slid on his coat and backpack. Susie handed him his phone. "No, you've already been so helpful. Thank you so much."

"No worries. I'm so excited for you! Now go! The app said your car will be here in three minutes."

"OK, I'll be at New York Memorial if you need me for anything. Wish me luck."

"Good luck!" Susie yelled after him as he walked down the hallway.

"Kevin, wait! Your phone!" He'd left it on his desk after Susie handed it back to him. She chased after him in the hall.

"Right, thanks. Geez, I'm all over the place." Kevin waved his hands in the air. "I can't believe this is finally happening! I gotta go!"

Kevin rushed out to the elevator, but he was too eager to wait for it. He flew down the eight flights of stairs and hopped into a black Mercedes.

When Kevin arrived at the hospital, the doctor was enthusiastic.

"Kevin, great news! Your blood matches with the donor kidney, and four of six antigens match."

Dr. Barton, the transplant surgeon, reviewed Kevin's chart as he spoke.

"Now the only thing we need to do is make sure your body will actually accept the transplant. We'll draw your blood and mix it with some tissue from the transplant kidney. If they mix well, that's a good sign that your body will accept the kidney. I'll send in a nurse to draw your blood, and we should know in about one hour."

Emma and Kevin exchanged a hopeful but nervous glance. She came straight to the hospital after she received Susie's text.

"If everything looks good, then we prep you for surgery," Dr. Barton continued. "I can't give you a firm time for surgery. It all depends on the condition the kidney is in and any testing we need to do. But it won't be long. The kidney will only be viable for a short while. Unfortunately, you can't eat or drink anything until then. We need your system to be clear. You will stay in this room, and we will continue to monitor your vitals. We need to draw a lot of blood to keep on hand in case of any complications. We don't expect any problems. It's just precautionary."

"Sounds good. So is the...I mean...do you already have...have you seen it? The kidney? The one that I'm going to get?" Kevin asked.

"It's not here yet. It's being medevacked as we speak. I'll run some tests as soon as it gets here. That's why your blood samples need to be ready."

The nurse walked in and drew several vials of Kevin's blood.

"Before I go," Dr. Barton said, "we do need to discuss possible complications. We can discuss it alone, or do you prefer for your girlfriend to stay?"

"Go ahead, Dr. Barton. We can talk openly in front of Emma."

Dr. Barton nodded.

"We don't expect any complications, but I'm required to tell you the potential risks. You might experience some bleeding or infection after the procedure. We will monitor you and prescribe medications as indicated. It's possible that you might experience urine leakage, or the vessel that carries your urine out of your body might get blocked. In that case, you might need a urinary catheter or another procedure to remove the blockage. In some cases, the new kidney doesn't start working right away. In that case, you might still need to do dialysis while we wait for the antirejection medicines to start working."

He said all these things that Kevin didn't want to hear. Kevin felt as overwhelmed as the day he was diagnosed with kidney failure.

"Like with any procedure, there are risks with anesthesia. You are not allergic to any medications, correct?"

"No. I mean yes...that's correct. I'm not allergic."

"OK, good. The anesthesiologist is going to start with a small dose to see how you do and proceed from there. If he notices anything unusual, he will stop or course-correct as needed. Do you have an advance medical directive?"

"Yes, I completed one when I registered for the wait list."

"Great. I'll ask the nurse to confirm that we have a copy," replied the doctor. "What about a will?"

Kevin's eyes grew wide.

"I don't want to alarm you. But these are standard questions I'm required to ask."

"No, I don't have a will."

"OK. I'm going to page a social worker to meet with you. I don't think you'll need it, but it's smart to have one."

"Um...sure...I guess."

Kevin didn't think to write a will. His hands were still shaking when he reached over to shake Dr. Barton's hand. "Thanks. I appreciate your help."

When Dr. Barton left, and Kevin and Emma were alone, Emma lay snuggled up to Kevin in the hospital bed.

"You won't need a will," she said as she held back tears. "This is a good thing! You might walk out of here completely back to normal!"

Kevin squeezed her hand and gently lifted her face to his. He looked into her eyes. "I'm scared, too."

She turned her face away from Kevin but snuggled in a little closer. They stayed like that, silent, for several minutes.

"Emma, just in case something does happen, I want you to have everything. It's not much, but whatever it is, it's yours."

"OK, but it won't be necessary. We're walking out of here together."

They were silent for a long time with nothing to do but wait. Nurses and technicians shuffled in a frenzy in and out of the room. They looked like they had never prepped a patient for a transplant. It made Kevin nervous, but he trusted Dr. Barton. Kevin read about him on the hospital's website. Dr. Barton was a renowned transplant surgeon in the tristate area.

A while later, Dr. Barton returned. Kevin knew something was wrong.

"I'm sorry to tell you this, Kevin. We have to transplant the kidney in someone else. Your antibodies rejected it after numerous tests. That's a strong indicator that your body won't accept the kidney. Another patient's antibodies were more compatible with the kidney. And that patient had five antigens that matched. You only had four. Normally four is very good, but if we have a patient that has a better match, we are required to give the kidney to the best match." Dr. Barton stopped talking and looked at Kevin with a dumb, robotic expression on his face.

Kevin's heart sank, and his temperature rose.

"I don't understand." He tried to remain calm, but Kevin's jaw was clenched, and it hurt his whole face. His tongue went dry.

"I'm sorry." Dr. Barton coughed uncomfortably.

"So a couple of hours ago, I was a match for a kidney, and now? Now…I'm not?"

"The chances are less that your body would accept it. If we give you the kidney, it's unlikely it would work. You would still have to resume dialysis, and you would have to take a huge amount of antirejection medications. Those medications would severely suppress your immune system and lead to other, potentially very dangerous, complications. We can't take that risk."

"But how do you know until you try! How can you possibly know?"

Kevin lost it. He shouted at Dr. Barton. Emma put her hand on Kevin's shoulder, but Kevin slapped it away and roared louder. He leapt out of the hospital bed, still wearing the gown.

"No! Someone please explain to me how the hell you could tell me that I was a match, and now all of a sudden I'm not! You haven't even tried, so how can you know if my body will accept the kidney? What if it does, and your assumptions are wrong? Then what?"

Dr. Barton remained calm. But two security officers were dispatched to the room. This wasn't the first time Dr. Barton had been in this situation. He felt bad for Kevin, and he remained professional.

"They're not assumptions, Kevin. Our tests showed that your body rejected the kidney. If I proceed with the surgery, the chances are very high that it would make your condition worse."

"So is it about the kidney not being a match for me, or is it about someone else being a better match? Because all I'm hearing is that someone else is getting *my* kidney!"

"When a donor kidney becomes available, we call several patients on the wait list in case of this exact situation. It's standard protocol to bring in multiple patients. We can't afford to let any organs go to waste, so we have to keep our options open."

Kevin knew it was hopeless. He tuned out Dr. Barton, and he punched the wall. He hunched forward with his head between his legs and his hands on his knees. He began to weep.

"I can't go back to dialysis. It sucks. I can't do it. It's been six years."

Dr. Barton still spoke like a robot. "I know it's rough. I'm sorry I don't have better news. We can just hope for another kidney to become available soon." He paused. He didn't know what else to say. "The nurses will get your discharge papers together." He walked out of the room and prepped to give Kevin's kidney to someone else.

"Wow, Kev. I'm so sorry, man." Max sounded genuine. "That's so rough."

"Just wait," Kevin replied. "It gets better."

CHAPTER 11
WESTWARD BOUND

After Kevin lost the donor kidney, he spiraled down a hole of self-pity and depression. He pushed Emma away. He barely spoke at work and at his dialysis treatments. He was *that* guy—the curmudgeon who snapped at tourists on the subway who walked too slow in front of him. He skipped the Christmas in July party, to which he'd gone to every year since he could remember. He didn't return phone calls, texts, or e-mails. He was more and more unhappy at work, and resentment brewed inside of him for his low status. Emma tried to be there for him, but the more she tried, the more Kevin pushed her away. She eventually found excuses to work longer and took more out-of-town gigs. Kevin knew that he had become one of those jerks that he used to make fun of. Even in those moments when he snickered at the cashier at the neighborhood bodega—the guy who had known him for years—he told himself to "just be cool." He told himself, "You don't have to smile or talk. But don't be an ass." Still, Kevin couldn't help it. And he hated himself for it.

For some reason, Emma stayed with Kevin through it all. He was this close to losing her and losing his job. He decided he had to make a change.

Emma encouraged him to enroll in New York University's part-time MBA program. She knew what he needed even when he didn't. He needed a new project, new people, and something new to learn. He worked full time at Logan, attended evening classes, and emphasized his MBA in entertainment. NYU's entertainment MBA program is one of the best in the country and by far the best on the East Coast. The only program ranked higher was in Los Angeles at University of Southern California, but he and Emma hadn't discussed Los Angeles yet. And Emma was still thriving in New York. The NYU MBA guaranteed that they would stay in New York for at least three more years. Kevin followed Emma's advice and enrolled in classes. He was thirty years old.

Kevin loved it. The people, the classes, the parties—all of it. His classmates came from every part of the world. He'd never had a friend from Korea or

Brazil—actually born and raised there. He learned how to make kimchi, he watched his friend compete in an MMA competition, he went mountain climbing with a semipro, he beta tested a classmate's energy drink. He would never have gotten to do half of those things without the graduate program. Not to mention the executives from major studios, who were NYU alums, who returned to campus for guest lectures and networking opportunities.

Kevin spent most weeknights at school events and networking happy hours. Sometimes Emma went with him, but her business was growing, and she had her own events most nights. They spent time together on weekends, but that was difficult to schedule, too, since their events spilled into the weekends. Neither one of them wanted to miss out, and all the events seemed important for their careers. They missed each other, and they both knew there was a problem. But they avoided it. They chalked it up to a phase that would end once Kevin graduated.

That was how Kevin's first year of business school, and eventually all three years, flew by. He was nailing it at work. He loved the hectic schedule of work and school and being distracted from dialysis.

Just a few months before graduation, the transplant office called again. They had another potential match. This kidney came from a live donor, a young, terminally ill woman who wanted to donate her organs. Kevin and Emma raced to the hospital and went through the same process as the previous time. Kevin was glad it was a different surgeon. He felt guilty for yelling at Dr. Barton, but Kevin was still pretty sure that he would have punched Dr. Barton in his fat face if he ever saw him again. The nurses did the blood work, the doctor went through the same set of required questions, and Emma stood by Kevin's side through it all. Kevin advised Emma not to get her hopes up, but he was really talking to himself. A few hours of frenzy passed, when the doctor returned with the same long face that Kevin remembered with Dr. Barton.

"Kevin, the patient gave us consent to take her kidneys just before she passed away. But after we put her under at the very end, the patient's husband demanded that we stop. He had agreed to his wife's wishes, but at the last minute he backed out. It's an emotional decision to let a loved one give away organs. He said it was too painful for him. He had a legal right to stop us as the holder of the advanced directive, so there was nothing we could do. I'm sorry."

The doctor left before Kevin could say anything. Kevin punched a plastic pitcher of water that was on the table next to his hospital bed. It splattered everywhere and splashed Emma and Kevin, which made Kevin even more raging mad. He knocked over a small table and punched the wall. Two nurses ran into the room, and the male one restrained Kevin. Kevin wrestled to break free and shouted, "I'm fine!"

Emma tried to hug him, but Kevin pushed her away. He practically shoved her.

"Goddammit! Leave me alone!" Kevin got dressed and stormed out of the room. "Don't bother following me!" he shouted at her.

Kevin wandered around the city for a while in total despair. He never wanted to step foot in another dialysis clinic again. He wanted to be normal. He didn't want to die. He wanted a transplant more than anything. He felt he had to choose between dying young without a transplant or continuing to live a shitty lifestyle on dialysis that just grew shittier each year.

What's the point? he wondered. *I could live for decades on dialysis, but the thought of spending so much of my life hooked up to that fucking machine with those fucking nurses who wear smiley-face pins on their scrubs and dress up in costumes for the holidays, who walk around the clinic smiling and "spreading cheer," when all they do is remind me that I can't walk around and smile and celebrate because I'm strapped to that fucking chair for twelve hours each fucking week for the rest of my shitty life.*

Kevin's chest heaved up and down as he recounted his story to Max.

"Sorry. I still get so angry thinking about it. It's like I can't talk about it without reliving it."

"No, man. I get it. That was your reality," Max sympathized.

"Anyway, after wandering around for a while, I walked back home after I blew off some steam. I climbed the stairs of our pre-war building, just to prove to myself that I could climb a few flights of stairs without being winded. It wasn't until I turned the key in the door that I thought about what I would say to Emma. She was curled up on the couch with a pillow in her lap and a tissue in her hand. Her eyes and her cheeks were red."

She got up when Kevin walked in, but he didn't look at her.

"I'm glad you're home. I was worried," she mumbled.

There was a long pause before Kevin responded.

"Sorry. I didn't mean to worry you. I just needed… some time…to think."

"It's OK. I understand."

"No, you don't understand!" Kevin slammed his keys on the counter. He didn't want to yell at her, but he couldn't stop.

"How could you possibly fucking understand? You have two perfectly functioning kidneys! You don't have this freak bulge on your arm. You're not stuck in that fucking chair on that fucking machine for hours and hours!"

Emma just stood there. She knew he needed to vent, so she let him. She knew him so well, better than he knew himself.

"Look, I'm sorry," he told her. "I know you want to help. But there's nothing you can do. I think we…"

"What if I give you one of my kidneys?" she blurted.

"What?" They stared at each other. "No! No way! I can't let you do that. It's too risky. What if it's a botched surgery? Then we'd both be screwed. Besides, you might not be a match."

"We can at least find out," she pleaded.

"No, I can't let you do that. It's beyond nice of you to offer. But no."

There was a long silence.

"Emma, I think we should take a break."

She stood there, stunned.

"I just think we're on totally different pages, and we have been for a while. It's just not working."

"I just offered you my kidney, and you want to break up with me?"

"I don't want to break up. I just think I need some space. I think it would be good for you too."

"You don't get to decide what's good for me!"

"OK, fine; then *I* need some space. It would be good for me."

"Why are you saying this? You're not in love with me anymore? Is there someone else?"

"No, there's no one else. And, of course, I still love you. But it's just not working anymore."

"What's not working? Let's figure it out and fix it. Don't just walk away!"

"You don't get it!" he shouted. "Without a transplant, I'm going to die! Who knows when, but it will be earlier than I'm supposed to! I can't be a good boyfriend or a husband to you or a father to children if I'm sick or too tired from dialysis. I can't work and earn a living and be responsible for more mouths to feed when I don't know how long I'll be around!"

Emma couldn't believe what he was saying. They both knew that plenty of people lived full lives on dialysis. Yes, it would be a challenge, but Emma expected them to take it on together.

"Kevin, we've been happy all these years that you've been on dialysis, right? Haven't we?" She waited for Kevin to reply, but he didn't. "We're working around it, within it, accepting it. That's how it will be for us."

"What if I don't want that? What if I don't want to do dialysis anymore? I want to be able to make that choice without worrying what it might do to you or, worse, if we ever have kids."

"Are you talking about killing yourself? Because that's what will happen if you stop treatment."

"Well, that's what's going to happen if I don't get a transplant too! So either way, I'm fucked!"

They stood in the middle of their tiny living room, facing each other but with miles between them.

"Look, I'll finish business school in a couple of months. I got an offer for a manager job with Logan in Burbank. I'm accepting the offer this week, and I'll start right after graduation."

"You're moving to LA? When were you going to tell me?"

"I don't know. It all happened really fast. I just need to do this."

Emma was wrung dry. She didn't have any tears left. She looked defeated.

Kevin told her that he would find a place to crash until graduation. "I'll stay in a hotel tonight and pick up my stuff tomorrow."

Kevin looked up at Emma, but she had turned her back away from him and stared out the window, hugging a throw pillow. He turned to leave. He opened the door and looked back one more time, but she was still turned away. He left, and the door softly clicked shut behind him. Emma collapsed onto the floor, buried her face in the pillow and sobbed.

CHAPTER 12
HEALTH SKYTOURS

Kevin rolled his eyes at Jeremy as they rode the elevator down to the lobby of Logan's Burbank studio. The whole department was already at the bar, waiting for them.

"I'm not doing a race tomorrow or volunteering. But you're right, I have to get up early for dialysis. Remember me? Your friend with the limp kidney?" Kevin asked sarcastically. "But it's cool. I can have *a* beer."

"I don't know how you stay so positive with all that stuff you have to do," Jeremy said. "But I'm glad you can at least celebrate your anniversary. Thirteen years...sheesh."

"So...the Blue Room, huh? That's where we're going tonight?" Kevin wanted to change the subject.

"The Blue Room," Jeremy answered awkwardly as they stepped out of the elevator.

Dialysis took more and more of a toll on Kevin. He knew that was how it would be. But that didn't make it easier. He felt and looked ten years older than he was. He only worked out one day a week, and he completely stopped lifting weights and playing softball. He never heard from the New York transplant agency again. He added himself to the California list as soon as he signed an apartment lease, but they never called. He actually forgot that he was on the list.

While they walked to the bar, Kevin wanted to tell Jeremy his secret. He wanted to tell someone… anyone. But he thought he might regret it as soon as the words came out of his mouth. That day wasn't just his thirteenth anniversary at Logan. It was his last day there, too. He had given his boss his two-week's notice and asked his boss not to announce his departure until after he was gone, that following Monday. By then, Kevin would be in New Delhi with no return ticket.

Desperate for a kidney, Kevin bought one through a medical tourism company. The company was based in India, and they advertised that they had dozens of donated kidneys for all blood types that were just waiting to be transplanted. They guaranteed a match within just a few weeks after he flew there. When he left the last happy hour at Logan, all he could think was that in about one month, he would have a new kidney, and he would never have to do dialysis again.

The company that sold the kidneys was called Health SkyTours. He read about them in a renal health magazine that was lying around in his dialysis clinic. Health SkyTours had a full-page color advertisement stating that they had kidneys for every blood type and that the kidneys came from Indian citizens with terminal illnesses who wanted to donate as their dying wish. A picture of a lanky, dark-skinned man covered the page. He wore a feeble smile. Underneath the photo, the caption read in broken English:

> When I learn that I am die, I scared. I worry after my wife and children, what they will do after I am gone? I hope and pray they will be OK. I do one last benefit before I am no more. If I am not alive, I stop someone else from happy life? This is why I donate.

Indian law mandates that donated kidneys only be transplanted in family members. According to this advertisement, the loophole was that terminally ill patients who wished to do so could donate to family or strangers once they passed away. The caption ended with, "I hope my wish for save kidney is of good karma for my family." The caption in broken English made it that much more intriguing and believable. In hindsight, Kevin knew he sounded naïve. But he wanted it to be true, so he convinced himself of as much.

Kevin spent thirty minutes on the Internet, researching the loophole, but he couldn't find anything to prove it or negate it. He called the toll-free number for Health SkyTours and spoke with a woman with an American accent. The woman listened gravely to Kevin's long history of dialysis and how his diagnosis came out of nowhere. She reassured Kevin that he could get a kidney. It would cost fifteen thousand dollars out of pocket for him to go to India for a few weeks to wait, get a transplant, and do some follow-up care. If he waited for a kidney in the United States, it could cost three hundred thousand dollars, and he had no idea how much insurance would cover. After the surgery, he would have to take a cocktail of antirejection drugs called immunosuppressives to ensure his body didn't reject the kidney. At home in the United States, the drugs could cost three thousand dollars per month. In India, the drugs would cost one-fourth of that price. No matter what, Kevin would have to take those drugs after a transplant. It was still cheaper for him to travel to India a couple of times a year and fill his suitcases with six months of meds at a time than it would be to buy them in America. That would be true even if insurance covered some of the cost. It sounded too good to be true. He knew it was, but he didn't listen to that part of his conscience. He was desperate.

Kevin asked the woman at Health SkyTours a host of questions.

"How long do I have to stay in India after the procedure? Where did the surgeons go to medical school? What is their track record? What if a kidney doesn't match or if I experience complications during the procedure or after I return to Los Angeles?"

"Whoa, slow down. You're based in Los Angeles?" the woman asked. "We have an office in Culver City on Washington Boulevard. If you're free tomorrow afternoon, why don't you swing by? This kind of discussion is always better in person. We're talking about your life, after all."

Kevin felt hopeful for the first time since the call he received from the New York transplant office. He missed Emma right at that moment. Kevin met her for an obligatory coffee on the morning that he left for Los Angeles, three months after they broke up. He didn't know how to address her. Should he hug her? Shake hands? Wave and smile? He opted to keep his hands in his jacket pockets and just said, "Hey." They sat through an uncomfortable thirty minutes and hugged good-bye more awkwardly than when they greeted each other. They wished each other good luck, and that was the end. They had zero contact after that, but in that moment, he wished that he could ask Emma her opinion about going to India. She would see upsides and downsides where he was blind. She would have supported Kevin in at least exploring the option, and then they would have made the right decision together. He knew it wasn't fair to wish for all that, especially after he broke up with her. On his own, he saw Health SkyTours through rose-colored goggles.

The Health SkyTours office was on the first floor of a high-traffic two-story strip mall. The hodgepodge of businesses included a nail salon, a Chinese food and donuts fast-food joint, a liquor store, frozen-yogurt place, and a hole-in-the-wall Mexican food restaurant. The Health SkyTours marquee read, "TRAVEL AGENCY," which Kevin thought was odd. It made the company sound like they booked vacations. A young woman of Indian descent, but who spoke with an American accent, greeted Kevin from behind a receptionist's desk. She wore a crisp, white physician's lab coat that came down to just below her knees, tall black pumps, and light-red lipstick. Her long, shiny black hair was combed perfectly and swayed gracefully. Kevin caught himself staring.

"Kevin?"

"Yes, hi."

"Hi, I'm Lakshmi. We spoke on the phone yesterday?"

They shook hands.

"It's nice to put a face to the name." Kevin was nervous.

"Yes, likewise." She smiled, her eyes shining bright. "I'm glad you came in. We have clients all over the country, so it's nice to meet some of them in person. We'll go back here to one of our conference rooms."

An equally beautiful Indian woman, who also wore a lab coat, emerged from the hallway and replaced Lakshmi at the reception desk. She smiled at Kevin when she passed him in the hallway. Kevin followed Lakshmi into a small conference room. Bright lights shone on the burnt-orange walls that were covered with photographs of exotic places and people. It could easily have been mistaken for a field office for *National Geographic.* Stunning images of the Taj Mahal, luxury hospital rooms, fancy hotel suites, and Indian natives in traditional clothes adorned the walls. Several photographs featured two people—a donor (who was Indian) and a recipient (a Caucasian in every photograph) with their arms around each other, smiling at the camera. The captions said things like "I'm grateful for the life I've been given by this generous donor," and "It is my dying wish to save a life."

Lakshmi invited Kevin to sit at a small round table while she took two bottles of water out of a mini refrigerator in the corner of the room. She handed one to Kevin.

"So. When we spoke yesterday, you said you need a kidney transplant. You've been on dialysis for ten years, right? Gosh, I'm so sorry. That must be really difficult." She cocked her head to the right and put her hand on Kevin's shoulder.

He nodded in agreement and grew slightly erect.

"When we talked on the phone, you mentioned that you had two false alarms with the transplant group in New York, correct?" Lakshmi asked.

Kevin nodded yes.

"Wow. Talk about cruel and unusual punishment. It's like the worst possible kind of tease." Lakshmi had taken the words right out of Kevin's mouth. She was so sympathetic. He wondered if she was teasing him in that moment.

"Let me tell you about what we do here at Health SkyTours. If we tell you we have a kidney, we *actually* follow through on it."

"That's refreshing," Kevin pitched into Lakshmi's sarcastic tone. "Are you a doctor? I just wondered because you're wearing a lab coat."

"I'm a nurse. I was working at a hospital for many years, but I got fed up with the American health care system, which is why I came to work here."

For the next two hours, Lakshmi gave Kevin a thorough history of Health SkyTours' operations, founder, and services. Kevin and Lakshmi discussed every topic, including medical-history forms that he would need to take to India, how to apply for a visa, safety, follow-up care, costs, food, lodging, what to expect when he arrived in New Delhi, background and education of each of the transplant surgeons, and how they found donors in India and matched them with people like Kevin.

"You will basically be on a luxury vacation," Lakshmi said. "Except, of course, for the short while when you're recovering from surgery. That won't be so fun," she said and smiled. "Literally when you step off the plane in New Delhi, one of our agents will greet you at the gate. He will basically be your personal butler during your entire trip. He will escort you through customs, through baggage claim, and to your private air-conditioned car. He will take you to your five-star hotel, and he will help you get settled in. A hot meal will be provided by room service in your room that day. We figure that you will be jet-lagged, so you will probably want to rest. The next day is when the waiting begins, and if you ask me, that's when the anxiety starts, too."

Kevin raised his eyebrows and cocked his head.

"I just want to keep it real. It is normal to experience anxiety. So there's no point in sugarcoating it."

Kevin liked Lakshmi's blunt, direct style.

"We will contact you as soon as a matching kidney becomes available. The longest any of our patients have had to wait is one month. Most patients are matched within a few weeks. In the meantime, we have relationships with the best dialysis clinics in New Delhi, which are conveniently located near your hotel.

We know the wait can seem long, and we've seen some patients grow impatient and decide to return to the United States without a transplant. It's such a shame when that happens. In the scheme of waiting for ten years, one month is nothing. We've learned that the best way to avoid those situations is to keep you busy. There's so much to see in India! This will be your first visit there, right?"

"Yes," Kevin told her. "I've always wanted to go there. I actually considered a silent meditation retreat in Dharamshala."

"Wow! I wish I had enough discipline to do something like that!" Lakshmi replied.

"Yeah, I'm not sure I do. But I'd like to try someday."

"That sounds awesome. Unfortunately, Dharamshala is a little too far from New Delhi to make that happen on this trip. Plus, if you were locked away for days on end in silence, we wouldn't be able to reach you! I can just picture myself in a parka, trekking up a mountain and storming into a peaceful temple to tell you we found a match."

They both laughed. Kevin couldn't help eyeing her from the waist down while she uncrossed and then crossed her legs as she laughed.

"But there is still plenty to see in Delhi and the surrounding areas." She caught Kevin looking at her, and she leaned in toward him. "The Taj Mahal is a quick day trip. Mahatma Gandhi's burial site is there, along with many other historical monuments. You can see the craziness of the markets if you are brave enough to visit Chandni Chowk and Janpath."

Lakshmi painted a dreamlike image of New Delhi, as if the stunning rainbow image of Indian spices that hung on the wall was what the city looked like everywhere, all the time. Kevin believed every word. She described the food: the wok-fried samosas that made your tongue melt and the steaming naan straight out of a clay oven. His mouth watered, and he watched her in amazement. Her dazzling act worked, and he found himself sitting on the edge of his seat. He shifted back in his chair and tried to stay calm. It all sounded so good—too good—and he was already hooked.

"I just have one last question." Kevin's stomach growled from all the food talk, and he hoped that Lakshmi didn't hear it. "Will I get to meet the donor? I mean, I assume you have to transplant the kidney soon after the donor passes away. Would I have a chance to meet him or her before then? It would be awesome to thank them before I take the kidney."

"Aw, you're such a good guy, Kevin." She squeezed his arm and smiled. He was aroused again.

"Nah, it's not that; it's just…I mean, how do you thank somebody for something like that?"

"Unfortunately, for patient privacy reasons, we can't set up an introduction. Plus, the whole thing is very sensitive. Sometimes the family members aren't happy with the patient's decision to donate. In some cases, the family doesn't even know. If they do know, then the family wants to be alone with the patient until they're gone. Our patients ask us that question *all* the time. We used to be able to host introductions; that's why we have these pictures on the wall. But we can't do it anymore. Believe me, I wish we could."

"I believe you," he told her.

"But we can do a couple of other things. If the family knows about the whole thing, we will invite them to meet you, in which case you could thank them. Or you can write a letter to them, which we are happy to deliver on your behalf. We can't give you contact information like their address, again for privacy reasons."

"OK, thanks."

"And before your transplant, we will give you a profile of the patient. It will have the patient's photograph; his or her first name; and some details about the family, such as if the donor has any children, what the patient did for a living, and what his or her specific motivation was to donate. Many donors also leave behind requests of the recipients."

"What do you mean?" Kevin wondered.

"Things like 'Please take care of this kidney, or please make sure this kidney was not given in vain.' Stuff like that."

"Wow, that's so powerful, you know? It just makes the whole thing so real."

"Yeah. Tell me about it," Lakshmi replied as she stood up. "This is a big decision, so I'm sure you need some time to think it over. Here's my card; feel free to call me anytime." She paused and let the word "anytime" hang in the air as she met Kevin's gaze head on. "As you already know, you can find the answers to most of your questions and everything we discussed today on our website."

Kevin glanced at the card. It didn't have her name or phone number; it was a generic card for the company with the toll-free number and the company URL. "Do you have a direct dial or a cell number in case I need to reach you?"

Lakshmi smiled flirtatiously. "Unfortunately, no. Everything is centralized. But if you call that number and ask for me, the operator will connect you."

"Do you have a packet of information or a brochure or something? I'm sure I'll forget some of the stuff we talked about today. It's a lot to take in."

"I completely understand. Unfortunately, we don't. But we keep our website updated daily. We figure everyone is on their smartphone. Plus, we like to think of ourselves as the good guys—you know, protecting the environment."

"Right. True. You know, your company would make a really interesting case study for business schools."

Kevin could feel the blood rush to his face as he tried to impress her with his business acumen. "You're helping people and the environment at the same time. You have a really innovative model."

Lakshmi smiled and maintained her gaze but remained quiet.

Kevin felt himself dripping with failed flirtation, so he decided to shut up and get out of there.

"Well, thanks again for all the info. I'll be in touch if I decide to do this."

Kevin and Lakshmi shook hands, and Kevin left. He devoured three samosas doused in tamarind chutney at the Indian restaurant at the other end of the strip mall before he drove home.

That night, he masturbated as he thought about Lakshmi. He imagined pushing her onto that small table in the conference room while he tore open her lab coat and her blouse, revealing two voluptuous breasts dangling in front of him. He imagined her sliding onto him until she took all of him in. She stripped down naked except for her black heels. She kissed him everywhere, even on the bulge in his arm over his graft. She understood how vulnerable he would be to show it to her.

"It's beautiful," she would tell him.

Kevin imagined squeezing her butt cheeks while she pumped her body on top of his faster and faster, while her breasts bounced up and down. She shouted his name over and over until they both burst with pleasure.

CHAPTER 13

THE PLUNGE

Across the next four weeks, Kevin researched Health SkyTours. They weren't on Yelp, and he couldn't find any reviews besides what was on the company's website. He searched "medical tourism," a term he learned while reading about kidney transplants in foreign countries. It was pretty common for Americans to travel abroad for all types of procedures, mostly plastic surgery and elective cosmetic procedures, such as breast implants and liposuction. But some desperate people had heart bypass surgery and knee replacements too. Kevin couldn't believe the sheer number of medical-tourism companies similar to Health SkyTours that were out there. But Health SkyTours was the only one with an LA office where he could meet someone in person, and they were the only medical-tourism agency that offered kidney transplants.

Kevin also cyberstalked Lakshmi. H [illegible]
her on LinkedIn and Facebook but cam [illegible]
Google search for "Lakshmi Health Sk [illegible]
was all he had to go on. He pushed hims[illegible] away from his laptop after searching for twenty minutes. He felt stupid for trying to track her down, and he decided it was best not to get involved with her anyway.

A couple of weeks later, on his way home from work on a Friday night, Kevin stopped at Apex Bar, just like he had almost every Friday night since he moved to LA. Kevin was shocked to see Lakshmi sitting at the bar. He did a double take. She caught Kevin looking at her, and she smiled. Kevin walked over with his hands gripped around the cross-body strap of his messenger bag. His heart pounded in his chest.

"Hey…Lakshmi, right? I'm Kevin. We met a while ago at your office."

Lakshmi threw her head back and laughed. Her thick, shiny hair glistened, and a small strand rubbed against her cheek.

"You're too cute, Kevin. Of course, I remember you. I really enjoyed talking to you. I was a little disappointed that I didn't hear from you again."

Kevin didn't know what to say. Was she flirting, or did she just want his business?

"Yeah, it's just been busy." Kevin rubbed the back of his neck and looked away when their eyes met.

Lakshmi smiled. "So…what are you doing here?"

"I live here. I mean, in this building. In the apartments above the bar."

"Wow, what a coincidence. Are you meeting anyone?"

"No, I'm alone. Just wanted to grab a drink before heading home."

Kevin liked to get there early before the bar transformed into a dance club. After ten o'clock, the younger crowd descended, and the tables and chairs were pushed to the side, while an electronica deejay set up his equipment.

"I'm alone, too. My friends bailed on me. Care to sit?" Lakshmi patted the barstool next to hers.

Kevin sat down and ordered a beer for each of them.

"Do you live around here?" Kevin asked. "It's kind of random to bump into you here."

"No, but I've been here a few times. Some of my friends live in the neighborhood. I like this place, and I was already here when my friends canceled. I thought I might as well wait out traffic and have a drink."

Drinks turned into dinner, and dinner turned into dancing. Kevin was a horrible dancer, but it was crowded enough that he could get by with the few small moves he had. Lakshmi swayed her hips in front of him and pushed her fingers through her flowing hair. Kevin couldn't stop thinking about his fantasy about her. Lakshmi was the first woman in several months to have that effect on him. It had gotten more difficult for Kevin to get an erection, which he knew was a side effect of dialysis. It had only become a problem in the last couple of months. When he initially arrived in Los Angeles, he was out almost every night, and two or three women rotated in and out of his apartment every week. He did the only thing he could think of to drown Emma out from his mind. But that grew old fast, and his reputation spread. It started to become difficult for him to meet anyone new.

Lakshmi was a welcome distraction. By that time of the night, they both had had more than a few drinks. When the music changed, Lakshmi wrapped her arms around Kevin's neck and started grinding against him. Her hips swayed from side to side, while she pressed her pelvis into his. She moved to the beat of the music. When the beat slowed, so did she, and when it picked up, she swayed faster and harder, never taking her body off his. Kevin held her tight and watched as her breasts rolled with her body.

"Do you wanna get out of here?" Kevin whispered in her ear. Hope practically dripped off his chin.

She smiled at Kevin and thrust her groin against his. "Yes, now!"

They made out in the elevator, and she continued to kiss Kevin, while he fumbled to unlock his front door. They stumbled inside, and Lakshmi immediately stripped. She stood in front of him, and he admired her voluptuous body. She took everything off except her black heels. She pushed him onto the dining table, just like in his dream. They had sex three times, each time more satisfying than the last. She slept over, and in the morning, they woke up spooning.

"Kevin, can I ask you something personal?"

"Sure.

"Are you scared? I mean to go through with the surgery in India? I mean, if you decide to do it, I would be scared if I were you."

Lakshmi seemed to understand him in a way that Emma didn't. Kevin told her the most vulnerable parts of himself and how he had always wanted to get married and have a family, but he wasn't sure that he could without getting a transplant. They talked and had sex all morning.

"Kevin, I've seen hundreds of patients return to the States with a renewed lease on life," she swore to Kevin. "It's like they get their whole selves back. I know it's a personal decision, but as a nurse and as someone who has worked directly in it for years, I can tell you it's safe. And the benefits...you just can't put a price on it."

She kissed Kevin and then forced herself out of bed.

"Thank you for being so open and honest with me. It means a lot to me." She got dressed, kissed him, and told Kevin to call her. After Kevin closed the door behind her and had a "holy shit, that really happened" moment, he saw her cell phone number scribbled on the whiteboard on his refrigerator. He saved it to his phone and took a shower.

The following Monday, three days after they hooked up, Kevin stopped by the Health SkyTours office after work. He had hoped to see Lakshmi again, but he had also made a decision. He wanted to go to India for the transplant. He knew the paperwork and visa-application process could take a while, and he was eager to get started. He stopped at the bank on his way there and picked up a cashier's check for six thousand dollars, the deposit fee. When he arrived at Health SkyTours, Lakshmi was nowhere to be seen. The other Indian woman whom he met during his first visit recognized him.

"Kevin, right? Nice to see you again."

"Hi. Good memory. Is Lakshmi here?"

She smiled at Kevin and raised her eyebrows as if she knew everything that had happened between him and Lakshmi.

"Yes, I'll get her for you."

Lakshmi sauntered into the lobby toward him. She smiled mischievously but spoke in a professional tone.

"Hi, Kevin, nice to see you."

"Hi. Could we go somewhere to talk?"

"Sure, right this way."

She led him to the same conference room. He eyed her figure from behind and felt aroused but could not get an erection.

"Are you here for a social visit?" she asked as she closed the door behind her.

Kevin smiled at her. He loved her playful nature.

"I wish it was personal, but I wanted to tell you that I want to have the surgery. I want to go to India."

"Really? Oh my gosh! I am so happy for you! I think you're making the right choice!" She kissed him. "You'll be a whole new man, I promise. No more dialysis forever!"

She took his check and left the room. She returned a few minutes later with a thick packet of paperwork filled with a visa-application form, medical-history forms, an e-mail request form to the travel agent who would book the airfare and hotels, and a slew of other documents.

"For some reason, we still have to do the final paperwork in analog. You would think with all the IT expertise in India, someone would figure out how to automate all this for small companies like ours."

Kevin didn't know what to say, but he was happy to stay there with her. They worked on the documents together for one hour until Lakshmi was satisfied that they were complete.

"If all goes well, you could be there in a few weeks!" she said.

Kevin felt nervous about the whole thing, but Lakshmi's excitement rubbed off on him. He didn't pay attention to the fact that she was a little too excited, like a mother is for a son when he wins an award at school. He only heard what he wanted to hear and saw what he wanted to see. Lakshmi went home with him again that night and spent the night at his place—almost every night that week. They weren't dating. She just showed up at his place after dark and crept away in the early morning hours. It continued for the next five weeks. When he came home from the Blue Room on his last night at Logan Studios, which was the last night before he left for India, she stood in the hallway outside of his apartment and leaned against his door.

"I thought you'd never show up," she said coyly and kissed him.

It was the perfect last night in Los Angeles. Kevin's flight to New Delhi left the next afternoon. He spent the morning packing up his last few items and then turned in his apartment keys. Everything else was already in storage except the stuff he took with him. Kevin was a light traveler. He packed the clothes needed for a couple of weeks, some toiletries, plus his MacBook, iPad, and iPhone. Lakshmi gave him a ride to LAX and kissed him good-bye.

"Good luck, Kevin. Look me up when you get back." She kissed him again but this time on the cheek. She hopped into her car and sped away like a coyote that chased a rabbit.

Kevin thought it was strange that she didn't ask him to call her if he bumped into any issues during his trip, but he didn't think too much about it at the time. Thirty minutes later, he sat alone in Etihad's first-class lounge. He checked in at an executive line for business class and higher, and he was the only person in line. An agent checked him in and then hailed an airline bellboy to usher him to the elite lounge. Kevin ate enough food for three meals and drank two glasses of champagne. He should have skipped the champagne, but he was pumped. He was on his way to get a new kidney, and he wouldn't be able to drink as much alcohol after the transplant, so he might as well do it now. He still had one hour to kill before his flight, and he had an urge to e-mail Emma. He hated that he still thought about her. She was there when he was diagnosed with kidney disease and when he thought he would get a transplant. Kevin had thought a couple of times about how cool the trip would have been if they were in Delhi together. She would have an opinion about going to India for the surgery, and he wished he could talk to her about it.

> Dear Emma,
> I'm probably the last person you want to hear from, which I would understand. But I figured I should tell someone what I'm about to do. I'm at LAX right now, about to board a flight to New Delhi to get a kidney transplant. I quit my job, saved a bunch of money, and bought a one-way ticket. I don't know when I'll be back. It could take a few weeks to find a match, and

> recovery could take a couple of months. I booked the whole thing with a company I found online called Health SkyTours based here in LA. They've helped hundreds of patients get kidneys.

As he wrote the e-mail, it occurred to him that he had never actually spoken to any of their patients. He only read their stories on the company website. He continued to type.

> Anyway, I just…wanted to tell someone…I wanted to tell you. Wish me luck. I hope you're doing great.
> —Kevin

Kevin didn't know what compelled him, but he added the website address for Health SkyTours to the bottom of the e-mail. He pressed "send" and refreshed his e-mail a bunch of times. He immediately regretted sending the e-mail. Why did he expect her to respond right away? *Because I'm an asshole,* Kevin thought and laughed at himself. He panicked when she didn't write back, and he felt like an idiot. He reread all nine sentences six times, and he rewrote the email in his head. *I should have written the part that I wanted to tell her that I'm going to India at the beginning of the e-mail, not at the end! Should I have written "Hope to hear from you soon" so that she knew that I was hoping for a response? What if she sees my name in her in-box and deletes the e-mail without reading it? Stop being such a pansy.*

He boarded the plane through the first-class jet way and tucked his backpack into the overhead bin. It was his first time in first class on an international flight. He couldn't get over the suite—it was as big as his cubicle at Logan. A twenty-inch HD television covered one wall. The seat could recline all the way into a full-sized bed. Folding tables adorned both sides of the seat, and the entire suite could be enclosed for complete privacy. He just had to press a button on a remote control, and the door automatically shut. Another button controlled the window blinds. A stewardess walked by with freshly poured flutes of Möet and Chandon, which he eagerly took.

As the airplane doors closed, Kevin refreshed his e-mail in-box one more time. Nothing. The plane had Wi-Fi, but he decided to turn on airplane mode; he wanted to detach for a bit and get in the zone for his journey. He stuffed his phone into his pocket as the prerecorded safety video played in English. His eyes grew heavy as the Hindi translation of the same video filled his ears, and the Indian flight attendant said, "*Apka swagat hai*" (welcome aboard).

CHAPTER 14
FOREIGN LAND

The chaos of New Delhi made the New York Stock Exchange look like a planned suburban neighborhood. Bicycles, three-wheeler autos, rickshaws, motorbikes, scooters, SUVs, compact cars, pedestrians—both animal and human—weaved in and out of traffic in a zigzag maze. Drivers ignored traffic lights. Pedestrians had the last right of way, and the occasional jab of a side-view mirror on their backs didn't bother people. The run-over-or-be-run-over attitude ingrained into New Delhi drivers meant the city was consumed by around-the-clock gridlock. The incessant, rhythmless honking escalated the mayhem. According to Delhi-ites, there was a method to the honking madness.

"You just have to understand the system to see the patterns," Kevin's driver tried to convince him. Kevin didn't expect to be in New Delhi long enough to decode the pandemonium, so he sat quietly in the backseat of the tinted black car and held onto the door handle for dear life. The driver chuckled and watched Kevin through the rearview mirror while Kevin fastened his seat belt.

"You Americans are obsessed with your seat belts. Most cars in this country don't even come with them. Look at this mess," the driver said, pointing to the traffic. "Our speeds are too slow for this belt to even help you."

Kevin didn't care. He double-checked that the belt was clicked all the way in, and tightened the strap. He arrived at his hotel in one piece but only after the driver almost collided head on with three different cars during the one-hour journey. Kevin leaped out of the car as they pulled into the hotel driveway, and the driver laughed at Kevin again. He escorted Kevin to the front desk and dragged Kevin's suitcase along. After Kevin checked in, a butler came over to assist him.

The driver turned to Kevin. "I will take my leave." He lingered for a few seconds, waiting for a tip. Kevin slipped him a few rupees while the butler introduced himself.

"Kay-win, sir. Welcome to India." The butler bowed. Kevin liked the way Lakhan pronounced his name.

"My name is Lakhan. It will be my honor to serve you."

Without waiting for a reply, Lakhan picked up Kevin's suitcase and started down the hall toward the elevator. He unlocked the room and held the door open while Kevin entered. He then followed him in and set up Kevin's suitcase on a luggage stand. Then he ordered room service, opened the curtains, and fanned a few business and lifestyle magazines on the coffee table.

"I just ordered a hot meal for you, Mr. Kay-win sir. It will arrive shortly."

"Thanks," Kevin replied.

"My pleasure, Kay-win, sir. Tomorrow morning, your breakfast come to room at seven o'clock. I am deeply sorry for the early time, but most important it is that you take dialysis immediately after this. Tomorrow morning at eight o'clock only I will meet you in hotel lobby. From there, we travel to hospital. The clinic for dialysis is in same hospital only where you will have transplant. Tomorrow your treatment will conclude by twelve o'clock in the afternoon. After treatment, I bring you here, or I take you to see sites. Whatever you like. Lunch we will have ready for both of these options. It will be my pleasure to show you Delhi."

"Thank you; that plan sounds great. But, please, call me Kevin. No need to address me as sir."

"Yes, no problem, Kevin," Lakhan said.

"I would like to see the Taj Mahal."

"Wery good, sir," Lakhan replied. "Ah! I said 'sir' again. Forgive me, sir. Ack! Please do not mind. It is my habit to speak with respect."

Kevin didn't know what to say, so he just smiled. "The Taj Mahal?"

"Yes! So many foreigners want only to see Taj. It is wery easy to wisit. But it requires a complete day. Perhaps the next day, when you do not have dialysis, we can see Taj. This is OK with you?"

Kevin nodded yes.

"Of course, we also must see if kidney is available; then we cannot go. We must stay nearby and be at hospital."

"Yes, of course. I understand."

"Wery good, sir," Lakhan said with a broad smile and shook his head from side to side. "On days you do not go for dialysis, I will call you at eight o'clock in the morning to tell you status of kidney. If no kidney that day, I suggest to you sites. You have choice if you want to go out or stay in hotel. If you need anything, you call me, and I will get it for you."

Lakhan handed his card to Kevin. Kevin was wrong. Lakhan was an employee of Health SkyTours, not the hotel.

"What if I want to go somewhere on my own?"

"This I do not advise you. You are visitor in my country and not understanding our ways. I keep your driver with me. He and I accompany you anywhere and anytime, day and night."

"OK," Kevin replied wearily. He didn't like being so out of control, but he was too tired to argue. "On days when I don't have dialysis, can you call me at nine o'clock instead of eight?"

"Wery good, sir. I will call at nine o'clock in the morning."

"Great. Thank you."

"You are most welcome, sir. Can I help you with anything else?"

"No, thank you. You've been very helpful." Kevin handed Lakhan five rupees.

Lakhan took it from Kevin without making eye contact and swiftly tucked the rupees into his pocket.

"You take rest now, sir. We shall meet tomorrow at eight o'clock in the morning, after your breakfast at seven o'clock."

Kevin liked Lakhan's English. It had a hint of a British accent, which gave him a refined air, yet many of his sentences were broken and incomplete. Kevin understood enough for it to make sense. He followed Lakhan to the door.

"Thanks again," Kevin said.

Lakhan smiled and waved as he left. The hotel was one of the nicest Kevin had ever seen. It reminded him of a Ritz-Carlton or Four Seasons, hotels he would never be able to afford back home. Adorned with intricate pillows, the king-size bed looked fit for dignitaries. The flat-screen television covered an entire wall, and the bathroom granite counters shone in maroon, brown, and silver. The crisp, white tiles in the shower, a separate hot tub, and double sinks glistened against the granite. The floor was made of white marble, and plush slippers were provided to keep his feet warm. Despite the stereotypes of Indian climate—scorching summers and flash-flood monsoons—Delhi was pleasant during fall. Kevin packed a light jacket and a few long-sleeved shirts, but he was comfortable in T-shirts and jeans.

He devoured the traditional Indian meal of roti, *dal tadka, aloo gobi,* and dahi and washed it down with half of a Kingfisher. He had had a lot of liquid on the flight, and he needed to cool it before his dialysis treatment the next day. He already felt a little bloated. He checked his e-mail again as he lay down in bed. Still no response from Emma. A part of him wondered if he would hear from Lakshmi, but so far she hadn't contacted him, either. It was seven in the evening in Delhi, and his friends and former coworkers were just getting out of bed to start the day. Kevin tucked himself in a little deeper under the crisp, cold covers. He flipped on the television and was surprised to find old Seinfeld reruns. He laughed out loud as he watched Elaine throw George's toupee out of Jerry's apartment window. Kevin drifted away into a deep slumber, while George ran down the street to recover his hairpiece.

The next day, Kevin abruptly awoke to pounding on his hotel door. He was disoriented and forgot for a few seconds that he was in Delhi. He glanced at his phone. It was 7:10 a.m. He leaped out of bed and let the hotel bellman in to set up his breakfast. Kevin welcomed the fresh cup of Darjeeling chai and slightly sweet cookies called "biscuits" that he had never seen before. They were called Parle-G, and the "G" stood for glucose. He ate something that looked like a pancake but tasted like a savory crepe. It was called *cheela* and was made of lentils. He dipped it in a tangy cilantro chutney and wished there were five more of them. He quickly showered and left his room in disarray to meet Lakhan, who was already waiting for him.

"Good morning, Kay-win, sir."

Kevin followed Lakhan to the car. On this drive, Kevin looked beyond the traffic into the markets and neighborhoods that they passed on the way to the hospital. Kevin had never seen anything like the intricate Hindu, Muslim, and Jain temples on almost every street. He saw a teenage boy hop onto the back of his friend's motorbike. They sped away as they laughed and talked and pointed at a pretty girl who walked on the other side of the road. He saw a group of children wearing uniforms gathered at the street corner as they waited for their school bus to arrive. A man left his home with a thermos in one hand and a briefcase slung over his shoulder. His wife walked out with him, and just before he walked away, she kissed him on the cheek and said something to him. Kevin couldn't understand it, but he imagined she wished him a good day at work.

On its surface, Delhi looked different from Los Angeles, but *people are people*, he thought. He even caught a small glimpse of the slums in Delhi, which were completely different from his experience in Los Angeles. He marveled at the patchwork homes made of old tents and tarps, people sleeping out on the streets, and the litter-ridden sidewalks. It reminded him of Skid Row in downtown Los Angeles, but he had never spent any substantial amount of time there.

The primary difference from Los Angeles, however, was the population per square mile. The Delhi metropolitan area was home to twenty million people, twice the population of Los Angeles County. Yet all those Delhi-ites lived in an area that was one-eighth the size of Los Angeles. Reminders of the population density were everywhere. Passengers hustled for a seat on city buses, and cars fought to fill open spaces on the roads.

Kevin expected Acharya Hospital to be as crowded as the rest of Delhi, but it was just the opposite. The hospital looked like a palace and a refuge from the chaos that surrounded it on the outside. It was truly one of the most beautiful structures Kevin had ever seen. The modern architecture reminded him of the Getty

Center with its glass walls and tall, cathedral ceilings, which let in plenty of natural light. The wide-open space felt organized and clean. Everything was white—the walls, the floor, and the hospital staff's uniforms. For a moment Kevin thought he had stepped into the future. Nurses in ironed white dresses and matching caps marched in groups of four through the hospital. Patients from every continent waited in the main lobby, wearing their traditional garb. An African woman wore a long colorful robe and a matching head scarf. An Arab man draped a traditional black-and-white checkered kaffiyeh around his head and neck. Many of the Indian men wore traditional kurtas, and the women wore saris. Kevin noticed, however, that some of the local Indians also wore Western clothes—jeans, skirts, pantsuits—it was a mix of Eastern and Western attire. He spotted only a handful of European patients and no other Americans. Kevin was impressed with the facility, and he felt at ease at the thought of having surgery there.

He felt much better after the dialysis treatment. All that fluid from the journey had caught up with him. But the treatment still drained him, and all he wanted to do was lie down. Lakhan took Kevin back to the hotel. Kevin skipped lunch and went straight to sleep in the middle of the afternoon. He woke up the next morning at nine, when Lakhan called right on time.

"Good morning, Kay-win, sir."

"Good morning." Kevin sounded like a chain smoker.

"Forgive me. Have I woken you?"

"Yes…no…it's fine."

"I have wery good news, sir. We have a kidney for you. We must haste to hospital."

"What?" Kevin shot straight up in bed. "Can you repeat that?"

Lakhan chuckled. "Sir, wery happy news. Your kidney is here."

"So soon? I thought it would take a couple of weeks!"

"You are unhappy, sir? I thought this is happy news."

"No! I mean yes! Of course, I'm happy! It's great! I…it's just different from what I expected."

"Yes, Kay-win, sir. I understand. Please quickly get ready. I will arrive at your hotel in thirty minutes."

When Lakhan showed up, one hour and fifteen minutes later, Kevin paced the hotel lobby and looked back and forth at his watch and the clock on the wall. He asked the front desk to call Lakhan's cell phone three times, but each time there was no answer. *Where is this guy?* he thought. *Will the kidney go bad if I don't get to the hospital soon? Should I grab a taxi? I wonder if my Uber app will work here.*

Lakhan finally arrived and made a beeline to Kevin with a big smile across his face. "Good morning, sir! Wery exciting day!"

"Yes," Kevin replied. "What took you so long to get here?"

Lakhan looked at Kevin with confusion. "But I am right on time, sir," he insisted. At that moment, Kevin remembered his friend Siddharth from business school, who was from India. Siddharth had told Kevin, "Indians are *always* late, but they will never say they are late. They will tell you they arrived right on time."

"Oh right. Of course, my mistake," Kevin told Lakhan.

They arrived at the hospital in one piece after another harrowing drive. The hospital staff welcomed Kevin with the same warm reception he received at his hotel. Indians were great at hospitality. Kevin felt like a king. One man offered to take his bags, another man brought him a bottle of cold water, and another man, the one in charge, shook Kevin's hand. He led Lakhan and Kevin to a small private room that could easily accommodate up to five people. A stern-looking woman who gripped an iPad joined them in the room. She led Kevin through a series of documents, confirmed his medical history, and explained what would happen next.

"I prepped for two prior surgeries in the United States," he told her with some arrogance. "I know the drill."

"Wery good, sir. Our process will be slightly different from the US, so please bear with us."

The woman's English was better than anyone he had spoken to so far in India. Kevin was impressed. She showed him a few more documents, but there was only one page that he had to sign.

"Now, we just need final payment. The balance is nine thousand dollars. How would you like to pay?"

Kevin pulled out a cashier's check from his backpack and handed it to the woman. She and Lakhan exchanged a satisfied look. She took the check from Kevin and stuffed it into an envelope.

She said she would give Kevin a typed receipt along with a packet of documents to take with him after he left the hospital.

"I'm surprised this is all happening so fast," Kevin mentioned as he wrapped up the paperwork. "I can't believe you found a matching a kidney so quickly. How often does that happen?"

"All the time," the woman replied.

In the same breath, Lakhan answered, "You are wery lucky; this happens wery rare."

Kevin looked back and forth at them quizzically. Lakhan and the woman exchanged a nervous glance. The woman finally broke the uncomfortable silence.

"What we mean is, we never assume we will find a matching kidney quickly, but since our program is very efficient...patients often get kidneys soon after their arrival. So...in these situations, we consider all of them to be lucky." Lakhan vigorously nodded in agreement, as if profuse head-shaking would convince Kevin.

A tiny spark inside Kevin's conscience lit up. It was the same speck of conscience that had poked at him when he first learned about Health SkyTours. It all sounded too good to be true. Kevin wondered, just for a few seconds, if his new kidney was too good, too. But the spark was a tiny minutia of emotion, like an annoying hangnail that he ignored. Back at the Health SkyTours office, Lakshmi had told him the organs were donated by terminal patients, and the full-color brochure confirmed it. He convinced himself it was all a legitimate operation.

Lakhan hastily rose from his seat and shook Kevin's hand.

"Good luck, Kay-win, sir. I wish you a good surgery and fast recovery."

Kevin handed Lakhan an envelope with fifty dollars as a tip.

Lakhan swiftly took the envelope and shoved it into his pocket. The woman smiled at Lakhan and gestured for Kevin to follow her down the hallway to the patient room. That hospital room was bigger than Kevin's Los Angeles apartment. A queen-size bed sat squarely in the middle of the room, facing the window, which looked out onto sprawling Noida, to the north of New

Delhi. Small side tables flanked either side of the bed. A four-person dining table and a three-drawer dresser filled one side of the room. A second bed—a twin bed for a family member—rounded out the furniture. An adjacent bathroom with a spa-style shower completed the suite. Kevin's suitcase was already there.

"I will let you settle in. The surgeon is looking forward to meeting you," the woman said. "His name is Dr. Mittal. He will visit you here in thirty minutes. He will start preoperative care and answer any questions you might have. In the meantime, I will leave this with you."

She handed Kevin *another* glossy color paper. It was information about the man who had donated his kidney to Kevin.

Kevin eagerly took the paper and waited for the woman to leave. He scoured the page and examined every detail. He thirsted for any information about his donor. The donor's name was Satyaraj Aggarwal, and he was from New Delhi. He had a wife and a daughter. He was thirty-eight years old (so young!) when he was diagnosed with pancreatic cancer, and it rapidly metastasized through his body. By the age of forty, he only had a few months to live. Mr. Aggarwal was a chartered accountant for a small family company in New Delhi. There were no other details. Kevin turned the page over, and he came face-to-face with a photograph of the donor and his family. Mr. Aggarwal's daughter stood between her parents. They all smiled happily. It appeared that the photograph was taken in their kitchen. The daughter held a chocolate birthday cake toward the camera and smiled with gusto. The cake read, 'Happy birthday!'

Kevin wanted to take more interest in the donor, Mr. Aggarwal, but he couldn't stop staring at the daughter. She had an alluring face and stunning, innocent eyes. He didn't know why, but she reminded him of his sister. Kevin instantly felt like he wanted to protect her. Right at that moment, the surgeon knocked and entered the room.

"Hello, Mr. Whitman. I am Dr. Mittal. I will be your surgeon." Dr. Mittal walked across the room and shook Kevin's hand. "Congratulations—you will have a new kidney today."

"Yeah, it feels surreal. I've waited for this for so long. I was just reading about the man whose kidney I'll get. There's not much detail, but it's nice to know a little about him and to see his face."

Dr. Mittal forced a smile but said nothing. He asked Kevin to sit on the exam bed, where he measured Kevin's vitals and reviewed his medical history.

"I need to draw several vials of blood for testing and for reserve during surgery."

Dr. Mittal towered over Kevin. He must have been close to six feet four inches tall. His stern expression gave him an unpleasant air, but his voice was friendly enough. He looked as though he was in his late thirties or early forties, not much older than Kevin. A sadness danced in Dr. Mittal's eyes. He didn't make eye contact with Kevin, and he quickly looked away whenever their eyes met. Kevin couldn't decide if he liked Dr. Mittal, even though he desperately wanted to.

"Do you have any questions?" he asked Kevin, as if he knew Kevin was sizing him up.

"Yes, one question. How often does it happen that you find a match for a patient within the first few days of arriving in your country? I expected to wait for at least a couple of weeks. And how can you be sure it's a match? I went through the matching process twice before back home. The first time, the doctor said the kidney wasn't a match. And the second time, the patient's family decided at the last minute not to donate the kidney."

"We must give a long wait window to patients so they are not upset if it takes more time to find a kidney. But most patients do get a kidney within one week of their arrival. No one complains if they can go home sooner."

"Don't get me wrong. I'm not complaining. I just wonder why it takes so long to find a kidney in the United States?"

"You provided us with your complete medical history before your arrival, so we know ahead of time which kidneys will match you," Dr. Mittal explained while he examined Kevin's chest and lungs.

"But don't you have to test for rejection risk? At least back home, they ran some tests where they mixed my blood and tissue with the donor's and waited to know if we were compatible. They couldn't do that ahead of time. They had to do it once I was there at the hospital."

"Are you questioning our methodology, Mr. Whitman?" Dr. Mittal took a half step away from the examination bed. Frustration swelled in his voice, but he still did not look directly at Kevin. "These rooms are full of patients who want a kidney. They will gladly take this one if you don't like our practices." Dr. Mittal practically sneered at Kevin. "You Americans! You think you know everything!"

"I'm sorry. No, not at all. I mean, of course, I want the kidney. I traveled halfway around the world for it. I wasn't questioning you. I just want to understand what you can do that we haven't been able to do in America. I think it's incredible that you help so many people."

Kevin immediately started to over-apologize and to compliment Dr. Mittal. Kevin didn't want anything to happen to his kidney, so he tried flattery.

"I read about you online, and I'm glad you're the one doing my surgery. I feel like I am in very good hands."

Dr. Mittal took a couple of deep breaths and resumed checking Kevin's back, eyes, and ears. They didn't speak after that, but Kevin could feel Dr. Mittal's heavy breathing. Kevin thought Dr. Mittal's heart might explode, as his breath was that loud. After Dr. Mittal finished his exam, he told Kevin, without looking at him, that a nurse would be in to provide final pre-op instructions.

"I will return with the anesthesiologist in thirty minutes to take you to the operating chamber."

Kevin breathed easier after Dr. Mittal left. He kicked himself for insulting Dr. Mittal. *Why did I have to open my stupid mouth? I just want to get this kidney and go home. I won't leave here without it…*

A nurse walked in and interrupted Kevin's thoughts. She gave him a fresh hospital gown and showed him the medical-grade soap and shampoo.

"You need to shower before going into surgery. Leave all your belongings in this room. You will return here after surgery. You can put any valuables in the safe inside the armoire. It has a numerical padlock. I suggest you pick your code and write it on a paper or keep it in your cell phone. You will be under the influence of a lot of medication. You might not remember it after the surgery."

After the nurse left, Kevin showered as instructed and stood in front of the full-length mirror as he draped the white gown over his aged body. He stared at himself and wondered if that's what he really looked like. Heavy bags sagged under his eyes, and crow's feet stretched from the outer corners. His eyes, which formerly shone bright white, had a yellowish tint, like old book pages marred by time. Chapped skin and dark spots marked his cheeks. He curled his fingers and could feel every part of his skin stretch, as if each small movement caused more cracking. He turned from the mirror in disgust and closed his eyes. He remembered a photo of himself from just a few years ago. It used to be his Facebook profile picture. He was dangling off a mountain and stopped to pose for a photo in the middle of a rock-climbing adventure. He was so happy. His bright smile illuminated the camera; his rosy cheeks were full of life. His tight T-shirt revealed his muscular frame. He smiled to himself. *I'll look like that again after all this is over.*

What happened next was a blur. Kevin was wheeled into surgery, but he fell asleep before he entered the operating room. When he awoke several hours later, he was lying on his back in the hospital bed and was in his hospital room. White and steel machines with digital monitors flashed numbers and beeped at random intervals. Tubes from his arms and legs dangled across the bed to their connection points on the machines. He couldn't feel anything except the heaviness of his eyes. He reached toward the surgery site in his thigh that was covered with a bandage and gauze. A nurse, whom he didn't notice was sitting near him, squeezed his hand.

"Do not touch, please, sir. It needs to heal."

The nurse called Dr. Mittal. He arrived a few minutes later.

"Your surgery went very well. Your body has accepted the kidney. It's not fully functioning yet, but that is normal. We will monitor you. If it does not fully function in the next three hours, we will initiate dialysis. We will continue to give you medication to assist the new kidney." He left without asking Kevin if he had any questions. Kevin immediately fell back asleep.

When Kevin awoke several hours later, his stomach growled with hunger, and he took that as a good sign. He shifted in bed and felt the aftermath of surgery for the first time. His whole face scrunched up when he adjusted in bed. The pain was so bad that he just lay still for several moments to muster the energy to try to move again. He tried to sit up again, but it was too painful. Kevin pressed the nurse call button that was attached to his finger.

"You slept so peacefully that I did not want to wake you," the nurse said cheerfully. "You will be wanting pain medication, yes?"

"Yes, please. It's very painful."

"Of course, sir. You had major surgery."

She was one of those nurses who had a permanent smile on her face. Even in the face of bad news, her face still looked as if it was smiling. It was tough to know if she was sincere. Her plump fingers practically covered the entire vial of drugs. She leaned over the bed, shifting part of her fat body onto Kevin's shoulder. It seemed that was the only way she could balance herself to safely inject him. She irritated Kevin. He missed Lakshmi. A nurse who looked like Lakshmi would keep his spirits up. He would want to recover fast to impress her. But this fat, smiley nurse just made him want to curl up into a ball. Her name was Kamla, and she was assigned to Kevin. She was by his side for the next month while Kevin healed.

The first few days with Kamla were rough, but he eventually grew to like her and then to really care for her. They spent twelve hours together every day. She bathed him, made sure he ate nutritious meals, and gave him his antirejection medications; and when Kevin was well enough, she was his physical therapist too. They walked around the room, up and down the hallway, and eventually visited other hospital floors. She taught him all the self-care that he would need to know after he left the hospital and after he left India.

Kevin would have to monitor his weight, blood pressure, temperature, and pulse every day. He would need to examine the inside of his mouth, including under his tongue, for any abnormalities. The slew of antirejection drugs might cause hair loss, weight gain, diarrhea, high blood pressure, and high cholesterol.

He would have to alter his lifestyle based on the risk of all possible side effects. He wouldn't be able to return to his normal workout routine. At most, he could walk for the first few months after surgery, and then, if his doctor cleared him, he might be able to do more strenuous exercise. And then there were all the antirejection medications that he had to take for the rest of his life, assuming the new kidney lasted that long.

There were four types of antirejection drugs, which were sometimes called immunosuppressives—drugs that suppress the immune system to prevent it from attacking the foreign kidney. They were all pills that had to be taken multiple times a day. If Kevin missed a single dose, or if he didn't take the medications at exactly the same time each day, he could trigger his own body to attack the new kidney. He was forced to carry a pillbox all the time—one of those boxes he only saw at drug stores and at his grandparents' house. It had seven little compartments, each one labeled with a letter—M, T, W, T, F, S, S, for each day of the week. He hated to be tethered to that stupid senior citizen's plastic box, but it was the only option to prevent his body from collapsing on itself. He put alarms in his iPhone as reminders. *It's still better than dialysis,* he thought.

During Kevin's last week at the hospital, he and Kamla took a stroll to the second floor, which he had never visited. When they stepped out of the elevator,

Kamla steered him toward the right, but Kevin heard a commotion coming from the left. Fortunately, Kamla was being paged through the overhead system, and Kevin had a few minutes alone. Kevin pushed his IV as he walked alongside it toward the ruckus. At the end of the hall, he peeked around the corner, and he couldn't believe what he saw.

In that state-of-the-art, gorgeous hospital, hundreds of sick people lined the walls and lay on the ground. Their skin was black as night and looked leathery as if overexposed to the sun. Many of them wore tattered clothes that hung limp from their skinny frames. Kevin didn't see any doctors or nurses. The groups of nurses with bright-red lipstick were nowhere to be seen. From the looks of misery on their faces and the way they hugged the wall, Kevin knew those people had been waiting for a long time.

Kamla found Kevin and scolded him like a child for walking away without her.

"You are not supposed to be here, Kay-win. Come now. Come. Do not trouble yourself with all this."

"Who are all those people? Why isn't anyone helping them?"

"They are locals. They are like rats. They multiply each day. It is impossible to treat all of them."

"You mean they're poor?"

"You wealthy foreigners think you know everything, but you do not. We try to help them, but there are too many. We do not have enough drugs, bandages, and hospital beds to treat everyone. Imagine if we gave all of them rooms, performed their surgeries, and prescribed all the drugs they need. How would you have surgery? We would not have any room for you! And we would not have money. Those people have no money to pay."

"So I'm responsible for all those people not getting proper care?" Kevin was offended.

"No, of course not, Kay-win." She paused and added, "But in a way, yes. How can we buy drugs to help the poor without making money? Patients like you come with unlimited money, so, of course, the hospital wants patients like you."

"Unlimited money? Is that what you think?"

"You may not be rich in your own country, Kay-win. But you are rich in India."

"So Indians are getting displaced from hospital beds by foreigners like me?"

Kamla sighed. "You are a smart man. Money is a universal language."

Kamla locked her arm in Kevin's and ushered him back to the elevator and to his hospital room. But Kevin couldn't shake his guilt. He hadn't thought about his impact on Indian residents. There were only so many beds, and he had occupied one for more than four weeks. It was so obvious! Americans were accustomed to complaining about low-wage labor from India (and other countries like the Philippines) that took jobs from Americans. What about all the foreigners like Kevin who displaced Indians in the health-care system? Through his rose-colored glasses, Kevin didn't think to ask Lakshmi about it when he visited Health SkyTours. She certainly didn't mention it, and, of course, the displacement issue wasn't listed anywhere in the marketing materials. Suddenly Kevin missed Emma. *Emma would have thought about the impact on locals.*

Kevin was discharged from the hospital one week later. During that week, he thought about the poor population, but he didn't know what to do about it. Besides, he got what he wanted, and he was already focused on his future far away from there. Dr. Mittal visited Kevin one last time on the day he was discharged.

"I can't thank you enough, Dr. Mittal. I feel like a new man. An entire month without dialysis!" Kevin sighed happily. "I don't know how I can ever thank you."

"You are welcome. You paid for a service, and you received it. My staff and I are proud of the work we are doing."

By then, Kevin was accustomed to Dr. Mittal's robotic speeches. *Doctors are the same on every continent.* Dr. Mittal instructed Kevin to visit a nephrologist in Los Angeles as soon as he returned home, and then at least every three months. He advised Kevin to walk but to refrain from any other, more strenuous, exercise.

"You can contact me with questions, although, of course, we will have to talk based on what you describe or what I can see over a webcam. It is better for you to get routine care locally."

Dr. Mittal handed Kevin prescriptions for the anti-rejection medications.

"This should last you six months. You will not be able to carry more than that with you back to the States. After that, it will be up to you to get your prescriptions from your doctor back home."

They shook hands, and Dr. Mittal left. Kamla and Kevin embraced for several minutes. He gave her a large tip—a few hundred dollars, which he wasn't supposed to do, but he wanted to. She stuffed it into her coat pocket and left Kevin for the last time.

The next day, Kevin settled into his first-class seat back to Los Angeles. He thought about staying in India to do all the sightseeing he had planned before surgery. But he was eager to go home. He didn't have a job or a place to live, but he was happier than he had been in a long time. Before he switched his phone to airplane mode, he refreshed his e-mail one last time. He hadn't heard from Emma or Lakshmi while he was in India. He had an urge to e-mail both of them, separately, to let them know he was safe and that he was headed home. But he decided against it. It was clear that they didn't want to stay in touch. Kevin flipped on the flat-screen television in his first-class suite and changed the channel to ZEE TV. He hummed along to "Yeh Dosti Hum Nahi Todenge" from the Hindi film *Sholay* as the plane took off from Indira Gandhi International Airport. He had watched the Bollywood classic at least six times at the hospital, and it still hadn't gotten old.

PART 3

Slum Life

CHAPTER 15
KIDNAPPED

After Kevin spent a few days with Max Cray, sharing his side of the story, Max decided to give Kevin a break and return to Juhi, who picked up right where she left off.

Juhi and her parents felt as though they sat in the back of the cavernous, rusted van for days. They were tossed like caged chickens on their way to the slaughterhouse. But it had only been two hours. They did not know where they were going or how long it would take to get there. Juhi's imagination ran wild with scenarios and possibilities, and in most of them, she and her parents wound up dead. Mummy and Papa fell asleep despite their battle to keep their eyes open. The blood inside and around Juhi's nose had dried, and she could feel it flaking off when she scratched her cheek. Her tears rewet the dried blood, and together they streamed down her face and got stuck in the depression at the center of her upper lip. Tears trickled from her right eye where the black eye had formed. The pulsing sensation that lingered after Mogambo punched her had subsided, but now she could not close her eye without squealing in pain.

A cold metal rod in the back of the van jutted into her right thigh, but there was nowhere to move. The seats had been pulled out of the decrepit vehicle, and it was filled with boxes stacked one on top of another. Somehow they managed to stuff Mummy, Papa, and Juhi in there, too. Her back rubbed against the steel grates that separated the drivers from the passengers, like the partition in police cars. She placed her school bag, which was still full of her textbooks and drawings, between her back and the grate to provide some cushion. In the commotion, she didn't recall grabbing her backpack; her kidnappers must not have noticed. Earlier that day, she had filled the backpack with her favorite drawings. She had planned to visit Pari after school, and Juhi wanted to show them to her friend. Juhi was grateful to have them, since she was forced to leave everything else behind.

She sat curled in a ball with her knees to her chest, and she rested her head on her knees. They ached from being bent for so long, and she wished there was enough room to stretch, even if for just one second.

She was careful not to move too much, though, because she would surely rub against Papa, who writhed in pain. Juhi's eyes grew heavy, but she could not sleep. Her ears were warm, and they pulsated to the beat of her racing heart. Every limb and ligament in her body was awake and aching, and now her stomach was, too.

She sunk her face into the fleshy softness between Mummy's neck and shoulder, seeking refuge. The sweat from Mummy's chin dripped onto Juhi's face, cooling and calming her at the same time. She tried to hold her head up, but it kept bopping and snapping like a woodpecker. Mummy wrapped one arm around Juhi and the other around Papa, who lay curled next to them. He moaned and shook as they traveled down the dirt road. Each rock that met the tires sent the van leaping in the air, followed by a heavy plunk when the van came back down. Papa groaned at each landing, teeth clenched, face crumpled in pain, exposing all of his wrinkles. Dirt from the van floor was creeping into Papa's wound, but they were helpless. Papa lay there, clumsily pressing the half bandage to keep it in place.

Their two kidnappers drove through the night in silence. Juhi was grateful that she was with Mummy and Papa, even though she felt strangely alone. She felt an ominous brooding of loneliness to come.

Juhi adjusted in her chair in Max's studio and shifted her gaze upward at no one in particular. She was in deep thought, transported to that moment in her history.

In the van, she cried silently as her mind drifted to thoughts of Mummy and Papa dying. They were right there in front of her. Papa's wound still trickled with blood. Juhi wondered how she would take care of Mummy if Papa died. As she lost her battle to keep her eyes open, Juhi drifted into dreams about how safe and happy she was just that morning and how she wished she had a time machine to go back to her morning chai and Parle-G biscuits.

Just before dawn, Mummy, Papa, and Juhi were jerked awake when the van came to a halt. Mogambo pulled the van door open and, without any warning, hoisted Papa up and dropped him into the wheelchair. Shocked, Papa screamed as the seat of the wheelchair dug into his wound. Mogambo kicked Papa for his outburst, which only made Papa howl louder. Mummy and Juhi scurried out of the van, afraid of being separated from Papa. Juhi's feet, legs, and thighs trembled under her as they tried to wake up.

Mogambo slammed the van door shut behind them and curtly sneered, "You are lucky. Kabir Singh arranged your new home. Usually we dump people in the slum, and they have to find their way."

He abruptly pointed to his right, jumped into the van, and sped away. When he was out of sight, Juhi remembered that her brand-new camera was still in the van. It had fallen out of the front pocket of her backpack and she forgot to put it back. She felt guilty for forgetting such a precious gift, but she took comfort knowing that she would never see Mogambo again.

A surly man stood a few meters away from them across the other side of the alley. He stared at Juhi, Mummy, and Papa with a hard expression and said nothing. He was old. Thick white hair covered his whole head. He used coconut oil to brush it back like a seventies film star. He wore a white *kurta pajama* and sandals and smoked a beedi. He must have been six feet tall, and he towered over them. Juhi and her parents stood there, confused and scared. Juhi pushed Papa's wheelchair across the alley toward the man, and Mummy followed. As they approached, Juhi noticed the man's hands. His skin looked like leather, and it was chapped. When they were close enough to him, he turned away from Juhi, Mummy, and Papa and ducked into a short, makeshift building and indicated for them to follow. It was the most unstable structure Juhi had ever seen. Referring to it as a structure was generous. It was hundreds, maybe thousands of rooms made from mud and bits and pieces of concrete, plastic, brick, glass, metal, marble, burlap, cloth, sticks, and wood slabs of all shapes and sizes. It looked as if the leftovers from a construction site were mixed together in a blender and regurgitated.

Juhi stopped at the gap between the open air and the structure. One more step would change their lives forever. She wondered if they should, in fact, follow the man inside that horrifying building or run away. The man whipped his head around and looked hard at Juhi, as if he knew what she was thinking. He turned back around and kept walking. Juhi looked at Mummy and Papa, but they were as bewildered as Juhi. Juhi decided to follow the man. She slowly pushed Papa's wheelchair inside, and Mummy followed. She turned back to look out to the main road where they had just entered, as if she expected a black drape to come crashing down and lock them into a house of horror.

Their new home was a vile, filthy slum. The smell was unbearable. It was a combination of feces and urine, mixed with the smell of burning animal carcasses, trash, and molded food. Someone nearby was cooking some sort of meat, a smell Juhi was unaccustomed to, and that on its own was enough to make her sick. She vomited and then dry heaved when there was nothing left inside of her. Mummy wrapped her handkerchief around Juhi's face. She tied a tight knot in the back so it would stay in place. It pinched Juhi's hair and neck, but it lessened the stench.

It was early in the morning, but the slum was already alive and in complete chaos. Women shouted, babies cried, pots hissed, pans clanged, fires crackled, brooms swept, water boiled—all against a backdrop of howling wind. The chill in the air ran through Juhi's entire body.

Juhi pointed at Max and then pointed at a window behind him.

"Imagine that window was shattered," Juhi said. "Now imagine that we removed the shattered pieces but kept the pieces that were still intact. Then we fill the spaces that had shattered with whatever we can find. We tie a long piece of cloth to cover one portion, and we use branches and sticks to cover another area, and then we glue chipped cement blocks together to fill another section. None of the spaces will be completely filled. It would be covered in tiny crevices and open holes, right? That is what the walls inside the slum were like. It was impossible to feel warm in the winter and impossible to escape the Delhi heat in the summer."

Juhi watched Max's expression, and she saw that he didn't understand the slum. He might not ever fully comprehend, but she could try to make it easier for him.

"Have you played a game called Jenga? I played it with Kevin on an evening he called 'game night.' Imagine the crisscross stacks of blocks, mismatched and struggling to stick together. That's what the walls are like at the slum," Juhi added to her explanation. "Last week, I went with Kevin to a place called Costco. Have you been there?" she asked Max.

He nodded yes.

"Three of those huge buildings put together," Juhi said. "The slum where I lived was that big. Each aisle at Costco was as long as one row of houses at the slum. Each room was a square home for two people or as many as fifteen. Each room was divided by the walls that I just told you about—made of cloth, branches, and brick. The rooms were no bigger than..." Juhi didn't know how to describe the size of the rooms. "I measured our room when we first arrived at the slum. I could lie down three times this way and three times that way," she said as she described the length of the walls. "Costco has very high ceilings, but the slum accommodated average-sized people. The tall man who met us outside the slum on our first day had to hunch over. An open gutter lined the perimeter of the slum. When we first arrived and followed the tall man down a narrow passageway, we walked alongside the gutter. I watched spoiled rotis, feces, spit, phlegm, candy wrappers, dead flies and bugs, old fruit, and other waste drift past us along a stream of urine. We walked past at least a dozen men who stood over the gutter and urinated straight into it, sometimes missing and leaking right onto the earth that made the floor of the slum homes. Rats and cockroaches were as much our neighbors as the other slum dwellers."

"There were no doors. The front of each house was covered with a makeshift curtain of some kind, such as a sheet of leftover metal, an old sari, or tarp. As we continued to follow the man deeper into the slum, I peeked behind one curtain and saw a family of three—a woman, a man, and a young child sleeping. In another, two half-naked boys played cards. In another, a woman squatted on the ground and cooked over a small fire. Some of the rooms had no curtain covering, and the people in the room were exposed, like fish in a glass bowl."

The tall white-haired man stopped in front of one curtain and pulled it back, revealing an empty brick room with a dirt floor. Juhi pushed Papa's wheelchair inside, and Mummy followed. When Juhi turned around, the white-haired man was gone. Juhi poked her head outside and searched in both directions, but he had vanished. The only items inside were a curtain that served as a door and a rusted metal bucket in the corner of the room—their toilet.

Mummy and Juhi helped Papa out of the wheelchair and laid him down on his back. He was delirious and fell in and out of sleep. His wound had stopped bleeding, but the gown was beyond soaked. Mummy delicately changed Papa into his own clothes and threw the gown into the corner of the room.

The ceiling was made of a flat metal sheet that lay at an angle on the four walls, with no anchor. When the wind blew, the sheet lifted up and created a draft in the room. Many of the bricks in the walls were chipped or eroded. The whole place was at constant risk of toppling over if someone breathed too hard. Juhi peeked through one of the holes into the room next to theirs and caught a glimpse of a filthy baby calling for his mother. The baby sat on the ground naked; his hair was a mess of knots and nests.

Slumped against one of the walls, Mummy and Juhi held onto each other, while Papa slept. Juhi's stomach growled. She shuffled around, trying to get comfortable in the dank, brick room. Little dirt clouds lifted off the ground when she moved her feet. This was the place they were forced to call home.

CHAPTER 16
A NEW "HOME"

When Juhi awoke, the sun shone through every crack in the walls and ceiling and made the metal ceiling shine like a halo. Papa still slept, and Mummy stirred on the ground next to him. Juhi tried to stand, but her legs buckled, and she fell onto her hands and knees. She tried again, leaning her whole body into the brick wall. The jagged edges scraped her face, while the blood rushed back into her legs. Hunger pangs consumed her, and she searched the crawl space for any indication of water or food. She looked down at Mummy and Papa in despair. She did not want to weep, but she could not stop the tears.

The shantytown had come to life again while they were sleeping. Thousands of people lived in this jungle of filth and disarray. She never felt more insignificant.

Her ears tuned into the sounds and smells surrounding them. A whiff of masala swept under her nose, and like an animal, her stomach moaned. She instinctively ducked out of their room under the curtain into that elongated passageway from where they entered. She ran. It was as if her nose was separated from her body and ran ahead of her, while the rest of her body tried to catch up. She leaped past row after row of rooms just like her own, tiny compartments filled with the poorest people she had ever seen.

The hallway broke off onto a bustling street, just like the scene from her nightmare of the girl who was separated from her parents. Cars of all shapes and sizes whizzed by; three-wheel auto rickshaws, bicycles, and motorcycles ducked and weaved through the maze of pedestrians, cows, dogs, and buses. Traffic moved in every direction; it was jerky and abrupt and lacked any rhythm. There was an endless clash of honking horns, police shouting, children laughing, bike bells humming, and motorcycles buzzing. It sounded like instruments in an orchestra that fought against each other to make the loudest sound. The commotion made her dizzy, and her stomach churned. She squeezed her eyes shut for a few moments, willing it all to go away, hoping that when she reopened them, she would be back in her living room in Gantak Mandi. But the sounds filled her head again, and instead of looking up, she focused on the ground, where she could tell her body and brain to march one step at a time.

A group of four children walked past her. They had emerged from the same narrow passageway that she had come from. The eldest of the four, a girl, looked Juhi's age. She carried a baby no more than one year old. Another girl, who looked like she was five or six years old, held a smaller baby, perhaps six months old. Their clothes were reduced to dirty rags. The four of them walked together, barefoot and with purpose, as if they were hunting. Their faces were youthful, but their eyes were weathered. Juhi followed them and stayed a few paces behind. They did not seem to notice her, or they didn't care.

They stopped in front of a small food kiosk, where fat, hairy men in dhotis and white *banians* (tank top undershirts) rolled dough, fried samosas, and poured steaming vegetables onto plates. Some patrons stood, while others squatted under the canopy, devouring their meals and sipping chai. Juhi's stomach growled so hard that she hunched over. She lurked around the corner as she watched the eldest girl beg at the kiosk.

The beggar girl walked straight up to customers and the cooks with her open palm stretched out. She held the one-year-old baby on her hip. She wanted money or food, whatever anyone might be willing to give. Everyone she approached ignored her, and a few shooed her away like a mosquito. She tried a different tactic. She put the baby down, turned on Bollywood music on her cellular phone, and together—she and the baby—started to dance. Their steps were synchronized, although the baby sometimes got off cue. Still, the baby smiled brilliantly. Passersby and patrons laughed and cooed, and some handed money to the baby. The girl quickly grabbed it out of the baby's hand and danced harder, which the baby followed. They had everyone's attention at the food stand, including the men preparing the food. The girl and baby kept dancing, and Juhi watched in awe. But there were four of them. Where were the younger girl and the other baby? That baby was left sitting on the ground, leaning against a pole, while the younger girl crept behind the man who served the plates of vegetables and *bhaturas* (fried leavened bread). She stealthily filled two lunch boxes with vegetables and placed a pile of bhaturas onto a large cloth napkin. She stuffed the food into the bag slung across her body, cautiously backed away, grabbed the baby, and casually stepped away until she dissolved into the city's commotion. The dancing girl watched, and once she was certain her partner was safe, she scooped up the one-year-old dancing baby and, with a subtle half turn into the street, vanished. The cook returned his attention to his pot and shouted when he saw the empty paper plates on which he had just poured vegetables. He ran into the crowd, searching for the young dancers, but they were already deep in the city's underbelly.

In that moment, Juhi wished she had listened to her mother, who encouraged Juhi to become a dancer. Juhi stubbornly refused, and now she had no chance of dancing for food. She walked a little further down the road to the next food stall. She stared at the vat of samosas frying in the large wok. A well-dressed woman stood in front of the counter, waiting for her order. Just as the waiter put her samosa box on the counter, the woman bent down to wipe dirt off her pants.

Juhi sprang forward on all fours, like a tiger, snatched the box, and ran like hell. Everyone in the food stall shouted after her. "Stop her! Grab her!" A few arms reached for Juhi. One arm even caught hold of her. Certain that she would go to jail, she looked up at the man who held onto her so tight that he cut off her circulation. He stared down at Juhi as if she was the most disgusting thing he had ever seen. His condescending expression triggered something Juhi had never felt before. She raged with anger and felt out of control of her own senses. Like a snake, she snapped her head back and bit into his hand so hard that she thought she might bite off his finger. He screamed and released his hold on her. Juhi bolted away, spitting out bits of his flesh and blood that were caught on her teeth and tongue.

When she was far enough away, and the shouts turned into faint background noise, she hid in a small nook between two shops. Her chest heaved as she tried to catch her breath. She held back the sobs that rose in her throat. She caught a glimpse of her reflection in a puddle of water at her feet. She stared at her likeness as if it was someone else. What had she done? What would she tell Mummy and Papa? She stole that box of samosas just like the doctor stole Papa's kidney. She turned away from her reflection in disgust. She lingered there awhile longer, just to be certain that no one chased her. As she weaved through the traffic back to the slum, she longed for her life to go back to the way it was. But deep inside, she knew that she had nothing to go back to. Kabir Singh would certainly kill all of them if they set foot again in Gantak Mandi. Juhi, Mummy, and Papa did not belong anywhere.

She returned to the brick room, where Mummy paced worriedly, and Papa still lay on the ground, half awake. Mummy pulled Juhi into her arms with relief. Juhi furnished the box of samosas, and Mummy wept. Mummy and Papa must have known that she stole them, but they never asked. They gorged on the meal and didn't spare a single crumb.

Juhi stole food for the next fifteen days. Some days she got lucky and grabbed enough to feed all three of them, while other days it was barely enough for one person. She was caught and beaten three times. They punched her face and kicked her in the stomach. "There are small scars around my nose that you can see if you look close," she told Max as she touched her face.

Juhi knew it was wrong to steal, but she thought they were wrong to beat her. After a while, she stopped caring if she got caught. She felt numb on the inside, and things that Kevin called "unimaginable horrors" stopped bothering her. Throughout the day, she cowered in the brick room, while drunk men shouted and beat their wives and children. Sometimes it sounded far away, and other times it could have come from the next room. Toddlers cried, mothers wept, teenagers yelled and cursed, men laughed and howled, families argued together and laughed together, mothers gave birth, couples got married, gunshots fired, people died, and police raided parts of the slum, which sent hundreds of people fleeing for their lives, only to return a few hours later to rebuild.

The thing Juhi hated the most about the slums was the sounds. Husbands and wives shouting profanities at each other drowned any hint of children laughing. Drunk men vomited; their flatulence, gunshots firing, women and children weeping, and the most vulgar insults surfed through the air. It never ended. Even when the sun went to sleep, the sounds continued. Sometimes a few seconds of quiet would pass. Those moments were like a drop of water trickling down her throat during a hot summer day. But then, like a torture mechanism, the slum erupted again in shouts and moans. The most private sounds could be heard out in the open for all to hear. Maybe slum dwellers got used to it; perhaps they did not hear it anymore. Or maybe, after a while, it was comforting. Juhi was amazed that after just a few weeks, she grew accustomed to sleeping on the dirt. She could even confess that she slept soundly on the nights that she was too exhausted to be scared. But even on the restful nights, as soon as her eyes opened, the sounds filled her ears all over again. It was as if the slum never wanted her to forget that she was there.

The sounds that scared her the most were the high-pitched squeals that came from young girls, old women, and every female in between. During their second week at the slum, Juhi was attacked for the first time. She ventured out for her daily food hunt, when a man, who also lived in the slum, stopped her. He lured her with a promise of a hot meal. He pulled out an aqua and purple-colored candy from his pocket and handed it to Juhi. He spoke to her the way a father speaks to his child. Juhi missed Papa's affection. Papa had been reduced to an emaciated mass, who slept most of the day and only opened his eyes to eat and urinate.

Juhi followed the man to his home, or whatever that place was. It was on the other side of the slum, at least a fifteen-minute walk through the maze of homes and filth. He invited Juhi to sit down on a mat that rested on the ground. It felt nice to not sit on the cold dirt. He handed her a plate of steaming vegetables and roti. Juhi didn't even chew the food; she just swallowed. He petted Juhi's hair while she ate, which she didn't like, but she couldn't object with the plate of hot food in front of her. When she finished the meal and handed him the empty plate, his face changed.

He put his hand on her shoulder and knelt in front of her. His nose grazed Juhi's, and his stale dirty breath filled her nose. She pulled away and tried to get up. But he pushed her down and sat on top of her. Juhi kicked and screamed, but he covered her mouth with a rag and squeezed her neck. He was so strong; it felt like the harder she kicked, the tighter he squeezed her body. She was certain that she was going to die.

He spat on her, pulled her hair, and tried to tear off her clothes. Juhi recognized the wild expression in his eyes—it was the thirsty face Mogambo and Gabbar made at Mummy. The man released her neck and used both hands to clumsily unbuckle his belt. Juhi tried to catch her breath while still wrestling with him. He laughed as if he enjoyed her struggle. Juhi screamed. She yelled for help. No one came.

Max sat on the edge of his seat. Juhi spoke like a robot. There would be many more attacks. This one was not as bad as those to come. The man slapped Juhi so hard across her face that her head hit the concrete, and her neck almost did a complete turn. He spat on her again. He pulled her dress up over her knees and held her face down with the palm of his hand. He lay down on top of her. Something hard between his legs skimmed her inner thigh. Juhi bit his hand that held her down and twisted his fingers. She bit wherever she could. She bit his neck and shoulders. He shouted and struck her across the face again. He stood up over her while she lay there on the mat, both of them exposed. He was fully erect. He smiled down at her ominously.

"Do not fight me. You will enjoy it," he whispered.

He closed his eyes and bent forward to lie on top of Juhi. Before he could sit on her, she reached for the little knife she carried in her sock and stuck it straight into his pelvis. She had stolen that little knife off a man who was busy chatting with his friends outside of a restaurant, one week after she arrived at the slum. She learned how to make swift, shallow stabs and how to pickpocket by observing other slum children.

"I am a fast learner," she told Max.

The man's eyes flashed wide open, and he fell to the ground, howling in pain. He grabbed onto his penis and rocked back and forth on his back while he screamed and cursed. Juhi stabbed him over and over in his arm, his stomach, his other arm, until she was confident he would not chase her. She ran. Her knife was in her right hand, lifted above her shoulder, ready to stab anyone who got in her way. She ran the whole way home with her knife drawn. Even after she was home, she would not let go of the knife. Mummy covered her hand with hers and gently massaged it until the knife dropped to the ground. The man's blood on the knife mixed with the dirt floor. Mummy wept when Juhi told her what happened, and Mummy held Juhi close to her for the rest of the afternoon. She refused to let Juhi leave the room for the next several days, not even to get food. She said they were better off starving. Mummy confessed to Juhi that Mogambo and Gabbar raped her every time they came to collect rent, and she feared that Juhi would be attacked again.

CHAPTER 17
SLUM DWELLER

Two weeks in the slum felt like ten years. Juhi couldn't pinpoint when it happened, but she had become a slum child. She still needed to learn their tricks, so she observed the other children like a hawk. They stole just about anything that was small enough to quickly stuff into a bag: food, wallets, jewelry, children's toys, books, clothes, and shoes. Other than food, which they saved for themselves, they resold the items at a fraction of their retail price.

The slum children had different schemes based on the situation. Each plan had a name, like a cricket team's playbook. They used hand signals and moved their eyes in particular motions to communicate with each other and to warn each other of oncoming danger. They all knew their roles in each conspiracy, what to do in case something unexpected occurred, and where to meet after it was all done. There was a minimum of three children involved in each plot, sometimes as many as seven or eight, depending on the size and quantity of loot they wanted to steal. To this day, Juhi has no idea if any of them were actual brothers and sisters.

They treated each other like family—generous and cooperative—yet each child still protected of his or her fair share. Disputes arose occasionally when earnings were divided. But the children settled them quickly; wrongdoers were swiftly silenced with several kicks in the stomach. The next day they would all be back together, planning their daily scams as if nothing had happened the day before. There was an unspoken understanding among them. Although they needed each other to survive, each child was responsible for him- or herself; while some children were clear leaders and others were followers, all winnings were divided evenly. Greediness was not tolerated. If someone was caught, he or she didn't tell on anyone else, and the others in the group would do everything they could to help him escape; any stealing someone did on their own, they got to keep it all. Everyone was responsible for taking care of any orphaned babies in the group. Babies were used like props to win sympathy. Food was always divided evenly, and older children were responsible for taking care of younger children. If someone was sick or needed to see a doctor, everyone gave money to pay for medication. If someone stole from anyone in the group, the group would punish the thief, which could include death, depending on the severity of the crime. Each group stayed on their own turf and did not infringe on the turf of other children. If there was a big area to be had, and others were already there, they would share the space, and if the other groups did not like it, they would fight to determine a winner. If a group tried to take someone else's area, the group that was there first had the right to fight back.

There were other silent rules, but Juhi never fully became an insider. The prerequisite to join a group was that you must be an orphan. There were scores of other bands of children who schemed, plotted, stole, and begged all day, but they had at least one parent or auntie or uncle who looked after them or at least lived with them. Many of the guardians were disabled or lepers or drug addicts, so children were left to survive and support their families on their own. Only a handful of children went to school. Their parents lost their belongings to gambling, but they still wanted their children to go to school. Or their parents were those who had love marriages and ran away together, only to be disowned by their parents. They were the "wealthy" ones in the slum. They had some skill or craft or a steady job as a laborer, and they earned enough money to support themselves. They could afford a living without forcing their children to work.

Juhi could not tell the difference between orphans and children with parents; they all looked the same to her. They all had sunbaked skin that was dark as coal, and they were covered in soil, clearly only bathing every few days or maybe once every week. Their black hair was filled with knots and pointed in every direction; many had lice and were constantly scratching their heads until they bled. Lots of young children were shirtless—even girls. Some had shoes and others didn't; their clothes were tattered, wrinkled, and covered in holes. Their fingernails were long and white, but they were filled underneath with dirt and covered in warts and calluses; their palms had rough lines, which were the sign of hard workers. They reminded Juhi of Kabir Singh's men, but she tried to block out their similarities so she wouldn't hate the children. Although Juhi was tempted to approach them when she saw them playing cricket or chasing a hollow tire frame down the street, she resisted. They never invited her, either. They didn't need her when they had each other. She was one more mouth to feed and one more person to divide earnings with. But they did notice her. They stopped and stared and pointed, just like people did in Gantak Mandi. Juhi was too intimidated by them to say anything, so she stared at them, and they stared at her until she walked away.

Juhi longed for a friend. She missed her school. But those thoughts quickly vanished. She had to concentrate on her next meal. And she had to find some sort of job to sustain her family. She needed money so Papa could see a doctor.

It had been two weeks since his botched surgery. The wound was clearly infected. It had since closed up, but it was covered with dirt, and who knows what other filth was trapped in there. His belly was also bloated, but they didn't know why. He hadn't bathed in the river the way Mummy and Juhi had learned, because he could barely sit up. Mummy had no skills and couldn't find any work. It was up to Juhi. In between stealing food, she spent her time observing the other children in the slum and thought about what she could possibly do.

Juhi had learned a lot about people while she lived in the slums. For people living outside of the slums, there is no distinction among people who live there. But inside the slum, a caste system thrives. Slum dwellers who have jobs shun crippled people, the mentally ill, and the beggars. Even beggars shun each other. A beggar with a light complexion frowns on a beggar with dark skin. But at the same time, they cooperated in other ways. It seemed like every day in India and around the world, there are stories about fights over religion. In the impoverished slums, Hindus, Muslims, Sikhs, Jains, and Buddhists coexisted and cooperated with each other. Occasionally, fights would erupt over Krishna and Allah, but they were quickly resolved, and just like the children, adults made up easily. Juhi decided that slum dwellers care more about survival than religion.

Just like the children, adults in the slum had rules, too. Slums are highly structured, yet still a convoluted mess of social, culture, and economic power. The basic rules that applied to the children also applied to the adults. Each adult had his or her purpose. The adults called themselves "entrepreneurs." Some slum men and women were construction workers on new houses for wealthy landowners; others paved public streets and built brick fences. Still others were *ironing wallas,* people who ironed clothes for the middle- and upper-class families in wealthy neighborhoods. They built shacks that were just big enough to cover their ironing board and one rod on which to hang clothes. At least four or five people worked there, all of them sitting on top of each other under that small space. One person was the ironer, one hung the clothes on hangers, one person went to pick up clothes that needed to be ironed, another delivered clothes that were already ironed. The larger, more successful shacks had two ironing boards and two ironers. During wedding season, frantic fathers and husbands raced to the shop carrying saris and *lehengas* that belonged to the women in their houses. The ironing wallas found creative ways to get power so they could heat the irons, such as running illegal wires to their huts directly from public electric wires. The more risk-averse ironers used ancient methods like filling an iron with hot coal.

Other common jobs for slum men were rickshaw driver, taxi driver, three-wheeler-scooter driver, tailor, waiter, package deliverer at an office building, dishwasher at a restaurant, chai maker, or samosa maker at a street-side food stall. Many men worked at hair salons. One man held the hair dryer and handed the stylist hair clips, while another man styled the hair—like a nurse handing a surgeon a scalpel. Women worked in kitchens at restaurants, doing whatever menial work needed to be done. They rolled dough for rotis, peeled vegetables, and cleaned. Women and girls cleaned homes. These were usually steady, full-time jobs and were considered lucky to get, easy to lose, and almost impossible to get back. In private homes, the slum women dusted furniture, washed clothes, mopped floors, and cleaned bathrooms. Men did not clean, not even those who were desperate for work. That was a job only for women. Slum workers are called servants, and are treated like servants too.

The women servants were not allowed to cook or to sit on the furniture, and they did not make eye contact with anyone who lived in the house. No matter how hard they worked or how honest they were, housemaids never earned the trust of their bosses. The middle and upper classes kept their drawers, chests, and jewelry under lock and key. Families were constantly suspicious of their maids. Maids tended to the children in the houses where they worked, only for those children to grow into adults who abused their servants.

People who could not find jobs—or just did not want to—worked in the black market. The most innocent among black-market workers were the boys and young men, who sold pirated books, music, and movies. They pawned stolen merchandise like Calvin Klein watches, Adidas tracksuits, Gucci handbags, Prada sunglasses, and Jimmy Choo shoes. They sold copycats too. Instead of "Gucci" handbags, women purchased "Cucci" bags for a fraction of the cost. There were men who worked a little deeper underground. They established drinking houses that stayed open all day and all night. Men gambled, drank, and pleasured themselves with prostitutes under these stalls.

The most sinister black-market workers sold drugs in large cartels. Their networks spanned across entire states of India. The cartels sold every kind of drug to anyone who wanted to buy—wealthy teenagers, college students, destitute women who wanted to drown their sorrows, and men who could not kick their addictions. It is easy for people on the outside to judge people who sell drugs and people who take drugs. But after Juhi had seen it from the inside, it wasn't so clear to her. Juhi hated the drug cartels; any good they brought did not outweigh the pain and suffering they caused. But drug cartels provided jobs to hundreds of slum people. There were jobs for growing, processing, selling, buying, and transporting drugs. Their networks were intentionally bloated to protect the drug lord and his immediate friends. Living in the slum, Juhi learned that men want to provide for their families regardless of whether they are rich or poor. A secure job gives a man pride. She knew Papa felt that way, and she saw it with the men in the drug scene, too. Drug gangs gave their workers a community where they felt loved and respected. Juhi saw mothers and fathers who traffic drugs spend all their earnings on their children's school tuition.

Still, the drug gangs were the most violent groups in all of India. They were ruthless, greedy, vengeful, and overstuffed with pride. Most of the drug lords were vile men with no value for human life, which made them capable of such violence that most people cannot even imagine. Juhi couldn't even repeat out loud some of the horrors that she had witnessed. Juhi hated the drug lords the most. Everyone from children to senior citizens shuddered at the mention of any drug lord's name. People talked about those lords as if they were great mythical beings with special powers. Only a very few people actually ever saw them, but stories floated throughout the slum about their grand clothes; their strong, muscular bodies; their gold adornments from head to toe; the great feasts that were laid before them every evening for dinner; and their connections to top government officials, the police, and Bollywood. Some people spoke of the drug lords as benevolent kings, while others cursed them.

Another group of crime lords incited equal fear, admiration, and terror as the drug lords. They were the villains who stole kidneys from living people. They cut poor people open, took their kidneys, and sewed them up halfway in makeshift operating rooms in the back of sinister buildings. The crime lords would promise thousands of American dollars to the kidney "donor" but found ways to cheat their victims out of every single rupee. The crime lords did not think of themselves as monsters. If you asked them, they would tell you they provided a service in a free market where there is supply and demand. Poor people needed money, so they were willing to sell a kidney; the middle-class people and the rich people who cannot wait any longer for a transplant had the means to buy a kidney. It was simple economics.

Max shuddered.

It was disgusting that people thought that way, yet many people agreed with it. If a man wants to sell his or her kidney, what right does anyone have to stop him?

But Papa was not offered money for his kidney. He would never agree to that! Kabir Singh just stole it, as if he owned Papa—as if Papa was a slave and Kabir Singh was his master!

Juhi was yelling now, and Kevin, who accompanied Juhi to her testimonial with Max, gently placed his hand on her wrist to help her calm down. Juhi did not realize she had become so riled. She took a few deep breaths to compose herself.

Papa was getting closer to death with each passing day. His swollen wound was covered in a blanket of pus. Mummy passed the hours in a sleeplike daze, attending to Papa the best that she could. She fell deeper and deeper into her mental seclusion, and she stopped speaking. She traded two of her gold wedding bangles for a gas burner. She exchanged two more for one pot, one pan, two spoons, one rolling pin, and a marble slab to roll rotis. Out of pity, the man who bartered with Mummy also gave her a large blue plastic tarp, which they spread over the dirt floor. She parted with her last pair of bangles for a sack of dal and rice. They ate out of the pot and pan and shared the spoons. Papa had to be fed. He was too weak to eat, and most of his meals dribbled down his shirt. Mummy grew clumsy over the flame, and she burned her fingers often. Juhi tried to talk to her the way she did at home, but it was not the same. At night Mummy held Juhi and massaged her back and ran her fingers through Juhi's hair until she fell asleep. While Juhi was out all day, trying to survive the next twenty-four hours, Mummy and Papa were left behind in that brick room with nothing to do but ruminate over their past and present. They were going mad, and Juhi could not help. She still had no options except to steal whenever they ran out of food.

On their sixteenth day in the slum, in the middle of the night, Juhi heard a cluster of soft footsteps gliding down her row of rooms. A few seconds after it passed, she ducked her head out and saw five children; the eldest was seventeen or eighteen, and the youngest was Juhi's age. They were hurrying toward the main road. She looked back at Mummy and Papa; they were in their normal stupor. Juhi stepped out and followed the group of children. They poured onto the sidewalk, passed through the shadows of the trees and buildings, and walked toward the city center that was now practically abandoned. At night the main road was unrecognizable. While the sun shone down, the street was flooded with traffic, but that night, she could count the number of cars on her fingers. She could hear her own breath. Juhi maintained a safe distance from them, but she stayed close. They quickened their pace, and she followed. They turned into a dark, rancid alley and whispered to each other, but Juhi could not hear them. They were masters at making themselves invisible, and they each hugged the buildings along the side of the alley as a large delivery truck pulled in.

Two men jumped out of the front cab and unlocked the back of the truck. The doors squealed as they folded open. At the same time, a man emerged from the back door of one of the stores. He told one of the deliverymen to come inside the store to pick up some leftover boxes. The other deliveryman, who was left alone in the alley, unloaded large rectangular boxes from the truck and counted them one by one as he stacked them. One, two, three, four, five, six. Seemingly out of nowhere, the two youngest of the children, a boy and a girl, stepped into the light. They held hands and cried. They produced tears on cue; it shocked and amused Juhi. They approached the lone deliveryman but sauntered and swayed as if they were drugged. The deliveryman stopped unloading and turned to them. They walked past him and turned.

"Our mother just died, and now we have nothing to eat and nowhere to go," wailed one of the children. Tears glistened in the alley lights as they dribbled down her cheeks. The man turned back to his boxes and pretended he did not see the children. He continued to stack boxes while they complained. They moved in closer so he would be forced to stop and acknowledge them. This time the boy cried.

"My mummy is dead, and we are all alone."

It worked. The man stopped pretending he couldn't see the children.

"What happened to her?" he asked with hesitation. He stared at the children and tapped his foot while he waited for them to answer.

"She was very sick, and we did not have money for a doctor."

"No father?"

"Our father left us when we were babies. We tried to find him, but we do not remember him. We do not even know his real name. Maybe he is not alive anymore."

The man frowned at the children. He had already been dragged into their mess more than he had wanted. The other children, who still hid in the alley, knew they had him. The two eldest boys peeled themselves off the building and tiptoed to the stack of boxes. They went unnoticed by the deliveryman, whom the crying boy and girl continued to distract.

"Mummy cleaned houses, but she lost her job when she was too sick to work. I went in her place, but the ma'am of the house said I was too young and that I should be in school. I asked her how I could afford to go to school when I needed money for Mummy's medicine. But the ma'am would not give me the job, so I was forced to clean public toilets and beg and pray for help..." The two children folded their hands in prayer.

The elder boys snatched the top box and carried it straight out of the alley without making a sound. They reached the end of the alley, turned the corner, and disappeared. The two crying storytellers continued to plead with the deliveryman until he shoved twenty rupees into the girl's hand.

"Thank you, uncle ji. Oh, thank you so much! We are very grateful! Now we might be able to cremate Mummy properly. Thank you, uncle ji, thank you!" The deliveryman thought they were too grateful for a measly twenty rupees, but he hoped it was enough to get rid of them.

He nodded and then shooed them away. His face dropped when he turned back to his work and saw only five boxes. He whipped around and ran up and down the alley, searching for the boy and the girl. He shouted, but he knew he had lost. He screamed profanities straight into the air and hoped that the children would hear him. The other two men came running out of the store. Juhi slipped away while they yelled and blamed each other. During those first few weeks in the slum, she had also learned to make herself invisible.

Juhi backed out of the alley and suddenly remembered that she was alone. The image of the man who attacked her flashed in her mind's eye. The hairs on her neck stood straight, and her pace quickened as she ran back toward the slum. A few streets away from the slum, she passed another alley. As Juhi ran past, she spotted two people. They were the boy and the girl who lied about their mother being dead. She stopped running and steadily ambled her way back toward them. She tried to make herself invisible again. Juhi inched closer and peeked into the alley. They did not notice her, so she went closer and hid fifteen paces away from them. The whole group was there, not just the boy and the girl. They squatted around the stolen box. At that moment, one of the older boys turned his torso, and his arm caught the light. His entire right forearm was covered in shiny gold and silver watches, and more watches were pouring out of the box. Each watch was in a large square box. Two of the children opened the boxes, one child examined each item, and another lined the boxes into neat rows. Scratched or broken watches were placed in a separate pile.

Juhi watched quietly as they divided the watches among them. They sat in a circle, and the child sitting closest to the pile passed out the watches like a card dealer. After they were all distributed, they each lined up their watches in a straight line, one line below the other, to confirm that they were equal. It was how they knew the watches were divided fairly. Juhi wondered why they did not count how many watches were in the box and divide that number by the number of children.

"In America, these watches sell for eight hundred dollars, maybe even two thousand dollars!" stated one of the older boys.

"Two thousand dollars?" The girl who put on the show for the deliveryman squatted on the ground and looked up at the older boy in amazement.

"How much do you think we can get for each watch?"

"You can probably get five hundred dollars, but I am going to sell mine for one thousand." The older boy made sure the others knew he could do things they could not.

Another younger boy chimed in. "One thousand dollars? How many rupees is that?"

"About sixty thousand."

The whole group whistled and hooted. Two of the boys celebrated their future riches with an impromptu bhangra dance. The entire group smiled and giggled but then quickly grew quiet as they each contemplated their strategies to sell the goods.

"So how much will we get with the watches we have if we each have ten watches?" The group went silent.

No one knew the answer. Juhi wanted to step out of the shadow to answer their question. She was excited to use simple multiplication again! It had been so long since she did any math. But she remained hidden and decided it would be safer to leave before they caught her.

Juhi turned to walk away, but her feet were like boulders. She wanted to see the watches one more time. She had never been so close to such valuable items before. If they each had ten watches, and each was worth sixty-thousand rupees, that was six hundred thousand rupees! Juhi grew fidgety at the mere thought of so much money. She turned away to tiptoe out of the alley, while the thieves swapped strategies to sell the watches. But since Juhi was an amateur in the slum, a pebble got wedged under her shoe. With her next step, it was propelled into the air and bounced off the side of the building across the alley. The gang of children looked up from their box and moved swiftly toward Juhi.

"Who's there?" one of them shouted.

Juhi tried to run, but she could not move. Her whole body trembled. The tallest boy in the group shoved her to the ground, flashed a light in her face, and drenched her in questions.

"Who the fuck are you? Why are you following us?"

"I saw her in the alley earlier!" said the other older boy.

Juhi wasn't as good at making herself invisible as she thought.

"What do you want? Do you think you can fucking steal from us? These watches are ours! Who sent you here? Who are you working with?"

"No...no...no one," Juhi replied. "I am no one."

"What are you doing here?"

"Nothing. I-I-I was just curious."

"About what? About how you can steal from us?"

"No...I do not want to steal from you. I just...I just..."

"What? You were just what?"

"I just wanted to learn...how to steal. You have been practicing for a long time...and I am just...I am just new."

They stepped back and laughed at her. A hand reached down and pulled her to her feet. They took their time eyeing her up and down. Juhi could see the girl's face soften as she realized that Juhi was, in fact, new to the slum. Juhi's clothes did not have any holes yet, and there were still some white spots on the sleeves. Juhi's hair was soft, not brittle like theirs, and her skin had not turned leathery. The other children calmed down except for the boy who was her age. He grimaced at Juhi, suspicious and unbelieving. Juhi lowered her eyes from his and avoided eye contact.

"I am sorry I followed you. I heard you leaving the slum; you walked past our room. I just wanted to see how the children here support their families."

"We do not have fucking families; we *are* each other's family." A few of them put their arms around each other in solidarity.

Juhi didn't know what to say. She was exhausted and past the point of fear. For the first time, she was desperate to return to the slum.

"Can...can...can I go now?" she stammered.

"We shouldn't let this bitch go!" shouted the suspicious boy. "I don't trust her. She is lying! She is fucking working with someone, and they put her up to this."

"I'm not working with anyone." She decided the only way to get out of there was to tell the truth. "My parents and I were forced to move to the slum two weeks ago. We are alone, and we have nothing. My father is sick. I need money so I can take him to a doctor."

They looked at each other, and Juhi wondered if they believed her.

"Don't worry about Sameer," the girl who was Juhi's age said as she put her arm around Juhi. "He was left behind by his family. He does not trust anyone."

She turned to the eldest boy. "She can go?"

He agreed. As Juhi walked away, she turned back toward them.

"If you each have ten watches, and you can sell them for sixty thousand rupees, you will each earn six hundred thousand rupees."

"How did you know that?" asked the tall boy, who now walked right up to Juhi, stood over her, and peered down.

"Ten times sixty thousand is six hundred thousand."

"You know math?"

"Yes, of course, I know math. I can read and write too."

A few of them howled and whistled. "You should have told us!"

"You don't need to steal! There will be plenty for you to do," the oldest boy declared.

"What do you mean?" Juhi pleaded. "Please tell me!"

But he just stared at her. Juhi didn't understand. She wanted to ask again, but she was no longer welcome. Juhi returned to the slum. Mummy and Papa were snoring. They hadn't noticed that she was gone. She fell asleep wondering what the slum children meant. She slept through the night for the first time since she arrived in New Delhi.

CHAPTER 18
A NEW JOB

Juhi's life took another turn the day after she met the young thieves in the alley. A line had formed outside her slum home before she woke up in the morning, and the tall boy from the night before stood over her and shoved her shoulder with his foot as she slept. Mummy and Papa were still asleep and oblivious to the commotion.

"Wake up," he said. "All those damn people outside are waiting for you." He pointed toward the curtain door.

Juhi stuck her head out and saw a line that snaked halfway down the row of the slum.

"What do they want?" Juhi asked as she rubbed the sleep out of her eyes.

"We spread word that you are smart. They want everything. Some want you to write letters, some want you to read to them. Others want you to count things for them, like their money or their food. They will pay you."

He caught Juhi's attention. She stared into his eyes to see if she could detect whether he was lying or mocking her. He was genuine.

"I do not have anything to write with." Juhi had one pen in her backpack, but it had dried out in the New Delhi heat.

"Here," he said and flung a black ballpoint pen at her. It grazed her cheek and left a skinny, long ink stain, but her own sweat washed it away a few minutes later.

"Consider it a gift."

"Why are you helping me?" Juhi wondered.

"I can see what your father went through." He looked down at Papa's half-dead shriveled body. "They did the same thing to my papa when I was around your age. We were taken from our village and dumped here. I have lived here ever since. I guess this place has not turned me into a complete monster yet."

Juhi stared at him. She wanted to ask so many questions, but her tongue was tied into knots. Her heart filled with empathy. The boy vanished before she could formulate a clear thought. She shuddered to think that she and Mummy and Papa might live there for so many years. He must have been five or six years older than her! For the first time, Juhi realized that living in the slum might not be temporary. She glanced at Mummy and Papa, slumped over like homeless people sleeping on a bench, and a sadness that she had never experienced before overcame her. A part of her died in that moment. Yet another part of her awoke with hope. She needed to devise a plan to earn a lot of money fast before that hope vanished.

She rubbed her hands over her face, and she urinated in the bucket before she invited the first person in line to step inside her slum home. The man was older and wore a white *banian* and white pajamas. His filthy, cracked, bare feet picked up dust as he shuffled across the ground. They sat on the tarp, while Mummy and Papa lay motionless. They continued to snore.

The man did not introduce himself to Juhi, and Juhi didn't tell him her name, either. She had learned another unspoken rule in the slum: only give as much information as is necessary. The man handed her an envelope addressed to "Sri Ravi Kumar." The return address read "Gupta" and "Jaipur" and a multitude of mailing codes. Juhi looked from the envelope to the man.

"Read the letter to me," he instructed Juhi.

She carefully broke the seal of the tattered envelope and unfolded the paper. It smelled like mold. The letter was from the man's brother.

"This letter is dated more than one year ago!" she exclaimed.

"Who would read it to me?" he snapped.

Juhi read the letter to him, and when she finished, he gave her two rupees and left. As he walked away, he said he would think about his reply and that he would return when he was ready for her to write it. The next group walked in. It was a mother with her two-year-old son and a newborn baby. She needed to complete a medical form for her baby's polio vaccine at the free clinic. She gave Juhi ten rupees.

"Where is the free clinic?" Juhi asked. "You can see a doctor for free?"

She nodded yes. She told Juhi how to walk there, but Juhi wasn't familiar with any of the landmarks the woman mentioned. Juhi copied the address from the form onto her left palm. On her way out, the woman said, "Look for the rice."

"Look for the rice?" Juhi looked up to wait for a reply, but the woman was gone.

The next customer, a young man, wanted Juhi to count his money. He asked her to write the amount on a small piece of paper that he put at the very top of his moneybag. Juhi asked him if she could tear off a small corner of the paper instead of taking payment. He looked at her sideways but agreed. Juhi scribbled the free clinic address onto the scrap paper and stuffed it into her pocket before her own sweat wiped it off her hand.

It was nine o'clock at night when the last customer left. She had helped at least fifty people and had earned two hundred rupees. That was less than five American dollars. Instead of payment, a few customers gave Juhi food. Still, Juhi felt uplifted for the first time since her life turned upside down. She even smiled. She fanned the rupees in front of Mummy, and Mummy forced a weak smile. Juhi tried to show Papa, but he had grown too sick to open his eyes. He slept all day, while slum dwellers filed in and out of their room. Juhi lay down next to him and held his hand. Silent tears streamed down her face. The next day she planned to visit the free clinic and see about taking Papa there. But when she woke, there was another long queue of customers outside her home, and the first one in line was nudging her to get up.

"Wake up. We have all been waiting for a long time now."

"I cannot help you today. I am going to the free clinic."

"I have been standing in line all night and so have these others. Do not leave. Someone will beat you."

He was an older boy, maybe nineteen or twenty; and from the way he stood over her, she thought he might beat her. When he caught a glimpse of Juhi's face, she saw his gaze turn to the "thirst." Juhi turned away from him but obediently sat down on the tarp with her pen. She gestured for him to sit down, too, and after he did, she slid back a bit to maintain some distance.

Another full day passed in writing letters, completing forms, and reading government notices and newspapers. She spent thirty minutes with a teenage boy who wanted to read and write text messages to a girl he met in the slum. Slum people had nothing, but they still had cell phones. The texting would have continued if the next customer had not interrupted by waving a cricket bat at the boy and threatening to beat him if he did not leave.

Juhi didn't ask for specific wages. She accepted whatever the slum people offered. She didn't know what to ask for. Besides, she was too mesmerized by the growing pile of rupees that lay next to her. The last customer that day, a middle-aged widow, left after dusk and paid her with three bowls of dal and rice. The customer had asked Juhi to write three letters, so Juhi thought it appropriate to exchange three for three. Mummy and Papa fell asleep right after they nibbled at their meal. They each ate about half of the food. Juhi was still exhilarated by her money pile and decided to go for a walk. It was dangerous to walk late at night by herself, but she felt suffocated in that cold, dark room. She stuck her knife in her sock and headed for the main road.

She walked in the general direction of the free clinic, trying to recall the landmarks that the lady from the day before—the one with the two babies—had told her. Juhi asked a few people along the way for directions. Every person told her something different, but they had all pointed in the same direction. The next street she turned on was empty except for a pack of wild dogs that searched for food. But as she approached the address that she had written on the piece of scrap paper, she saw a line of people that started at the front entrance of the clinic and stretched for at least one kilometer. Some of the people moaned in pain, others coughed up phlegm and blood, children wept, mothers prayed, and fathers paced. Like the people waiting outside her own room at the slum, these people waited all night to see the doctor who would return the next morning. There were two doors at the front entrance. The left door read "Free Clinic," and underneath there was a painted picture of a plate of steaming rice. "Look for the rice," the woman had said. All the people waited in front of that door.

On the right, the door read "Paying Customers," and there was a picture of a chicken. No one waited in front of the chicken door. But Juhi had money! Yet there was no possible way that Papa could lie there all night. The trip to the clinic alone could kill him; he was already too frail. She sat down in front of the chicken door, and the people in the rice line shouted and spat at her. They reminded her that they were there before her, so they would see the doctor before her.

"Hey, *benchod!* (sister fucker). We've all been waiting here! Go to the back of the line!" After one man shouted at her, several others joined him. She wanted to pull out her rupees from her pocket and gloat in front of them. But the fear of being beaten or robbed, or both, stopped her. She ignored them and prayed that they would grow tired of shouting and insulting her. And finally, after a while, they left her alone. She wondered if she looked as determined as she felt.

Juhi tried to stay awake for fear of being attacked. But her eyes grew too heavy, and the next morning, a woman dressed entirely in white shook her awake. The nurse asked if Juhi had an appointment. Juhi shook her head no, and the nurse nudged Juhi toward the rice line. When Juhi realized what was happening, she resisted and revealed the money in her pocket.

The nurse looked from Juhi's hand to her face and released her hold on Juhi's shoulder.

"Follow me." She turned toward the clinic and led Juhi past the rice line.

The men who shouted at her the night before stared with their mouths agape as Juhi zoomed past them. She felt guilty that she enjoyed walking past the rice line, but she couldn't help it after the insults they had flung at her.

The nurse told Juhi to wait in a small room that had a chair, a bed, and a small table with a computer.

"Why do the doors have a chicken and rice on them?" Juhi asked the nurse.

"How else are they to know where to line up?" she snapped. "So you can read, and you think you are special because you have light eyes and a pretty face? You have some money, so that makes you better? You probably got it by fucking some of those assholes in that line."

Juhi was confused by the nurse's hostility. But she quickly recognized the same jealousy cast on her by the ameer girls at her school in Gantak Mandi. Maybe the nurse was a slum dweller herself.

"Most of *these* people cannot read, and they have no money. But they can recognize pictures. Rice is cheap. Chickens are expensive," she explained.

Juhi later learned that in Indian Parliament, all political parties have assigned symbols that appear on voting ballots to assist illiterate voters. The lotus flower is the symbol for the Bharatiya Janata Party, one of the largest parties in India. An open-palm hand is the symbol for the other major party, the Indian National Congress. The then prime minister of India, Manmohan Singh, was from that party.

Juhi admired the nurse's clean, ironed uniform. Juhi wondered how the nurse's crisp, white hat stayed on her head even when the nurse nodded her head back and forth. But Juhi decided not to ask her. It would probably just irritate her more.

The doctor arrived a few minutes later. He was a short man with a thick mustache. He wore a white coat and black pants. His white shirt was wrinkled and had a green chutney stain down the center. A few crumbs stuck out of his mustache. He reminded her of Dr. Rao, and her muscles tightened.

"What is your name?" He tapped the computer keyboard without looking at Juhi. Juhi didn't reply. *Only tell as much as is necessary*, she reminded herself.

He asked her again, "What is your name?"

"I am not the patient."

"Then why are you here? Do not waste my time!" He raised his voice at her.

"I do not want to waste your time. My father is sick. The doctor in our village stole his kidney two weeks ago. My family and I were dumped in the slum. We have been living there ever since, while Papa grows weaker. He is very fragile, and I have no means to bring him here. He needs medicine. I will pay."

The doctor shifted his gaze onto Juhi and frowned. He had heard stories like hers before.

"He is at the slum right now?"

"Yes."

"You must find a way to bring him here. I cannot travel to the slum to see him."

"But how can I bring him?"

"That is not my concern. If you want to give him medicine, you must bring him here."

"OK, I will find a way to bring him," Juhi replied with despair. "How much will a visit and medicine cost?"

"You seem like a smart girl." The doctor stared at Juhi. "And beautiful too. How will you get the money?" He raised his eyebrows, and Juhi saw craving dance in his eyes. Her stomach tightened. There was a long pause before she could reply. She used every muscle in her throat, jaw, and tongue to prevent her voice from quivering. She didn't want the doctor to know that she was frightened. A few months earlier, Juhi would not have understood what he implied. But now that she was another rat in the slums, she understood all too well.

"My family has managed to earn an *honest* living." She drew out "honest" as it left her mouth. "My older brother works at the construction sites."

Juhi felt compelled to create a fictional older, muscular brother. This man already knew that her papa was sick. Perhaps he would assume she was an easy target with no one to protect her. Juhi's antics worked, and the doctor's insinuations stopped.

"Your father will need antibiotics, and I will need to clean the wound. This would normally cost several thousand rupees, but this is a community clinic." He puffed his chest with pride. He paused to let Juhi compliment him for being a noble servant to the poor. She stared at him quietly, unimpressed.

"It will cost one thousand rupees for a visit, plus the cost for drugs. I do not know what drugs he needs until I examine him. You have to bring him here. I do not see patients in the slum," he repeated with condescension.

"I will bring him here." Juhi handed the nurse five hundred rupees for the visit, the required amount for any doctor consultation. She hurried toward the door, eager to distance herself from the doctor. Juhi didn't know if she could trust him. But she had no choice. She had to trust someone, even a proud, disgusting doctor.

It took Juhi several days to save enough money for another doctor's visit plus medication. She needed extra money to pay for someone to take Papa to the clinic. She decided to use the money she had already saved to buy just enough food to provide for her and Mummy and Papa for those few days. If they did not have enough food, they would be forced to fast until after Papa's doctor visit. And Juhi would have to collect all fees in rupees—no more bartering for meals. That would offend several of the slum people, but Juhi had no choice. If she bartered, it could take an extra day or two to save enough money. She could not afford to delay. With each passing day, Papa lost hope. He began to mumble about wanting to die peacefully. He was only forty years old, but his eyes and body were those of a man twenty years his senior.

On her way back to the slum, she stopped at a *sabzi* stand to buy vegetables. She had learned that it was cheaper to buy raw food and cook it than barter for prepared food. She purchased one pound of rice, dal, and just enough okra for one meal. She shouldn't have done it, but she decided to indulge in three two-liter bottles of clear, crisp water. She had almost forgotten what clean water looked like. It was almost too good to drink. The food was enough for three days, if they only ate once each day. They had grown accustomed to skipping meals, and Mummy and Papa no longer ate much anyway. When she stepped foot back into the slum after meeting the doctor, Juhi shouted into the open air for the entire slum to hear.

"Reader-writer *walla* is here and ready to help!"

Like rats, dozens of people appeared from nowhere, and a queue had formed even before she stepped into her room. The customers clapped and cheered when they spotted her. It made her feel good. And then she felt sad that it made her feel good, that anything in the slum could spark joy. It was as if she was admitting that she and Mummy and Papa were like the rest of the them.

Before she invited the first customer in, Juhi decided to set a price list. She scribbled her fees on a scrap piece of paper that she had snuck from the clinic. None of her customers would be able to read it. But she wanted her rates to be in writing; that way, no one could accuse her of cheating them. Bargaining was a way of life in the slums, and she hated the whimsical way that the price for everything changed based on the mood of the vendor. Bargaining for every little thing was exhausting, and constant worry about being swindled made her lose faith in people. But it also helped her harden her attitude. As far as she knew, Juhi was the only person in the slum who was educated. Her customers had no other place to go. It would take two weeks to earn enough money for Papa if things stayed the same. She couldn't wait that long. Juhi drafted a price sheet and drew symbols just like the rice and chicken signs at the clinic.

FEES

Reading: Ten rupees per page (Symbol: book)
Writing: Fifteen rupees per page (Symbol: pen)
Counting and Calculations: Fifteen rupees per minute (Symbol: abacus)
Texting: Two rupees per incoming and outgoing text (Symbol: cell phone)

She expected some customers to protest, and, of course, they did. The old customers who had already come to see her complained and tried to bargain. But she looked at Papa, who lay still on the dirty tarp, and she held strong to her fees. She kept a logbook of clients who owed her money. She was naïve to think they would pay her. From the next day on, she demanded customers to show her the rupees before she helped them. But then some customers showed her the rupees and still refused to pay. Then she demanded customers to pay her as they went along. After she read one page, the customers paid ten rupees. But still, some customers handed her five rupees and claimed it was ten. So she revised her policy again. For each page, she demanded half before she started to read or write and the rest after each page. She also refused anyone who did not have cash. The line outside her room stretched long and steady from morning until night. She could afford to refuse customers who could not pay according to her rules.

Word had spread in the slum that Juhi had wizened up about her fees, but she didn't get as many complaints as she expected. Maybe she could have charged more, but by that time she was earning 940 rupees per day. She calculated that she could work twelve hours each day. She spent about ten minutes with each customer, so on most days, she met up to seventy-five clients. She did equal amounts of reading, writing, and math. The doctor wanted one thousand rupees for a visit, plus the cost of medication.

But Juhi didn't know how much the drugs would cost. Three days later, when she had enough money for a visit plus extra for medication, she took Papa to the clinic.

CHAPTER 19

PAPA'S MEDICINE

Juhi paid a *sabzi walla* (vegetable seller) thirty rupees to help lift Papa off the ground and onto the sabzi walla's bicycle-drawn cart to take Papa to the clinic. He pedaled through New Delhi's streets with Papa lying there, fully exposed and oblivious. Mummy stayed behind at the slum, and Juhi followed Papa on foot. She ran alongside the bike and dodged and weaved through pedestrians, motorcycles, rickshaws, three-wheeler autos, and cars. The anaconda-like queue at the clinic stretched out in front of the rice door just as it did on her first visit. Only one other patient stood in the chicken line. In front of the clinic, the sabzi walla lifted Papa again, but this time off the pallet. The sabzi walla must have taken pity on them, because he was very gentle with Papa, which surprised and pleased Juhi. Perhaps it was his nature, because he transported delicate tomatoes, beans, melons, and other foods that easily bruised. Together, they laid Papa down on the ground behind the first patient in the chicken line. Papa looked dead; he was motionless, and his eyes were closed. When their turn came to see the doctor, the sabzi walla helped again to lift Papa onto the patient bed.

The doctor removed the heavily soiled bandage that Juhi had awkwardly taped almost one week ago. He shuddered at the sight of the wound and held his breath. It smelled terrible—like a dead rat. Papa's eyes were closed, but he grimaced as the tape was pulled from his skin. Underneath, swollen skin and purple-and-black bruises surrounded a long, thick scar. The stitches clumsily held his skin together, and between the threads, pus oozed out in a continuous stream. It was painful to look at. Juhi couldn't imagine what Papa felt.

"It is very infected. I am not sure I can treat it. You should have come sooner," the doctor scolded Juhi, as if she chose to wait that long.

Tears welled up in her eyes, and her throat filled with sobs. She tried to swallow it down while the doctor continued to examine Papa, but the thick drops already traveled down her cheeks. He injected Papa with an antibiotic, which he said would fight the infection. The medicine woke Papa up a bit. He opened his eyes, and when he saw the doctor, he became combative and tried to slap the doctor, but his weakened arm just flapped toward the ground. His bulging eyes met Juhi's, with fear stricken across his face. Juhi placed a firm hand on his head and whispered in his ear.

"It's OK, Papa. This is a good doctor. He is going to make you better," Juhi lied. She had no idea if he was a good doctor, but she had to try.

Papa eyed Juhi suspiciously. It was the first time that he had looked at her with distrust. He tried to get up from the bed, but he just flopped back down. He tried to speak, but fear tied his tongue. He just made desperate grunts and moans and jerked uncontrollably. He looked like a fish caught on a rod as it's pulled out of the water. He tried again. This time he managed to speak in fragments. The doctor stepped away from Papa, staring at him with a needle in his hand, pointing up as if he were ready to shoot it at someone.

"Stole my kidney…my tooth…horrid doctor…why me…dumped in this hell hole…I loved Kabir…forced to leave…" Papa recited particular details of their real-life nightmare, and as he started to lose his breath, the doctor approached Papa again. Helpless, Papa fell back onto the table and wept.

"Please! Let me go!" he pleaded. He folded his hands in namaste and looked up at the doctor. "Please just let me go. Do not harm my family!"

Juhi clutched Papa's arm and buried her head in his lap. Her tears soaked his exposed belly. He patted her head and stroked his fingers through her hair. The doctor used that moment to inject Papa with morphine. The doctor said it would stop the pain and calm him. Papa fell asleep less than one minute later, and the doctor continued to treat Papa. He delicately wiped the wound clean. Juhi could see that even the doctor felt compassion toward Papa and toward their helpless situation. Yet he also did not seem to want to get involved. They were not his problem.

Juhi suspected that the doctor had seen other people like Papa who had kidneys stolen. The doctor probably knew something about the criminals who took them too. Who were they? Where did they live? How did they find wealthy people in villages and concoct scams together? He would be in a position to report it to the police. But he was not a good man, a man with integrity or the kind of man who would use his education and influence to fight back. He just wanted to make money and look away when things got ugly.

Before the doctor replaced Papa's stitches with new, clean ones that actually sealed his skin, the doctor rubbed another clear solution all over the wound. He explained that it was a numbing cream. It would help with the pain, at least through the night. Juhi handed the doctor one thousand rupees, and in return he gave her a bag filled with large, square bandages, tape, and alcohol-drenched napkins. He instructed Juhi to change the bandage every night after wiping it with alcohol.

"His wound is very badly infected," the doctor repeated. "Whoever did this to him did not sew him up properly, and it appears they used dirty instruments. Given what you have told me, I can assume the wound has been exposed to dirt and other harmful elements. I must be frank in telling you that your father has slim chances of recovering, and the infection has likely already spread to other organs. We can treat him with antibiotics to reduce the infection. Chances are small that it will kill the entire infection, but it will at least bring it down. This is the only recourse."

Juhi clung to Papa and pressed her face tightly against his. "Please, doctor, we have to try."

"Antibiotics are expensive. He will need to take one pill three times per day for a few weeks. And he needs to start taking them right away."

The doctor read the question spread across Juhi's face. "Each pill costs three hundred and fifty rupees, so three pills per day is one thousand and fifty rupees."

One thousand and fifty rupees per day? Juhi would have to work more hours or change her fees. But if she changed her fees again, she would certainly be beaten or raped.

"My brother and I will do what we have to," she reminded the doctor about her fake older brother.

While the doctor examined Papa, he brushed the front of his body against Juhi as he walked past her. She had to bear it. If she accused him of inappropriate touching, he would claim he had to stand that close to Papa to do his job, and if she did not like it, she should have moved out of his way. If she confronted him, she would offend him, and he could take revenge by harming Papa or by withholding treatment. The doctor knew he could get away with it. Juhi didn't understand the satisfaction it brought him to brush his elbow against her breast or his arm against hers. She would be a victim of this many more times with many more men long after she left that slum. The only explanation that she could think of was that the men exerted power over her, and they loved it. Also, that it felt dangerous, somehow increased their excitement. They were giddy when they could get away with it. Juhi's master, who adopted her after she left the slum, enjoyed that power, too.

Juhi maintained a straight face despite her disgust. She told the doctor that she would return to the clinic every morning to buy three pills. He nodded at her, and without acknowledging Papa, he left to treat his next patient.

Papa was still under the morphine spell when the sabzi walla laid him down back on the pallet. Juhi offered to pay him for waiting during Papa's appointment, but he refused the additional rupees. He was the second person to show Juhi any kindness. The first was the boy who gave her his pen. She knew she would never forget either of them.

As she followed Papa back to the slum, her mind raced into action, and her pace quickened.

I will work more hours each day! The medicine will work, and Papa will get better; then he can find work, and we will have enough money to rent a decent place to live. Until then, Mummy and I will eat one time each day. Papa will have three full meals until he recovers. If I cannot earn enough for food and medicine, I will beg at night or steal food just until Papa gets better.

They still had enough dal and rice for two more days. She was exhilarated about her plan, only for her heart to sink when she returned to the slum. She had told her clients that she would not be available that day. The hallway outside her room was empty. She would have to start saving the next day.

That night, she talked excitedly to Mummy and Papa about her plan. She wanted them to feel encouraged and reassured that Papa would be fine. Mummy faked a smile for Juhi's benefit. It was difficult to imagine Papa getting better—a gray shadow seemed to surround him, as if one of his legs was already dangling in the afterlife. Mummy and Papa could no longer trust any doctor—particularly one who cared for poor and destitute slum people. Juhi did not confess to them her suspicions, too.

Papa was already asleep because of the busy day and side effects of the medicine. Mummy lay down in her usual place and fell asleep a few minutes later. At night, when it was quiet, Juhi missed Gantak Mandi. She missed walking to school with her friends. She missed running to the farm to surprise Papa and walking home with him, singing and laughing and telling each other what happened at school and on the farm that day. She missed Mummy greeting her with a kiss and a hug. She missed drawing.

Juhi didn't make any friends at the slum. That unspoken rule to only share as much as necessary made any friendship impossible. Many slum children played together, but she was an outsider, one of the "lucky" ones because she had parents. When she walked by a group of children playing in the slum, she slowed her pace, hopeful that they might invite her to join them. They never did, and she was too shy to ask. The faces of the pack of child thieves from the alley showed up in her dreams. She never saw them again, but their serious, hardened faces; wild hair; tattered clothes; and harsh hands and fingers were detailed canvases in her mind that needed to come out. She desperately wanted to draw, but she reserved her pen for her work.

She was grateful for her job. She was happy to practice writing, reading, and math. She worried that she might forget those things because she wasn't in school. She even felt happy in spurts throughout the days that followed, because she learned about many new things that she never could have imagined. She wished she could erase some of it, but other things came in very handy. She learned to bathe in a river without fearing the cows that also bathed just a few meters away. She turned her head away when she saw children and adults drink from that same river.

She could balance a water jug on her head and carry additional jugs in each hand without spilling a drop! Her customers too taught her things. She learned about government protections for slum dwellers, and municipal laws, and the countless forms that are mandatory to gain access to public and government services. She could recite laws against slums, and the possible punishments for people who build them. She learned to listen to the general mood of the slum—something in the air—if there was pending anxiety and rumors that the police might come to tear it down. She had become a master at rebuilding.

She held a gun and loaded a bullet for the first time. A group of men came to Juhi to divide a box full of bullets. She didn't ask any questions. She could guess where they came from—they were stolen from underground gun sellers or bought as bribes from police. Almost everything that entered and exited the slum was stolen, but that fact was never discussed. She quickly counted the bullets and distributed them evenly among each person. Thankfully, that group did not fight; but other times fights broke out when one person got greedy while she divided their goods. After those scuffles, their gas burner would be turned upside down, and the tarp that covered the ground would be dusty, twisted, and turned in every direction. Mummy and Juhi learned to cover their few belongings and move them to a corner each morning. They covered them with old rags that Juhi found in the trash.

Juhi divided and distributed just about everything: purses, sunglasses, and watches. By now she could easily spot the differences between real goods and imitations; beedies and cigarettes; and bottles of alcohol and sometimes drugs, which were called "special medicine." She helped young boys who sold pirated books and DVDs in the streets to memorize titles based on the cover artwork. She read personal letters and wrote responses, and she became familiar with the intimate details of other slum families. She learned how to use a smartphone and taught others to recognize the symbols on the screen. Juhi learned how to pickpocket. She knew just from a glance who the evil people were in the slum and who the kind people were. She never again saw the man who had attacked her.

Sometimes she worked fifteen to twenty hours each day, but it was not enough. All of her earnings went to Papa's medicine, and they had nothing left for food. Papa was starting to heal, but the doctor said medicine was only part of it. He needed proper nutrition. She earned enough to eat one bowl of dal every other day so that Mummy and Papa could eat at least two meals each day. Mummy and Juhi must have each lost seven kilograms since they arrived in New Delhi. Papa had lost even more. Juhi was lucky to get three or four hours of sleep, and many days passed without even a small break for a glass of water. It reflected in her work. She rewrote letters at no charge because her hand grew weak and couldn't grip the pen. Many times, she counted and distributed items all over again because she lost count. She fell asleep while reading letters out loud. A small itch inside of her started to grow larger—it stunk of resentment toward Mummy and Papa. While she slogged all day, they sat in the room day and night. Of course, she had compassion for them, especially for Papa. But sometimes her hunger led to anger—they could eat properly with just a little bit more money.

And besides the money, Mummy and Papa no longer comforted her. The flicker of hope in their eyes turned to smoke. They barely spoke all day. Mummy still held Juhi at night, but her frail body was cold. Mummy and Papa awoke each day with deep sorrow in their eyes, and they also fell asleep that way. Some days Juhi was forced to choose between purchasing food or Papa's pills. She didn't have the time or energy to steal and beg. Many nights her growling stomach kept her awake.

A few weeks passed, and by then Juhi had lost track of what month it was and how long she had been in the slum. She estimated the days by the texture of her skin. Her arms had already turned into slum leather, and her legs started to follow. Her forehead and cheeks had changed weeks ago. Her skin hung looser and looser with each lost kilogram. She estimated that three months had already passed. It was around that time that they grew so desperate that Mummy became a prostitute.

CHAPTER 20

MUMMY

Mummy's decision to sell her body was simple. She could not bear to see Juhi withering away. Her family needed money, and the slum had a supply of boys and men who thirsted for women. Although Mummy and Papa spiraled into insanity while they lived at the slum, they were still completely devoted to each other. Mummy held Papa all day while he rested; she massaged and bathed him, and she even found someone to yank out that rotten tooth that plagued him. Juhi figured that with all that Mummy did for Papa, she didn't have energy left for Juhi at the end of each day.

A mother will do anything to protect her family, and Mummy was no different. She sold her body so they could eat. Some days she returned home, badly beaten and bruised, the bottom half of her sari dark and soaked with blood. Juhi begged her to stop, that they would find another way, but when Mummy pressed Juhi for alternatives, she had none. Juhi proclaimed that she would fast and let Mummy and Papa eat because she was young and resilient. But Juhi's mother asked, "How can a mother eat in front of her starving child?"

Mummy's plight worsened. Some nights she did not come home, only to return the next morning, drugged and bloody. Then Juhi's worst fear finally came true. Mummy did not come home at all.

One day passed and then two and then three and then an entire week. Juhi searched for her everywhere. She sneaked around the slum, spying on the rooms of her regular clients. She must have peeked into every home in the slum. She didn't know what to do, so she searched everywhere that she could think of and many places that made no sense. But what child would just let her mother disappear? Juhi stuck her head in trash cans and crawled on her hands and knees in alleyways, searching for any sign of her. She even traipsed through the outhouse. Her real-life agony followed her in her nightmares, and it still haunted her to the present day. She dreamt that she was bathing in the slum river, and Mummy's hard, cold, lifeless body floated past her.

In a daze, Juhi roamed the slum, talking to everyone, sometimes mumbling into thin air, asking if anyone had seen her. Juhi carried Mummy's portrait with her. It was one of the many that she had drawn. Somehow, in the harshness of the slum, her backpack full of her drawings had stayed intact. She held Mummy's portrait high in the air as if more people would pay attention that way. This particular drawing was of her smiling warmly while all three of them ate dinner at their Gantak Mandi home. The image felt like a dream, like something that was never true. Juhi chased after women who looked like Mummy from behind, only to be disappointed.

Juhi never saw Mummy again, and she never found any trace of her. Now that she was thousands of miles away in America, Juhi knew that she would never know how Mummy vanished. Juhi paused again and cried uncontrollably.

"Juhi, would you like to take a break?" Max asked.

"Yes, I think that's a good idea," Kevin replied for her.

But Juhi protested. She still had not told them about Delhi's black market. She wasn't going to stop until they heard the entire story. Her sorrow was real, but she had lived with it for so long that she tucked it away in a mental compartment and trudged ahead.

"No, I want to continue," she said. She wiped her face and piled the soaked tissues on the desk next to her. She sat up straighter in her chair and repeated, "I want to continue."

No one argued with her.

Papa's heart broke in half when he finally accepted that Mummy was gone. And just two weeks after Mummy disappeared, Papa's infection won. He passed away gently in his sleep, right there in the middle of their slum room. The night before, Papa and Juhi fell asleep cuddled together; when she woke, his heavy, lifeless arm was still wrapped around her. Juhi used whatever money she had left to cremate him.

Juhi's face took on a hazy glow, as if she was daydreaming.

"Life is funny. Papa only left the slum twice during the few months he lived there. The first time, he left to visit the doctor. The final time was when there was nothing left of him but ashes poured into a clay pot..." Her voice trailed off.

For three days, she walked aimlessly around New Delhi, half asleep and half awake. Her backpack full of drawings was all she had left of her former life. She could not look at her portraits of Papa and Mummy. They made her angry, and she was tempted to rip them apart into a million pieces. Other times she wanted to throw them in the fires that burned in the trash cans and watch as the crayon melted and smeared their faces. She knew it was not their wish to die or to leave her, but sometimes it felt like they abandoned her in that horrible place.

She started to go mad. Sometimes she imagined that Mummy and Papa were alive, and they spied on her from behind a wall and pointed and laughed at Juhi, while she shivered in the cold air. She imagined that they plotted the whole thing because they stopped loving her. In those moments, she whipped her head around like a crazy person and searched behind walls and in dark shadows, expecting to find them laughing and eating *kaju burfi* and hiding from her. She knew none of it was true, but she had moments where she thought it might be.

For a long while after Mummy and Papa were gone, it seemed like the life they had together was not real, as if it never happened. She imagined that a cruel person implanted those memories in her brain to make her think they were real. She grasped her hair and shook her head violently from side to side to dump the memories out like a waste bin turned upside down. She wished she had died, too. She felt guilty for feeling relieved that Mummy and Papa were gone. She didn't have to watch them suffer, and they didn't have to watch her suffer.

Juhi's face erupted like a broken dam, and her eyes gushed as she told Max her story. It was almost five o'clock in the evening. She looked older than she had at the start of the day. Kevin stood up from his chair and scooped her into his arms. She dug her face into the soft fleshy part of his neck and let her sobs pour out of her.

"Why don't we call it a day?" Max suggested. His tone dripped with compassion as he wrapped up the session.

The ride from the studio back to Kevin's apartment felt long, as if it happened in slow motion. Juhi had run out of words; her story had left Kevin speechless. Although he knew most of it, he was hearing it for the first time in its entirety. Juhi could see that he loved her and cared for her even more.

Juhi slumped down in the front seat. Kevin placed his supple hand on her forehead before he started the car and lightly brushed his fingers through her hair. It felt nice, and for the first time, she did not push him away. He hummed the tune of the Gayatri Mantra, a Hindu prayer that Juhi's mother sang to her while she helped her get ready for school. Kevin knew that Juhi loved the tune, so he learned it by watching YouTube videos. His pronunciation was a little off, but she appreciated his effort.

Om
Bhur Bhuvah Svah
Tat Savitur Varenyam
Bhargo Devasya Dheemahi
Dhiyo Yo nah Prachodayat

She relaxed as the mantra vibrated throughout the car. The familiar song filled her ears, and she felt her heart calm down. For a few minutes, Juhi felt like she was still the little girl from Gantak Mandi. She sank deeper into the seat cushion, and her mind drifted into dreams of Mummy.

CHAPTER 21

BABAJI'S HOME

When Juhi's eyes opened the next morning, the stars still danced in the night sky. The dark bedroom was peaceful. It was the first time since her arrival in the United States that she woke up without anxiety or adrenaline racing through her body. She tucked her body in a little deeper under the covers and curled up her toes. She felt happy for the sense of calm, yet she was eager to return to Max's studio to share the rest of her story. She hated to admit it, but Kevin was right. She felt better—lighter—after telling her story to a captive audience, even if it was just one man and his crew. She no longer carried all that great burden by herself. Now that Max knew what he knew, if he did nothing about it—if he didn't share her story—then to Juhi he was just as bad as the thugs in India. She took comfort knowing that by sharing her story, she honored her parents' memory.

When Juhi and Kevin arrived at Max's studio, Juhi took her seat across from Max and next to the interpreter. She started right where she left off the day before.

After Mummy and Papa died, she ended up in a different slum. It was smaller than the first one. Everyone knew each other, and to Juhi's surprise, they were neighborly with each other. Her heart was numb, but her stomach was still awake. She read and wrote for money, and she bought her first meal as an orphan, a nomad, a family-less wanderer. She found a little unoccupied corner in the slum and made that her home. It was just a patch of dirt. She slept there and helped customers there. Five days passed until one special client visited her. When he walked in, every person in the slum scurried away like cockroaches in the dark disturbed by a lamp. She stayed seated on the floor, her heart pounding in her chest, and she stared up at the tall brooding man who smiled down at her.

His name was Sunardas Shetty. He was the best-dressed man she had ever seen. He looked like a sixties Bollywood star. His wide-rimmed sunglasses completely shielded his eyes and part of his cheeks. He had thick, curly hair, which looked freshly combed, and a thick black mustache to match, which covered most of his upper lip. He was tall, and his crisp pants were as white as clouds. *How does he keep them so clean and perfectly ironed?* His red button-down shirt was tucked into his pants, which made his shiny golden belt buckle glisten in the sunlight and accentuated his round belly. When he slowly removed his sunglasses, she noticed that each of his fingers was adorned with a gold and ruby ring. He knelt down so they were at eye level. He referred to her as *beti,* a term of affection a parent calls his child. It sounded nice.

"Are you hungry?" he asked.

Juhi was frozen like a mummy.

"Where are your parents?"

Juhi didn't move. She stared at him.

"Do you know who I am?"

Juhi nodded yes.

"Wery good." He clapped his hands together, slightly threw back his head, and smiled at Juhi. "Will you come with me to my home? You can meet my children, and you can have a nice, warm meal. And then you can sleep and take a bath if you want. You look as if you have not done either in a long time."

Juhi tuned into how exhausted and hungry she was. He placed his hand on her head with slight pressure. It was an affectionate touch that made her miss Papa. She didn't trust Sunardas Shetty. She didn't trust anyone. But he was the first person to show her any kindness since Mummy and Papa died. She wanted to enjoy it for however long it would last. She also figured that if he hurt her, it would get her that much closer to joining Mummy and Papa.

"OK," she whispered and looked away from him.

He clapped again, smiled, and stood up. He helped Juhi put on her backpack and held her hand as they walked out of the slum. Other slum dwellers peeked out of their rooms and watched them walk away. She couldn't tell whether they were jealous or wanted to warn her, or both.

"My name is Juhi," she said, looking up at him timidly.

"I am Sunardas Shetty. But you already knew that. You and the other children call me Babaji."

Other children? Juhi was excited and scared.

His house was the biggest one she had ever seen. It was made of white marble and stone, and it was clean and cool all the time. It was probably bigger than a cricket field—it was that big! At least a dozen children lived there. He told Juhi they were all his, but now she knows they were like her, other slum children who stole for Babaji. Babaji took her to the backyard where the children played hide-and-seek. He told them to gather around.

"This is your new sister, Juhi. All of you come quickly and shake hands."

One by one, they obligingly shook Juhi's hand. They all told her their names, but she was too overwhelmed to remember any of them.

"Juhi, these are your new brothers and sisters. Be kind to them, and give them time to get to know you. But first, let's get you some dinner."

Juhi's stomach growled at the mention of food. She followed him to the grandest kitchen in the world. At least five different cooks chopped vegetables, stirred curries, baked naan, and seared meat. Pots and pans of all shapes and sizes sizzled and boiled and steamed. A separate whole table was covered with *burfi* of every kind—cashew, pistachio, almond and so forth. There was a whole tray of warm *gulab jamun* and the welcoming smell of fresh chai.

"What would you like, Juhi?" Babaji faced her and opened his arms wide like a bird flapping its wings.

In those early days with Sunardas Shetty, he looked right into her eyes when he spoke to her. His piercing stare still haunts Juhi.

"Everything!" Juhi blurted and then immediately regretted it. Mummy would be ashamed that she showed such poor manners.

But Babaji laughed and called for one of his servants to fix Juhi a plate with a little bit of everything.

"But no meat, please. I am vegetarian," she added softly, almost in a whisper.

"Wery good," Babaji replied. "Bring a little bit of everything, but veg only!" he shouted to his servant.

Once one plate was full, the servant handed it to Juhi and went back to fix the next plate. She instinctively sat on the floor, but Babaji invited her to sit at his table.

"You will take all your meals at this table from now on."

Juhi's heart soared. She feasted like a baby lion cub eating flesh for the first time. Masala and chutney dripped off her face and fingers. Turmeric and paprika stains dotted her shirt. But she didn't care. Babaji laughed at her affectionately, which put her at ease and reassured her that it was OK to eat more. She wiped three plates clean and still devoured a plate of sweets.

After the meal, Babaji led Juhi to the second story of his home. A beautiful spiral staircase made of the same white marble as the rest of the house connected a hallway of eight rooms together. It was quiet. It seemed they were the only ones up there. The hairs on the back of her neck stood straight. With her full, bloated belly, she looked down at her feet and concentrated on the steps. Nothing was free. She would have to pay for the meal. She tried to calm her pounding heart but instinctively made her hands into fists. He opened the door to one of the bedrooms. It had the largest bed she had ever seen, with beautiful, crisp, white bedcovers. Almost the whole bed was covered in a rainbow of decorative pillows—aqua, mustard orange, maroon, and deep green. The room felt cool. It smelled like cinnamon.

"Come in," he said to Juhi, showing all of his white teeth.

She stayed still in the hallway and looked down.

"Do not be frightened. I am your father now. A father does not hurt his child, does he?" He didn't wait for a response. "This is your new room."

Juhi looked at him suspiciously. She knew what men wanted from girls. She saw what they did to Mummy. The man who tried to rape her in the slum told her she would like it and that it was not going to hurt. She wanted to run, but she knew she wouldn't escape. At least five of Babaji's men waited downstairs and guarded the multitude of entrances and exits. It would be worse to run and be caught. It might mean being raped and beaten. If she stayed put, she might just be raped and spared a beating.

She slowly walked closer to him. She stood at the edge of the room and took one step over the divide between the hallway and the room.

"This is yours," he said and scanned the room with his eyes. "It is just for you. You will sleep here and bathe in that bathroom."

He stood in the middle of the bedroom and walked casually to an adjoining door. It led to an attached bathroom. Juhi followed him with her eyes but stood still, half in the room and half out.

"I can see that you are tired. You can take a bath and then sleep. There are fresh clothes and a towel for you in the bathroom. I will leave you now."

He turned to walk away, and she took another step into the room to move out of his way. He was leaving?

He was just going to walk away and not take anything from her in return for the meal?

"Babaji?" He turned back to look at her. "Thank you."

"You are welcome, *beti*."

Juhi bathed in complete privacy, behind a locked door in the most beautiful bathroom that had a curtain, steaming hot water, and lavender soap. She washed her hair and scrubbed the dirt from under her fingers and between her toes. She let the water rush all over her. She wanted it to last forever. She used every last drop of the hot water and reached for the clothes that were laid out for her. She loved them. There was a fresh pair of panties—the first she had had in months—and a beautiful yellow frock with English letters. It read on the front, *Little Rockstar!* But she didn't know what that meant. She didn't care, because the dress fit her perfectly. Babaji had also left a new pair of pearly white socks that had a little frill at the top. There were new matching pink-and-yellow shoes. She slipped them on too. There was also a new pair of soft pajamas. She desperately wanted to sleep in the dress, but she decided Babaji might scold her if it was wrinkled. She slipped into the pajamas and neatly folded the dress. She dumped her old clothes in the waste bin and was happy to let them go. She still had her pocketknife, which she hid in her new socks. She climbed onto the bed and slid under the covers with her backpack right there under the covers with her. She slept for two days.

On the third day, Babaji sent one of the other children to check on her. A girl who was older than her poked Juhi a few times until she opened her eyes.

"Babaji is calling for you," she said, and then she left the room.

Juhi showered and brushed her teeth in that glorious bathroom and wore the new frock. She tiptoed down the stairs, and at the base, she looked around the large foyer, uncertain of where to go. One of Babaji's men who guarded the front door slightly cocked his head to the right toward the kitchen.

"Juhi, *beti,* I am glad you are awake." Babaji came toward Juhi as she climbed into a seat at the kitchen table. "You must be hungry."

She ate another bountiful meal, and afterward Babaji instructed her to join the other children outside. On her way out, Babaji asked her what she liked to play.

"I like to draw," she replied and turned away to go outside.

The other children welcomed Juhi. "Look, she is awake!" exclaimed a few of them.

Another girl, Simran, complimented Juhi's dress. For the rest of the day, Juhi played hide-and-seek, hopscotch, *karem,* and jump rope and ate popsicles, ice cream, and *pani puri.* She didn't think about Mummy and Papa for the entire day except when she climbed the stairs back to her room that evening. It was the longest guilt-free stretch of time that she had since Papa died, and now she felt guilty for enjoying herself all day. But it was hard to concentrate on her guilt. She felt like a child again for the first time since she left Gantak Mandi. And when she returned to her room that night, she was delighted to see a new desk covered with beautifully decorated boxes of fresh pens, pencils, coloring markers of every color, paints and brushes, crayons, and a stack of notebooks filled with crisp, white pages full of possibility. She was too exhausted from playing and eating all day to draw, but she ran back to the living room to thank Babaji. She wrapped her arms around his neck and buried her face in his chest. He hugged her back.

"Thank you, Babaji! Thank you so much! I do not deserve it."

"Yes, you do, *beti*," he said, laughing.

If you only knew that I am responsible for my parents' deaths, you would agree that I do not deserve anything, Juhi thought.

As she climbed into her new warm, soft bed, she stifled a smile. She was happy for the first time since she could remember, but she also felt guilty for feeling happy. Her eyes grew heavy, and she drifted into a dream where she drew in her new notebooks, while Mummy and Papa smiled down at her.

One month went by. She spent her days swinging in the yard, playing hide-and-seek, and drawing. In between activities, she feasted on every food and dessert imaginable, and she had gained back the weight she had lost. She thought of Mummy and Papa often, and she thought that they would be happy that she found such a nice home. The slum seemed like a distant past, like a bad dream with no beginning or end, with a hazy line between fantasy and reality. She referred to the other children as her brothers and sisters, and she genuinely started to accept them as her family. Her closest sister was Anjali. Anjali was one year older than Juhi, and she had been living there for three years. Like Juhi, Anjali was an orphan whom Babaji plucked from the slum. She was very young when her parents had died, and she did not remember them. She joined an orphan pack in the slums for a while before Babaji found her. Juhi liked her so much because they were similar. They both still believed that good existed in the world, even though they had few reasons left to believe in them.

Juhi was with Anjali when Juhi kicked a much older, taller, and stronger boy right between his legs. The girls watched the boy slowly fold over to the ground onto his side, like a falling tree. He moaned and clutched his crotch. Anjali and Juhi knew him as the crude teenager who worked at a neighborhood *paan* stand. Tawdry clientele flanked the kiosk continuously, and they shamelessly stared at women as they walked by. The boy, however, did not just stare; he also taunted Juhi and Anjali. The day Juhi kicked him was no different. He howled and whistled from afar, but then he walked up to them and blocked their path. He whispered with a wild look on his face, the same thirsty expression she had seen so many times. He told them that he dreamed about massaging Anjali's succulent breasts while sucking on Juhi's.

"After that, you bitches can take turns stroking me and sucking on me."

In those situations, Anjali and Juhi usually kept walking; they avoided eye contact and pretended to be blind and deaf. This enraged him, and he yelled in their faces. He called them "worthless whores who dared to ignore him." But they held strong and avoided any actions that he might interpret as an invitation or an insult. In that neighborhood of contradictions, no one stood up for them or shamed him for his behavior—not even his own father, who sat by idly behind the *paan* kiosk. For some reason, no one took action until unless the boy actually hit the girls. Strangers ran to Juhi and Anjali's rescue only after the boy shoved Juhi to the ground and slapped Anjali across the face. Why was it OK to spew offenses and insults up until they resulted in bloody noses and knees?

Although Anjali's curves were as round as Juhi's, Juhi knew that her face begged for attention. She was accustomed to the stares and the under-the-breath comments and the overt ones. Anjali and Juhi endured hoots and whistles and uninvited poking and cupping in the constantly crowded streets. Where do men learn to graze a woman's breast with their elbows as they walk by? And what sort of pleasure does that bring? Just like the doctor in the slum, Juhi knew she would never understand it. The worst part about it is that it was impossible to trace. The offense was over almost as soon as it started, and the culprits had already moved on to the next victim before Juhi could look up to identify her attacker.

Anjali tolerated the boy's insults and did not hit back. Juhi wished she could do that—it is what Gandhiji taught. But she couldn't. It was a bad habit. When he slapped Anjali so hard that her whole body whipped around, and she fell to the ground, he laughed out loud. Instead of helping Anjali back to her feet, something burned inside of Juhi, and she kicked the boy right between his legs. Juhi didn't think about his friends who were watching, who would certainly chase them and beat them, or worse. She didn't think about the fact that if the roles were reversed, Anjali would not have had the guts to stand up for Juhi the way Juhi did for her. Juhi didn't care. The boy fell to the ground, and his friends came to his rescue. They chased Anjali and Juhi all the way to Babaji's home. The girls zoomed past the security guards and turned

to watch as the guards seized the boys, who
ed at them even after the girls were safe behind the
mansion gates.

After that day, Anjali and Juhi were inseparable. They were partners in every game, and they ate all their meals together; both of them loved to swing their legs under the table, happily nibbling on *chaat* and *kachoris* and sipping chai. They held hands while they walked, they sang to each other, they recited poems, and Juhi even started to teach Anjali how to read. If one of their older siblings pushed Anjali, Juhi pushed back, and Anjali even did the same for Juhi a couple of times. Juhi drew pictures for Anjali all the time. She drew flowers, the sky, the two of them holding hands. Juhi sketched Anjali's profile in pencil and kept it for herself, along with the other portrait sketches of all the faces that haunted and delighted her. Just like she always did, she wrote Anjali's name at the bottom-right corner of the page, along with her age and the date that Juhi drew it. Juhi loved Anjali's bright smile, her skinny but sturdy frame, and her firm grip. Anjali's eyes were spared of the sadness that existed in the other children's eyes, including Juhi's. When Anjali held Juhi's hand, Juhi felt safe. She made Juhi feel like she belonged somewhere again.

But the friendship wouldn't last. After one month at Babaji's home, he approached Juhi after breakfast and asked her to accompany him to his office. He had a special task, and only she could do it. By then, Juhi really believed that Babaji was like a reincarnation of Papa, and she was devoted to him—father and daughter. She was proud to be able to help. Some of the hardness that came with living in the slum had faded in that month of luxury, and she began to trust again.

Juhi expected Babaji's office to be as beautiful as his home—a top-floor office suite with glass windows, shiny doors, and doormen fighting to open the door for him. Instead, they rode in a three-wheel auto rickshaw for twenty minutes and stopped in front of a kiosk the size of a closet. Two filthy men stood behind a counter that faced the street. The kiosk overflowed with cereals, biscuits, chips, crackers, *Haldiram* packets, and every other packaged snack item imaginable. Babaji sold snack foods? The two men stood at attention like military men when Babaji stepped out of the auto rickshaw.

"Hello, sir," they said in unison, swinging open the counter door to let him and Juhi in. Juhi couldn't fathom that two more people could fit in that tiny kiosk.

Babaji didn't respond as he walked past them, and he held Juhi's hand firmly. The kiosk was deceiving. Off to the left of the kiosk, there was a small room labeled "inventory." It was a long, narrow passageway filled with even more snack foods. Juhi followed Babaji into the narrow room, single file as it was too narrow to walk side by side. Customers who stood outside the kiosk would not have been able to see them back there, and vice versa. Babaji tapped his foot three times with a two-second pause between each tap. All of a sudden, the ground opened in front of them. It was a manhole! A man, another of Babaji's servants whom Juhi had never seen before, stood at the bottom of the hole. Babaji climbed down first, and once he was completely underground, he looked up at Juhi and raised his arms toward her. Juhi sat down on the ground and dangled her legs in the hole. He grabbed her around her waist and pulled her in, and the barefoot man who opened the hole closed it again.

CHAPTER 22
THE CAVE

"Come, let's go," Babaji said. He faced Juhi, but she couldn't see him in the darkness under the kiosk.

The hair on Juhi's neck and arms stood straight. She stepped cautiously while her eyes adjusted to the blackness. The barefoot man, Minku, walked ahead of her and carried an oil lamp as a guide. They walked through room after room. They seemed to be descending lower and lower into the ground. She expected a fire-breathing dragon to turn the corner at any minute and bite her. It smelled worse down there than the makeshift latrines in the slums, and the stench grew nearer and nearer. She gagged repeatedly until Babaji wrapped his scarf around her neck to cover her nose, just like Mummy did when they arrived at the slum.

The body odor absorbed into his scarf did not smell much better, but it blocked the other stenches.

They turned one last time and stopped a few feet from the grand finale—a factory of some kind. Someone might have thought they were producing a breakthrough pharmaceutical. The workers, at least thirty of them, wore face masks, hair nets, gloves, and bootees over their shoes. Each of them intently hunched and peered down over their desks. Small pieces of colorful paper, leather binding, rubber stamps, razors, string, pens of every size and color—all these materials lay in organized bins next to each worker. The dinginess of the cave mismatched the cleanliness of their work. The spotlight lamps on each desk were the only source of light. They spoke to each other in whispers, as if they also worried about waking a sleeping dragon.

Juhi was the only girl. Everyone else was male between the ages of fifteen and fifty years old—the men she feared the most. She was grateful none of them paid her any attention.

"Papa!" she whispered to herself under her breath. It was a bad habit calling for her Papa when she was frightened, even though she knew he would not come.

That day in the cave, she learned something that she wished she could unlearn. Babaji was manufacturing counterfeit documents. He made American passports, visas, and other immigration documents. He gave Juhi her first lesson in counterfeiting, but he did not call it that. She heard the word "counterfeit" for the first time when she arrived in the United States. Babaji told her that they were patriots. He said they helped Indians find a better life in the United States, where they could earn more money and send it back to their poor families in India. He told her that she would be helping hundreds of her fellow countrymen. He told her it was her duty. It was her privilege, since she was young and educated. Didn't she want other parents to be able to afford good schools for their children?

"Your papa as proud of you, wasn't he?" he asked Juhi. "I am proud of you too. How nice would it be for other children to be the pride of their parents? Your mummy and papa would be proud of you for helping others."

During that first lesson, she received a United States passport. A small, square photograph of her against a white background with her ears showing was copied onto the first page. Babaji had taken that photo of her a few days after she arrived at his home, but she didn't know why, until now. Above the photograph, on the front inside flap, was a picture of an eagle and olive branches and the United States flag. Underneath was a blank line for her signature. The page with her photograph listed her full name, her birthdate, and a bunch of other numbers. Her name was correct, but the birthdate was wrong. The following pages were blank, but each had a unique design. One was of a lady who carried a torch high overhead. She wore a crown and a robe. Another picture looked like the beaches she had seen near Kevin's home in California. Her favorite was one of the faces of strange men carved into a mountain. She dreamt of climbing that mountain and hanging onto the nose just as one of them sneezed.

Max and several of his crew members laughed as they listened to Juhi describe Mount Rushmore.

Babaji explained the symbol of the eagle on the front of the blue book, which carried olive branches and arrows in its claws. He said it was America's most famous symbol, just like the Indian flag's emblem with three lions and the Ashoka Chakra. He told her that people use the blue book to travel outside of their home country. He said hers was just a toy model that she would use to replicate hundreds more just like it. One of those factory men must have made it, but it was sloppy. The corners were not cut properly. They were supposed to be rounded edges, but Juhi's passport was slightly square. The font on pages four and five titled "PERSONAL DATA AND EMERGENCY CONTACT" was two points smaller than the standard, but Juhi wasn't sure if anyone else besides her would have noticed, and she kept her mouth shut. The lamination and electronic coding within the page with her photo were beautiful. But the ones she made were much more precise. Her bar codes were flawless, and on the rare occasions when Juhi and the other counterfeiters did hear back that a passport worked, it was usually one of hers. She quickly graduated from passports to visas and green cards to the most coveted role, making dollars. The American twenty-dollar bill was very beautiful, but the fifty-dollar bill was her favorite. It was the biggest challenge because of all the blending colors. She never mastered it. For the first several months in the cave, she didn't know that she was doing something illegal. When she realized it, she was in too deep to feign innocence.

Babaji did not know that Juhi had studied English. Juhi decided it best to keep it a secret, but she didn't know why. She let Babaji's men teach her the English words that they wanted her to know. They probably never imagined that she would ever end up in the United States.

There was an entirely different area on the other side of Babaji's mansion, a much darker place that was constantly covered in gray shadows. Once Babaji enlisted Juhi in his illegal schemes, she was no longer welcome in his house. She was moved to a cabin in that dark place behind the main house. There were four cabins in a row. She had one to herself. Her cabin had a bathroom and a shower, but there was no kitchen and only one window that was covered in steel grates. Meals were anonymously delivered through a square flap in the door. Babaji locked her in there, and she only left when Babaji or one of his workers fetched her. Inside the cabin, she slept on a squalid mat with a single sheet. For some reason, Babaji showed some small kindness by moving her notebooks, pens, and sketches to the cabin. Everything was gray—the walls, the light inside the room, and even the small curtain that covered the inside of the window. Juhi was barely tall enough to reach the top of the window. Luckily, Babaji had a lot of work for her, so she did get brief moments to be outside each day. It was on the trips in and out of Babaji's compound that she caught glimpses of the people who occupied the other cabins. It seemed that at least five or six women lived in the cabin next to hers. They were older—teenagers and some women in their twenties. They did not look at her. She came to know that they were "Babaji's girls." They were just for his pleasure. As she was dropped off at the cave one afternoon, the driver, one of Babaji's assistants, told her how lucky she was to have her own room. There were actually ten women sleeping in that small cabin next to hers, twice her original estimate.

"They are just for him," the driver leered at Juhi through the rearview mirror. "You have so much privacy. So much space for anything to happen." He turned his head around to smile at her.

Juhi looked away but knew this was not the last time he would look at her like that.

When she arrived at the cave, the workers were just as they were the day before. Her lessons in passport making resumed. She eventually had her own desk like the others, but for the first two weeks, she sat on a mat on the ground. A young boy delivered meals to the cave. He was paid handsomely to stay quiet about the underground dealings. Juhi received one roti and only enough vegetables for half of the bread. It was dark when she arrived at the cave, and it was dark when she left. She worked there every day with no days off. Most days, no one spoke to her except her instructor. She missed her brothers and sisters at Babaji's house. Did Anjali miss Juhi as much as Juhi missed Anjali? She didn't see Babaji on her second day in the cave. She missed him too. She wanted to know why he moved her from his home and into the cabin. She would not complain, though; it was still better than the slum.

The third day was much like the day before. Babaji was absent again, and she longed for a friendly face. Four more days came and went. After one week of learning counterfeiting, her instructor said she showed much promise. She had already made her first flawless green card and recognized all the denominations and major symbols on US dollars. On most nights, when she returned to her cabin, she was too exhausted to draw. But she managed to sketch a scene of the cave with all the men working, a portrait of the lunch-delivery boy, and several drawings of her instructor.

Juhi thought the other workers in the underground cave didn't notice her. But she was wrong. They did, and they raped her when Babaji wasn't there.

On the eighth day in the cave, her instructor sent her to the deepest room in the cave to put a box of supplies away. No one else was there, and she was grateful for her headlamp. On her tiptoes, she slid the box onto its rightful shelf, but she almost dropped it when muted voices behind her whispered her name.

"Juhi," one said, breathing deeply. She heard at least two other men giggle.

She turned around and came face-to-face with three men.

"The instructor asked me to put that box away," she stammered as they drew closer to her and closed the gap between her and the only exit. They were silent. She could hear their breath. Their nostrils flared like hyenas before a kill. She tried to reach for the knife that she kept in her sock, but the man to her left grabbed her arm and twisted it like a wet rag. The other man grabbed her legs and threw her onto the ground. She kicked and screamed. She didn't know if anyone heard her, and she wasn't sure it mattered. They would easily ignore her. She bit one of them—the man who held her arm. But it just made him more determined. He shoved her face into the ground and knocked off her headlamp. Someone shoved a dirty rag into her mouth. They called her *benchod* (sister fucker) and *kuththi* (bitch). In the blackness, all she could see was the whites of their eyes. While the other two pinned her down, she heard a third man unbuckle his belt. He pulled his pants down, and then he yanked off Juhi's pants too. She felt her panties slide down her legs. He laid on top of her and pressed his entire body onto her. She couldn't breathe. He thrust inside of her with a giant push. It felt as if her body was being torn apart. He pushed harder. She wanted to die. Her head knocked repeatedly against the stone ground, and blood streamed down her scalp. He grunted the way the bad men did when they were alone inside the house with Mummy. He pushed faster and faster until he suddenly stopped. He rolled off her, and she heaved for breath. She shriveled up into a ball while she tried to recover. But then one of them pulled her legs straight again, and the second one and then the third one pleasured themselves inside of her. They all smelled like body odor. After they were done, one of them kicked her in the stomach, and another one urinated on her. They left her there while she fell unconscious. The next day, her instructor found her, badly bleeding from her head and between her legs. He draped her in a blanket and rushed her to Babaji's home, where she stayed for several days. She was back inside the house, not in the cabin, but still in a separate section than her original bedroom. Babaji's servants and doctors nursed Juhi back to health. No one asked her about the incident.

Babaji visited her on the fourth day of her recovery. He said she would go back to work because that would be best for her health. He saw the terror in Juhi's eyes and promised it would be different. He assigned a security guard to stay with her at all times, who even stood post outside of her room while she slept. He told Juhi that her safety was his highest concern. He said that in addition to the security guard, he himself would stay with her as much as possible. If he went to meetings, she went with him. She didn't eat with Babaji in his grand kitchen, though. She sat outside the kitchen on the floor with a plate of food that one of his servants gave to her.

Many days passed when the only things Babaji ever said to her were commands: "Juhi, come here. Get up. Sit there. Eat now." Other days he was much more talkative, and he told her about his meetings and taught her about his business. He had important meetings with police commissioners and powerful government officials. Sometimes Babaji waited in the car while Juhi went inside offices or approached someone waiting on the side of a street to pick something up or drop something off for Babaji. She never knew the contents of the items that she picked up for him, but she was happy to do it. She was happy to be with Babaji and out of the cave. But eventually he made her return there. On that first day, something unexpected happened. Babaji wanted to talk about the night that she was raped. Babaji asked everyone to stop working, and in the center of the largest room, Babaji called Juhi forward from the shadows where she lingered. Much to her horror, Babaji asked Juhi to point to the culprits. On the night they raped her, she caught glimpses of their faces before they knocked off her headlamp. She drew their hideous faces in her sketchbook as she lay restless after the assault. She wished she could erase their faces from her mind.

Juhi hesitated. What if they retaliated against her?

As if Babaji read her mind, he said, "Tell me who it was. You are safe."

She stood in the middle of the room, looking down, and pointed at the first one and then the second and then the third. They looked away from Babaji in shame. One of them burst out, "She asked us for it! She said she wanted it! What could we do?"

Babaji practically leaped across the room and slapped him across the face. Juhi's attacker fell to the ground and wept like a school boy. No one moved. Babaji stood over him and called for his servant.

"Minku!" he yelled.

Minku ran to the commotion; his rapid footsteps echoed through the cave. He slowed as he approached, holding something shiny behind his back. He pulled a machete out of its case and stood with it held high in his hand. Everyone gasped and took a step back. Now the three perpetrators shook in fear and cried and pleaded with Babaji. They folded their hands in namaste and, on their knees, bowed to Babaji and begged for forgiveness. He ignored them, and one by one they were commanded to hold out their right arms. They quaked with fear.

Minku whipped the knife, severing each of their right hands from their bodies. One of the loose limbs landed near Juhi. It rolled on the ground and the toe of her shoe stopped it. Juhi vomited so violently that she thought all of her insides would come out. She imagined her own organs lying on the ground next to the bodiless hands. The three men, now with only one hand, shriveled in pain. They reminded her of the lepers in the crowded train stations. Blood oozed out of their wounds, just like it oozed out of Juhi on the night she was attacked. In that macabre seen, the blood formed a shallow river in the middle of the factory. Its metallic smell sent Juhi on a dizzy spell; her stomach churned, and she vomited again. But Babaji was accustomed to such morbid scenes. He spat on the three shriveled men, who lay in their own pools of blood and vomit.

"I had half a mind to castrate you, but this way, the whole world will see you are crippled. This is a warning. If any of you even try to touch her, just see what will happen."

After that day, Babaji's workers kept their distance from Juhi. They still looked at her with thirst and whispered dirty comments under their breath. She heard them, but they never did more than that. Juhi felt empowered by Babaji's actions, but she still lived in fear every day that one of the workers might turn on Babaji or act on his thirst. She stayed close to Babaji and was quiet. The people in Babaji's circle who did not know her might have assumed that she was mentally challenged or some kind of savant. She had become his most skilled counterfeiter, but she was practically mute. Entire days passed when she didn't speak, and when she tried to use her voice, it stuck in her throat. Through the course of staying close to Babaji and learning his business, she saw that Babaji only cared about her so long as she was useful to him. He would have gladly fed her to the cave workers as soon as he was done with her or if she ever crossed him. But at that time, she was his most prized possession. He put her on display when he negotiated deals.

"Men become stupid around beautiful girls," he said.

He dressed Juhi in beautiful frocks and shiny white shoes, with colorful clips in her hair. He said they were rewards for her hard work, but the truth was that people were far less suspicious of a girl who was dressed well than a girl in rags. Juhi couldn't remember all the places she had been in and out of with Babaji, but most of them were dark alleys or at dinner tables in the back of expensive restaurants. She even slipped into places where all the men were drunk. She never had to introduce herself. These meetings were so swift that sometimes she wasn't sure that they had started. She would walk into a place, a man would hand her an envelope, or perhaps she exchanged envelopes with someone, and she walked back to Babaji's car. Babaji made thousands of rupees by using Juhi. By the time she understood just how big a criminal Babaji was, she didn't care. She had lived under lock and key for so long; she was too defeated and too tired to care. She didn't care about anything, except that she never wanted to live in a slum again.

Babaji gave her three hot meals a day; he provided security and a covered place to sleep. She thought about running away, but she knew that if she escaped and he found her, he would torture her and then kill her. Plus, there was no way to run or anywhere to run to. His men were vigilant, and someone was always watching her.

She was numb, as if ice had been rubbed over her whole body. She forgot Mummy and Papa. They felt like a dream of a happier place—like a cruel joke amid her hopelessness. One day passed and then one week, and eventually months went by when she didn't think of them. She questioned if they had ever existed at all. Their portraits that she drew were buried deeper and deeper into her backpack as her memory of them furrowed in her mind and in her heart.

One year passed working for Babaji; it had been two years since she was dumped in New Delhi. By then, she never left his side. She even moved back permanently into his house and in a side room next to the master suite where Babaji slept. Her room and Babaji's room were guarded by the same men.

She knew that if he only drank chai in the morning without eating any food, it meant he did not sleep well. If he sat at the table and opened the newspaper without saying a word, he was angry at someone. If he wore his black snakeskin shoes, they were going to visit a judge or a politician. Every morning, the barber visited the house to shave Babaji's face. Every other Tuesday, he stayed for an extra hour to trim Babaji's hair and groom his fingers and toes. Juhi and Babaji traveled to the cave in the mornings, where she was now in charge of overseeing the training of new recruits. She seldom made fake documents any longer. After her training responsibilities were finished, she spent the rest of the day doing whatever Babaji wanted. On one particular day, they visited a new place—somewhere she had never been before.

CHAPTER 23

THE BLACK MARKET

Acharya Hospital was the most beautiful place Juhi had ever seen. The white lobby glistened and smelled as if *aarti* had just concluded—fresh incense burned continuously. Perfectly spaced rows of chairs lined the perimeter of flower beds. There was even a fifteen-foot-tall tree right there in the middle of the lobby. Nurses, doctors, technicians, patients, and families all hustled and bustled in a world of organized chaos. Everyone was attractive—as if there was a prerequisite to be beautiful just to enter the building. The walls were made of glass, from top to bottom, which delivered beaming sunlight all day.

Overhead, doctors' pages and hospital announcements filled the air.

"Dr. Bhalla, please report to room two-zero-two immediately."

"Visiting hours are from nine in the morning until seven in the evening. Please visit the front desk for a visitor badge."

"Code red. Trauma en route. All emergency teams stand by."

Each message was repeated in English, Hindi, Vietnamese, Korean, Portuguese, and other languages in a continuous stream. While messages blared overhead, they also appeared on the dozens of screens mounted throughout the lobby. They ran commercials for the hospital gift shop where women could purchase Fair and Lovely lotions, Lakmé makeup, real Prada and Gucci bags, and brand-name sunglasses. Many of the Acharya Hospital doctors had commercials to educate patients about gastric bypass surgery, breast implants, knee replacements, and facelifts. Nurses who walked by wore bright-red lipstick, which sparkled against their crisp, white uniforms. They wore large buns in their hair; their white tent hats were pinned strategically in place. They smiled constantly and walked in unison, as if they were windup toys that were turned loose at the same time. Babaji had been there before. He knew exactly where to go.

Juhi and Babaji rode the elevator to the third floor and walked down a long hallway with patient rooms on either side. Juhi peeked inside each room. She wanted to know what diseases and ailments plagued each patient. They stopped outside of a small room that was labeled "Lab." It was across the hall from a series of patient rooms.

"Sit," Babaji told her and pointed to a chair outside of the lab.

He went in the lab alone, and Juhi did as she was told. Nurses and doctors shuffled along in the halls; Juhi went unnoticed. She counted the number of tiles that lined the hallway's belly. It was long enough for a nice game of hopscotch, and suddenly she had an urge to play. But she resisted. She sat in the chair where Babaji had left her, and she didn't move. As she ticked off the tiles that lined the hall as far as she could see... fifteen, sixteen, seventeen...her eyes followed their trail to the wall across the hallway that intersected the ground. It led to a patient's room, and the door was open. She leaned over in her chair to see the patient, but suddenly Babaji reappeared.

"Get up! Let's go!" he barked at her and took her hand in his.

He wanted people to think that he was Juhi's father. No respectable criminal would hold the hand of one of his slaves. That was the only time Juhi visited the hospital. She liked it there, and she wished she could go again.

They sped away from the hospital and drove to a much more secluded and sinister building in a different section of New Delhi, called Vasant Kunj, one of Delhi's most dangerous neighborhoods. They entered a dilapidated building, marked by broken windows that were covered with thick tarps. The filthy entryway smelled of stale urine and rotting, dead mice. Babaji and Juhi followed a man through the main hall past one room and then another. It felt like another one of Babaji's caves.

Juhi could hardly believe what she saw next. She found herself standing in the middle of an operating room. To her right stood a hospital-style bed. To her left, several medical machines beeped and hummed. Bright lights clung to the ceiling and shone down on a large, rectangular table covered in supplies—a scalpel, gauze, gloves, needles, and thread. There was a sink and a large refrigerator. Large trash cans lined one side of the room. The filthy floor and walls gave the whole room an old, decrepit feel. It reminded her of the doctor's office in Gantak Mandi.

"How many do we have today?" Babaji asked one of the men who was already in the operating room.

"Five," he replied.

"Just five?" Anger swelled in Babaji's voice. "Why so few? What the hell am I paying you for?"

The man looked away from Babaji sheepishly.

"We have seven patients waiting at the hospital, and two more will arrive tomorrow," Babaji said sternly. He spit as he spoke.

"Yes, Babaji. We will find more today and tomorrow. We will have enough."

Babaji walked to the other room, and Juhi followed.

"Juhi, you will be stationed here from now on. You will make counterfeit documents about the people we take kidneys from."

His words rang in her ears. He saw her shocked expression.

"Do not be so naïve, Juhi. You are not a little girl anymore," Babaji reproached her. "Why the hell do you think I adopted you? I know Kabir Singh. I arranged for your father's kidney to be donated."

Juhi's heart almost leaped out of her chest, and she started to shake. She wanted to scream, but her mouth went dry. *How dare you say that Papa's kidney was donated? It was stolen, and he died, and my life is ruined, and Mummy and Papa are dead!*

Juhi wanted to charge at him, to spit in his face and slap him a million times, but she just stood there, paralyzed and in shock. Babaji watched her for a few seconds, and then he turned away. There was something in the way he turned his back on her...the flippant disregard for her...for her family. The paralysis left her body, and she found her courage.

"It is not a donation when he never volunteered his kidney. You stole it! You killed him, you fucking bastard!"

Years of rage caught up with her. She sprang forward like a cheetah and leaped onto his back. She wrapped her hands around his throat and squeezed. She bit him wherever she met flesh. She scratched and kicked. Babaji threw her onto the floor and drew a gun from his pocket. He pointed it at her torso.

"How dare you cross me!" he thundered. The veins in his neck popped, and his face burned red. "I did you a favor, you stupid *benchod*! Kabir Singh wanted to take both of your father's kidneys. I persuaded him to take one. I told him it was more humane to let the poor man live. After all, he had two mouths to feed. If your papa could not take care of his family after I spared his life, that is not my fault. My business saves lives. I am giving organs to people who will die without them. Sometimes when I do not have enough to give, I have to take what I need. Villagers beg me to buy their organs. They need money to feed their stupid fucking families, and I help them. I make lives better for everyone."

Juhi couldn't believe the words coming out of his mouth. She lay on the ground and stared into the barrel of his gun.

"Do as I say, or I will kill you," he said. "If you try to escape, I will find you, and I will kill you. You have nothing to fear. Except torture and death. And if you cross me, you will suffer!"

He struck her across her face with the gun. Her nose tore in half and bled down her face and neck. Tears filled her eyes. She shriveled into a ball and wept for a long while. She thought that her worst loneliness came after Mummy and Papa died. But this was worse.

She thought again about escaping. She dreamed about killing Babaji and running away. In her dreams, she ended up back in Gantak Mandi, where she would warn her old friends about Kabir Singh. She imagined killing Mogambo and Gabbar and then Kabir Singh too. She frightened herself with her thoughts of murder. Babaji was a murderer, not *her*. But was she lying to herself? If she was helping to steal kidneys, was she not as guilty as him? Her choices were to kill or be killed. Sometimes she thought she would rather die than help Babaji. But Mummy and Papa would be disappointed in her for giving up on her life. They would beg her to find a way out.

"Juhi, you are so thoughtful and creative," Papa used to tell her. "You are one of the smartest people in our entire village. You can do anything you want."

One week in Babaji's kidney clinic felt like months and months. After just a couple of weeks, she came to accept that she would never escape, and even if she did, Babaji would find her. He would delight in torturing her before killing her. He might take *her* kidneys too. Still, she decided that if she ever had a chance to run, she would take it. At least she would have tried and not given up.

During the next six months, she became an expert in the organ black market. She met the men and women who were hired by Babaji to travel to the poorest villages in the outskirts of Delhi. They approached the head of each family with a job offer. They told the villagers to meet them the next morning at a specified location, and the "workers" were loaded into a van and brought to the underground clinic. Babaji trapped them, and instead of giving them a job, Babaji forced them to sell their organs for a promise of several thousand American dollars. Like an assembly line at a slaughterhouse, their kidneys were carved out of their bodies in that shack of an operating room. Afterward, the victims were dumped in wheelchairs and moved out of the operating room into an adjacent dingy recovery room. The room housed at least three or four victims at all times. They lay on dirty beds and were not given any medication to reduce their pain. Meanwhile, their organs were carefully handled with white, shiny gloves and were artfully placed in clean ice chests. The surgeon and nurses gently carried the ice chests to the refrigerator, where they placed them inside. Screams of pain from the victims flooded the shanty. For Juhi, the aftermath was the worst part of it all. She hated the cries of terror when the people were told what they were really there for. But she hated the recovery more. The fear in their eyes. She saw Papa's face again and again. The victims were never paid what they were promised—sometimes one-eighth of the amount. If they fought back, they were beaten. One of Babaji's thugs liked to poke his filthy fingers into the raw wounds of the victims, and he giggled as the victims writhed in pain.

Juhi's job was to create fictitious stories about each "donor." She wrote elegant copy in Hindi, and then someone translated it into English. She still had not divulged that she knew English. She drafted ridiculous tales about patients who were on the brink of death and who wanted to give life to fellow humans. She made a list of the deadliest and most common types of cancer and, in a round-robin style, switched off which one she incorporated into her stories. She hated to see the pictures of the victims and their families. Everything about the operation was a lie, but for some reason, Babaji wanted the pictures to be real. She was forced to include a family picture in the packet of materials. The Westerners always wanted to know the man or woman who was so generous to offer a kidney. She hated the fucking Westerners who were stupid enough to believe anyone would donate their kidney to a stranger. She forced herself not to think about the person who received Papa's kidney. She would want to hunt that person and kill not only that person but also his entire family. She would want them to suffer like her. But that would not bring Mummy and Papa back. It would just make her as bad as Babaji. Even if Juhi wanted to hunt for Papa's kidney, she had no chance of escape. Babaji's men watched her like a mama elephant watches her calves. Plus, no records existed. Even if she wanted to find the person who took Papa's kidney, she would never be able to.

In Babaji's organ circuit, after the kidneys were stolen, the victims were dumped in slums like bags of rotten vegetables. That way, they couldn't warn the rest of the village or neighboring villages. She learned how the market worked with the Westerners too. Babaji set up fake companies in Western countries and advertised in medical magazines, newspapers, and online. He promised a matching kidney to Westerners who would die without them. The surgery would cost them very little compared to a procedure in their home country. It was all done under the guise of humanitarian gestures. The Westerners were told that Indians who were on the brink of death chose to donate their organs as their last wish. Juhi did not understand how Westerners could be so easily duped. *Do they think their lives are more important than an Indian's life?* She hated all the rich, selfish Westerners. Juhi felt her temperature rise as she directed her comments at Max, at Kevin, and the camera crew in the room.

"Most Westerners have to wait a long time for a transplant in their own countries, so they go to India instead. In India, they only have to wait a few weeks compared to years. If they only knew..." Juhi's voice trailed off.

The Westerners didn't go to Babaji's dingy operating theater for their transplants. Babaji bought his way into Acharya Hospital with bribes to almost every department. He bought surgeons, nurses, and the people who handle patient admissions and organ transplants. The leaders of the hospital—the ones who smile on Acharya Hospital commercials and talk about how much they care for and respect patients—all knew Babaji and what he was doing. But they did nothing to stop it. Those surgeries brought millions of rupees to the hospital. Hospital leaders justified it in their minds that one inhumane act paid for the health care of hundreds of other innocent patients, including the poor and needy patients. It became easier to look the other way as the business grew. Westerners recovered in beautiful hospital suites and had nurses who waited on them all day and night. After one month, they traveled back home in first-class airplane seats. They were told to see their own doctors back home and that it would be difficult for the Indian doctor to provide any follow-up care unless the patient was back in New Delhi. Patients rarely returned. They went on to live healthy lives with stolen organs beating in their bodies. Juhi also read, but wasn't sure if it was true, that most Westerners get their health care bills paid by their employers. In some cases, companies knew or suspected that transplants in her country were illegal, but no one wanted to verify the facts. It was not their problem, and they wanted to save money. Why pay one hundred thousand dollars for a surgery in America, when you can spend fifteen thousand dollars in India? The employee would return to work sooner instead of waiting for a transplant for years and years, all the while taking sick days off work while he or she waited for a kidney. She began to wonder if the system was set up to intentionally take advantage of poor villagers.

PART 4

Redemption

CHAPTER 24

KEVIN RETURNS

Kevin thrived when he returned to Los Angeles with a new kidney. Across the next two and a half years, his health remained steady, and his career blossomed. He grew accustomed to the antirejection medications, and the side effects waned over time. He earned more than enough money to cover the three-thousand-dollar monthly cost of the drugs, thanks in part to his insurance. He didn't mind spending the money in the United States instead of going to India every six months to refill his prescriptions. That just wasn't practical; he didn't know what he was thinking when he actually considered flying halfway around the world twice every year. He visited a nephrologist every three months, and as long as things were fine, his nephrologist was happy to treat him.

Instead of rejoining Logan Studios, Kevin started his own business and became a highly sought-after entertainment-marketing consultant. He landed contracts from all the major studios, which gave him flexibility to travel for quick getaways to San Francisco and Vegas or more exotic locations in Central and South America. He started dating again, but he kept things casual.

He decided not to call Lakshmi when he returned to Los Angeles. She was in the past. She served her purpose. She helped him decide to travel to India. Besides, he decided that she had probably forgotten about him. He didn't contact Emma either. He thought about calling her many times, but he never got around to it. She hadn't responded to the e-mail he had sent on his way to India, and that still bothered him. She didn't seem to care if Kevin was dead or alive. He decided not to care about her, either. To cope, he encouraged a revolving door of women in and out of his luxury, high-rise condo.

But as Kevin approached the third anniversary of his new kidney, things changed. His body swelled again, and his urine was foamy…again. He developed a fever, and when it escalated above 102 degrees, he rushed to the emergency room.

His new kidney was failing, and he had to get emergency dialysis. The graft in his arm had shut a long time ago. He was forced to get another emergency death tube catheter in his chest. During the dialysis treatment, a new nephrologist—not his regular doctor—came to check on him.

"Hi, Kevin, I'm Dr. Scrivener."

"Nice to meet you, Dr. Scrivener."

Dr. Scrivener was old. He was the kind of doctor who said things like, "In my day, there were no dialysis clinics. Patients went to the hospital, and the machines were twice as big."

Dr. Scrivener reviewed Kevin's chart and asked questions at the same time. "It looks like you had a transplant two and a half years ago, but now that kidney is failing."

"Yeah. I went to India to get a transplant."

Dr. Scrivener peered at Kevin with suspicion. "You went to India?"

"Yes."

"And you paid for a transplant, or did a friend or relative donate it to you?" Dr. Scrivener's tone was loaded.

"I paid for it," Kevin replied with confidence.

"Did you know that's illegal?"

"Well, sure, it's illegal here. But not over there."

"No, it's illegal there too. India has laws that say it's illegal for anyone to pay for an organ, whether they are Indian or American or from anywhere else."

"I'm pretty sure you're wrong, doctor. I went to a prestigious hospital and reviewed all the documents they gave me."

"Well, that's fine. But I know what I know, and you know what you know. Regardless, you have two options. If I treat your failing transplant, I'm required by law to report you to the authorities. Or, I can give you a prescription for dialysis and be your dialysis doctor but not touch your transplant. In that case, I don't have to report you."

"Doc, come on. I'm telling you my kidney is above board. It was a legit purchase."

"Those are your options, Mr. Whitman. What would you like to do?"

Kevin couldn't believe what he was hearing.

"From a medical standpoint, I can't treat you without complete details about your surgery. I need a postoperative report at the very least, and it needs to have details written by the surgeon about how your surgery was conducted and what medications they gave you. I assume they gave you a receipt and a half-page summary of the surgery that said you received a kidney and that it was done with 'standard operating procedures?'"

"I have it on my phone. I'll show it to you." Kevin searched his phone. "I've been seeing a nephrologist four times a year since my surgery. He had no problem seeing me, and he knows all about my transplant in India."

"Why didn't you go see your regular nephrologist today? Why did you come here?"

"Because...it's the middle of the night, and my doctor's office is closed," Kevin replied, with an "um, isn't it obvious" tone.

"What's your nephrologist's name?" Dr. Scrivener inquired.

"Dr.—wait. Why should I tell you? You're probably going to tell me that he did something illegal, too. No way. I'm no snitch."

Dr. Scrivener stared at Kevin. He could easily discover Kevin's doctor. "Did you find the report?"

Kevin practically shoved his phone in the doctor's face as if to say, "Take that."

The doctor frowned at Kevin as he passed Kevin's phone back. "Did you read that? It's only four sentences."

"Patient received kidney from donor. Procedure conducted under standard operating procedures for kidney transplant. Anesthesia given. Patient recovery normal."

"This tells me nothing. It's not even signed by a physician."

"Aren't you required to treat me by law?"

"I am required to stabilize you in emergency situations, which I did. Like I said, I'm only required to ensure your dialysis needs are met. And given the legal issues around your transplant, I will not treat your transplant concerns—unless you want me to report you to the authorities. You have until the end of this dialysis treatment to make a decision. Let me know what you decide."

Dr. Scrivener turned to leave the room.

"You can't just walk away!" Kevin shouted. "You can't just tell me I have to go back on dialysis!"

"I didn't say you have to go back on dialysis permanently." Dr. Scrivener came back into the room. "If you want treatment for your kidneys, you need to find another doctor who might be able to revive your transplant. Or you can let the failing kidney stop working altogether and get back on dialysis. Those are your options."

"What if I refuse treatment and die instead?"

"That's certainly your choice."

Dr. Scrivener's tone was as sterile as the medical equipment surrounding him.

"You call those options? Practically drowning myself in drugs or attaching myself to this fucking machine? Well then, fuck you!" Kevin lunged forward, but he fell back. He forgot that he was still hooked to the dialysis machine.

Dr. Scrivener shoved Kevin in the dialysis chair. Their faces were so close that their noses almost touched. Dr. Scrivener was strong despite his age.

"You're lucky I'm giving you an out! I have half a mind to call the cops on you right now. You stole a kidney from some poor Indian and had some kind of botched surgery. You want to blame someone, blame yourself!"

Every nurse, patient, and physician in the immediate area was staring. Two security officers ran to the scene. One of them restrained Kevin, and the other calmed Dr. Scrivener as he walked away.

Kevin thought about filing a lawsuit against the doctor and the hospital. But the truth was, the hospital had done nothing wrong. Obviously, Dr. Scrivener shouldn't have been physical with Kevin, but Kevin asked for it. Besides, Dr. Scrivener was the beloved head of nephrology. In those hospital hallways, he walked on water. The incident would pass without mention.

Kevin returned home and searched through his files. He found the one-page document about the donor, Satyaraj Aggarwal, and tossed it aside. He found brochures about Acharya Hospital that he picked up during his stay, but he didn't have anything else. He discovered the generic receipt. It was not itemized. It just read "medical services." Kevin felt stupid for not thinking to read the postoperative report before he left Acharya Hospital. *Could it be true that I bought a stolen kidney? How could it be against the law when a company is operating in Los Angeles and at a prestigious New Delhi hospital? It can't be true. Could it?*

Kevin visited his regular nephrologist—the doctor who treated him after he returned from India. But when he arrived at the doctor's office, a nurse and a physician's assistant took Kevin into a private room.

"Where is Dr. Merano?" Kevin knew something was wrong.

"Unfortunately, Dr. Merano can no longer treat you," explained the nurse.

"What do you mean? He's been seeing me for two and a half years. Why can't he see me?"

"He received a call from Dr. Scrivener. I understand he recently treated you at the hospital. Is that correct?" The physician's assistant stared at Kevin as if he were a cop interrogating a criminal.

"He refused to treat me. He asked me for the name of my nephrologist, but I refused to tell him. How the hell did he find out that I see Dr. Merano?"

"Dr. Scrivener sees patients at the hospital, but he also sees patients at a few dialysis clinics around town. He must have had access to your patient record from one of your previous clinics."

"Isn't that illegal? Like a violation of HIPAA or something?"

The nurse and physician's assistant exchanged an uncomfortable glance.

"Kevin, given the history of your transplant, unfortunately, Dr. Merano can no longer treat you. I'm very sorry," the physician's assistant said with an empty coldness, as if he recited remarks off a notecard.

"That son of a bitch! I refused to snitch on him to Dr. Scrivener, and now he's just going to abandon me? My kidney is failing, and I need a doctor. I'm a fucking American citizen! I have health insurance!"

"I'm very sorry," the physician's assistant repeated with absolutely no hint of an apology.

"I'm going to sue his ass! I didn't do anything illegal. He's just being a pansy! Getting scared off by one phone call from some doctor? You got to be kidding me. Well, fuck him! Fuck all of you!"

Kevin visited five different nephrologists across the next two days. He had to get a dialysis treatment the next day; he couldn't wait. Every single doctor told him the same thing as Dr. Scrivener. Kevin conceded to accept a dialysis prescription, without treatment for his transplant. But that's what he really needed—to find out what was going on with his new kidney and if it could be fixed.

Kevin called Health SkyTours, but he got an endless busy signal every time he called. Their website said, "Under Construction" and listed the same toll-free number that came up busy. Desperate and out of options, he called Lakshmi. He was greeted with a robotic recording that said her number had been disconnected. He drove by the Health SkyTours office, but a "For Lease" sign hung crooked from the door. Cobwebs covered the top corners of the doorway. He searched for them on Google and Facebook, but he came up empty. Health SkyTours had vanished into thin air.

He tried to contact Dr. Mittal at Acharya Hospital, but the operators said there was no doctor by that name at their hospital, nor had there ever been a "Dr. Mittal" at their facility. He scoured the hospital website for their physician directory, but there was no trace of Dr. Mittal or Kamla, his nurse. There was no trace of them anywhere on the Internet. It was as if they never existed.

Kevin was frantic. How could everyone disappear? He remembered the butler and found his card stashed away in a desk drawer. Kevin called the number at least fifteen times. It rang endlessly. He didn't know what to do. On a whim, he looked at websites for other hospitals in New Delhi. Maybe Dr. Mittal had changed jobs? Just as he was about to give up after two days of searching, Kevin stumbled upon a photograph. It was a group photo of the physicians at a different hospital in Delhi called Shivaya Medical Center. In the back corner of the photograph, Dr. Mittal smiled broadly at the camera. Kevin searched the staff directory, but there was no Mittal. He scrolled the staff's thumbnail photos, and next to Dr. Mittal's picture, it read "Dr. Dinesh Mehra." The biography listed all his accolades and professional accomplishments. There was no mention of Acharya Hospital.

What the hell? he thought. Kevin's stomach churned. He had no choice but to contact Dr. Mittal or Dr. Mehra, or whoever he was. It was three thirty in the afternoon in New Delhi. He called Shivaya Medical Center twice, but no one answered. On the third try, an operator connected Kevin directly to Dr. Mittal's office.

"Dr. Mehra?"

"Yes, how can I help you?" Kevin recognized the doctor's robotic voice.

"This is Kevin Whitman from Los Angeles. You did my kidney transplant two and a half years ago at Acharya Hospital."

The doctor fell silent. Kevin continued.

"I've been experiencing some complications, but my doctors here won't help me because I don't have a detailed postoperative report. They said they need that, or they need to talk to you directly to understand what you did during my surgery."

The doctor remained silent, but Kevin heard him breathing into the receiver.

"So would you be able to send me a report? Or would you be willing to talk to my doctor?"

"I'm sorry, but I have no recollection of your procedure. If you needed a report, you should have gotten it at the time of surgery. Quite frankly, I cannot even be sure that you are telling the truth. It sounds like lies to me. I never worked at Acharya Hospital."

"Excuse me? You told me your name was Dr. Mittal. Your assistant was my nurse, Kamla. You gave me a kidney transplant, goddammit! Now you're saying it never even happened!" Kevin screamed into the phone.

"I did no such thing! Now leave me the hell alone!" the doctor shouted back and slammed the receiver.

Kevin fell onto his hands and knees, and his iPhone cracked as it hit the hardwood floor of his condo. He didn't know what to do.

He lay in despair for a long time. He reached for his laptop and did a Google search for kidney trafficking in New Delhi. The search returned more than one hundred hits. One of them was a cable news online article dated three days earlier. It was about a nabbed criminal who orchestrated dozens of stolen kidneys from poor villagers in remote parts of India. The article read that the kidneys were sold to Americans and Europeans, who were duped into believing that the kidneys were donated.

Kevin vomited. He bought right into a shady organ racket ripped from the headlines, and now no one would treat him. The dialysis treatments held him over despite his failing kidney. But he couldn't go back on dialysis. Kevin would rather die. He spent the following week contemplating his next move. All signs pointed to one inevitable decision. He would have to return to India and confront Dr. Mittal. Kevin didn't want to talk to any more American doctors. What if he *had* broken the law, and what if one of the doctors reported him? He still wasn't entirely convinced that he had done anything wrong. And even if he did, he was the victim!

Kevin didn't know what he would say to Dr. Mittal. What the hell was he getting into? Organ trafficking? The criminal underbelly of India? But he was desperate, and he was already in the middle of it. He flew to San Francisco to renew his visa at the Indian consulate. He was the third person in line, but it would still take the entire day for his documents to be processed. He needed to blow off some steam. As he walked through the city, he passed a boxing gym. Maybe he could punch the bag around for an hour? A few doors down, though, he found a shooting range. Kevin signed up for a same-day class.

He held the handgun in his palm. The cold metal was heavy. He felt safe just touching it, even though he didn't know how to fire it. His aim was off, and his hands shook. The instructor promised him that he would improve with practice, so he signed up for another class on the following day before he left San Francisco. He improved only a little, which was due more to luck than skill. But that would have to do. He boarded a flight to New Delhi that night.

Thanks to the power of the Internet, Kevin scheduled dialysis treatments at a clinic near Shivaya Medical Center in Delhi. It would have been easier to return to the clinic at Acharya Hospital, but he didn't want to risk being recognized. He rented a cheap room at a midrange hotel near the hospital. He hung around the hotel lobby and staked out one of the butlers. He followed the butler out of the hotel and into the adjacent parking lot.

"Hey!"

The butler turned around to face Kevin. "Yes?"

"I need help getting something." Kevin pulled five hundred dollars in folded bills out of his pocket and flashed it just long enough for the butler to see before shoving it back into his pocket.

The butler didn't say anything, but he looked at the money with thirst.

"A handgun and bullets. I need it by tomorrow."

The butler looked into Kevin's eyes as if to ask what this American in India needed with a handgun. Kevin stared back without saying anything else.

"Tomorrow? It will cost one thousand dollars in cash."

"Fine, no problem. I will meet you here at this same time tomorrow."

The butler agreed, and Kevin walked back to the hotel. He had no idea what to expect the next day, but the butler was there right on time. The butler handed Kevin a grocery bag. Inside, the gun was wrapped. Kevin unwrapped it and examined it. He had no idea what to look for, but he pretended like he knew what he was doing. When he was convinced that it was legit, Kevin handed the butler one thousand dollars. He put the grocery bag in his backpack and walked away. He checked into a different hotel later that day.

For one week, Kevin visited Shivaya Medical Center, hoping to find Dr. Mittal. For the first three days, he hung around the hospital for twelve hours but left disappointed. But on the fourth day, Kevin finally saw him. Dr. Mittal was in the hospital lobby, at a small table that was hidden behind a large staircase. Kevin cowered so Dr. Mittal wouldn't see him. He followed Dr. Mittal up the stairs to the fourth floor and kept a safe distance. Kevin tracked Dr. Mittal down a hallway and into a suite labeled "Nephrology." Kevin didn't go inside. He hid behind a utility closet door for the rest of the afternoon until Dr. Mittal came out. Kevin followed him back down the stairs and out of the hospital. Kevin could feel his anger growing with each step as he followed behind Dr. Mittal. Outside, it was dark without a star in the sky. When Dr. Mittal reached the parking lot, Kevin grabbed him from behind and pulled him into an adjacent alley. Kevin shoved him to the ground and pointed his handgun right at Dr. Mittal's face. Kevin's hand shook, and he was terrified that he would accidentally fire the gun.

"Do you remember me? Open your fucking eyes!"

Dr. Mittal wept. His eyes were clamped shut. "Who are you? What do you want?"

"Don't pretend like you don't remember me! I called you, and you hung up on me! You did my transplant almost three years ago, and now I'm sick. You're going to fix it, or I will kill you!" Kevin pushed Dr. Mittal harder against the ground.

"OK, yes. Just don't kill me."

Kevin pulled the doctor to his feet. Dr. Mittal straightened his glasses and looked at Kevin. The gun was still pointed at him.

"Kay-win Whitman," Dr. Mittal said, still shaking. "I remember you."

"Good. Then you will remember what the fuck you did to me! None of my doctors will touch me. They say you gave me some bogus procedure! Let's go!"

Kevin tied the doctor's hands together with a plastic tie that doubled as handcuffs. He saw the cops do that on a reality television show and purchased a couple of ties online before he flew to India. Kevin pressed the gun into Dr. Mittal's back and led the doctor back to the hospital.

"Not there," Dr. Mittal said. "I can't take you there without raising suspicion. You see, I am no longer doing *those* surgeries anymore."

"Then where?" Kevin demanded. "What do you mean *those* surgeries?"

"You must know it by now, Kay-win. You bought an illegal kidney off the black market. There is only one place that is safe for both of us," Dr. Mittal stammered.

They got into his car. Kevin couldn't drive in India, so he had no choice but to untie Dr. Mittal. Kevin pointed the gun at Dr. Mittal. Twenty minutes later, they stood outside of Babaji's makeshift clinic.

Kevin's stomach tied up in knots. The shack looked like it would topple if the wind blew hard enough. *Dr. Mittal would treat me there?* He was way in over his head, and he thought he might die there. He had no idea what he would do next, and he was terrified of shooting himself with the gun.

"Don't say anything. I will do the talking," Dr. Mittal said.

"How do I know this isn't a trap? What the hell is this place?"

"This is where we steal the kidneys," Dr. Mittal said flatly, as if that was normal.

Kevin's stomach tightened further. His worst fears rose to reality.

"So the kidney I got was not donated by a dying man with cancer? You stole it from him?"

"I didn't remove it, but yes, I was part of the ring that stole the kidney and gave it to you," Dr. Mittal replied. "I grew too scared of being involved with all that. Your surgery was the last one I did for them. After that, I bought my way out of the illegal racket, but I was forced to change my name and leave the practice I built for fifteen years. They will be surprised to see me—and to see you. White people don't come here. I can't give you any assurances. You just have to believe me. They might kill you, or me, or both, but they might not. I guarantee that if you walk in there with that gun pointed, they will shoot and kill both of us before you step one foot inside."

Kevin had no choice but to follow Dr. Mittal's lead. Before they approached the clinic, Kevin forced Dr. Mittal to repeat his confession. Kevin recorded a video on his iPhone. Dr. Mittal protested, but Kevin waved the gun at him.

"Who is behind all this?" Kevin wanted to know.

"A very powerful man named Sunardas Shetty," the doctor replied.

Kevin took pictures of the run-down building and Dr. Mittal's license plate. Kevin e-mailed them to himself, but he told Dr. Mittal that he e-mailed them to an American journalist with the *Los Angeles Times.* He told Dr. Mittal that he instructed the journalist to investigate Dr. Mittal or Dr. Mehra and Sunardas Shetty if the journalist didn't hear from Kevin the next day.

"If you screw me, I'll screw you!"

Dr. Mittal trembled. He was obviously frightened to be back at Babaji's clinic and thrust back into the illegal racket. He would have believed anything Kevin told him. Kevin returned his phone to his pocket but left it on record mode, fully expecting that his phone would be stolen or the battery would die. But it didn't hurt to try to gather some evidence. In hindsight, he felt stupid for not thinking of it during his first visit. He hid the gun in a nearby bush and nodded at Dr. Mittal when he was ready to enter the clinic.

Dr. Mittal rapped on the door three times with a distinct pause between each knock. A peephole slid open in the wooden door. Dr. Mittal announced himself. The suspicious eyes from behind the door eyed Kevin up and down. The voice behind the door spoke to Dr. Mittal in Hindi. Dr. Mittal explained who Kevin was, including the fact that he really did need treatment. The peephole suddenly shut. A few minutes later, the door opened, and Kevin followed Dr. Mittal into the main entrance. The stench of stale urine and something rotting was overwhelming. Kevin immediately gagged and doubled over to vomit. Dr. Mittal handed him a handkerchief.

"Cover your nose and mouth. It will help."

A surly man patted both of them down, and somehow the guard didn't notice or decided not to take Kevin's phone. They walked through the main entry to an adjacent room—a makeshift operating room. As clean as Kevin's hospital room was at Acharya Hospital, this place was the opposite. Kevin's heart sank at the thought of a poverty-stricken man, woman—or worse, a child—being forced into surgery in that wretched place.

The man in charge of Babaji's clinic reprimanded Dr. Mittal for returning to the clinic, with a swift blow to the head. Dr. Mittal fell to the ground. His forehead was split open, and blood dribbled down his face. Dr. Mittal had compromised their whole operation by showing up with Kevin. Dr. Mittal begged for mercy from the ugly man in charge, but Kevin knew Dr. Mittal was a dead man. Maybe he was, too.

"Dollars!" Kevin blurted. All eyes turned to him. "I have money!" He removed one thousand dollars from his backpack and waved it in the air. "I will pay you if you let him treat me."

Ten minutes later, Dr. Mittal had a bandage around his head and took an ultrasound of Kevin's kidneys. He did a biopsy and proceeded to run blood samples in the decrepit lab. As Kevin's body was rejecting the new kidney, Dr. Mittal would have to pump him with new doses of antirejection medications. Dr. Mittal fetched the medicine from a refrigerator and connected the IV pole and the vial and needle. He was alone, so he fumbled through it. Usually nurses administered the medications. His hands trembled. He was preoccupied with the wound on his head and what the thugs would do to him after he treated Kevin. Kevin couldn't care less about what happened to Dr. Mittal. He would only protect Dr. Mittal for as long as Kevin needed treatment. Kevin still needed dialysis treatments too, but there was no machine at the back-alley clinic. Kevin was at their mercy.

Kevin grew drowsy from the heavy medication, and he passed out despite his efforts to stay awake. He knew the thugs would search him as soon as he slept, but he didn't care. The only things he kept in his backpack were a change of clothes and copies of the documents he had received from the hospital after his first surgery. He was smarter this time around. He stored the original hospital documents, his passport, several thousand dollars, his laptop, an extra iPhone and charger, and his iPad in a bank safe-deposit box. The thugs wouldn't find anything valuable.

He woke up in the middle of the night. Medicine still flowed into his arm, and Dr. Mittal was asleep, sitting upright in a chair next to Kevin. His backpack and clothes were a ransacked mess on the ground, and the thugs finally took his phone. The clinic was quiet; the thugs were nowhere to be seen. While Dr. Mittal continued to snore, a girl entered the room. She carried a tray of food and set it on the table next to Kevin. She turned around to face him, and Kevin almost fell out of the bed.

She was the girl in the picture—the one they gave him of his donor's family. She was the girl who stood between her parents, smiling, holding up her birthday cake. Kevin would never mistake her hazel eyes and angelic face.

"My name Juhi," she said in broken English. "I feed you."

Kevin saw that she wanted nothing to do with him. He couldn't move his arms because of the IVs, so he was forced to let her feed him. He couldn't take his eyes off her. Kevin thought, *What is she doing in such a horrid place? Is she really the daughter of the man whose kidney I purchased? Maybe Juhi knows the true story about my kidney? Was it actually donated, or was it, in fact, stolen?*

Juhi felt Kevin staring at her, and her body tightened. She had never sat so close to a white person before. Juhi thought, *He doesn't look rich. I thought all Westerners were rich.* Juhi decided that Kevin was nothing special. She decided that she hated him.

In silence, Juhi fed Kevin bite after bite of dal and rice. She wouldn't look at him. Kevin continued to stare, and he wanted to speak, but he didn't know where to start. Kevin began to ask her, "Where is your father?" but they suddenly heard footsteps, and Juhi quickly shoved the last bite of food into Kevin's mouth and scurried away.

"Babaji's men abused me when I was alone with them at the clinic," Juhi chimed in. Max interviewed Juhi and Kevin together for the first time. "It had become part of the routine," she continued. "They ate breakfast; then they raped me. They completed their morning work, ate lunch, and then they raped me again. Then they took a nap. They each took a turn with me every day. I grew numb to it, except I feared that I might get pregnant. I started to menstruate while I worked at the clinic, and the last thing I wanted was to be bound to those men forever with a baby that no one wanted."

When Kevin arrived, it was the first time that an American stayed at the clinic, so the routine was off schedule. As a result, the gang didn't attack Juhi as often. In that way, she was grateful Kevin was there, and she didn't want him to leave.

Dr. Mittal treated Kevin for two more days. On the third day, he showed improvement when he began urinating again, and the color returned to his skin. It was also the day he mustered the nerve to talk to Juhi. They found themselves alone for a few moments when the man in charge at the clinic called Dr. Mittal into another room.

"Juhi, do you live here?"

She looked at Kevin with fear in her eyes.

"Don't be scared. I don't want to hurt you. I just want to know if you're the daughter of any of the men who work here."

"None of these men is my father," she replied sternly.

"Do you live here?" he repeated.

"No," she replied. *Never share more than what's necessary,* she remembered.

"Why do you work here? Shouldn't you be in school?"

She looked at Kevin as if he was an alien. She didn't trust him, and it bothered her that he was interested in her.

"I don't want to hurt you. I want to help," Kevin told her.

"Why you help me?"

Kevin didn't know how to respond. "Because you don't seem happy here," he blurted.

"Happy? It's been many years since I am happy. You think you can make me happy? I am happy if you can bring my mummy and papa alive again," she whispered, and anguish swelled in her voice. Her eyes danced with fear and a wildness that scared Kevin.

There was something in Kevin's voice and eyes that compelled Juhi to tell him everything. Maybe it was because he was American, and she had never spoken to a white person before.

She told Kevin that the slumlord stole Papa's kidney and sold it to some man like Kevin.

"My family taken from home and left in slum New Delhi. We had nothing. Mummy and Papa died, and I am alone for two years. Babaji take me as his slave. Bring me here. They rape me every day, beat me, and starve me. Soon I will die here."

Kevin couldn't believe what she was saying. He thought, *I ruined her life. I'm responsible for her parents' death, and if Juhi was correct, I would be responsible for her death, too. Dr. Scrivener was right along. I stole a kidney in an illegal scam. I became a thief and a murderer in the same breath.* He dry-heaved and hyperventilated. He wanted to tell Juhi that he had her photograph. He wanted to tell her who he was, but he couldn't breathe. She watched him choke and didn't move for several seconds. She wanted to let him die, and he didn't blame her.

But Juhi knew Babaji's men would kill her if they found a dead American at the clinic. Juhi gave him water and gently pressed on his forehead to calm him down. She ran away into the adjacent room as Babaji's men entered the room.

When Kevin woke the next morning, his kidney was functioning again. Dr. Mittal wrote all the documents that he would need in order to receive treatment back in Los Angeles, including a falsified document that Kevin's kidney came from a willing family member. But Kevin wasn't sure he would need the documents. As his health improved, he felt confident that Babaji's men wouldn't let him leave the clinic alive. He knew too much. He saw too much. That night, when Dr. Mittal and the gang finally fell asleep, and even the man who guarded Kevin dozed off, Kevin disconnected his IVs. He collected his clothes and tiptoed out of the clinic. He almost blew it twice—he forgot about the horrible stench, and his gag reflex almost woke everyone. He made it out safely, rummaged in the bush for his gun, which was still there, and slipped away into the night.

He found a cheap hotel, and the next morning, he retrieved his gadgets from the safe-deposit box. He was free. If he went to the airport right then, he could be on the next flight home. He wanted to leave and never return. But something tugged at him to stay. He saw Juhi's face every time he closed his eyes. The guilt made him fifty pounds heavier. He knew the men from the clinic would search for him. They probably had already killed Dr. Mittal after they realized that Kevin escaped. They would undoubtedly interrogate and beat Juhi.

CHAPTER 25

ESCAPE

Kevin made it halfway to the airport and turned around. Flashes of his dead sister's disapproving face kept flashing in his mind. Each time Kevin closed his eyes, Stacey looked more like Juhi, and Juhi looked more like Stacey. If only he hadn't looked at his phone while driving through the intersection, he could have avoided the accident that claimed her life…

Kevin hailed an auto rickshaw and went back to the dingy clinic. He struggled to direct the driver; the place looked different in daylight. But once he found it, he hid in an alley across the street, with a direct view of the clinic entrance. He waited there for one hour, but nothing happened. No one left the clinic, and no one entered. Another hour passed, when a black sedan pulled away from the clinic onto the street. He saw

Juhi sitting in the backseat next to a large, frightening man who wore large sunglasses. Kevin knew immediately that that was the man who enslaved her. Kevin wanted to race across the street, reach in through the window, and strangle him. But all he could do at that moment was follow them.

He hailed another auto rickshaw, and the small three-wheeler struggled to keep up with the sedan. Juhi's car stopped abruptly in front of the New Delhi train station, the third-largest station in all of India. The place was a maze of travelers, vendors, beggars, police officers, stray dogs, and luggage carriers. Three hundred trains across sixteen tracks serviced five hundred thousand passengers every day! Kevin had never seen anything like it. He strained to keep Juhi's car in view amid the parade of people. The side door of the car swung open, and Juhi and Sunardas Shetty stepped out. Juhi wore a tattered backpack, and Shetty carried nothing. They walked into the station together, holding hands. They crossed the bridge to the first platform. Then Shetty released Juhi's hand and nudged her forward. She slowly walked toward a group of brooding men who waited a few hundred feet away. One of the men carried a black briefcase. Shetty stayed back and watched Juhi as she inched toward the men. The oncoming train whistled in the distance as it approached the station.

Juhi trembled. If she took any misstep or made any wrong move to make Babaji or the other men suspicious, they would shoot her in broad daylight and leave her there to die. The train drew near as she walked toward the men with the briefcase. She didn't know Kevin was there watching the whole time.

When she finally reached the men with the briefcase, they handed it to her just as a train pulled into the platform next to them. A sea of passengers disembarked. They filled the platform, including the space between Babaji and Juhi. He watched her without flinching. She felt Babaji's eyes burning a hole in her forehead. She knew he clenched the gun in his pocket. He was ready to shoot her at any moment. She walked toward him steadily as the train picked up steam again. She inched her way closer and closer to him. He watched her, and she watched him. The train whistle howled again and shifted to a faster gear.

Suddenly, Juhi shifted her gaze to an open train car just a few feet away. Shetty followed her gaze and then looked back at her. He drew his gun from his pocket and waved it in the air as he frantically pushed through the crowd toward her. She hopped onto the train just as Shetty caught hold of her leg. But the train sped up again with a billowing shake that knocked Shetty to the ground. He shouted and cursed her as she drifted away.

Call it kismet or intuition, but Kevin had a feeling Juhi would jump onto a train. He found himself treading closer to her while she approached the men with the briefcase. He got close enough to jump on the train right after Juhi did, and luckily just before it picked up steam; otherwise, he would have been pulled under the tracks. Kevin shouted for Juhi, but the train's roar drowned all other sounds. He frantically traveled up and down the train, straggling through every car, looking for her. By the time he jumped on the train, he was at the tail end of it, and Juhi was somewhere in the middle. There were fifty cars on that train. He walked deeper toward the back of the train, oblivious that his search took him in the wrong direction.

Juhi knew the trains well. Her train would stop in a few minutes at Delhi's much smaller station, Sarai Rohila. It was impossible for Babaji to beat her there, but his men could be dispatched there by the time she arrived. She had to get off that train. Babaji's men would surely jump onboard, and they would never stop hunting her. She devised a plan to sneak off the train and embark on another, with the hope of disappearing forever. As the train approached the station and slowed to a safe pace, she jumped off the moving car along with a group of other jumpers to avoid attracting attention. She slipped into the underground tunnel.

She ran along the tracks but struggled with the weight of the briefcase and her backpack. She gagged at the foul stench of human waste, burnt tar, and garbage all mixed together in a soup that soaked through her shoes. She had to cover her mouth to stop herself from vomiting. She ran. It wouldn't take long for Babaji to think about sending one of his men down into the tunnels. As she gained speed, she heard a man shout her name. She recognized him as one of the men from the counterfeiting cave. He closed in on her, and the ground began to rumble as a train approached. If she didn't find a space to hide, the train would run straight over her. She ran faster, and her captor followed suit. The train's headlight flooded the tunnel. Its rumble filled her ears and shook the walls around her. She looked back. The man still pursued her with a wild look in his eyes. The rumbling train and the man drew closer. He was in arms reach of her, and his hand grazed her backpack. A few feet in front of her, there was a small opening in the tunnel, an oval-shaped carving in the wall, as if it were a safe hole designed for people on the run just like her. Her captor grabbed onto her just as she stepped into the opening. The train thundered past her at exactly the same moment. She watched in horror as the man was sucked under the train and crushed alive. She covered her eyes and shook violently at the sight of such carnage. After the train passed, she gasped for air. She had to keep moving. Someone from Babaji's gang would come looking for the crushed man. Her legs felt like cooked spaghetti. She kept her gaze at eye level and didn't look down so she could avoid the crushed man's maimed body. She stumbled along for a few feet, but it was too much for her. She vomited, and she could barely breathe. She hunched over, clasping the briefcase, and retched for several minutes. She thought about giving up and letting Babaji find her. But then she thought about what he would do to her. She put one foot in front of another until she found herself running. She found an opening in the tunnel onto a platform and hoisted herself into a bustling crowd that waited for an approaching train. It was headed southeast to Bihar. She hopped on and cowered in her seat.

In the meantime, Kevin was still on the first train that Juhi had jumped onto. He continued to frantically search for her. He ducked and weaved through car after car but saw no sign of her. Passengers filled every open space. They stuffed themselves into the train, and those without a seat hung out the sides over the tracks and clung to the handrails. If she was on the train and spotted him, it would be easy for her to hide from him and easy for him to overlook her. It didn't help that he stood out so much. Practically every person stared at his light-brown hair and blue eyes as he went up and down the train.

Kevin was on the Shane Punjab train that traveled for eight hours and three hundred miles northwest to the city called Amritsar. Along the way, it stopped throughout the vast state of Punjab. As Juhi traveled farther away from him to Bihar, he continued to search for her on the wrong train. He grew weary and was overcome with helplessness. He squeezed into an empty seat in a sleeper car between two elderly men. It felt good to sit down after hours on his feet. He couldn't help it when tears streamed down his face. He didn't know what to do next.

CHAPTER 26

RIDE TO BIHAR

Juhi sat in her seat on the train for three hours without moving. Her heart pounded as her imagination ran wild with notions that one of Babaji's men, or Babaji himself, saw her get on the Bihar train. She willed her body to stay still, but she could not hold her urine any longer. With her backpack still strapped on, she clung to the black briefcase and walked to the bathroom at the front of the car. She tried to keep her legs crossed as she walked; otherwise, she was certain that she would urinate on herself. The bathroom was just an open hole that she had to squat over. One misstep, and she would be swept under the train and crushed like the man who had chased her. She peeked down the hole and watched the tracks race by underneath. The fierce rumble and shake made it difficult to balance. She didn't let go of the briefcase. She didn't know what was inside, but she still felt desperately attached to it. She managed to pull down her pants and underwear and squat while balancing herself on the far wall. She shut her eyes as she urinated, willing herself not to look down.

She pulled her pants up and rinsed her hands in the filthy sink one at a time, never letting go of the briefcase. She wanted to open it, but she wasn't safe on the train. She had already gained the attention of a group of men who sat in the aisle of seats two rows from her. If the briefcase contained anything remotely valuable or interesting, she would definitely be attacked. Even in the lavatory, she knew someone might be watching her. She returned to her seat and nestled herself next to a mother traveling with her three young children. Juhi wanted to blend in, and even though she desperately craved to be away from Babaji and to have her independence, she felt less alone when she sat with that family.

During the twelve-hour train ride, she got up twice more to relieve herself. Those were the only times she left her seat. She didn't talk to anyone, and she fought with her tired, heavy eyes. Her stomach growled, but she didn't move.

She disembarked at Patna, Bihar's capital city, that has a population of two million people. She could easily hide there. But first she would have to escape the bustling train station without attracting attention. A sea of taxi drivers, rickshaw wallas, and food vendors waited outside the train station, ready to pounce on weary travelers. They were like a pack of lions that eyed a herd of elephants. Juhi's face would attract attention. It always did. If she exited and walked off alone, surely a gang of men would follow her. As she stood on the platform, she watched for a family, any family that was exiting. She spotted one and walked behind them but close enough to seem like she was with them. The young girl in the family was Juhi's age. She looked at Juhi curiously but said nothing. Then, to Juhi's surprise, the girl smiled at Juhi and extended her left hand. Juhi took the girl's hand in hers and smiled back. The girl's parents were too distracted trying to remember where they parked their car to notice Juhi. Juhi exited the station holding the girl's hand. She walked with the family well past the station to the neighboring, less-crowded parking lot. She released the girl's hand as they approached her family's car. The girl still said nothing. She just looked back at Juhi, smiled, waved, and took her seat inside the car. Juhi waved back and slipped away toward the street.

She didn't know what to do next, and she was too exhausted and hungry to think. She needed to find food and a place to sleep for a few hours. It occurred to her to steal some food, but she hesitated. She wanted a fresh start in this new place, and she didn't want to attract attention. She could find a slum and offer to do a couple of hours of writing and reading, but she didn't have the energy for that. And how long would it take her to find a slum? And what if someone in the slums in Patna was connected to Babaji? What if someone recognized her? She found a row of trucks parked in the lot. They looked as if they had been there for several days. Juhi squeezed into a small crawl space between the last truck in the row and the parking-lot wall. It was just big enough for her to fit with her backpack and briefcase. She lay down and used her backpack as a pillow. She clung to the briefcase with her whole body and wrapped her arms and legs around it, as if it were a body pillow. She drifted off to sleep like that. Her growling stomach would have to wait.

When she awoke, the afternoon sun beat down on the concrete. She was sopping wet with sweat. She felt disoriented and frantically searched around her to remember where she was. Her head pounded in the harsh sunlight. As the memory of her escape flooded her mind, she remembered the briefcase. She whipped her head around to make sure she was alone, and then she slowly pressed on the side catches to release the locks. She searched around again to ensure no one was watching. What she found inside was beyond anything she could imagine or hope for.

She traced her index finger over the top row of crisp American dollars wrapped in bundles with rubber bands. All the bundles contained one hundred bills, and each bill was one hundred dollars. She didn't dare take out all the packets. She needed to move to a safer location to count the money. But at a glance, she guessed that there were at least ten bundles. Her head swam in circles as she did the math—one hundred thousand dollars! She took one bill out of the top bundle and examined it. She was a master counterfeiter, and she wanted to know if the bills were real. She held the bill close to her face and searched for the usual mistakes found in counterfeit money. The shading in the right eyebrow of the man on the bill, Benjamin Franklin, was perfect. The intricate webbed design across the top and bottom was impeccable. And most of all, the bill had that smell. The smell that could never be replicated. The smell reminded her of a crisp, white cloud that provided shade on a hot day, fresh and airy. She always wondered how new dollars got that smell.

To both her horror and delight, the bills were authentic. She had to get out of there and find somewhere safe to hide. Babaji would not easily let go of such riches. She took three one-hundred-dollar bills out of the top bundle and slid them into her backpack between two of her drawings so that the bills wouldn't wrinkle. She carefully closed the briefcase, double checked, and then checked again to ensure it closed tightly. Once she was convinced it was sealed, she listened for any sounds around her. She crawled out of the space and walked swiftly out of the parking lot. Her mind raced, and food was the last thing that she could think about.

That was Juhi's first time being completely alone since Sunardas Shetty found her in the slum. The same vast emptiness she felt as she wandered from one Delhi slum to the next filled her heart and stomach. She was grateful to be out of Babaji's grip, but her sixth sense detected a looming danger that challenged any appreciation for her newfound freedom. Her survival instincts kicked into gear. Her mind raced. *I need to get off this road. I need to disguise myself. I am already attracting attention. A young girl walking alone with a backpack and heavy briefcase on the side of the road? I look like a young calf at a watering hole.*

She wandered into a crowded market. It was exactly what she needed. She found a couple of boys, younger than her, hawking pirated books. She knew they were novices by the way they walked up to shoppers but then hung back at the last minute, exposing their lack of confidence and experience. She made eye contact with one of them, and the boy walked over to her. She slightly tilted her head to the right, signaling to the boy to follow her into an alley.

"I will give you this for six thousand rupees."

Juhi held a crisp American bill out toward him. The boy's eyes widened. She thought he might drool. He reached toward the bill but hesitated. He looked at her as if he came out of a trance.

"Where did you get that?" He looked at her with narrow eyes.

Juhi liked him. He was smart to be skeptical. But she knew he didn't care where she got it. She knew that he wanted it.

"That is my own business," she replied.

"Why should I give you six thousand rupees? The exchange rate is forty-eight rupees for one dollar."

Wow! Juhi thought. *The boy knows math.*

"Yes, but this is a perfect new bill. It does not have any marks or wrinkles. It is worth more than a dirty, old one-hundred-dollar note."

The boy contemplated for several seconds, while Juhi grew impatient.

"Never mind." She unzipped her backpack and slid the bill back inside.

"Wait. No. I will take it."

She held the bill in her hand and waited for the boy to hand her the rupees.

"But I do not have that much money on me. I have to run back home to get it."

"No, you must give it to me now."

She knew he was bluffing. The boys who sold pirated books kept loads of cash on them. They accumulated it quickly because most of their customers could not resist buying at least two or three books at a time. This boy wanted to trick her. He wanted to tell his father or brother or boss or whomever he was working for.

"But I do not have that much right now," he said.

"OK, then forget it." She put the bill in her backpack again and turned to walk away.

He ran after her in a panic. "OK, fine. I will pay you now."

He reached into the satchel wrapped around his body and counted six thousand rupees. He held the wad toward her at the same time that she held the American bill out to him. They snatched the notes from each other's hands at the same moment. The boy held the bill up into the light to admire it. While the boy was distracted with his good fortune, Juhi ducked out of the alley and disappeared into the crowd. She knew that as soon as he walked away, he would brag about his shiny American money, and within minutes, a swarm of his friends would be searching for her. She weaved in and out of the crowded bazaar toward a busy street and dissolved into the bustling city.

She trudged along through the city. Her hunger awoke like a sleeping lion as she walked past a dhaba, and her nose filled with aromas of masala, piping hot potato patties, and *chole bhaturas.* She forced herself to ignore her hunger pains. She had to conceal herself and the money. She found another market, and she used the rupees that she had just exchanged to buy new clothes that would conceal her. She also purchased a duffel bag to transfer the money. After she dumped the money into the duffel bag, she buried the briefcase in an empty field near the market. By that point, exhaustion and hunger overtook her. She stumbled upon a temple. In India, you can count on finding a temple nearby; they are everywhere—like Starbucks in America.

Inside, there were a handful of parishioners. A woman dressed in a bright yellow sari held her baby on her left hip. She reached up to chime the bell that hung from the middle of the ceiling. A man stood with his eyes closed and hands folded in prayer in front of the carved marble statues of Hindu gods. His mouth moved as he silently recited a mantra. Juhi sat on the white marble floor all the way in the back corner. The cold stone cooled her skin. She felt her breath soften. She did not pray; she did not feel like it. Instead, she sat with her back against the wall and enjoyed a few moments of freedom from her heavy load.

A *sadhvi*—a female priest—draped in a white sheet approached Juhi. She stood over Juhi and smiled.

"You look hungry. Come," she said and continued to smile.

Juhi gathered her bags and followed the sadhvi without hesitation. At that moment, she truly did not care what happened to her, as long as she could eat something—anything.

Juhi followed the sadhvi through a hall off the north side of the temple and into an open courtyard filled with long tables and benches. Off to the side, a group of men hovered over stoves and frying pans. A dozen people sat at the tables and ate in silence. They looked like her—poor and alone.

She sat at an unoccupied table and placed her backpack and duffel bag to her left. She put her left hand on top of the bags, while her right hand rested on the table. The sadhvi handed Juhi a plate of saffron rice, two rotis, dal, saag, and dahi. The sadhvi still wore the same affectionate smile on her face, and she invited Juhi to eat. Juhi tore into the roti and scooped the vegetables into her mouth. The monk watched Juhi and maintained her strong hospitable stance. Juhi was still hungry after eating every morsel of rice and vegetable, but she did not ask for more food, and none was offered.

The sadhvi sat next to her, and Juhi felt her body tighten.

"What is your name?"

"Pari," Juhi lied. "Pari Kumar." Her childhood friend, Pari, was the first name that came to her.

"It is nice to meet you, Pari. I am one of the monks who lives here at the temple. My name is Kripaji. You look as if you have not slept in a long while. We have rooms for girls like you. You can take rest here for a few days and take your meals here, too. In return, you can help with chores such as cleaning, or if you possess any skill that might be useful?"

Juhi listened quietly and observed the nun for a few long seconds. Her muscles softened. She heard stories of girls and boys lured to temples with hot meals and warm beds, only to be abused or sold. Still, she had also learned to trust her instincts, and she liked Kripaji. Plus, if Babaji was hunting for her in Patna, he would not dare to enter a temple.

"Thank you, I would like that very much," Juhi accepted the offer.

Kripaji smiled and invited Juhi to follow her to a room off the courtyard. It was a closet-sized room that had only two furnishings—a bed with clean white sheets and a lamp. Across the hall was a clean bathroom with hot running water. After Kripaji left, Juhi took her backpack and duffel bag with her into the bathroom. She removed the new items she had purchased from her backpack and balanced them on the sink's ledge. She laid out a new shirt, pants, and panties, as well as soap for her body and hair, a toothbrush, toothpaste, and a hairbrush. She had also purchased a hat and scissors, which she kept in the backpack.

She soaked in the hot water and lingered for a long while. She loved the heaviness of the water in her drenched hair. She watched the soapy water rinse off her body and circle down the drain, as if it washed Babaji off of her. She did not have a towel, but she didn't care. Her new clothes clung to her wet body. She scooped up her backpack and duffel bag and sat in the courtyard, where her skin and hair dried in the beating sun. She loved the feeling of her skin baking. She wrapped strands of her hair around her fingers and brought them to her nose. She was grateful for the fresh scent.

As she dried off, she grabbed a broom and swept a small area of the courtyard. She might as well show her willingness to repay the kindness that she had received. She kept her bags close and only walked three steps away in each direction away from the duffel bag. When she finished sweeping a small radius, she moved her bags over a few feet and swept the new area. She did this three or four times, until she grew sleepy. She put the broom away, and with bags in tow, she returned to her room. The door did not have a lock. She put the bags on the bed facing the wall away from the door. Then she slid into bed and snuggled against them. She pulled the white sheet over the bags and over her small frame, and she drifted into sleep within minutes.

Juhi slept for half a day. When she opened her eyes, Kripaji stood over her with a plate of steaming food in her hand.

"You have been resting for a long time. Will you come eat something?"

She handed Juhi the plate of food and left. Juhi devoured the meal, slid the plate under the bed, and went back to sleep. When she woke again, stars filled the night sky above the courtyard. All was still in the courtyard. She sat up in bed and listened for any noises. The temple and dormitory were silent. She unzipped the duffel bag. A manila envelope rested underneath the bundles of money. She peered inside and emptied it onto the bed. Inside was a pocket-sized notebook filled with handwritten notes in English and Hindi.

Juhi cracked it open to a page in the middle. At first the notes did not make sense. It was some kind of list. Each page had the name of a place—a village or city, and next to it was the name and phone number of a person. Underneath was a list of other names. There was one name per line, and next to the name was the number "1" or "2" in parentheses. There was a date and time at the bottom of each page.

She flipped to the first page and found more names of places and people. She turned the pages swiftly three or four more times and then turned back one page because something caught her eye. She read "Gantak Mandi" written across the top of the page. Kabir Singh's name and phone number were next to it.

Gantak Mandi—Kabir Singh 95-84-12-93...
Sameer Ghanekar—1
Govinda Satyagiri—2
Rajeshswami Birla—2
Satyaraj Gupta—1 (September 21, 2010)

She read each name aloud, and she almost dropped the book when she saw Papa's name at the bottom of the list. Her whole body shook. This was the list of Gantak Mandi victims. The "1" next to Papa's name meant one kidney. Papa was the only person with a date next to his name. She would never forget that date. It was the day after her twelfth birthday.

She snapped the book shut and sobbed into her pillow. Papa was in a notebook with hundreds of other names and places, like inventory at a clothing store. She opened the book again and stared at his name. She concentrated, as if it would help her discover who wrote it. She swept her index finger across his name and then across the other three names. Those uncles listed under Papa—she was friends with their daughters. Those names did not have dates next to them. She wondered if those uncles suffered Papa's same fate. If Kabir Singh did catch Govind Uncle and Rajeshswami Uncle, that would mean they were dead. The "2" next to their names made their fate more unfortunate than Papa's. But then she wondered if that was true. They would not have suffered like Papa.

She combed through the rest of the book. Each page listed a new location and at least a dozen names. The final two-thirds of the book listed future dates. She was holding the roadmap of victims. She shuddered at the notion and dropped the book again, as if blood seeped from its creases. She heard approaching footsteps, so she threw the book back into the duffel bag and turned off the lamp. She quickly covered herself and her bags under the covers and turned her back toward the door just as Kripaji peeked in to check on her.

CHAPTER 27

PUNJABI JOURNEY

The moon shone bright in the night sky when Kevin stepped onto the platform. He guessed it was around 11:00 p.m. He disembarked at Amritsar, the final stop on the Shane Punjab line. Despite the late hour, the station bustled with activity. Dozens of armed soldiers walked up and down every platform, surveying the crowds. The air swelled with the continuous thunder of fighter jets. He quickly learned that Amritsar was situated a mere thirty miles from the India-Pakistan border. Amritsar was a proud city and patriotic; a heavy military presence was a welcomed everyday part of life for its residents.

He scanned the platform for any sign of Juhi. As the crowd thinned, he shifted his thoughts to where he would sleep that night. His phone ran out of juice on the train, and his iPad needed a Wi-Fi connection. He decided to surrender to the aid of a taxi driver—whichever one looked the kindest among the barrage of them that surrounded him as he exited the station.

"Luggage?" the driver asked Kevin in English as he eyed Kevin with curiosity. Westerners typically arrived with hard-shelled suitcases on four wheels, but Kevin only carried one backpack. Kevin shook his head no and slid into the backseat.

"Hotel?" he asked as the driver turned the key in the ignition. The driver didn't understand and turned around to face Kevin.

"Hotel?" Kevin asked again. He pantomimed the universal sign for sleep by clapping his hands together and resting them against his cheek. He tilted his head and closed his eyes just for a second.

"Acha! Tusi kamra chayya!" (OK! You need a room!) the driver exclaimed in Punjabi. He nodded emphatically and turned back to the steering wheel. He continued to nod and smile at Kevin through the rearview mirror. Kevin had no choice but to assume the driver understood him and to hope that he would take Kevin somewhere decent.

After thirty minutes, the taxi finally came to a stop. Kevin tried to take mental notes of the trip and remember landmarks just in case he needed to find his way back to the train station. The taxi pulled into a long, curved driveway. An attendant wearing a red-and-gold vest and a matching turban opened the taxi door and greeted Kevin.

The hotel looked fancy. The front facade was made of glass, and the lobby appeared modern and clean. Rows of large vases overflowed with beautiful flower arrangements. Bright lights sparkled in the high ceilings of the main lobby. Kevin paid the driver and said one of the few Hindi words that he still remembered.

"*Shukriya.*" (Thank you).

For the first time in India, Kevin blended right in. Though all the hotel employees were Indian, practically every hotel guest hailed from the western world. As Kevin made his way to the registration desk, he overheard guests speaking in French, British English, Australian English, and Catalan. He craved an American accent, and he felt a tinge of homesickness.

The Golden Temple Grand Royal Hotel and Spa had a room with a king-size bed available that night. It was off-peak season for tourism; otherwise, a last-minute room would have been impossible to reserve, the front-desk attendant explained. Kevin handed over his credit card and fell sound asleep in his room ten minutes later.

Prayers at the Golden Temple began daily at two thirty in the morning. By the time he rose from his slumber and cozied into a chair on the balcony with a blanket wrapped around him, devotees had already been singing *kirtan* for six hours. He couldn't believe his luck. His third-story room had a spectacular view of the temple. He knew nothing about that most sacred temple before he arrived in Amritsar. But he understood at first glance why it was called "the Golden Temple." Lavish gold plates adorned the exterior walls of the highest two floors. The dome and minarets at the very top were also shrouded in gold. The temple shone in the morning light against the reflection of the pool that surrounded it. The temple was one of the most beautiful, peaceful places he had ever seen.

Kevin ordered a carafe of chai and breakfast from room service. While he waited for his meal, he showered and thought again about Juhi and what to do next.

India is home to one billion people, but its landmass is half the size of the United States. Juhi and Kevin were just two people in that congested country. He wanted to find her, but how? He debated giving up altogether and just returning to Los Angeles. But there was no reason to return. He had nothing and no one to go back to. He was convinced that if he left her behind, he would not be able to live with the guilt. Even if he never found her, he had to at least try. His health was back on track, now that the kidney was working again. He even imagined that her papa's kidney inside of him might be oozing fatherly affection into his bloodstream and told him not to abandon Juhi.

He roamed around Amritsar for three days, aimlessly searching in markets, bazaars, and crowded streets. He stared at young girls who remotely resembled Juhi, as if he willed her to appear. Despite thinking about her all the time, her face faded from his memory. He kept her family photo from the flyer in his pocket. He would never forget her eyes—he could recognize her if her whole body was covered and nothing shone but those two bluish-green pearls. None of the girls he saw in Amritsar had her eyes.

He suffered through horrid nightmares—images of the slumlord beating or raping Juhi; her hunched over her father's dead body, holding his bloody, pulsating kidney in her hand. Sometimes in his nightmares, she held the kidney out to Kevin, and she screamed at him for stealing it. After two nights of chilling dreams, he couldn't close his eyes. He tossed and turned but found no rest. He lost his appetite altogether on the fourth day. He felt hungry, but as soon as he sat in front of a plate of food, he wanted to vomit. He wondered if Juhi had food to eat, wherever she was. He spent twelve hours each day wandering through the city, hoping to catch a glimpse of her. He went in circles. Soon, shop owners shooed him away. His sluggish walk, the restlessness in his eyes, and his loose clothes that hung from his body made him a boorish site that scared market patrons.

He stumbled over to a nearby public park and slouched on a bench. Overcome with despair, he felt a sense of duty to keep living; otherwise, Juhi's father's kidney would go to waste. But he also couldn't bear the guilt of what he had done to Juhi and the lives that he ruined. He wished that he had never come to India. He even thought that he would be happy doing dialysis again.

A group of Americans sat across the way from him. They looked at him and then at each other. One of them—the only man in the group—walked over to Kevin.

"Hey, are you OK?"

Kevin didn't reply, and he didn't move. The man looked back at his friends who watched and shrugged back at him. He turned back to Kevin. "Do you speak English? Maybe I can help?"

Kevin looked at the man as if he just realized someone was talking to him.

"Yes, I speak English."

"Great. I'm sorry to pry. You look like you could use some help."

"I don't think you can help me."

"Maybe I can't. But maybe I can?" the man said cheerily.

"I'm sort of lost. I'm looking for something that I lost five days ago."

Kevin decided not to tell the man that he was looking for a person. A girl. He felt insecure about how that might sound.

The man didn't know what to say. Kevin was right. The stranger didn't know if he could help. But he tried anyway. "I'm sure it will turn up," the man replied.

Kevin avoided making eye contact.

"Why don't you join my friends and me? We're headed to our favorite dhaba just two blocks from here."

"No, thanks," Kevin replied. "I'm gonna stay here."

"Aw, come on," the man insisted. "You haven't lived if you haven't had the potato *tikkis* at this place." The man waited for a response, but Kevin didn't move. "Just one meal. After that, if you think we're weird, we'll leave you alone."

Kevin reluctantly stood up from the bench and stood in front of the man. He and Kevin were almost the same height.

"I'm Kevin." He extended his hand toward the stranger.

"Hi, Kevin. I'm Greg. Nice to meet you." Greg shook Kevin's hand.

"Kevin walked with the group—Greg plus two women, Samantha and Ashley, to the restaurant. Greg had met Samantha and Ashley in graduate school five years ago. After graduation, the three of them moved to India to work full time for a nonprofit organization focused on clean water. They had been in India for the past two years and considered themselves the next best thing to Amritsar natives.

"We live in Amritsar, but we travel to surrounding areas that are more remote," Samantha explained. "We work directly with citizens in villages to bring them clean water and to show them how to get it themselves. Our goal is to leave behind a model that is sustainable and self-reliant so they aren't dependent on charity and NGOs."

"Our organization has done some incredible work," Greg added. "But it's taking longer than we expected. We didn't anticipate how isolated each village would be from the next. So if we're successful in one village of, say, about five hundred people, there aren't resources for locals to go to the next village to replicate it. So we do it ourselves. But we've found that what works in one village may not work in the next. Politics plays a big role, too. Some communities are more open to foreigners than others. And in some villages, decisions are made by a single head patriarchal figure, while other villages are more democratic. So now we've given up on putting a deadline on our work and shifted our goals to focus on the geographic area that we want to cover before we can say we've achieved our goal."

Greg passed Kevin a cup of chai and a plate stacked with two steaming-hot spiced potato patties. "You have to eat these with chai. Anything else just won't do it justice."

Kevin's appetite returned, and he felt stronger after the meal. Perhaps the company made him feel better, too. He hadn't realized how much he missed speaking conversational English with other native speakers. But he didn't feel like talking too much. It was just nice to listen. He was glad that Greg and his friends didn't ask him much. Kevin wouldn't know how to explain why he was in India. He wasn't sure if it was even safe to share that he had a transplant, because, technically, he was a criminal. Plus, he already felt like a monster for ruining Juhi's life. He didn't need three strangers judging him.

Kevin passed the rest of the day with Greg and his friends. It was their day off, which they only received once per week. They tried to make the most of it. They showed Kevin around Amritsar as if they had lived there all their lives. Shopkeepers, restaurant owners, street-food vendors, and locals who traveled by bus, train, bike, rickshaw—everyone seemed to know them, and they seemed to know everyone, too. As the sun went down, and the moon rose, they decided to head back to their apartment. They called it a "flat," and it was a two-bedroom apartment in a tiny, tucked-away hostel just a few blocks from Kevin's hotel. Their building was stuffed with foreigners and locals alike—all people who were working, many of them for nonprofit or NGOs. They invited Kevin over for a nightcap, but he just wanted to get back to his hotel. Greg scribbled down his cell-phone number and the Amritsar address for their nonprofit organization. Greg and his friends practically begged Kevin to swing by their workspace the next day. Kevin thanked them, but as he walked away, he thought that he would never see them again.

Kevin appreciated the mental break from his own issues. But it all flooded back and drenched him as he walked back to his hotel. He spent the next two days sifting for Juhi through the city streets and returned to his hotel disappointed each day. He stayed up all night, looking at flights back to Los Angeles. It took a while to find the right train that would take him back to Delhi and would connect on time to a flight home. He reached into his wallet for his credit card, and the scrap of paper with Greg's address floated to the ground. It was late, but Kevin decided to call anyway.

A groggy voice answered, "Hello?"

"Hey, Greg. I'm sorry to call so late. It's Kevin. We met the other—"

"Hey, Kevin! I was hoping you would call!"

"Yeah, well, I'm thinking about going back to LA. I don't think I'll find what I came to look for."

"Man, I'm sorry to hear that," Greg replied earnestly. "Samantha, Ashley, and I actually wanted to invite you to join us on a trip. We're headed out into the field for a couple of months to visit a bunch of villages. We could use another pair of hands. And I thought that maybe you could look for whatever it is you're trying to find. Maybe it's not in the city. Could it be hiding out in the villages?"

Kevin hadn't thought of that. Maybe Juhi had decided to stay away from big cities. But even if she did, he had no idea if she was in Punjab. She could be clear on the other side of the country. Still, the idea intrigued him, and it would give him an excuse to stay in India.

"Wow, that's really nice of you. I don't know what to say."

"Well, say that you'll hold off on going back to the States right now. You can swing by our office tomorrow, and I can give you more details. If you don't like what you hear, no harm no foul. You can still catch a flight the next day."

Kevin pushed his credit card back into the snug slot in his wallet. He lay in bed on top of the covers and thought about Juhi.

CHAPTER 28

VILLAGE LIFE

Kevin was in the field with Greg, Samantha, and Ashley for two months. Two months turned into four months, and four months doubled into eight months. He was glad that he thought to purchase a one-year supply of his medications before joining Greg and his team. It was just luck and economies of scale. Kevin's kidneys were fine, and he felt good. But he saw no sign of Juhi during that time.

He trekked south across Punjab, sometimes veering west toward the border and other times headed east toward China. He learned everything there is to know about clean water, the lack of it in some places, and how to get it. He became a legit employee of the nonprofit organization "Clean Water Now!" just like Greg, Samantha, and Ashley. They were patient with him and taught him how to dig wells, how to collect rain water, how and when to use nonpotable water, and how to purify water to make it safe for drinking. They even taught him some Hindi and Punjabi. For the first few weeks, Kevin was a fish out of water. He could hardly converse with the locals, and he had a tough time adjusting to their simple living. He felt irritated with the number of national religious holidays that shut down schools, the government, and many private companies too. At the time he thought, *No wonder the infrastructure in India is so behind!* But he didn't think to admire the religious tolerance that they enjoy. Again, at the time, he was annoyed that children got so many days off from school. *It's obvious that education is the best way out of poverty, but the villagers don't seem to care about education.* It took him a while to get over himself and his superiority complex. A few humbling moments brought him back to earth.

The first moment was when he learned to drink out of a communal water bottle without putting his mouth on it. Every Indian person Kevin met was a master at sharing drinking water out of a bottle. It didn't look difficult, but Kevin practically choked each time he tried, not to mention he drenched his shirt and also wasted a lot of precious water. The villagers could hold the bottle high, tilt back and open their mouths wide, and pour and swallow at the same time. He had to pour it into his mouth, swallow, and then pour again. When ten other people were waiting for their turn to drink, he held up the group and disrupted the rhythm. The villagers laughed at him because it took him twice as long to drink water as everyone else. Fresh besan laddoos made of chickpea flour and ghee were passed around the village when he finally drank and swallowed from a bottle at the same time. Typically, such a dessert is reserved for holidays such as Diwali or Raksha Bandhan, but even he thought it was worth celebrating.

He slowly started to fit in and felt more comfortable in his own skin. The villagers started to accept him and opened up to him. He played hide-and-seek and cricket with the village children. The children enjoyed teaching him their language, Punjabi, but also loved to laugh hysterically at his pronunciation. They squealed with joy while he agonized over rolling his "r's" and softening his "t's." They also loved it when he taught them English. They wanted to play with his iPhone and iPad, and they freely touched the white skin on his face and arms. They were so fascinated by his light complexion. The villagers called him "Kaywin," just like the butler on his first trip to New Delhi.

Kevin kept an eye out for Juhi every step of his journey. Whether he traveled in sports utility vehicles through thick brush or visited schools and homes, he had one eye out for her all the time. Sometimes he thought he saw her, and his heart would pound as he made the group stop the car and he called out her name. Each time, no one looked back, or the locals looked at Kevin as if he was crazy. Kevin grew close to Greg, Samantha, and Ashley, but he never told them his story. They asked on occasion if he had any luck finding what he chased, but after a while they forgot about it. Samantha, being the existentialist out of the group, convinced Greg and Ashley that he was really searching for his life's purpose, and they had helped him find it—or at least gotten him one step closer.

They slept in people's homes, and if none were offered, they pitched tents. They saw wild snakes, elephants, and other exotic wildlife but luckily without incident. He became a master at going to the bathroom in nature and burying his business to disguise the smell and to promote sanitation in the villages. It had been months since he felt the urge to check Facebook or to check his e-mail. For the first time, he lived in the present moment, and he was actually happy. It helped that his kidneys kept up with him, and he grew stronger in the field than he had ever been back in the States.

He thought about Juhi every day and never forgot that he was there to find her. One night, as he nestled into his sleeping bag, he dreamed about reuniting with her. He dreamed that he would ask her to join him in the field with the nonprofit organization.

In other dreams, he took her back to New Delhi and settled down with her as a brother/dad figure. Still, in another dream, he helped her to find a foster family that would love her and take care of her. In every single dream, he forgave himself, and Juhi too forgave him. But those were just dreams.

CHAPTER 29
WARNINGS

Juhi stayed at the temple for two more days, but she could feel Kripaji becoming more interested in her and more intrusive. Kripaji wanted to know what she held so dearly in her backpack and duffel bag, and it would only be a matter of time before she demanded to know. Juhi worked dutifully at the temple. She helped with cooking and cleaning and plotted an escape at the same time. Kripaji would not just let her walk out of there.

Juhi went to bed early one night. When she was certain that everyone had retired to bed, she slipped into the bathroom. She gathered her hair into a low ponytail and cut it straight across. The bundle of hair fell into her hand, and she stuffed it into a plastic bag. She continued to cut off her hair to make it shorter and shorter until she resembled a boy. She changed into her new pants and shirt that she had saved, which no one had ever seen her wear. She had purchased a hooded sweatshirt so that she could keep warm and use it as a disguise. She draped it over her head. When she was satisfied that she looked different enough, she gathered all her belongings and swept away any evidence of her new hairstyle. She tiptoed into the temple and dropped two hundred dollars into the donation box. She slipped out through a back door that she had discovered was usually unlocked.

In the dead of night, she walked toward the market where she met the boy whom she had given the one-hundred-dollar note. At that time, she had noticed a little concealed space in the alley where she could stay for the night. At sunrise, she planned to go back to the Patna train station and leave Bihar forever. She had already been in one place for too long.

She climbed onto the first train that arrived at the Patna station. It was headed to Punjab. She wondered, *Was Babaji already searching for her there? Maybe he followed that first train to Punjab and stayed there? Maybe he grew tired of searching for her there and left?* She didn't know if she was headed toward danger or running from it, but she took the train anyway. She told herself that she would take the first train that arrived in Patna, and she just couldn't think about it anymore. That feeling of just wanting to give up overwhelmed her at times, like that particular day at the train station. She had to make a decision, and her instincts told her to travel to Punjab. The first stop was Rajpura, a small city situated north of New Delhi and south of Chandigarh, Punjab's capital. She combed through the kidney notebook for villages that were listed near Rajpura. There were five. Each village had a list of ten to twelve names, which equaled fifty-five victims and eighty-two kidneys scheduled to be stolen. She wanted to visit them—all of them, if she could. She made a list of the villages she would visit in order, starting from the south of Punjab and headed north. After she grew tired of examining the notebook, she pulled out a wrinkled, blank paper from her backpack and a few pencils. She sketched Kripaji, and on the back, she scribbled the dates of her stay at the temple and its exact location. She slipped the completed black-and-white drawing into her bag and fell asleep as the train roared forward.

The jerk of the train leaving Ambala stirred her awake. The next stop was Rajpura. She gathered her bags and sat on the edge of her seat. She covered her head with her hoodie and jumped off the train. She exited quickly and mingled with the crowds. She walked for half an hour and then stopped at a dhaba for a samosa and chai. She bought a second and then a third samosa after the first two did not fill her. She attracted far less attention disguised as a boy, and she kicked herself for not thinking of it sooner when she lived in the slums. Next to the food stall, a small shop sold trinkets and snacks, as well as hats, sandals, and even walking shoes. As her sandals were tattered, and she would end up doing a lot of walking, she purchased a pair of white walking shoes and threw her old sandals in the trash.

Then she walked…and walked. For dozens of miles, she walked toward the first village listed in the notebook. The further she traveled away from the train station, the lonelier she felt. After a while, only tractors and motorcycles passed her. Buildings and houses were less frequent and were replaced with lush open fields. The air was fresh, like she remembered in Gantak Mandi. The main road was paved in some places and melded into a dirt road in others. She covered her mouth and nose with a scarf to keep dust away. The weight of her bags forced her to stop more than she wanted. The day began to melt into night as she approached the first village, Neelapur. She came across a small roadside store, but it was closed. She decided to stop for the night, and she slept on a grassy patch behind the store, completely alone and undisturbed.

The next day, she waited for the store to open and asked the owner to point her toward the house of Srinivas Atwal. He was the first person on her Neelapur list.

"His house is the third one on the right, just up the road," the store owner shared happily. She was surprised that he was not curious about her. Perhaps he was accustomed to strangers passing through the village. Fifteen minutes later, she reached the Atwal home, which was more of a hut than a house. Two toddlers played with sticks in front of the door. A round woman who stood inside watched Juhi as she approached.

She didn't think about what she would say until she stood outside their door. Her tongue went dry and twisted in her mouth.

"Is this…is this the house of Srinivas Atwal?" she stammered.

The toddlers stared at Juhi, and then they looked at their mother.

"Yes. Who are you?"

"I am Juhi."

"Juhi who?"

"I have come to speak with Mr. Atwal. Is he home?"

The woman eyed Juhi up and down, and then she disappeared into her home. A minute later, a man in a white banian undershirt and dhoti came to the door.

"Hello, who is there?"

"Sir, my name is Juhi. I have come to talk to you about something important. Might I come in?"

Mr. and Mrs. Atwal exchanged a look and then looked at Juhi. He opened the screen door and waved for her to enter. She approached slowly and smiled at the children, who stared at her with wide eyes. She assumed they must rarely get visitors, particularly strangers. She tried to appear as calm and friendly as possible. But her heart pounded, and her voice shook.

Mr. and Mrs. Atwal invited her to sit down on the straw mats in the middle of the room on the floor. They were similar to the ones her parents had in Gantak Mandi. The house smelled of spices, seasonings, and fresh vegetables. Her stomach growled. She coughed in a silly attempt to mask the sound.

"You do not know me, and what I am about to tell you might seem unbelievable. But I came here with only good intentions. My papa was a farmer in our village." She decided not to say "Gantak Mandi." Perhaps they had heard of it or even knew someone there, and then she might be discovered. "As he got older, the farm owner got frustrated that Papa had slowed down in his work and made mistakes. The landowner felt cheated for investing in Papa. Papa worked on the farm for more than thirty years, and the farm owner expected at least ten more years out of Papa. The farm owner made a deal with a man in New Delhi to steal one of my papa's kidneys and sold it on the black market. After that, Mummy, Papa, and I were taken from our home and dumped in a slum in New Delhi. There were other people in our village whom the farm owner wanted to take kidneys from, so he got rid of us before we could warn them. The surgeon left my papa in such a horrendous state that he died in the slum. My mummy also died in the slum. I have been alone for the past two years. After my mummy and papa were gone, a slumlord took me in as his personal slave. I escaped from him just a few days ago. I found a list of people whom he plans to target, and your name is on that list. I came here to warn you."

She leaned over to show them Mr. Atwal's name in the notebook, but they looked away. Instead, Mr. Atwal and his wife stared at her with anger across their faces. They simply could not believe her story, and they turned away when she showed them the notebook. They were probably illiterate, but it was also obvious that they did not believe her.

"This is impossible!" yelled Mr. Atwal. "How dare you come into my home and say all these lies? Get out of here! We know these thieves like you who come to our village with schemes. Get out!"

Juhi didn't expect their response. She backpedaled.

"No, please, Mr. Atwal. I am not trying to cheat you. I am telling you the truth!"

Mr. Atwal rose and practically leaped in front of Juhi as if he were going to strike her. She scrambled to her feet and moved away from him. But she continued to press. She had traveled all that way. She just wanted to be heard. She had to try.

"Please, Mr. Atwal. Do you know Amar Batta? He is the man who has arranged for your kidneys to be stolen!"

But by then, Mr. Atwal had had enough. Amar Batta was Mr. Atwal's boss—he owned the small steel plant where Mr. Atwal worked. Mr. Atwal did not believe her. He chased Juhi out of his house and shouted after her as she ran away. She ran back in the direction that she had come from, and when Mr. Atwal finally gave up his pursuit, she ran into an empty field. She rested against a mango tree and wept.

She stayed under the tree for the rest of the day and drifted in and out of sleep and despair. How could Mr. Atwal get so upset when she was only trying to save him? At nightfall, Juhi walked back to the train station. Along the way, she prayed that Babaji's men would not show up and steal Mr. Atwal's kidneys.

The next morning, she embarked on the Punjab train headed north. She was getting closer to her own village, and the notion of seeing it again both excited and frightened her. She hadn't decided if she would return there. It was very risky, but she wanted to warn the others—her old neighbors. She feared that she might be too late.

It took one hour to get to the next stop due to some mechanical errors with the train. Normally, that trip would take thirty minutes. She reached Hardinwar in the late morning. She could not see or think straight because of the hunger pangs emanating from her belly. She ate three rotis, dal, and masala vegetables at the food stand at the station. She wrapped a *laddoo* and a *burfi* in a napkin and stuffed them into her pocket for later. Just as she did in Rajpura, she asked for directions to the next village on her list, just outside of Hardinwar. It was called Banthirna, and it was half the size of Neelapur. A sheep herder who passed her on the one-lane road pointed up the road when she asked for the first family on her list. By the time Juhi arrived there, the sun was in full force, and she was drenched in her own sweat. She had not showered in several days, and she was embarrassed by her foul stench. But the land was dry as a bone, and there was no place for her to freshen up. She knocked on the door at the house of Amit Khare. No one answered. She knocked harder. Soft footsteps came to the door, and a man swung it open.

"Who are you?" he asked sharply.

"Sir, my name is…uh…Harsha. Harsha…Timbani."

He waited for her to state her business.

"I came here with some important information. I do not want any money or food—I am not a beggar. I am not a thief. I just came to speak with you."

He eyed her up and down just as Mr. Atwal had. His gaze struck her confidence. A woman joined Mr. Khare at the door. She had compassionate eyes. She examined Juhi and then opened the door. She invited

Juhi to sit on one of the chairs—not on the floor—and brought Juhi a glass of water.

She told the same story to Mr. and Mrs. Khare that she had told the Atwals. But this time, at the end of it, she added, "When the men come for you, they will do one of two things. They might tell you that they will pay you handsomely for your kidney. But the truth is that they will not pay you. They will make excuses and find ways not to pay you anything. Or they will make up an entirely different lie and then trap you in the doctor's office and steal your organs the way they stole my papa's."

She also told them about the notebook and that that was how she knew to visit them. She didn't show them the notebook, but she mentioned the name of Mr. Khare's boss—the man who had arranged for his kidneys to be stolen.

She sipped on the water they had given her, and her hands shook. Mrs. Khare noticed, and it was obvious that she believed Juhi, even though her husband was not convinced.

"You have no reason to believe me," Juhi said. "I know this must sound like some childhood fantasy and drama. The only thing I can offer is money. I will pay you not to be bribed or tricked when the men come for you."

Juhi removed five hundred dollars from her pocket and placed it on the table that sat between her and

Mr. Khare. He looked down at the money with wide eyes and then looked at her.

"This is some of the American money that made the slumlord rich. This is money that he made by stealing from people like my papa. I stole this money from him, and I am giving it back to the people who he wants to harm. I do not want what happened to my papa to happen to you."

Mrs. Khare put her hand over her heart. But now Mr. Khare really didn't believe her.

"Why are you giving this money away? Why don't you want it and make a life for yourself?"

"Because I do not need it, and I do not want it. I have no family. I have no one. Eventually my old master will find me, and he will kill me when he does. Until then, I will try to warn as many people as I can and give the money to people who can use it. I do not want it. I do not want anything," she repeated.

To show her sincerity, she rose from her chair and walked toward the door to leave. She left the money on the table. She did not want to leave an impression that she wanted something in return by lingering too long.

On her way out, she said, "I hope you will heed my warning when they come for you." She walked out, turned back onto the main road, and headed north to the next house. She visited five houses that day. It was the complete list for that village. Each family hesitated when she told them her story and left the money. They also greedily took the five hundred dollars. She prayed that she was doing the right thing. She wanted to get rid of the money as fast as she could. Its weight was becoming unbearable, and she was attracting attention to herself, as more and more people became aware that she was handing out American dollars.

The next village was fifteen miles away. She would have to walk the whole way. She waited until nightfall and decided to make progress in the cool darkness. She walked halfway there through the night, slept for three hours, and reached the village by midmorning. The first name on the list was Sumit Sarna. She practically collapsed from exhaustion on his doorstep as she knocked on the door. A young woman, about twenty years old and pregnant, ran to Juhi just as she fell to the ground. The woman yelled for someone to fetch a glass of water. She held Juhi's head up and squeezed her cheeks to pry open Juhi's mouth. Juhi stirred a little, and the woman called for someone else in the house—perhaps her brother—to carry Juhi into the house.

They laid her down on a mat on the floor for several minutes, while the pregnant woman placed a cold compress on Juhi's forehead. Juhi regained her senses, and she sat up, but she was still clearly disoriented. She panicked when she realized she didn't have her backpack and duffel bag. She jumped to her feet and ran to both items that rested along a wall on the other side of the small room.

"Wait!" the pregnant lady implored. "You are not well. Please sit down and drink some water."

Juhi brought her bags over to the mat and sat down with them tucked close to her. The pregnant woman put a plate of food in front of her. Without any further invitation, Juhi devoured every morsel without breathing or looking up. She didn't care if she looked like a savage, because that was how she felt.

Once some color returned to her face, she thanked the woman for the meal. And she remembered why she was there. She asked the pregnant woman if Sumit Sarna lived there. He was the woman's father. He was in a back room in the house, alone and not to be disturbed. The pregnant woman—Jigna—seemed scared to even mention her father's name. Jigna's mother died a couple years ago, so it was just Jigna, her thirteen-year-old brother, and their father, Sumit. Juhi wondered who the father of the unborn child was, but she was too scared of the answer to ask. Sumit worked on the farm in the village, but he was hurt in an accident one year ago and could no longer work. He turned to drinking and had grown into a violent drunk. Jigna's teenage brother dropped out of school and went to work on the same farm where his father had worked. They lived off Jigna's brother's wages. Jigna said she did not know how they were going to afford to feed a new baby.

Juhi decided not to insist on speaking with Mr. Sarna. Instead she told her story to Jigna and her brother. They listened intently, and unlike the visits in the first two villages, they believed her wholeheartedly. Juhi also decided not to give them five hundred dollars. She had seen enough drunkards in her short life to know Jigna's father would squander it within one week. Instead, she offered to buy their family a goat, a couple of chickens, and some seeds. They could milk the goat to feed the baby and plant vegetables in their own little plot of land. As the brother knew how to farm, he could manage it. They could sell the chicken eggs for some additional money. Juhi showed the money to Jigna, and Jigna cried. She could not believe Juhi's generosity. She quickly wiped away her tears and ushered Juhi out the door as she heard her father approaching. Jigna told her brother to stay behind while she took Juhi to buy a goat and seeds. As Juhi and the pregnant woman rushed away, they heard Sumit slap his son across the face as he usually did in his drunken rage.

Juhi left Jigna after she purchased the items. Jigna insisted that Juhi return to her home for another meal, but Juhi refused. She had several other houses to visit that day, and she wanted to move on. Besides, she did not want to see Jigna's father. Juhi waited for Jigna to walk away and out of sight before she turned in the opposite direction and headed toward the next house.

As Juhi visited each house, she recalled the lessons about sustainability that Ms. Nisha had taught her at her school in Gantak Mandi. That was how she knew to buy a goat and chickens and seeds. She thought that if she gave families a source of a steady income, they might be less destitute and less desperate to fall for bribes and promises from Babaji and his gang.

CHAPTER 30

WORLDS COLLIDE

For the next six months, Juhi traveled hundreds of miles on foot and by train. In that time, she gave away thousands of dollars, and she still had plenty left to give. She knew that only about 50 percent of the people she met actually believed her, but 100 percent of them happily took the money. She stopped giving it away and insisted on buying more goats, chickens, and seeds for each family. In some families, the women were talented basket weavers or makers of beaded jewelry. She purchased supplies for them so they could start a small business. She purchased bicycles for the women who had to travel longer distances to get to the market or to places where it might have been dangerous for them to walk alone. Her load of money was getting lighter—which she appreciated—and she was glad that she could warn families, even if they did not believe her.

As soon as the duffel bag was light enough, Juhi transferred half of the remaining money into her backpack. She decided that she would give away ninety thousand dollars and keep ten thousand dollars for herself. That sum was arbitrary. She had no concept of how much ten thousand dollars was or what it could buy her. But she remembered from her counterfeiting days that ten thousand dollars was the maximum amount of money that travelers could carry in cash in and out of India and the United States when traveling by plane. She hadn't given any thought about leaving India, but that large sum sounded good to Juhi.

She moved swiftly from house to house and village to village. She set a limit to stay no longer than thirty minutes at each home, and she only stayed that long if she was offered a meal. She made sure that no one followed her, and if someone did, she knew how to hide. Her hair was growing long again, which accentuated her femininity. She was approaching fifteen, and her figure was starting to fill in. She grew increasingly aware of the boys and men in the houses she visited, and if there were no women at the houses she went to, she skipped them and moved on to the next one.

After four months, she woke up in the morning, and the hairs on the back of her neck stood straight every morning. She had an unshakeable feeling, like a looming danger that was inching its way closer to her. Everything was fine for two more months. She kept copious notes of every family and villages that she visited. She recorded the amount of money she gave each family or what she purchased for them. At night, when she could not sleep, she drew pictures of the villages and the people she met. Their names and the particular details about them blurred in her mind, but she remembered every face.

She had a routine. She traveled at night or in the early morning hours to beat the sun. She visited homes until evening. Then she found a quiet, hidden place in the outdoors where she could sleep until midnight, and then she would travel to the next destination. Eventually she arrived in a small village outside of Ludhiana and made her way to the first home on her list.

Juhi was surprised to find the entire family outside in front of the home, working with a group of four *ghoras*—white foreigners. She stopped just shy of the home and hid behind a giant tree. Her skinny frame was completely hidden by the fat tree trunk. Her heart pounded as her mind raced. Were the ghoras working for Babaji? Had they finally caught up with her? She shouldn't have assumed they were there for her. After all, she never saw any ghoras working for Babaji. Still, she couldn't help but wonder and worry. She strained to listen to their conversation.

"See, it's actually pretty easy to dig a well once you know how to do it. I mean, don't get me wrong, it will take time, but it doesn't take a lot of skill to do it," explained the tall man with glasses. One other man and two women hovered in the circle with him and nodded as the tall man spoke in broken Hindi.

"With three men in your home, you could probably have it done in a couple of days."

Juhi smirked at the sound of the ghora speaking in Hindi and Punjabi. His pronunciation was actually pretty good. Juhi's concerns washed away, but she listened for a little while longer just to be sure. A short time later, the group dispersed, and the Indian men began to shovel the earth. The foreigners stayed nearby but were distracted with some sort of contraption in the back of their vehicle. One of the Indian women from the home stood off to the side to observe the foreigners. Juhi approached the woman, who didn't notice Juhi until she was just a few feet from the house.

"Hello," Juhi said to the woman. She was getting ready to ask the woman if they could talk inside.

"Juhi?"

Kevin was awestruck. He stared at Juhi without blinking. He walked toward her with caution. He had turned his head around for one minute toward the SUV to help unload the materials for the well. When he turned back around, Juhi was standing there talking to the Punjabi woman.

"Juhi, is that you?"

The color left Juhi's face, and she turned white as a ghost. She did not recognize Kevin right away. In fact, she had completely forgotten about him. She ran.

Kevin chased after her.

"Juhi! Wait! Please! It's me, Kevin! I was the patient at the clinic in New Delhi. I don't want to hurt you. Please don't run away!"

Her memory of Kevin flashed in her mind. He was the American who dared to return to India after his kidney failed. Juhi remembered hating him. She thought he was stupid to come back. But she was also impressed by his courage. She stopped running and turned to face him. She would not be able to outrun him.

"Kay-win?" she panted.

"Yes! Yes, it's me!" He ran up to her. He wanted to hug her, but he stopped himself.

"What are you doing here? I do not understand. You sneaked out of clinic. Why you are still in India? Babaji look for you for many days. Your doctor—Babaji kill him."

"I know," he replied. "I mean, I didn't know about the doctor, but I assumed Shetty would kill him when I went missing. But I had to get out of there before they killed me too." He was about to confess that he stayed in India to find her, but he couldn't find the words.

"I felt much better after receiving treatment, and I decided to stay in India for a while. I'm working with those other Americans for a nonprofit organization." He pointed to Greg, Samantha, and Ashley. "We help villagers access clean water."

An awkward pause filled the space between them. Kevin finally broke the silence. "What are you doing here?"

She looked away from him. Kevin watched her and waited for a reply. He was ready to run after her in case she bolted. She felt as haggard as looked. She had lost a lot of weight, and the bags under her eyes were as heavy as her duffel bag. Her hair was longer and shorter on different parts of her head. Her clothes were tattered and covered in stains. But her eyes still shone bright, especially when she faced the sun.

"My friends and I are staying here tonight. We have space in the females' tent with Ashley and Samantha. And we have plenty of food and hot water. Why don't you stay tonight?"

He paused for a reaction, but when Juhi remained silent, he tried again to fill the space between them. "I bet Samantha and Ashley could spare some clothes too, so you can wash yours."

Juhi only understood about every other word of Kevin's English, but she understood the sincerity in his voice. She hated him when she had met him at Babaji's clinic, and she wanted to hate him in that moment.

But the truth was that it was the best offer she'd had in a long time. The idea of sleeping in a tent and washing her clothes was too good to pass.

"I will tonight." She folded her hands across her chest.

"Great!" Kevin said, trying to control his enthusiasm. "Let me introduce you to my friends. I'll let them know we'll have a guest tonight." They walked back to join the group, when Kevin stopped and turned to her. "What do you want me to tell them? I mean, how do I explain how we know each other?"

Juhi replied bluntly, "The truth."

"OK." Kevin hesitated. "That sounds good…it's just that I haven't told them about my transplant."

"You tell them now," she replied. If Kevin sought any sympathy from her, he would be disappointed.

"Yeah, I guess I…" he responded. "I hope they don't judge me," he whispered under his breath.

Kevin's friends welcomed Juhi. Kevin didn't say much.

"Juhi and I met in New Delhi. She is one of the people I was looking for when I met you guys."

Juhi looked at him with surprise. "Why you look for me?" she gasped. "Are you working for Babaji?" She panicked and slung her backpack over her body and started to walk away. He followed her, and she ran.

"No, Juhi! Please! I'm not working for Shetty, I swear. You're safe. I too escaped him, remember? Please stop!"

He caught up to her and grabbed her arm. She tore free, and he released her. He held his hands in the air as if he were surrendering.

"I don't want to hurt you. I want to help you. Look, I promise to explain everything. But I can't right now, not in front of them." He signaled to his friends. "But I promise you with my life that you are safe. I will make sure of that. I have so much to tell you."

She didn't know why she believed him, but she agreed to stay. They walked back together toward the group of Americans.

"All good?" Greg inquired. He looked back and forth at Kevin and Juhi.

Juhi put on her best fake smile, and Kevin made a thumbs-up sign. The Americans didn't ask anything else about her.

Samantha and Ashley offered Juhi some clean clothes and showed her where she could take a hot bath. They gave her a couple of American protein bars to eat. They said they would fill her up until dinner, which was in a few hours. Kevin, Greg, Samantha, and Ashley went back to work on the well, and Juhi decided to use the time to talk with the family about the kidney list and why their names were on it.

But she was too distracted by Kevin. All the questions and the eerie coincidence played out in her mind. *Was it really a coincidence?* she wondered. Kevin kept looking back at her to make sure she was still there.

In all that time that Kevin searched for Juhi, he imagined dozens of scenarios of finding her. He imagined what he would say and how they would interact. Their actual reunion was nothing like what he had imagined.

As the afternoon passed and their work started to wind down, Kevin knew that he would have to tell Juhi everything that night; otherwise, he might explode. Plus, he knew she wouldn't stick around if he didn't tell her what he knew. Kevin started to grow restless as the Americans prepared dinner. Juhi sat across from him at the campfire. She didn't look at him.

Kevin finally awkwardly announced, "So I guess you're all wondering how Juhi and I met and what she's doing here now?"

"We're a little curious," Greg confirmed.

"Yeah, I can imagine. And I want to be completely honest with you, since you've been such great friends to me."

Greg and the girls exchanged glances.

"The truth is that I paid for a kidney transplant in New Delhi. Or, I should say, I paid for a kidney, and it was transplanted in me in New Delhi. The kidney came from an Indian, which is why I came to India from LA to have surgery. I arranged it through this company that told me the kidneys were voluntarily donated by Indians, but it turns out that wasn't true." Kevin paused. The next part would be hard to explain.

"The kidney was taken illegally from a living person and sold on the black market under the guise of being legal and safe."

"Oh my gosh!" Ashley exclaimed and put her hand on her chest in disbelief.

"Yeah, I know. Unfortunately, it gets worse. I wanted that kidney so badly. I had a hunch that it might be shady, but I ignored my conscience. I regret it so much, and I wish I could take it back." He looked down as he spoke. He was too ashamed to make eye contact with his friends, let alone Juhi.

"After my transplant, I was doing great, and I returned to LA. But after a couple of years, the kidney started to fail. I got really sick, but none of the American doctors would treat me because I was transplanted in India. They said they needed to talk to the surgeon who did my operation or see notes about the procedure. I tried to contact the doctor, and it was like he didn't exist. There was no trace of the company that arranged the whole thing—it just disappeared. Their offices were closed, the telephones were disconnected, and they were wiped off the Internet. From LA, I searched the websites for all the hospitals in New Delhi, hoping to locate my surgeon, and I finally found him. He was at a different hospital and went by a completely different name. I was dying, and no one would treat me in America. So I came back to India and confronted the surgeon. Long story short, the doctor tried to deny me at first. He said he didn't know me and that I must have confused him with someone else. I then threatened him. I pulled a gun on him."

"What? Where did you get a gun?" Greg exclaimed. "I mean…what? Is this for real?"

"I had no choice! I was dying, and I needed help. That doctor was the only person who could help me."

The group fell silent.

"The doctor took me to a shady clinic in a seedy part of New Delhi. It was one of the places where they did surgeries to steal organs. When I received my transplant, I was at one of the best hospitals in New Delhi. That's how they do it. The recipients get royal treatment, but the people they steal from get botched surgeries in back-alley clinics. Juhi's dad's kidney was stolen almost three years ago."

Greg, Samantha, and Ashley gasped and looked at Juhi. She had been silent the whole time. She was eager to hear Kevin's side of the story. *Would he try to make himself sound innocent? Would he take responsibility for ruining the lives of whosever kidney he now relied on?*

"Juhi's family lived in a village not far from Punjab. After the kidney was stolen, her family was kidnapped and dumped…"

Kevin stopped and asked Juhi to share her story with Greg, Samantha, and Allison, which she did. Sadness filled her eyes. She didn't spare any details. They listened keenly to every bit right up to that moment and what a strange occurrence it was that they reunited in a small, remote village.

Juhi had only shared her drawings with her mummy, papa, and a few friends, but she unzipped her backpack and passed around portraits of her parents, landscapes of Gantak Mandi, her drawings of Mogambo, Gabbar, Sunardas Shetty, the first Delhi slum, and her two best friends, Pari and Shilpa. Ashley and Samantha wiped away tears, and Greg fought the lump in his throat. Kevin couldn't look at Juhi. He still couldn't bring himself to reveal the truth to her.

CHAPTER 31
CHANDIGARH

Kevin and his team took the next day off from work. They planned for a fun day in Chandigarh. They said they wanted to do something special for Juhi. Kevin kept his distance from Juhi to avoid having to talk to her, but he kept a close eye on her to make sure she didn't run away. He didn't tell her the truth after that first night of their reunion.

Juhi agreed to stay with them in Chandigarh. She felt comfortable with the ghoras, and she was exhausted too. That same feeling of wanting to give up that came and went—it swelled inside of her when she met the Americans. She decided that she didn't care if they turned out to be Babaji's cronies. She would be caught and killed and be closer to Mummy and Papa.

They started the day at a café with chocolate pastries and sweet masala chai. They rode the roller coaster at

Fun City, toured the botanical garden, visited the butterfly garden, went bowling (Juhi won!), and ate every delight they could find, including freshly grilled corn on the cob smothered in *ghee* and masala, piping hot samosas with tamarind chutney, and puffy *chole bhaturas.* As the hours passed with the Americans, Juhi grew more convinced that they were not Babaji's gangsters. They were the first ghoras that she got to know. She liked them.

Halfway through lunch, Juhi slid her duffel bag toward Greg, who was sitting next to her at the round table.

"I want give you." She looked directly at Greg, Samantha, and Ashley. "Your water work. It has five thousand American dollars."

They dropped their forks and stared at her in disbelief.

"Juhi, we can't take this from you." Greg pushed the bag back toward Juhi.

She put her hand up in the air to stop him. "Please take. I am villager you help. My village maybe you go to later? This money very heavy. I am tired. Please... too much burden. You take."

The Americans looked at each other, unsure of what to do. Greg eventually picked up the bag and put it next to him.

"Juhi, this is really generous of you. Thank you. We can help a lot of people with this donation."

Samantha and Ashley hugged Juhi. Greg shook her hand and smiled with appreciation.

"Juhi, that is an incredible gesture, but maybe you should hold onto some of the money in case you need it?" Kevin turned to Juhi and spoke with disapproval dripping from his voice. "What I mean is, you could get on your feet with that money and use it to start a new life."

"You not my papa, Kay-win," Juhi replied curtly. "I spend money how I want. Babaji will find me. He loves his money. He kill me. Better you take than he find it."

The table fell silent. It startled them to hear her speak of her own death with such frankness and detachment.

"I still have money for more villagers. I keep some too."

"So you're planning to continue with that? To visit the rest of the villages?" Kevin asked Juhi with surprise. He should not have assumed that she would stay with him.

"Yes, I must," Juhi replied. "What else I do?"

Kevin was silent.

They spent the second half of the day at the Rock Garden, Chandigarh's forty-acre park filled with sculptures made entirely of recycled garbage. The sculptures towered over even the tallest person in the park, and hundreds of them filled the plot. Juhi loved their magnificence. During all that time in the slums, she was surrounded by trash. She never dreamed that it could be turned into such beautiful art. The waterfall with the sculptures of women holding water jugs on their heads—that was her favorite. The statues reminded her of Mummy. She sat on the edge of the waterfall for a long while, and her tears mixed with the pool.

They ended the day at the railroad museum, located inside the Chandigarh train station. It was filled with stories about the tragic trains that traveled between India and Pakistan during the bloody partition, and it related the history of the rail expansion across the entire state of Punjab. Juhi loved the miniature train replica that ran in circles inside a glass case in the center of the museum. She watched as it trudged past open fields and stopped at a miniature red light. The horn blew as the train pulled into the tiny station. Kevin watched Juhi without taking his eyes off her. But he still didn't say much to her.

As they made their way out of the museum and onto the platform, they became entangled in the mass of travelers who waited for the late train out of Chandigarh. Kevin walked just a step behind Juhi, while Greg, Samantha, and Ashley were a few paces in front. Just as Juhi approached the exit, she looked up and did a double take. A man stood there staring at her and blocked the exit. Juhi stopped dead in her tracks, and Kevin followed so close behind her that he bumped into her.

"Sorry! Are you OK?" he asked her. Juhi's face went ghost white. In their fumble, it was enough time for Babaji's thug to approach.

"Hello, Juhi," he snickered, revealing his yellow, gapped teeth.

Juhi couldn't help but look at his right arm and the missing severed hand. It hung limp next to his body, like a cord with the plug cut off.

"I have been looking for you for a long time. Just think that I was getting ready to leave Punjab. I was convinced that you were too smart to still be here. But I guess you are as stupid as you look." He smirked grimly and licked his red-stained lips.

"Who the fuck are you?" Kevin reproached the man in English.

Babaji's thug looked at Kevin and then back at Juhi.

"Yeh kaun hai?" (Who is this?) he demanded from Juhi.

"Mere dost," (My friend) Juhi replied.

"Yeh koi dost nahin hai. Yeh hai wahi benchod American jo clinic mein tha!" (This is no friend. This is that fucker American from the clinic!)

The thug stepped up to Kevin and shoved him with his chest. He whipped out a gun with his left hand and poked it into Kevin's chest.

"Wah! Kya kismet. Main ek saath aap donon ko paaya." (Wow, I have great luck! I found both of you together!)

"Juhi, what's he saying?" Kevin asked.

"He says you should run away and forget about me before he changes his mind and kills you."

"I'm not leaving you, Juhi." Kevin looked directly at the thug.

Juhi used the moment to pull her pocketknife from her sock. Greg, Samantha, and Ashley had continued walking ahead without realizing what was happening. By then, they were out of sight.

Juhi inched closer to the thug to make him think that she was ready to follow him wherever he wanted to take her. But he still had his eyes on Kevin. Juhi swiftly stabbed the thug on his right side straight through his abdomen. She pushed the knife in as far as she could. He yelped and fell to the ground.

"Run!" Juhi took Kevin's hand and pushed through the mass of travelers.

The thug screamed for Juhi. By now a crowd had formed around him, and confusion broke out as Juhi and Kevin weaved through the maze of people. The man pulled the knife out of his side and rose to his feet. They made it to the bridge that connected one platform to the next. The man aimed his gun and fired twice. The masses of people screamed, and people ran in every direction; some dropped to the ground. Kevin and Juhi kept running, and the man chased after them. Greg, Samantha, and Ashley were still in the crowd. They ducked as the gunshots fired through the air.

"Look! Up there!" shouted Samantha as she pointed at Juhi and Kevin. "Where are they going? What's happening?"

The thug ran through the crowd with his gun swinging in the air in his left hand. As the thug pushed through the crowds, dripping blood all over, Greg stuck his foot out, and the thug went tumbling to the ground.

"Run, Kevin!" Greg shouted.

Greg tried to hold the man down, but he was too strong for Greg. The thug got back on his feet and struck Greg across the face with the gun. Sirens approached the station, but the police were too late. The man slipped out of the station and jumped into a car that waited for him. The car sped away before Samantha and Ashley could note the license plate.

Juhi and Kevin didn't look back during the commotion. They shoved their way through the crowds onto the next platform as a train approached. Kevin was worried that they would get separated in the sea of people, so he held onto Juhi's arm so tightly that he cut off her circulation. The train's engine revved. They waited impatiently to board. Juhi should have kept her head down, but she couldn't help looking around for Babaji. And then she saw him. He stood there, just a few feet in front of her. Her entire body stiffened. Kevin looked at her and then in the direction that she stared. Babaji didn't look at Kevin. He didn't take his eyes off Juhi.

He smirked as if he was victorious. She wondered how someone could make a smile look so hateful.

"I want my money." He walked toward her.

Juhi froze. The train slowly started to propel forward at a snail's pace.

Kevin maintained his grip on Juhi's arm. He squeezed it tighter and looked at her.

"Run," he whispered. But Juhi didn't move. "Run!" he shouted, and without letting go, he ran down the platform, knocking over travelers. He dragged Juhi along. She put one foot in front of the other and kept pace with Kevin. Babaji ran after them, shouting profanities. The train had gained some speed, and just as Kevin had seen her hop on a moving train in New Delhi to escape Babaji, he lifted her and practically tossed her onto the moving train. Babaji screamed. Kevin jumped on after her, but his left leg got caught between two steps. Babaji grabbed onto it and yanked it. Juhi thought Babaji would rip off his leg. Kevin kicked, but Babaji's grip was too strong. Kevin held on tight to the train railing and swung his other leg out the door and rammed it into Babaji's face. Babaji fell backward and slammed his head onto the concrete platform. He cursed Juhi and Kevin as they sped away.

Juhi cried uncontrollably for the next two hours. Kevin embraced her in his arms, and she let him. Everyone in their car stared at them. Kevin ignored the looks, and Juhi was too preoccupied to care. She couldn't stop shaking, and it took her a long time to calm down.

"We have to get off this train," Kevin told Juhi.

"He never stop hunting me," she replied hopelessly. "No matter we run, he find me. I am too tired."

It was Kevin's turn to cry. "Please don't give up on me. Not now. I'll take care of you."

Juhi didn't understand Kevin. He was a burden to her. It would be much easier for her to run on her own. He stuck out in a crowd, and together they were the most unlikely friends. Plus, she didn't want to be responsible for his death. The weight of her parents' deaths was already too heavy. The train was headed back to New Delhi. She suggested they disembark there and part ways.

"You help me in Chandigarh. Thank you. You go back to New Delhi now. Go back to your country. Do not return," Juhi advised him.

"I won't leave you."

Juhi had run out of things to say. The next four hours passed in silence.

"I think we should go back to New Delhi," Kevin declared and broke the long silence.

Juhi thought he was crazy. "I know that Shetty is there, but you know that place like the back of your hand. You know how to hide there. At least until we can figure something out. He won't expect you to be there."

"What '*we*?'" she asked him.

"The only way you will ever be safe is if you leave India, Juhi. Now that I too have seen him, I know you're right. He will never leave you alone until he's killed you."

"How I leave India? You take me?" she scoffed.

"I don't know. Maybe."

He knew the idea was ridiculous, but he could not think of anything better.

"What would you do instead? Keep riding trains to different towns and run for the rest of your life? Is that practical?"

"You give hopes of America. This is practical?" she shouted back. Kevin turned away from her.

"What you do here? Why you care? You have kidney. Go home now. Leave me!"

Kevin looked at her with such heaviness. She didn't understand.

"At least do this one thing for me. Let's get off at the next station. It's the last one before New Delhi. It's late, so we'll spend the night there. And then in the morning, we'll go to New Delhi. Once we get there, let's decide whether we go our separate ways. It doesn't make sense to ride this train into New Delhi. Shetty will definitely be there waiting for us."

He was right. Juhi knew he wouldn't leave her alone. They disembarked at the station outside of New Delhi and slept in a small field. There was a small hotel there, but it was too risky to arrive there together. Kevin gave Juhi his sweatshirt, which she wore like a blanket. As they lay down, Kevin made sure to leave a lot of space between them. They watched the stars twinkle in the night, and Kevin finally mustered his courage.

"Juhi, since we might not see each other again after tomorrow, there's something I need to tell you." He paused. "The reason I don't want to leave you…it's not just that I met you at the clinic and that I pity you. It's more than that."

He waited for her to say something. She listened without moving.

"The real reason is…oh God…how do I say this? The real reason is that all this…everything that happened to your family, everything that has happened to you…it's my fault. It's *all* my fault."

"I not understand."

"Your father's kidney. It's mine now. I'm alive because of him…because of you."

Juhi sat up and looked at him, completely dumbfounded. *What was he saying? He was the American who received Papa's kidney? How could it be? There were no paper records. How did he know this to be true?*

Juhi picked up a rock and threw it at him. She wanted to speak, but she couldn't form any words. She moved her mouth, but no sound came out, except for fits and grunts.

Kevin ducked, and he tried to move closer to her. She leaped to her feet and screamed at him to stay back.

"Please, Juhi. I want to tell you everything." He held out the one-page color brochure that was now wrinkled and worn. It was the picture from Juhi's twelfth birthday, the one of her with Mummy and Papa; it was faded, and the corners were folded.

"They told me at the hospital that your father was sick, and it was his dying wish to donate his kidney to save another life. When I saw you at the clinic, I recognized you right away. I couldn't believe you were the same girl from the photo, but you're unmistakable."

He paused again and waited for a response. Juhi was paralyzed.

"When I was at that clinic, and you told me what happened to your parents and what had become of you, I couldn't live with myself. I had no idea that the kidney I received was stolen. I couldn't just get back on a plane to the States and leave you behind. I had to find you. I wanted to somehow make things right. So I went back to the clinic to find you. But when I got there, you were leaving in a car with Shetty. I followed you to the train station. I saw you jump onto the train, and I ran after you. I jumped on it, too. I searched every car in that train for you. I went all the way to Amritsar, and I looked for you every single day." Kevin was crying now as he tried to form the words. "I'm sorry, Juhi. I'm so very sorry for what I have done."

She stood up. She wanted to charge at Kevin. She wanted to strangle him. Her mind swam in a garbled, complicated mess as Kevin's confession washed over her. She held the one-page flyer in her hand and started to walk away. But then she whipped back and charged at Kevin. She wanted to yell or scream or punch him, but she was mute. Finally, overcome with emotion, she hunched over and vomited. She heaved loudly and sobbed. Kevin tried to come closer, but she pushed him away and kicked at him. He backed off but stayed close.

"Juhi, I'm so sorry," he repeated.

She fell to her knees and held her head in her hands. Her tears formed a small puddle in front of her. She stayed like that for a long time until she turned to Kevin.

"Lie down!" she demanded.

"What?"

"Lie down! On your stomach!"

Kevin did it. He looked scared, like she might stab him the way she stabbed Babaji's thug at the train station. He lay down anyway.

Juhi walked over to him and lifted his shirt. She put her palm on his back. She lowered her face and rested her cheek there.

"Papa?" she whispered.

CHAPTER 32

DISCOVERED IN DELHI

When Kevin awoke, Juhi was gone. He scanned the area, and there was no sign of her. He jumped up and quickly gathered his stuff. He was about to run down the one-lane road toward New Delhi, when she appeared out of nowhere carrying two cups.

Steam rose from the chai that she handed to him. She took a sip from hers but didn't say anything. "I thought you left," he told her.

"I thought it. But…"

"But what?"

"I did not sleep. I think and think. I hate you. You ruin my life. I hate you," she repeated. "But part of Papa lives in you now. How I can let go?"

His heart sank. "I want to help you, Juhi. I want to take care of you."

"I do not need you take care of me," she hissed.

"I know you don't need me to take care of you. But I still want to."

Something changed inside Juhi. A desire to survive had replaced her despair and helplessness. It was as if the knowledge that some part of her family still lived, some part of her papa still pounded with every heartbeat—that was worth living for.

They made the trek to New Delhi. They walked all day and reached the city by nightfall. Juhi navigated, and Kevin followed. They spent the night in a hotel that Juhi had passed at least one hundred times when she had lived with Babaji. But she had never been inside, and as far as she knew, he did not do any of his business there. It was a seedy place, the kind where it was common to see foreigners with beautiful young Indian girls.

They entered separately, and Kevin rode the elevator to their room a few minutes after Juhi. They took turns showering, and they ate food that Kevin purchased at the restaurant next to the hotel. Juhi slept in the bed, and Kevin slept on the floor. Kevin turned the lights off, and Juhi lay down. After a few minutes, she said, "I have passport."

"What?" Kevin exclaimed and darted up from where he was lying on the floor.

"I have passport. American. They gave me in Babaji's cave. I used as my model for others that I make."

"It's fake?" Kevin clarified.

"Yes. But it is very good. No one would see."

Juhi turned on the lamp and reached inside her backpack that she kept in the bed with her. She fumbled through but could not find it. Finally, she dumped all the contents onto the bed. Hundreds of sketches and drawings covered the bed, along with worn pencils and markers and crayons. Wads of cash were mixed in among the drawings. She pushed the money aside and reached for her drawings. Kevin looked on and picked up one of Juhi with her parents.

"These are your parents?"

"Yes."

"I recognize them from the brochure photo. You drew this?"

"Yes."

"It's beautiful."

Kevin picked up a few more drawings. She had sketches of her parents, the bad men in Gantak Mandi, the slums, Sunardas Shetty and his mansion, his gangs of thugs, the counterfeiting cave—her whole life after the kidnapping was sketched and laid out right there in front of them. He had seen a few of her drawings back in the Punjab village, but this was a full view of Juhi's talent and her life after the kidney was stolen.

He examined the kidney notebook. He saw the page for Gantak Mandi, and he could not stop staring at the date next to Juhi's father's name. It was a date that he celebrated before he met Juhi—it was the date that he got his life back.

"Juhi, you're really talented. I mean *really* talented. You could be a professional artist. People would buy these."

Juhi smiled vaguely, as if Kevin lived in a fantasyland and she knew the truth. She handed him her passport that she found at the bottom of the pile. Kevin couldn't believe how real it looked. His mind raced. *Could they get past security at the airport with her fake passport? What if they were caught? What if they let him go back to America but detained Juhi?* He wouldn't do anything that might separate them.

They rested in that hotel for two days and devised a plan. But everything they came up with was too risky. After a while, Juhi was frustrated, and Kevin was cranky. They took a break from brainstorming.

"Why don't you stay here and get some rest? I'll go next door and pick up some food. Maybe some food will get us thinking again," Kevin suggested.

Juhi locked the door behind him. The food took longer than normal to prepare. Not only was the line long, but the stove seemed to be broken, and there was only one working burner. When the food was finally ready, Kevin packed it to take back to the hotel. He pulled the bag of food over his hand so it dangled off his wrist, and he held two scalding cups of chai in each hand.

But when he returned to the hotel, he could feel that something was wrong. The door to their hotel room was wide open. He rushed in and found Juhi standing there with both hands in the air. A man pointed a gun at her. It was the one-handed man from the Chandigarh station that Juhi had stabbed. He was thirsty for revenge.

He turned around when Kevin entered the room.

"Welcome, my friend," he said in English but with a thick Indian accent.

The thug waved his gun in the air to signal for Kevin to stand next to Juhi. She was wearing her backpack. There was not a trace of any of her drawings or the money or her passport. She must have returned everything to the backpack before the gunman showed up. It was a reflex for her to put on her backpack when other people were around. Kevin's backpack lay on the bed just a few feet from him. The man with the gun turned to Juhi and spoke in Hindi.

"I want to tie you up and rape you again, you stupid bitch! I lost my hand because of you. I want to make you suffer, and then I want to kill you. Stick three bullets right in the back of your ugly fucking head! But Babaji wants you for himself. Let's go!"

"Juhi, what's he saying?"

"He wishes to kill me, but Babaji wants to do it himself."

"Do not talk to him!" the man yelled at Juhi. "Where is the money?"

"I do not have it," Juhi replied.

"What do you mean you do not have it? Where is it?"

"I gave it away."

Kevin looked back and forth at Juhi and the gunman, as if he was watching Wimbledon. He couldn't understand anything.

"You stupid whore! Who did you give it to? Babaji is going to skin you alive!"

His rage got the better of him, and he struck Juhi across the face. Juhi collapsed to the ground. The man pointed his gun at Kevin, but he was sloppy with his left hand. Kevin threw one of the scalding cups of chai on his face that sent him screaming and writhing in pain. He dropped the gun and clung to his face with his one hand. Juhi scrambled to her feet and grabbed the gun. Kevin snatched his backpack, and he and Juhi ran to the door. The one-armed thug followed clumsily, but Kevin threw the second cup of chai on him and then punched him in the stomach twice until the thug collapsed.

Kevin grabbed his backpack, and they ran down the stairs to the first floor before exiting through a side door of the hotel. A car was running just outside of the exit—it was the thug's escape car. His partner, who sat behind the driver seat, shifted into gear and chased Kevin and Juhi down the street. The car was catching up with them fast. Kevin ran into the street and stopped a young man who was riding a motorbike. Kevin pulled out whatever cash he had in his pocket—three hundred dollars—and handed it to the driver. Then he pushed the guy out of the way and jumped on. Juhi hopped on behind him, and they took off just as the thug's car approached them. He didn't know how to drive on the left side of the road, but it was easier on a motorbike than a car. Kevin zigzagged between traffic and tried to shake the car, but it followed in close pursuit.

"Which way to the airport?" Kevin shouted to Juhi.

Maybe they could get rid of him if they could get past a security checkpoint.

"Keep straight on this road for a few kilometers and then turn right," she yelled back. Juhi looked back, and the driver's eyes met hers. He was another one of the three who had raped her in the cave.

"Kay-win, we will never make it there. Even if we do, he will catch up to us."

She was right. He had to think of something else. They turned on to Panchsheel Marg Road. Juhi knew where to go.

"Trust me," she said. "Stop the bike! Come on, we can get away if we run!" She jumped off the bike and ran. "Come, Kay-win! This way!"

"What are you doing? He'll catch us!" He ran after her.

"American embassy!" she shouted. "Throw the gun into the bushes; we will never get in with a weapon."

Kevin threw the gun. Their assailant followed them and tried to catch them before they entered the embassy. But he was too slow. Juhi and Kevin walked behind the first barricade and then the second, and they joined the line for the Americans. Kevin looked back to check if anyone else chased them. They were clear for the time being.

The embassy guard examined their passports—first Kevin's and then Juhi's. The guard eyed them once over and then again. It took just a couple of minutes, but it felt like a lifetime. The guard finally waved them in, and for the first time, Juhi was safely barricaded away from Babaji in a fortress that he could never penetrate.

CHAPTER 33
EMBASSY ROW

"So let me get this straight," the embassy official said to Kevin. "You walk in here with an orphan girl from the slums who has a counterfeit American passport? And you want the US government to look the other way so you can adopt her and take her back to the States to live with you?"

"Yes," Kevin replied, having spent the last two hours retelling their whole story.

"Are you out of your mind?" Matt Pearson was the head of counterterrorism at the US Embassy in Delhi. He was paged out of a meeting to meet Kevin and Juhi.

"I know it sounds unbelievable, but she will never be safe in India. I feel responsible for her, and I want to take her back with me," Kevin replied.

"Does she even want to go with you?" Officer Pearson asked Kevin. He then turned to Juhi and asked, "Do you want to go with him to the United States?"

"I do not know. It is not safe for me here."

Officer Pearson frowned at Kevin. "You are throwing out some serious accusations here, Mr. Whitman. My team has been tracking this Shetty guy for months. We know he's making fake dollars and fake documents. But we've never been able to prove it."

"We can prove it," Kevin said. "We have proof. And not just about the fake money and passports. We have proof of his involvement in kidney trafficking in India and the US."

"Oh yeah? Show me," Officer Pearson said with skepticism.

"Juhi, will you show him?" Kevin asked Juhi.

Kevin begged Juhi. She didn't like to share her drawings with strangers. She didn't like the American officer, and she could tell that he did not like her, either. She didn't want his fat, sticky fingers touching her things.

"Juhi, please. It's the only way," Kevin said.

She reluctantly unzipped her backpack and piled her drawings onto the table. Officer Pearson picked up a few and barely glanced at them. He threw them back onto the table and looked at Kevin.

"A little Indian girl's drawings? That's what you have to show me?"

"Look at them again," Kevin replied patiently, although he resented the undertone of racism in the officer's tone. "They're not just a little girl's drawings. Look at the details. She captured specific places with building addresses and license-plate numbers and names of people and dates. Look at the faces. They're as clear as photographs."

Officer Pearson picked up a drawing from inside the cave. It showed two men hunched over their desks, making fake visas. He could make out the serial numbers on the documents—numbers he could trace through the embassy's computer system. His face softened as he examined another and then another drawing.

"Show him the notebook, Juhi," Kevin requested.

She took the black notebook from her backpack and slid it across the table to Officer Pearson.

"This book lists all the villages and every person Shetty targeted for black-market organs. Flip toward the end of the book. Juhi spent eight months alone, wandering from village to village to warn each of those families. She gave each family money from the one hundred thousand dollars she took from Shetty as an incentive to not accept Shetty's bribes."

Officer Pearson examined a page from one of the villages near Ludhiana.

"Look at the notes she kept—all the accounting she documented of how much she gave to each family and how much she has left."

"According to this, she still has ten thousand dollars. So where is it?" the officer asked, as if he had caught them in their own lie.

Kevin turned to Juhi. She pulled out the wads of cash from her backpack and placed them on the table.

"They real. I am master at copy your money. I know fake money. This real."

Officer Pearson took a bill off the top of the stack and held it up into the light as if he would know if it was authentic.

"We'll see," he said.

He picked up the phone that sat in the middle of the table and dialed a three-digit extension. "I need someone to run serial numbers for potential counterfeit currency. Can you send Agent Henderson down here?"

Agent Henderson, a much kinder-looking man than Officer Pearson, arrived a few minutes later, carrying a laptop with him. Agent Henderson ran the serial numbers for a handful of random bills throughout the stack through their computer system, and they came up as authentic.

"Hmmm..." Officer Pearson said. "You both will have to wait in here for a while so I can go over this whole thing with some of my colleagues."

After Agent Henderson left, Officer Pearson called his assistant and asked her to join them.

"This is my assistant, Nancy. She'll stay here with you and get you anything you need."

"How long will it take?" Kevin asked calmly.

"As long as I need it to," Officer Pearson replied.

"It's just that Juhi hasn't had anything to eat or drink today. If it's going to be a while, maybe she could have some food?"

"And what about you?" Officer Pearson asked.

"Well, I haven't eaten either, but I'm more concerned for her."

Officer Pearson smiled at Kevin, which took Kevin by surprise. "Nancy, make sure they get some food."

"Juhi's vegetarian," Kevin blurted.

Officer Pearson rolled his eyes. "Nancy, please help them get some salad or whatever it is that vegetarians eat."

He gathered up Juhi's drawings and stuffed them in a manila envelope. She stood up in alarm and eyed the envelope. Officer Pearson looked from her to Kevin.

"They are *her* drawings, Officer. It's all she has left of her parents. Would it be possible to leave just one of them here? Maybe one of her with her parents?"

Officer Pearson sighed and shuffled through the papers. "Will this one do?" he asked and placed it on the table. It was one of Juhi watching Mummy and Papa as they slow-danced together.

"Thank you," Kevin said.

"I'm going to bring these all back," Officer Pearson said, referring to the drawings. But Kevin knew the government would confiscate them, and they would likely never see them again.

When Officer Pearson returned three hours later, Kevin and Juhi were hunched over the conference table, asleep.

"Oh, for Pete's sake, wake up, Mr. Whitman!" Officer Pearson knocked on the table with his knuckles. Kevin wearily opened his eyes.

"Do you want to wake her up? She needs to hear this."

Kevin leaned over and gently put his hand on Juhi's head. She stirred and then sat straight up. Kevin quickly moved his hand away. She didn't like to be touched.

"I cross referenced some of the details in these drawings with the intel my team has gathered over the last few months, and yours checks out. There's also some new things in here that will help us track Shetty."

"That's good, right?" Kevin asked.

"Yes, it's very good for our investigation, but my hands are tied when it comes to your situation. We're willing to let you go back to the States free and clear without pressing charges for buying and stealing an illegal kidney. But our protections only extend to US citizens. We can't let her go with you."

"But if you just push her out of here, Shetty will kill her!" Kevin exclaimed.

Officer Pearson stared at Kevin.

"You can't do this! You can't use her for her evidence to your advantage and just leave her to be murdered! I know there is something that you can do!"

"I'm afraid there isn't," Officer Pearson replied flatly. "It's impossible to let her go with you, let alone let you adopt her with no questions asked. Do you know how long normal adoptions take? It can take years! And you expect us to approve something like this overnight?"

"Well...well...there's more information...about Shetty...that's not in the drawings. Juhi knows where he lives. She knows the exact location of the counterfeiting cave and the clinic where they steal organs. She knows every hotel and restaurant where he has his meetings."

"I need to know all that information to stop this guy," Officer Pearson said. "Those are all crucial details for us to be able to catch him in the act."

"How much is it worth to you?" Kevin asked.

CHAPTER 34
HOME

Juhi and Kevin landed in Los Angeles thirty-six hours later. All she had was her backpack and one of her drawings. Kevin made a deal with Officer Pearson that Kevin would adopt her, and he would be her legal guardian, free and clear. They also gave her an Indian passport and a US green card. After several years of living in this country, she could choose to become a US citizen. Kevin had to agree that she would visit the senate committee to tell her story. In exchange, she gave Officer Pearson all the additional information she knew about Sunardas Shetty. She waited until they were safe in a hotel in Los Angeles to tell the rest of what she knew. The embassy people wanted her to tell them on the plane to the United States and then tried to ask her again before they exited LAX airport, but Kevin insisted that she wait. He was worried they would turn the plane around or force her to stay in the airport before they cleared customs. Even though she was exhausted by the time they reached their Los Angeles hotel, Juhi stayed up for the next two hours with an embassy official and dictated every other detail that she could remember. Kevin stayed up with her.

⸻

"Wow, Juhi. I don't know what to say." Max released a long, heavy breath and shrugged as if to release a giant weight off his back. "You didn't get to tell your story to the senate the way you had hoped, but it still led to the capture of Sunardas Shetty and many of the criminals who worked with him. And I hope you feel better telling your story to me. I am committed to making sure your story is heard by the masses." Max detailed his timeline for filming and releasing a documentary about Juhi and Kevin and organ trafficking.

"You showed tremendous bravery in the work you did to warn all those villagers. You also saved a lot of Americans from being duped into purchasing illegal organs," Max added.

"That is up for debate," Kevin interjected. "I should have known. Any American with half a brain should know that if it is difficult to get a kidney in America, and it's ridiculously easy somewhere else, there's something shady going on."

Max looked at his cameraman to make sure the tape was still rolling.

"I like say one thing," Juhi said in English.

"Please go ahead," Max replied.

Juhi looked at the translator who was exhausted but continued to speak on Juhi's behalf.

"After I testified before Congress, the Americans all say that I am brave for sharing my story. You also say that I should be grateful for the Americans for rescuing me."

Max shifted uncomfortably in his chair; Kevin did, too.

"I am grateful to be away from the slum and from Babaji. I am not a poor orphan that you show on your news. The Americans did not save me. I did not ask for it. Please do not misunderstand. My life is better here. India is no longer my home. But if America is so great, and you all believe the Americans saved me, how can such a thing happen in the first place? You blame other countries, but you are part of the problem."

Juhi stopped talking and sat back while the translator spoke on her behalf. Everyone in the studio fell silent. The tick-tock from the wall clock filled the quiet room.

Max was stumped. He struggled to find words until he finally said, "You make a smart point, Juhi.

Companies like Health SkyTours shouldn't be allowed to operate anywhere in the world."

Juhi just stared at him and had nothing else to say.

"So what's next for you?" Max asked, wanting to change the subject.

"I want to go to school. I know I am behind, but I am a fast learner," she switched back to speaking in Hindi.

"I can tell. Oh, I remembered one more thing I wanted to ask you. Harsha Timbani—the name you used while you traveled through the villages. How did you pick that name?"

"One of my final lessons at school before I was kidnapped was about slavery around the world. I learned about the American slave trade and the underground railroad. Harsha Timbani—she was the Indian Harriet Tubman."

⁂

The next day, Kevin woke up early to make breakfast. He would spend the day looking for a job. He decided to retire from consulting; it required too much travel, and he wanted to be at home with Juhi. He bought a small home close to the beach in Santa Monica. He thought the vastness of the Pacific Ocean would appeal to Juhi after she spent the last few years living a cramped life in small spaces. Kevin's home was on a quiet cul-de-sac west of Bundy between Santa Monica Boulevard and Broadway. Some reporters still lingered outside, but as the story had been in the news for a few weeks, most of them had moved on. Juhi rode a new bike that Kevin purchased for her around the cul-de-sac. It was her first bike, and she fell off from it the first few times she took it for a ride. But she wanted to start straight off with two wheels instead of four.

"I'm fifteen years old, Kay-win! What teenager uses training wheels?" He agreed reluctantly.

While she rode around, Kevin was in the house, preparing dinner. He tried his hand at dal and masala vegetables. He still wasn't used to the blasts of steam from the pressure cooker. His first few bouts of cooking tasted horrible, but it showed signs of improvement. Juhi never complained, and she ate everything on her plate. She showed him how to cook, and he watched patiently. And she did not hesitate to give Kevin plenty of feedback after each meal.

Someone knocked on the door just as he switched off the stove. He opened the door and almost fell backward.

"Emma? What are you doing here? How did you know...?"

"You've been all over the news, Kevin. Didn't you think I would see?"

"I guess so. I hadn't really thought about it. It's been so long." He couldn't believe it. It was like the moment when he turned around and Juhi was just standing there in the village, right in front of him. "Do you want to come in?"

Emma hesitated for a minute and bit her upper lip. Then she propelled forward and embraced Kevin. "I'm so sorry—for everything," she cried into his shoulder. "For not responding to your e-mail when you went to India. For not being there for you."

Kevin's body tensed and then loosened as he held her. It was like they never skipped a day together—it was safe and comfortable, and the feeling of her was like nothing he had ever experienced but familiar at the same time.

"I'm sorry, too," he said. "I'm glad you're here. We were just about to have dinner. You hungry?"

Emma nodded. "Where's Juhi? I want to meet her."

"She's out riding her bike. She'll come inside in a few minutes. She'll be so happy to meet you."

"Isn't she a little old to be riding around on a bike?"

"She said she always wanted to ride a bike as a child, and she didn't get to. So I bought her a bike. She doesn't care if she looks childish. She wants to look like a child. She wants to be a child."

Just then, Kevin and Emma heard a crash, and Juhi screamed. The bike wheels stumbled in a pile of pebbles that got wedged in the spoke. Juhi went tumbling to the ground.

"Papa! Papa!" she yelled.

Like a Bollywood hero, Kevin ran to her. The California wind whipped through his hair, and he scooped her up in his arms.

THE END

ABOUT THE AUTHOR

Mamta Jain Valderrama is a writer, speaker and entrepreneur. Formerly a healthcare strategist, she learned about the difficulties involved in kidney transplants and the daily suffering of those living on dialysis. These important social-justice issues inspired her to write *A Girl in Traffick.*

Valderrama graduated from George Washington University with a bachelor's degree in journalism. After working as a reporter, she went on to receive her MBA from the University of Southern California, where she wrote an award-winning business plan centered on medical tourism. As a first-generation Indian

American, she has visited many of the beautiful and intriguing places she describes in her novel, both in the United States and in India. She resides in Los Angeles with her husband and daughter.

Visit www.MamtaJainValderrama.com to learn more.

BOOK CLUB DISCUSSION QUESTIONS

1. Prior to reading *A Girl in Traffick*, what, if any, was your opinion on organ donation? Should it be legal for strangers to donate to other strangers? What about family members donating to each other? The most common kind of kidney transplant occurs with cadavers. What is your opinion on living organ donation?
2. What did you know about organ trafficking prior to reading *A Girl in Traffick*? Most people would agree that any kind of trafficking is deplorable. But what is your opinion on free commerce and supply and demand? Do you think there is room for a legal marketplace for the buying and selling of kidneys? What about other organs? Should such a market be contained

domestically? What about international trade and imports and exports? Consider that most trafficked kidneys come from poor communities and are purchased by and transplanted into wealthy people. Many times the people who sell their organs and the people who buy them are desperate. The former are desperate to get out of poverty, and the latter are desperate to save their own lives.

3. As of the time of publication of *A Girl in Traffick*, Iran is the only country where the buying and selling of organs is legal. What are your thoughts on this?
4. China is famous (or notorious, depending on your perspective) for taking organs from Chinese prisoners and transplanting them into Chinese nationals who are in need of organs. Do you agree with this policy?
5. Do you think Juhi was right to forgive Kevin and accept him in the end?
6. How do you feel about Kevin and his decision to buy a kidney in India? What about his decision to stay in India to find Juhi?
7. Many people remember the elaborate food descriptions in *A Girl in Traffick*. What, if anything, stuck out to you?
8. Juhi's arrival at the first New Delhi slum was a turning point in her life. How did she change?

As a young, attractive girl in a huge city, what do you think of her survival instincts?

9. After Juhi stole Sunardas Shetty's money and fled from his grip, she decided to stay in India and warn other future victims about organ trafficking. What do you make of her decision to stay in India and to give the money away? What about her decision to give the remaining sum to the American NGO, other than the $10,000 she kept for herself?
10. If you could ask the author any question about *A Girl in Traffick*, what would you want to know?

40567651R00268

Made in the USA
Middletown, DE
16 February 2017